PROVOCATION

DONALD McMASTER

PROVOCATION

ARCADIA

Provocaτion

First published 2012, by Arcadia
the general books' imprint of
Australian Scholarly Publishing Pty Ltd
7 Lt Lothian St Nth, North Melbourne, Vic 3051 tel: 03 9329 6963 fax: 03 9329 5452
email: aspic@ozemail.com.au web: scholarly.info

A Cataloguing-in-Publication entry is available from the
National Library of Australia

ISBN 978-1-921875-81-6

Cover design and typesetting by Art Rowlands
Cover talent c/o Vivien's Model Management
Printed in Australia by Tenderprint Pty Ltd

Set in Fairfield LH 45 Light 11.5/25pt

This book is for my lovely daughter Kristi

While we were together with our fine Thoroughbred horses at Hillsburgh Ontario, and later at Ourimbah on the Central Coast, it was my daughter Kristi who bore the brunt of my doubts and frustrations during that long period of writing. I hope she will continue to live her life as if it is a grand adventure, and retain that indomitable courage of youth — to act as if she knows she cannot fail.

Author's note

Sun Tzü, *The Art of War* (512 BC)

Excerpts used for heading each chapter are from an archaic text of an ancient Chinese General Sun Tzü. For long ago in the Kingdom of Wu, in a place we now call China, a treatise was written by the venerable Sun Tzü on *The Art of War* (512 BC). An English translation was first published by Lionel Giles in 1910 and it is now in the public domain.

Some forty years ago (1972) a bamboo scroll of Sun Tzü's *The Art of War* was discovered during an archaeological excavation of a tomb, at the foot of Mount Yinqueshan, in the Linyi region of Shandong Province. Archaeologists were sorting through funerary objects when they found archaic bamboo strips inscribed with archaic characters. Once assembled these strips formed the complete ancient scroll of the venerable Master Sun. The find authenticates the precise order of the original text, which had already come to us from historical sources. Dating of this new archaeological find indicated that the text was indeed written well before the invention of paper, and this accords with the purported era of Sun Tzü's writing.

In places where I have used extracts of this ancient text, I have not always done so verbatim: sometimes I've used poetic licence to enhance Giles translation's with the visceral impact of Anglo-Saxon words, while still retaining the archaic flavour of Sun Tzü's writing.

CHAPTER 1. ONTARIO

Attack your enemy when he is unprepared,
appear where you are least expected.

Sun Tzü, *The Art of War,* 512 BC

Although I didn't know it, this was the night they killed him. I didn't know who *they* were then, didn't know the devastation they would bring us. Didn't realise the delicate balance of our marriage was such a fragile thing.

My lights were on low beam as I drove with snow drifting down in small flakes reflecting white in the headlights. The Blazer was skittish as a weanling colt as we fishtailed up tenth line, trying to stay on the road.

"Hell of a party. I've had too much to drink."

"I'll drive if you can't hold your liquor." Giselle's breath carried a frowsy whiff of red-wine tannins that reminded me of Christmas.

"You're in no better shape," I said. Giselle flicked me one of her looks so I added, "I've got a migraine coming on, going to crash when we're home."

The planes of her face reflected soft in the dashboard glow.

"Not before, I hope." She hadn't said it with a smile, her mouth was set in a thin red line. "Slow down, there's a car."

A splash of light swept past with a roar, then a backwash of snow squished on the windshield, blinding us. Giselle stared through the window into the night as if she was contemplating eternity; moonlight gave a sheen to her blonde hair. Corrugations in the road slid the unbuttoned coat from her breasts. She didn't seem to notice. I never knew what went on in her mind and I didn't know it now, she seemed so far away.

When our line of spruce came up on the left, I dropped the Blazer down a cog, revved the motor and wheeled into the banked snow of our driveway. Giselle fell against me as we turned, radiating a feminine warmth, while I kept enough speed going to make it to the garage through the blinding snow.

The dark closed in around us when I killed the motor. We got out to the shock of cold — cold the way it gets in Canada. Dead cold. The hairs in my nose froze like needles and snow crunched underfoot. The air carried a hint of ozone, as it does in a storm. I rammed my hat down and buttoned my sheepskin coat, feeling like Clint Eastwood playing *The Mad Trapper of Rat River*. Dragging a glove off, my wedding band slipped and fell in the mush. As I bent to retrieve it, I flashed a smile at Giselle. She stood silent like a child awakening — a silence that weighed on me like a stone.

"Has to be thirty below," I said plugging the motor into an outdoor socket, to stop the engine freezing overnight. The hot metal already making those odd ticking sounds as it does in the cold.

Giselle made it to the grand old Ontario farmhouse ahead of me. I could barely see her through the flying snow, struggling with the frozen lock at the door. Following in her tracks, sinking to my knees in the white stuff, I was aware in some part of my mind that something was wrong.

"I'll check the horses," I yelled.

Giselle burst through the door of the house with a rattle of windows. I didn't wait to hear her reply; the wind picked up, curled round the corner and carried her voice away.

A new horse came in last night, one we had pinned our hopes on. We were depending on him to pull us out of the morass I'd gotten us into. I hoped he'd turn our fortunes around. Though under that desire, a rational side of me knew that many things could happen with horses, too many things — none of them good.

Trudging uphill through the drifts, I edged past the double doors of the barn, where I snagged my coat on a bolt and stood a moment in the dark — listening. The horses were quiet, though when I spoke to them the mares greeted me with the low sound of their snickers.

A chestnut nose poked over the half-door, *Red* the lead mare, her muzzle soft under my hand. The others hung back in the dark. Now this was something I should have picked up on, something I should have noticed, though at the time I missed it. Sounds came, a shake of a head here, a swish of a tail there, the stamp of an impatient hoof. Something was wrong. That's when it hit me: Where was *Tuff*? Dog should have jumped me well before I made it to the door. Where the hell was he? Peeking out of the barn I expected to see him bounding through the drifts — nothing.

Snapping on the lights I found the fluorescents had died in the cold, except for one at the end that switched on and off — as if panic-stricken. The hot flash of an electrical short sounded each time the light came on, with the smell of burning plastic. The tube settled into a steady oscillation, bathing the barn in a bluish light for a trice, then pitched into darkness for another — with what sounded like a dangerous splutter each time.

Anxiety flicked to fear as I walked along the row of horse-boxes in splashes of light. The outlines of each animal burned into my retinas with each flash. The mares hung back and stamped their hooves. That by itself was unusual. *Jet Stream* swished her tail at the back of the stall and wouldn't look at me. When I walked past *Shandy's* box, he pressed hard up against the back wall, as if trying to make himself small and quite invisible.

Something moved, but all lay silent in the dark. The fluorescents flashed again and bathed us in light. *Killer* sprang from the stallion door, his usual spotless paws a dark smudge. This feral Tom goes out of his way to slash unwary visitors with his claws, like he's practising Kung Fu. He sat a few feet away glaring at me. The cat picked up a front paw and began cleaning it with his tongue — distastefully. He was that kind of cat. I snarled a demented hiss and he ran.

There was no stallion to greet me over the stable door. Most farms have a separate barn for their stallions, but on my place, I kept him in the only barn I had, with the mares. Horses are like humans in this way, isolate them from females, as some cultures do to their young men, and men become aggressive, hard to handle — even murderous. Leave stallions with mares in a herd and they become gentle and protective of them.

Alaric had come off the plane last night. Perhaps he was now *cast* with his legs hard against the wall. Sometimes horses need a helping hand to get their legs under them so they can then stand.

The stuttering light gave a strobe effect, snapping one scene at a time. The shutter clicked and registered an image; blood marring the white blaze of his face upon the straw. His legs were stiff, like no horse sleeps. The shutter blinked where splintered bone had pierced his chestnut hide. A cloying scent arose to meet me: a wet, metallic scent of blood.

Another click of light revealed the bloodied axe discarded on the straw. *Alaric* lay in death at my feet, his belly opened. Who had done this thing?

"BASTARDS, MISERABLE BASTARDS," I shouted in the night.

Another snap of light. Walls reflected an arterial graffiti. And even as my belly heaved, I felt guilty for not being there to protect him. I'd broken that tacit agreement men have, to protect those within their care. Cradling *Alaric's* head I sat while tears blurred my sight, and I fought to make sense of it.

Migraine tightened like a ligature. The migraines had started some time ago when things first began to go wrong. Pain now claimed my thoughts while I sat, legs straight in the straw, my back hard against cold stone. Hopes dashed on the stable floor.

A horse coughed and I roused myself to action. No good can come of staying here. Whoever had done this had gone and I could freeze here in the barn. I threw some hay to the boarders then trudged through the snow to the house and phoned the police.

Migraine drove me to bed in a sea of hurt. Giselle had passed out cold. Drifting in a codeine twilight, my drug-fuzzied mind imagined the scene in the stable. Snibbing the lead would not have been easy for someone who didn't know horses. *Alaric* would have struck them. That first blow hadn't killed him. The axe had smashed his facial bones without striking the brain, that's why there was such a mess. *Alaric* had struck them. They must have panicked and cleaved at his spine.

Tearing my mind away from that disaster, I thought of Jennifer our daughter, away overnight with friends. How could I shield her from whatever malevolent being this was? How would I protect us all from what evil lay out there?

Lying snug in bed I watched a shaft of light shine through the window.

Watched the moonlit shadow of the birch tracing its fractal branches infinitely slowly across the ceiling.

CHAPTER 2. **DUNCAN**

He who knows when he can fight and lies in wait for an enemy, while his enemy does not, will be victorious.

Sun Tzü, *The Art of War,* 512 BC

The wind had died and snow covered the earth in its white stillness. Nothing marred the pristine surface. Our farm looked like a Christmas card — perfect. A wonderland of snow and tiny firs, poking their dark heads from under a white blanket. Reality was different. Reality was biting cold. Reality was screeching wind. Reality was hard work.

Sound drifted from the radio and I caught the tail end of the weather report: temperature at the airport was thirty-three below. Even if you grew up here, even if you spent your entire life battling cold winters, you never got used to it. Despite thirty-million souls living in Canada, right now in midwinter, I thought they were mistaken about the country being habitable.

After feeding the horses, mucking out and fighting a migraine hangover, I found *Tuff* in a drift by the garage — stiff with *rigor mortis* and the cold. It shocked me to see him half-buried in the snow, his four limbs rigid. *Tuff* was a tough hombre; when riled he'd crouch and go silent in that intense fang-drooling way Dobermans have. *Tuff* would not have let the killers pass, he would have had them. With us he was part of our family, a pal, a puppy, energetic and eager to please.

Tugging a glove off, I leant across *Tuff's* body and stroked him with my bare hand, as if it were a sacred ritual. His hair felt stiff and alien to my touch. I couldn't bear to look at him. I left him in the cold.

Police came in the morning. They had refused to send a car last night when I'd phoned, assuring me it could wait, something about a five-car pile up on Caledon Road. A car wreck had taken precedence. At the time, it didn't seem as if it should. I hadn't gone back to *Alaric's* box until we met the detective in a black and white, when it pulled into our yard on Sunday morning.

"Duncan McKinley," I said, when the cop extended his hand.

Detective Greiner was taller than me: lean and wiry, with that haunted Hungarian look his name implied. Opening the stall door, a visceral stench washed over us, a softening up for the real thing. *Alaric* seemed smaller than he'd been last night, smaller than he'd been in life, a dark chestnut with a muscled neck like a bull. He'd been a Group II winner in France before a tendon injury. He'd filled the box with that mystical quality of horses, he had carried our hopes for the future. The box seemed huge — the horse diminished. Blood had by now congealed into a dark spray on the walls and ceiling, on the headstall and his straw bedding. His wounds blackened.

"Oh — no," Giselle said when she saw the gutted *Alaric* for the first time. She'd stepped across the threshold, drawn by a morbid curiosity, a curiosity that transfuses us all. I wondered how she would react?

"Stand back," Detective Greiner ordered.

He was systematic, I'll say that for him. He took a slow look around, then scribbled incantations in his notebook.

"The axe?"

"Mine."

Realising as I said it, that the bastards had picked up the axe from the woodpile. It meant they hadn't planned to kill him. Not like this anyway. Greiner snapped Polaroids of the horse. A flash of light. *Click* and *whirr.* Again and again from every angle.

Flash, click, whirr.

Giselle pointed to something on the back wall and murmured to Detective Greiner while I stood stone faced. *The wall?* I strained to see, then when Giselle moved aside, I saw the mark missed in the night.

A hand dipped in blood had made a crude sign on the stone.

Click, whirr.

"The hell's that?"

"Our only *clue*, is what that is," Greiner said, putting the camera down and scribbling a diagram. He studied the blood splatter a moment. "Two of them," he said looking around, "one held the horse while the other swung the axe." Greiner pointed to the bloodied footprints in the straw, then added: "Wound's too deep for a one-hander."

"Seems right," I said, "I know the first blow didn't kill him."

"What… How ya figure that?"

That's when I realised he'd misunderstand the remnants of my Scottish burr.

"The blow's too low, it missed the brain. Can you send a vet with Forensics," I said.

Greiner laughed. "No. No vet, not on our budget. Ya can't lift prints from stone anyways. Not like they do on TV." He almost smiled.

"Can you at least *try*?" I said, "There must be a print here somewhere." He looked at the blood and raised an eyebrow, so I added, "Forensics is the only way to get this sick bastard."

Greiner said nothing and shook his head.

"Why *Alaric*?" Giselle asked of no one in particular. By this time she was looking queasy, a shade paler than her usual robust self.

"Yeah," said the cop. "Why'd they go directly to your *new* horse?"

"Someone must have wanted to hurt us."

"Anyone with reason to?"

"Of course not, at least… no one I can think of — no."

Greiner looked at our other horses peering over their stalls, tossing heads, stamping hooves, impatient to be out. "Well, somebody sure did. And how *did* they know which horse?"

"He's a chestnut with a blaze, a stallion — there's only one."

Greiner scribbled again in his notebook.

"You have insurance?"

"Yeah, signed the policies when he shipped a few days ago."

What I didn't tell him was that it was all on invoice. Fact is I didn't know precisely what it covered, or what I'd paid. I was hoping the company would honour the deal. Have to say that in this matter, as in others, ideas come easily to me, acting on them is harder. I tend to let things go. It allows me a way out, if things go bad. Along with that I have a cavalier disregard for money that's not healthy in any business. My vagueness annoyed Giselle, especially when I didn't know if we could cover the next mortgage payment. Now I'd have to cancel *Alaric's* stud bookings, they too were gone.

"What was he worth?" Greiner asked, his *bic* poised over the pad.

"Eighty grand."

"That much, huh? That's a lotta horse."

"Yes, but then we might get that for a single foal. Well... a foal out of a stakes-winning mare anyway."

"Got stakes-winning mares, have you?"

The mares were out picking at grass through the snow in our home field. The leading chestnut looked over and pricked her ears, as if she knew we were talking about her. I glanced back at Greiner and *Red* ambled towards us, her belly swinging. The other mares came too, unwilling, snatching a last tuft almost in defiance, as they left their patch to follow.

"Just one," I said, "*Intrepid Red's* my only stakes winner. Her breeding goes back to *Eclipse*, an undefeated chestnut a quarter century ago. Anyway *Alaric* drew plenty of mares from other breeders, he had a full book."

"Is there *money* in that?" he asked.

"*Absolutely*, that's where the *real money* is."

"I see." Greiner said puzzled, "But why go all the way to France to buy a horse?"

"Around here they are all inbreeding to *Northern Dancer*, now that his grandsons have done so well. *Ferdinand* won the Kentucky Derby last year. *Shahrastani* won the English Derby and the Irish too at the Curragh. His sire *Nijinsky* did the same. He's *Dancer's* best son. The thing is, around here most brood mares are already related to him."

Greiner's gaze shifted from the mares and fixed on the woods across the road. It seemed that I'd lost him. Despite this I ploughed right on.

"On the other hand *Alaric's* an outcross with robust genes. Biologically it's important not to inbreed *too* much. All animals, including us, have evolved instincts to avoid it."

"Yeah, like they get six-fingers and such in the Appalachians."

"Exactly, in places like Turkey, Pakistan, even the Appalachians, where they're in the habit of marrying their cousins, or worse, they run into puny growth, weak immunity and other more serious genetic disorders."

"Hmm," he said changing tack, "getting your insurance payout will sure be a bitch."

All I got out of that was a gut-twisting dose of anxiety. Greiner turned to Giselle, he must have figured that in a state of shock she'd be more helpful.

"So how is the horse business, Missus McKinley? Heard the bottom dropped out of it — with the recession and all."

He took a moment to look around the yard. And I could see his mind ticking over in its appraisal. Greiner must have thought the farm run down, compared to those flash places with four-board fencing like Harry Hindmarsh, and Quentin Nash, down the road. Not to mention E P Taylor's five-thousand magnificent acres of Winfield's Farm, where *Northern Dancer* stood, due east of us at Oshawa. Hardly a fair comparison.

"Well," I said, answering for her. "We're doing all right — till now. *Alaric* shipped the day before, we were hoping for better things."

Giselle pursed her lips again into that thin red line.

"Ah," he said, gazing at me, letting the silence build.

"Ah, *what*? You suspect me. You think I'd kill my own horse — *Christ!*"

Turning on my heel I walked back to the house, as dignified as I could manage in knee-deep snow. Then banged the door shut, leaving him alone with Giselle. I wanted the bastards who'd done this. I wanted forensics. I wanted fingerprints. I wanted a vet. I wanted the samples analysed. And I wanted it all right now — *Goddamnit*.

Migraine tightened a noose around my head.

I headed for the phone.

CHAPTER 3

The rising of birds in their flight is a sign of ambush.

Sun Tzü, *The Art of War*, 512 BC

A cold North Westerly blew in trailing snow, like the foam of breakers in a great white sea, a cruel and barren tundra. While I was standing in the stirrups galloping a horse, in the powder of my snowploughed track, a police van slithered up the driveway. My breath came hard in a dense cloud with each driving stride. Shards of ice flew in the wind stung my face.

Sitting back down I pulled the horse up beyond the gate, then trotted back to greet them, the colt skittish under me, hyped from the run — pulling hard. He skipped into a canter as we came to the barn, his bound like a stolting antelope. He humped his back to buck, then shied like a cat at something unseen in the snow. Luckily I was centred and sat him easily, going with him, enjoying the buzz.

I love to work with horses, they feed my battered soul. Adventure is part of it. Horses are so damned unpredictable, so quick to flee, dangerous to be around. That whiff of excitement gave me something primal I got from nowhere else. Horses are so direct and their behaviour so obvious. In the next field *Intrepid Red* laid her ears flat, pulled a face, and lunged at the colt I was riding, smacking her teeth on the rail between us. *Red* was telling him to stay away.

Prey animals form herds to maintain vigilance against predators and exploit a wisdom of the herd in finding forage. Stallions with a band of mares will scout the terrain, looking out for predators in ambush. It's the lead mare, the highest on the totem pole, that leads the herd to new pastures. Horses have a collective memory of the land they roam and all its hidden dangers. As with other social animals, their overarching reason for herd attachment is for sex and their ultimate protection in numbers.

We exploit their social structure. We tap into it and this makes our mastery possible, mastery of their strength and lightening speed by puny men like me. We understand horses because they have the same pair-bond attachments and interplay of dominance and submission that we do. For humans and horses, life is a sexual dichotomy, though many would not admit to such a thing.

What I knew was that caring for mares and their foals healed me in ways the rest of the world did not. I loved the way mares cared for their own; loved the way they took to higher ground and stood vigil. I too stood vigil.

That morning I was home alone, except for Giselle's cats, and I reflected on the nature of horses. Reflecting how deeply they resent those who mistreat them, the way they carry that forever, and seem to know when they are treated unfairly. Horses will lash out. Their sense of fairness is like that of humans, though horses don't have the deceit of humans and believe me — that's a big difference.

Being Monday, Giselle had gone to work at Ciba-Geigy, in Mississauga, while Jennifer went to school in Guelph. They would be home tonight and I was looking forward to seeing them. Without *Tuff* sniffing for the scent of groundhogs, only an occasional car along the road disturbed the frosted stillness, a snowbound silence that is winter in Ontario.

Later, when the police turned up, I showed the technoid to *Alaric's* box, unsaddled my horse and brushed the sweat from his trace-clipped hide. The glacial air formed a rising mist that enveloped the colt. My eyes watered and I dried them with my sleeve. The man in blue worked his *Leica* and examined surfaces with a magnifying glass like Sherlock Holmes.

After drying the colt I put him away and entered *Alaric's* stall, careful to keep clear of the blood. The visceral smell augmented the scent of ammonia in the stall. The technoid knelt to scope the brass nameplate on the headstall — frowning when he saw me. He didn't want to be disturbed. A dark powder now lay on surfaces that should be clean, and seeing *Alaric's* corpse now rekindled my guilt.

"No prints so far," Technoid said.

"You will keep looking?"

"Sure, won't find anything though."

"Why the hell not?"

"Cause they were wearing gloves, eh?" He chuckled at his wit.

"How can you possibly know that?"

"Was thirty below last night. *Everyone* was wearing gloves. Besides..." he pointed to the sign on the wall, "Scrawl's real thick. Had gloves alright, or fat fingers — eh."

He had that rural habit of ending sentences with an inflection. It irritated me beyond reason. Now he hammered his point home. "Sure, we can print leather. Ain't nothing here though ... they'd have got rid of stuff with blood on it, eh."

"Look at this place. Christ, they'll have blood all over them."

"I've seen it before," he said. "They'd have gotten a kick outta it — that's for sure."

"Got a *kick* out of it — Jesus!"

"There's a lotta sick puppies out there. They could have shot the horse instead, eh."

"Might have worried about the neighbours hearing?" I said, "Damn that mark must *mean* something."

"Seen a lotta strange folk," Technoid said. "No telling what's in their tiny minds."

"You *are* sampling the horse's tissues, I take it."

"What for? He weren't *poisoned* with an axe, eh."

"No," I said slowly, "though perhaps you might find something, *anything* — human blood maybe. The horse would have struck them."

The technoid looked at me sadly and shook his head.

"*Human blood*. Chrissake, look'it," he swept his arm around the blood-soaked stall, "there's no way."

"We're missing something — *I know it*. I'd like pathology to check."

"No way. We can't justify it, eh. Not a case like this — it's a *horse* for *Chrissake*."

"He's an eighty-thousand dollar horse."

"Well he *was,* eh."

Now that did give me pause. "There has to be *something*."

"Look't, I'll take the damn dog if it makes ya feel better. You get the Vet school to run pathology on the horse. It'll cost ya though."

"Yes, I already phoned. Too rich for my blood."

With a slow burning angst I left him to it and wrestled instead with a recalcitrant snow blower for the rest of the morning. It did nothing to improve my mood. I love animals, nature and the great outdoors. What I do *not* like is the bowels of a damned machine. I'd rather be messing with horses than with metal that doesn't mesh.

Murray called next day to ask about his filly. Murray's an old friend and a client. A good client. He's also a surgeon at Toronto Western. When I told him what had happened to my horse he was more than a little worried about his own filly we had.

"What mad bastard would kill a horse with an *axe*?" I asked.

"Psychiatric wards are full of them," Murray said.

"I want to get forensics on *Alaric*. Can you do that for me at the hospital?"

"What do you expect to find?"

"Maybe blood from the killers. All we have now is that mark on the wall. Toxicology might give us something."

"Not much, Duncan. Blood's a problem too, now that it's clotted."

"Damnit, police aren't giving it their best shot. They're not taking it seriously. They're not going to solve anything."

"What about your local vet for tissue tests?"

"He doesn't have facilities. And I sure as hell can't afford the Vet School."

"Hmmm," he said, "do you know how to take tissue samples?"

"I've done it before with infected mares. Still got the tubes here someplace."

"Good. Can't get there myself, but you get the samples to me, I'll run them at the hospital. Someone owes me. I'll call you back on what to collect."

In the interim I made a fresh cup with a new Kenyan blend I'd bought on my last trip to Guelph. *Kenyan* because Arabica coffee grown at high altitude tastes better. In this case it tasted as if they'd over done the roast, or perhaps it was my mood. A burnt aroma emerged when I poured and the coffee tasted bitter. I added a spoon of sugar.

Murray phoned back after seeing his colleague.

"Get the tubes here today," he said, then gave instructions. "And wear surgical gloves to avoid contamination."

Collecting the specimens, I wrote Murray's name and a number in Texta, on the side of each tube. The youngest son, Ahanu Pasquale, from a family of Native Americans down the road, agreed to deliver them as he was already heading to Toronto.

He pulled up in our yard in a battered old pickup and I gave him twenty bucks for the job. Ahanu came by whenever he could think of an excuse, not that he had much inclination to chat. A quiet kid to the point of silence who seemed just a tad too willing to run errands for us. It made me think he might be into something. I clapped Ahanu on the shoulder and he let out the clutch. The decrepit pickup took off down the gravel road trailing a dark plume of exhaust.

CHAPTER 4

It is essential to seek out enemy spies who have come to spy against you, treat them well and to bribe them to serve you. Give them instructions and return them to their camp. Doubled spies are used to spread false rumours.

Sun Tzü, *The Art of War*, 512 BC

From the study I looked out over the white expanse of our universe. A white broken only by five-thousand firs and spruce I'd planted in an asymmetric pattern along the fences, so they'd look natural. The last owner had told me, with some pride, that his grandfather had chopped down every last goddamn tree on the place. Now a metre or so above ground, my thousands of treetops held an ominous green, so dark they looked black against the snow. The fields were enclosed with board fencing and the firs stood out in stark lines against it, scattered ranks of soldiers, black coated in the frosted glare.

Brood mares were running together in the home field that day along with a few boarders. They stopped walking and dug every now and again in the snow for a few stalks of winter grass. The horses loved to be outside, even on the coldest days, and they needed the exercise to keep them healthy. They'd be all right no matter how cold, as long as they had a warm barn to go back to and hard feed. As long as they didn't get wet with freezing rain or wind-driven sleet.

As I watched, *Red* shied suddenly and bolted. The herd caught her first move and ran with her down the fence line, raw power at a hundred miles an hour, snow flying like dust. They did a grand circle of the field then stopped, heads up, sides heaving at the far end facing toward the woods across the road.

From the window I could hear the hard rasp of their breathing, see the heat rise from them like mist. Every magnificent line, from their pricked ears to high tails, alert and streamlined for flight. My soul soared at the sight. Prey animals, flight animals, fine-tuned by evolution and bred to run.

Whipping the camera from the desk, I clicked a shot as the mares took off again, then turned the lens toward the woods to see what startled them, holding my old Nikon and its telephoto lens hard braced. A smudge of movement in a stand of cedars a half-mile away. Turning the focus ring I accidentally clicked the shutter, then swore at wasting the shot. Peered again through the lens. Nothing. Two crows lifted in the wind, from snow-packed cedars. As I marched the lens along the horizon, it magnified a battered pickup down the road. Coyote live in them there woods, fox too and wolves. I'd seen an odd man or two among the foliage after deer. Predators all.

As I stood at the window a phrase ran through my mind: *A master of all he surveys.* It had a false ring to it. I was no more master here than I'd been elsewhere. More like a breathless constructor of a house of cards. A Banker's slippery cards, cards that I'd assembled from a precarious deck. By holding my breath, I was trying to stave off whatever it was, whatever's out there in the universe that makes them fall.

With the mortgage due at the end of the week finances were close, not to mention the eighty-thousand on the stallion that I owed the Royale. Anxiety knotted my gut in a way that thoughts of hard money bring. I don't know if it's that way for everyone, but it is that way for me. My work-worn farmer's hand was shaking when I reached out for the phone.

When I spoke to the bank manager, he didn't exactly threaten me, but he warned me that the bank would not tolerate another missed mortgage payment, as they had on my overdraft. I looked across to the Beech woods while he spoke. Sunlight reflected off the snow, trees swayed, stirred now by a breeze.

The manager suggested putting the farm up for sale to pay off our debt. He recommended the bank's tame estate agent for Chrissake. I hung up the phone. Damn. Shylock wants his bread while my dreams die. It wasn't just the land: What about my precious horses, all those gorgeous foals? How could I provide for Giselle and give us all a home? If I lost the farm I would lose her. What would Jenny think? The crises snowballed in my mind — way out of control. I stood to lose everything. Better cancel *Alaric's* bookings and make that damn insurance claim.

Searching files in a bottom drawer I was aware that I was a touch short of panic. I fired up my trusty Mac and ran the spreadsheet modelling the fiction of our cash flow. Pixels on the screen settled into numerals, then shifted when I changed dates and added recent bills. The computer hesitated for a split second, as if it was thinking, before spitting out the next row of numbers.

The Mac didn't tell me where to get the money, only that I was $5,268.92 short of the next mortgage payment. Doesn't sound like much. Let me tell you, when you don't have it, when your credit's maxed out, when the tractor's thirsty and horses need feeding — it's a mountain.

While at my desk I ran the insurance documents through the scanner, opened a folder in the electronic ether and slipped them inside. Then composed letters to Thoroughbred Insurance, the Bloodstock Agency and to the bank about the whole calamity and printed the lot. A first step taken. I guessed there'd be forms to fill and there were phone calls aplenty.

After typing invoices, I made some calls, then left a few callbacks. I was fighting a rising panic, afraid of failure — afraid of loss. The loss of my horses, the loss of my farm, maybe the loss of my wife and our home.

Why was *Alaric* killed? Was it a warning? But of what?

As I sat a while focussing on the problem, as if sheer cerebral processing alone would solve it, the sky darkened and rain streaked across the windowpane. I ran down the stairs two at a time to get the horses in the barn.

When I caught *Red,* she nuzzled my armpit as I opened the gate and led her to the barn. She knew what I was doing. The others came with us running loose. The brood mares kept behind her until I put *Red* away. Then without a leader they blitzed up the centre aisle with a clatter of hooves.

They stopped in a herd of disarray in front of the closed barn door at the end, breathing hard. I caught them one by one while they stood with their heads down, not meeting my eyes, looking a trifle ashamed. We had an old stone barn. One of the lovely old-fashioned kind you see in Ontario, with room upstairs for hay and feed. We'd built the horse-stalls with timber, back when we first bought the place, back when we had enough money to do so. Dismay at *Alaric's* death churned inside me, and left me feeling sick with the thought. Questions remained a cancer in my brain — destructive and unresolved.

The barn door opened and someone slipped inside — a familiar silhouette against the light. She stroked *Red's* neck when the mare reached over the door for her. I watched the androgynous shape of my daughter as she strode through the barn to her horse. She was willowy with long hair falling down her back. She had a natural confidence some teenagers retain from childhood, before they're battered by the world. She was fast getting to the stage where she knew it all. Indeed, she already thinks she knows a hell of a lot more than me. That wasn't hard right now, for I didn't know what was going on any more.

Jenny was almost as tall as me, though thank God she has her mother's looks. Though she has my light-brown hair rather than Giselle's platinum locks. She sensed me watching, turned and then smiled when she saw me walking towards her.

"Hullo Jen," I said, "it's good you're riding today."

She came over and wrapped her arms around me. She was whip thin and lumpy at the same time. It wasn't often she hugged me now, since she'd reached that awkward age where girls no longer admit affection with grace.

"It's a bitch about *Tuff* and *Alaric*. I can't really believe it's happened. That someone actually did this — how could they, Dad?"

"Don't..." I said, "please don't, not now."

Jennifer glanced at *Alaric's* stall and shivered. The mare in the stall beside us pawed at the ground and Jen stepped back startled.

"*Jesus* Dad he's still there. I didn't expect that. There's blood *everywhere*."

Her hands went up to her eyes. She'd glimpsed *Alaric's* ruined carcass, an ugly spatter on the walls, the entire bloody catastrophe.

"Ground's still frozen," I said, "can't bury him yet, besides it's a crime scene." I stepped in front of her to bolt the stable door and block the wretched view. "Don't look at him," I said, "no good can come of it." I put my arm around her and steered her away. Our horses still needed to be worked. "Take *Shandy* outside to saddle him. And keep an eye on the weather, a storm's closing in."

"Yes," she said, stroking her horse's neck, with a furtive glance at *Alaric's* now firmly bolted stall. "Yes," she said again with a sniffle and a straightening of her back, "today I'm starting him on leg yielding."

"Good, you know how to do it: keep it simple. Just a couple of steps to one side, until he gets it. Leave the other side till later, maybe next week."

"Dad, I don't understand. *Who did this to Alaric?* Who could hate us that much?"

"Don't know. I *do* know they've hurt me. They've hurt all of us," I breathed out hard in a sigh, "I don't know if we'll survive."

"What... What do you mean?"

I didn't answer — I didn't know. For the life of me I didn't know why I'd said it. Some part of my brain had slipped its leash and released unconscious fears. I *was* afraid. Afraid for myself, afraid for my family, afraid for all of us. We were stepping into the unknown. I knew that with *Alaric's* death everything had changed.

I held Jenny in my arms. Holding my daughter gave me strength, strength to find my way back, somehow I felt that just for a while, I had lost my way.

By the time Jenny finished riding I had Texas Chilli on the boil. Turning it down I left it to simmer, stirring gently every now and then — whenever I remembered. Jenny took a shower while I caught the evening news on TV. In New Zealand two French secret agents had just been sentenced to ten years jail for sinking *The Rainbow Warrior*. CNN replayed dramatic footage of the aftermath of the sabotage in Auckland harbour, an action now known by the codename: *Opération Satanique*. I translated this to *Satanic*.

On the tube a silver-maned newsman stood in the drizzle at dawn interviewing survivors. I watched the re-run footage of a blonde with bedraggled hair, shivering with an army blanket swept around her like a poncho. She was answering the reporter in staccato sentence fragments between fractured sobs. Her boyfriend, a Green Peace activist, had gone down with the ship. So when French agents of Sécurité were finally dragged into court the charge was murder.

The news shifted to Ronald Reagan and Mikhail Gorbachev in Reykjavík, who in a joint communiqué denounced the policy of mutually assured destruction. The year was 1986 and the cold war was beginning to thaw. "The end of MAD," the reporter added his jokey style, "Now that wasn't so hard now, was it fellas?"

Sports took over the tube after the news, and in Canada in winter, *sports* means only ice hockey. Giselle's Volkswagen chugged up the driveway as Wayne Gretzky slammed in another goal with a smashing clunk. The crowd roared as if they were cheering for her, as the *Golf* hit a patch of ice going into the garage and revved like a rally car in full cry. The Volkswagen convulsed for a few heart-stopping wheel spins, then churned in. She cut the motor just as I added my secret ingredient: *El Paso's* enchilada sauce. Then silence. An absolute silence that comes with winter snow.

Giselle stumbled into the house, shucked her coat and brushed away the snow. I melted at her smile when she turned and saw me. She wore a tailored suit and carried a leather attaché: her long blonde hair twisted up, held with a jade clip — perfect. A turquoise teardrop nestled at her throat in that flawless notch between her collarbones, a perfect match with her eyes. Giselle's fair hair contrasted with the smooth tan of her skin and navy suit. She radiated femininity, health and bursting fertility.

I wanted to take her in my arms. Wanted to breathe in her delicate aura, I wanted to kiss her even tan all over. Wanted to make love to her right then, right there, on the floor. I never did. Sex had to be on her terms. She had to shower first and fold her clothes neatly on the bed. She had to be the one to reach out. She had to be the one who had control. I closed her in my arms, held her tight and kissed her hard on the mouth.

"You're looking worried," she said with a lilt in her voice, "more grey hairs."

I touched my hair, couldn't help it, sensitive as I was to my golden brown turning a steely grey. Bad enough having a weather-beaten face without ageing hair.

We had a quiet meal. Restrained is what it was. Candles on the table flickered while the wind bayed in the night outside. Chilli bit my tongue and left a festive aftertaste, hot and tomatoey with chunks of roasted beef. I washed it down with *Sangria,* the citrus tang of Spain — perfect. Giselle stuck to *Perrier*, spring-water shipped all the way from France. Jennifer had *Coke*.

Jenny wanted to talk about her horse, how naughty he had been when schooled. I indulged her readily for we had shied away from talking about *Alaric's* demise. We wanted to shield her from a harsher reality.

"*Shandy's* not naughty," I said. "Horses are not deliberately disobedient. They're not *deliberately* anything. The trick is to reward him for everything he does even half right."

"*For everything?* You mean pat him for taking a single step away from my leg?" She said sounding incredulous, and in what was essentially a challenge.

"*Sure*, stroke him for *each* step in the right direction. And always finish instruction by going forward."

Jenny made a face: "You're telling me to pat him even if the movement's *not* correct?"

There's scepticism in her voice. Teenagers know better. What I know, what all parents know, is that she won't listen; she won't take on board what I say. I say it anyway.

"Make it easy for him. Put him against a wall for leg-yielding, so it's hard to get it wrong. Shape his behaviour with reward and punishment."

"You want me to *punish* him?"

"*Absolutely*. Growl *NO* in a low tone. If he doesn't respond then shank him. Use the whip if mounted — just the *once*." Jenny rolled her eyes as if to say *what does he know*. Too slow to read the signs I continued, "*NO* is enough punishment for high-strung Thoroughbreds. Warmbloods are slower, they need more stick."

I'm now in rant mode. Jenny is in revolt.

"You mean *punish* him, even for stepping on my foot?" she says.

"*Especially* for stepping on your foot. For doing *anything* wrong. Don't gabble as if he's a native English speaker. Just say *NO*. It becomes a reflex, so that when you're riding and he starts off on the wrong lead or whatever, when you say it he'll understand. Horses can learn about half a dozen words if you are consistent and distinct."

Jenny fidgeted. She'd run out of tolerance for *wise thoughts of the old one*.

"Had to yell at him today," she said, in what I sensed as a challenge.

"Oh Jen, *never* shout at horses. They are frightened by it, they don't understand. We're the smart ones."

Giselle flicked a look at the talking heads on the tube. More footage of last years footage of Auckland harbour came on TV, bedraggled survivors in tracksuits and ugh boots with uniformed police looking stern standing around on the dock. There's a body being pulled from the water, then a thirty-something newswoman with the wind in her face, mouthing platitudes. I plough right on, unwilling to heed the wind.

"Just growl *NO* and ask *Shandy* to do it again. Asking him to repeat a movement is understood by horses as punishment."

Giselle got up from the table to get a second helping of chilli from the kitchen. It seemed like a silent rebuke. She tuned out when we talked horses. Giselle wasn't into them, not in the way we were. She did enjoy the farm, enjoyed walking in our enchanted woods, but at heart she was a material girl. She worked in personnel, among the smart suits, hiring and firing people. A world where people are commodities — human capital. Being such an attractive woman she found that people liked her, opened their hearts and told her their innermost thoughts. Giselle attracted friends among her colleagues that swarmed to her like flies to rotting meat, although underneath it all she was not anyone's friend — not ever.

She lived in a corporate world. A world apart. A world I didn't belong to, a world she thought I didn't measure up to. I was the one who got anxious. I was the bleeding-heart, soppy animal-loving touchy-feely type. Like me, our daughter Jenny was compassionate, concerned about the world's wrongs and the starving tribes of Africa. She too had an affinity with horses, although from time to time I had seen a glimpse of a certain glacial toughness that I'm sure she'd inherited from her mother.

Giselle was glad to get away to work in the mornings, leaving the farm and our problems behind her. I understood it. I'd like to leave them too. In a way I envied her private and separate world.

"Any news?" She asked me.

"Forensics came. A technician anyway. Told me the killers wore gloves."

"Oh, did they take samples?"

"Well no, except for *Tuff*. No point in *Alaric's* toxicology."

"I was hoping for something more positive," she said, and her mouth pressed again into that thin red line. The turquoise pendant I'd given her bobbed up and down at her throat as she swallowed, then turned away.

There are rituals to married life. And at the core of them is sex. In the bedroom I removed a half-asleep moggie from my side of the covers. Sliding under the duvet against an inert Giselle feigning sleep, I enclosed her in my arms, felt her heat radiate against my belly. Aching for reassurance, I stroked her skin, savouring its oiled smoothness, there was a flicker of muscle underneath. She wears a nightdress, wears it like armour. She has panties on underneath. Never vulnerable, even in sleep. My hand slid over the well-toned muscles of her rump, across the slip of silk, snagging on lace at the seam.

Raising myself on an elbow I kissed her neck and whispered softly in her ear, "Feel like a cuddle?"

"No, dammit — I don't," she answered in croaky irritation.

"Don't think I can get to sleep," I said, "I'm wound tight."

With that I slid my hand across her breast in a caress that raised a nipple. A twinge of desire lay tense in my palm. Her body betrayed it, for she shivered when she felt my touch, stretched then rolled over, flinging off the duvet.

"Okay, now I am awake, you want me to give you a medicinal? Is that it? It's all about *you* isn't it. Doing what *you* want. It's the only way you know how to be intimate."

Damn. I'd triggered the entire fuckin' catastrophe. Sex in marriage is a gift, a gift from one sensual being to another, although it is always a gift you have to want to give.

"What about *me*? She said. "What about *my* needs?"

This came with a whine in her voice.

"What *are* your needs Giselle? What is it you want?"

There was silence, and in this silence Giselle rolled onto her belly away from my hand, taking the duvet with her. Her rump a sensual swell under the covers. Cold descended and my bare skin tingled. The moon was now hidden by cloud. There's a light breeze and birch outside tapped on the window.

I lay on my back listening to her ragged breathing and the birch tapping in the dark.

A sadness bled my soul.

CHAPTER 5. GREINER

If you know your enemy and know yourself, you need not fear the result of a hundred battles.

Sun Tzü, *The Art of War*, 512 BC

Guelph in Southern Ontario is reputedly the home of the northern Mafia, it is a town where the mob protects their women and they raise children in an ambience of understated wealth. Rumour has it there is an underworld truce, there's no organised crime, and not much violence in this town.

Guelph lies at the centre of what used to be a rich farming belt that extends southwest from Toronto. Now that farmers were the new-age poor, in our brave new world of global enterprise, it falls on academe to fund this town. Its presence takes the form of a brownstone university that dominates the high ground. It's an austere institution, without the leafy niceness of New England's Ivy League. There is a practical Protestant ethic here that produces treeless environs. Since trees shrink farmer's yields, a relentless logic has led farmers to lop trees, with such a ruthless aggression the land is now stripped bare. It's an ancient arboreal aggression that successive generations of farmers have maintained around here for over two-hundred years. Few trees remain.

Nat Greiner thought about this as he drove to work, thought about how pragmatism had brought a certain dourness to its citizens. He considered Guelph a practical, though unlovely town. Fittingly, the veterinary school, not a ditzy faculty like fine arts, is the university's crowning glory. Nat didn't know if they even had a faculty of fine arts. He rather doubted it.

Greiner thought it an easy tour. A duty sought by those more concerned with raising kids than raising Cain. He thought of himself as a dependable guy. A first generation immigrant. His parents had fled the Russian terror, in the Hungarian revolution of '56. His father became an x-ray technician, instead of the doctor he would have been in Hungary. So over the years he had become bitter. Despite this, Nat had been brought up with a great respect for Canada. He did hate the winters though.

The police station where he headed was a red-brick lockup a few blocks from the *Church of our Lady.* Greiner changed down with a crunch from the dodgy gearbox and wheeled into the police lot. The snow was churned to mush by an unholy mix of sump oil, salt and vehicular traffic of the good and the bad.

Greiner had been attracted to Guelph for the same reason as the Mafia, a quiet place to bring up children. He had three now, two boys and a girl. After six years in this low-crime backwater, Nat was champing at the bit for a big case, a case that would give him a decent jolt. Something exciting to advance his stagnant career. Maybe get him a move to Toronto. Now that would be a welcome change. He felt neglected in middle age, as if life had passed him by.

Yesterday he pulled a fresh case in Saint Catharine's, not far from Guelph. A domestic that got weirder by the minute. When the cops tried to untangle them, the two teenage girls went ballistic. Screaming, clawing their own faces with their fingernails, for Chrissake. Flinging obscenities at their parents and tried to stab their mother with a bread knife. Nothing fatal, just dramatic. Hard to figure.

When the case first came Greiner's way, none of the other cops would touch it, then RCMP bought into it when things got interesting. The Mounties already had a psychologist, John Hackman in Toronto on secondment. He had made a name for himself profiling crimes in British Columbia. Hackman looked like Clarke Kent, Greiner thought, one of those who speak in unpronounceable words.

Toronto had sent him out to Guelph for this case.

That was another thing Greiner had to look out for.

A buckram hardcover lay on his desk when Greiner got in, with a sticky-note from Hackman. *Read this!* Jeez, as if he didn't have enough to do. Greiner turned the book over and read the lurid blurb on the back.

> Between 1450 and 1750, more than 100,000 people — mainly women — in Europe and colonial America were prosecuted for practising harmful magic and worshipping the devil. Tens of thousands were executed, after being subjected to bestial tortures.
>
> *Witch Hunt* examines this persecution and the religious hysteria that inspired it, tracing its roots back to the savage suppression of the heretical Waldensian sect by the Catholic Church. With the creation of the inquisition, and the publication of the book *Malleus Maleficarum*, the *"Witchfinder's Bible"*, the craze spread across Europe and reached as far as the United States where, despite the infamy of the Salem Witch Trials, it was soon dismissed by a more rational population.
>
> Although witch trials continued in Scotland until 1727, Norway until 1760 and Hungary until 1777, the growth of scientific reason gradually gained ground from the witch hunters.
>
> Strangely, in light of this murderous activity, there is no evidence a confederation of witches ever existed. There were no medieval covens, secret betrothels of Satan, sacred group-sex rituals, concerted acts of cannibalism, destruction of babies, crops, horses or cattle by witches. These notions were pure fiction, an imagined folklore, fantastic dreams and confabulation, many confirmed in lurid detail by false confessions under the most horrendous torture.

Greiner was still going through the girls' transcripts with Hackman in the interview room when Dispatch called. The call caught him when he was about to bring up the subject of the book on his desk.

"Constable Kern for you John. Anderson girls came in again."

"Uh huh."

"Parents have got to them."

"Jesus."

Hackman stood, grabbed his camelhair coat and slid it over his tailored suit. Then he downed the last of a day-old Danish before reaching again for the phone.

"Hackman here. Where ya at?... okay... we're on our way." Then to Greiner struggling with his coat while draining dregs of a lukewarm cappuccino, "Come on Nat, girls are at the Crisis Centre. You'll get to meet 'em."

At the centre, Birgit the police counsellor glared when Hackman introduced Greiner.

"Run that by me again," Hackman said.

Birgit resented him for interrupting the briefing. Resented him for being a man, resented him as an outsider, resented his intrusion into her domain. Hell, this woman resented him being alive.

Greiner was naturally drawn to the girls. Honey-blondes with hair that framed their clear-skinned faces and spilled down their backs to their waists. Angela couldn't be a day over thirteen. Bizarrely they were dressed in white satin pyjamas that contrasted with their tanned skin.

When Nat turned his eyes to her, Angela took a breath and arched her back. Her high breasts demanded his attention, like headlights on high beam. He revised his assessment: *Hmmm, thirteen going on twenty-three — this girl is dangerous.*

Angela's mouth lisped in a high-pitched child's voice as she spoke.

"We *had* to go. They *made* us do it."

"That's all right," said Birgit soothing, "go on dear."

"Mommy drove us to the woods. Started off a full moon that night, then clouds blew in and covered it. Light was skinny after that."

"*Skinny*?" Hackman asked to make sure he'd heard her right.

"Yes, you know like kinda thin."

Hackman continued to write in his notebook. The girl shook her head in irritation, then pressed on.

"She made us drink something that made us feel, well... you know, like *funny*."

"*Funny*? How does that feel exactly?" Hackman asked.

"Fuzzy headed — dizzy."

"Okay," Hackman said as he wrote: *Psychotropic drugs ???*

"She took off our clothes, then dressed us all in white. People stood among the trees and each of us lit a candle."

"You know these people?" Greiner asked.

That earned him another glare from Birgit. He could see a hard time coming with her riding shotgun on the girls.

"Yeah, seen 'em. Don't know their names."

"*Where* have you seen them?"

Another glare from Birgit. There was silence as they all looked at the girl waiting for her answer. "Don't know," she said with a practised flick of hair.

Silence lay between them as they digested that little bit of theatre. Greiner crossed his arms and rearranged his features.

"You've seen them before and you don't know where? Well, I *can* see we're going to have a hell of a problem with this Goddamned testimony."

The eldest girl fixed him with a glare, and in that instant he had the impression she had sized him up, *she knew what he wanted.*

"Maybe know one of them. A girl from school."

"Oh, and what's her name?"

"Ah — Jenny."

"Really Detective, let the girls tell their story."

Greiner bit the inside of his cheek and mumbled something no one could discern. The girl started once more.

"Mommy dressed Nicole too and she looked radiant."

They all looked at Nicole, two years younger, the same blonde hair, but still a child.

"Why did she do that?" Nat asked.

Birgit shushed him. The girl ignored the question and carried on as if he'd been unspeakably rude to interrupt.

"They filed past an altar, and took a kind of a communion."

"Oh, what kind of communion — precisely?" Hackman said.

"They sipped blood. Blood that stained their black robes."

"*Black* robes?" Hackman asked.

"Yes, all with hoods like monks. Well, all except for the High Priest."

"And what did he wear?" said Hackman.

"He wore a red cloak and a mask."

"Okay, the head honcho wore red: What next?" Greiner said impatiently.

"They forced us to into the circle while chanting. Then stopped at the altar."

She paused, aware of the effect she had on them. The girl was a natural, she had their full attention.

"Where did the *blood* come from?" Hackman asked.

"What blood?" she said, looking back at them, her face a study in blank.

"The blood you drank."

"From the horse — silly," she said and glanced at her sister.

"They killed a horse?"

"Yes, of course they killed it."

"Did you see them kill it?" Greiner asked, getting into the act now when it involved evidence. She looked around at each of them in turn, then shook her head.

"Please answer that *aloud* for the record," Birgit said.

"No. *No*, I didn't see a horse." she said, "That all happened before we got there."

"How do you know about the horse then?" Greiner asked the obvious.

"Someone said."

Angela stopped. Her face formed the sulky cast of a naughty child.

"Go on dear. Tell us what happened," Birgit interjected.

Angela looked around to make sure all eyes were on her. She leaned back and flicked the blonde hair from her face again in a practised move.

"They made me lie on the altar, face down. A priestess tied me there. She wore a gown like Maid Marion, gathered under the breasts."

"Maid Marion? You mean as in Robin Hood?" Nat said.

"Of course the *movie*, what else? They took off my robe. The altar was cold on my bare tummy."

She paused again, then wet her lips with the very tip of her tongue. The slight blonde girl looked directly at each man in the room. Greiner was all too aware of the effect she had. He noticed Hackman wrote *Borderliner?* in his notebook. *What the hell was that?*

After more urging from Birgit, the girl said, "Don't know what all happened 'cause I blacked out."

"Were you still there on the altar when you came to?" Birgit asked.

"Yes, yes I was. People were chanting and there's this big black dog."

"A Doberman?" Greiner said. "What the hell was it doing?"

Greiner became impatient with the séance; he wanted something concrete, he wanted evidence. *What fuckin' planet was this kid on?*

The girl squirmed in her seat, fidgeted for a while with a fingernail and shot a look at the door.

"It's alright Angela," Birgit said, shooting Nat a killer look that would have stopped a bullet. She leaned forward, touching the girl's forearm, "Tell us everything dear."

Angela squirmed again in her seat. *She's got worms*, thought Nat.

She looked down at her hands in her lap savouring the moment. Nicole stared at her sister, murmuring from time to time and nodded her head when Angela spoke. Greiner sat immobile; he'd had it with this lot.

Hackman re-lit his pipe and gave a couple of thoughtful draws. Greiner thought he was obviously trying to decide: *Did he really believe this shit*?

"I know it's hard, but you must go on dear," Birgit said.

"The High Priest stood behind me. And when he pushed into me, I screamed. Others came and did me the same way."

The girl stopped, then stared off into the distance. No one spoke. Chairs creaked as the cops leaned back, except for Hackman, he leant forward keeping his eyes on the girl. She gave a skittish smile, which carried an overlay of embarrassment.

Angela shifted her unfocused gaze to the door.

"About the sacrifice?" Birgit prompted.

"The priest had a dagger and I thought he was going to stab me, instead he cut the rope. When I sat up, he plunged the knife into the dog's heart. It yelped once and went limp, hanging by its spiky collar."

"Jesus," Greiner said, then mindful of evidence, "Which *side* was he stabbed?"

The girl paused, and shifted her eyes up and to the right.

"Right, I think. Yes, I'm sure of it: Priest stood behind the dog, bending over him — *right* side for sure."

"You getting this on tape?" Greiner asked.

"I've got it," Birgit answered. "So, we have a High Priest in red with a mask."

"Think back Angela, tell us anything that might identify the priest," Hackman said.

"Oh," she said, surprised. "I already *know* who he is."

Now she had them in the palm of her hand: Nicole, Birgit and the men, everyone in the room lavished their attention on her. She looked so calm, so regal, she looked like she adored that feeling.

"The High Priest," she said, pausing for effect, "is my father."

Birgit insisted on terminating the interview right there. She had a policewoman take the girls to the women's shelter. She'd get a court order to keep them in care, out of the clutches of their parents. They'd have no trouble with this evidence.

"I'll get a policewoman to stay with them."

Hackman looked again at Greiner: "Well Nat, what do you think?"

"Hell of a story. Thing is, do you believe it?"

"I'm inclined to," Hackman said. "Children don't usually lie about this."

"Look'it," said Birgit, "I've worked with them in therapy. Girls trust me."

"What's with the white pyjamas?" Hackman asked.

"Wouldn't change their clothes when we picked them up," she said and shrugged. "We found their mother in the bath, drunk and close to passing out. Father was missing. Girls refused point-blank to get dressed."

Nat came in on that one, "Why the hell would they do that?"

"Their stories support each other," Birgit said, "what more do you want?"

"It's so way out," said Nat. "This crap is hard to believe from where I sit."

"Believe it," said Hackman. "A lotta cases just like it. The States has been flooded with them."

"*Flooded*. How *many* exactly?"

"*Thousands of cases*: so many the FBI can't handle them."

"So if it's in the States, why's the RCMP interested?" Nat asked.

"It's not *only* the States. We've had cannibalism here for Chrissake: a baby in Ottawa. In Kingston — mutilations: cats, dogs, and heads bitten off chickens. All ritualistic stuff."

"Have these cases been through the courts?" Nat asked, wondering why he had missed it.

"Not yet. We're still putting it together. Thing is," said Hackman, "does the girl's story fit your case?"

"I'm shocked how well it fits — *everything*," Nat answered, fiddling with his notepad. The page glares back a blank reproach.

"You've seen the transcripts. It's time to nail this case down. Take the girls out to McKinley's place. Make 'em show us where it happened, see if they recognise him."

"Yeah sure, I'll arrange it. So tell me: What do their parents say?"

"Parents deny everything," said Hackman. "Mum's a drunk and Dad's a flake. He's like a sideshow carny with pubic fluff on his face: a wee goatee. They go to church on Sundays, pay their rent on time, manage a *Seven Eleven* south end of town."

Greiner fiddled with his pen for a moment. "Yes, but what about this Satanic stuff?"

"Mum says the girls have an intense fantasy life," Hackman responds.

"Yes," Birgit added, "the girls are imaginative, emotional and highly suggestive. Of course they fantasise, that's normal. They're barely in their teens."

"So they made it up," Nat said.

"No, it doesn't mean they made it up. I've used the latest methods — even hypnosis."

"*Hypnosis?*" Nat asked.

"These girls have a lot of pain in their subconscious, along with post-traumatic amnesia. We help them recover their memories."

"Will hypnosis stand up in court?"

Nat Greiner looked to Hackman for an answer, thinking about how the hell he was going to back it up in the witness dock.

Hackman frowned and fiddled again with his *Bic*, clicking the damn thing faster and faster. "Hypnosis is a worry, we all know it's not admissible. Though it is *very* convincing."

"Okay then *hypnosis is out*," said Nat.

"No," said Hackman, "not entirely. I've seen Birgit question them under truth serum — sodium amytal. We had a physician administer the drug. That we can cite in evidence."

"How the hell did ya get permission for that?" Greiner asked incredulous.

"Permission was easy; parents wanted them to fail. Wanted it to go away. They gave permission." Hackman got up, tired of explaining, he was getting ready to leave. "We did a polygraph, with the best in the business."

"But they're not *reliable* with children," Nat countered.

Hackman looked at the door, then turned again. He'd underestimated Greiner: "You're right they're not. Nor with pathological liars, drunks or schizophrenics — or anyone else that's psychotic. Hey, now I've gotta go."

"Wait up," Greiner said, "it's me that has to get the evidence to solve this case. Help us out here. How can you be sure they aren't lying?"

"We did a voice print," Hackman answered, "FBI lent us a voice-spectrograph. They developed it at Quantico with the Army's psych ops. Records speech on high-fidelity tape and analyses pitch and resonance. "

"How is that specro-thingy better than a polygraph?" Greiner asked him.

"It picks up the slightest quaver in their speech. There's not a hint of deceit in these girls. They're not lying. I'd stake my reputation on it."

"You may be doing just that."

"Okay, gotta go, meeting at the courthouse in ten."

"Question is, will their story stand up in court?"

"It'll stand up in court, believe me," Hackman said stuffing notebooks and pens into a brief case to make his escape. "There's also forensic. She's not a virgin; at least they've established that much. And recovery therapy jogs their memory. I'm outta here."

As he headed for the door Greiner swung around to the policewoman.

"How did you do it then Birgit?" Nat asked her, "The memory recovery bit."

Hackman paused in mid-stride when he heard that, waiting to hear her respond.

"Painful memories are repressed. Children don't trust adults, and recalling trauma is painful, so the girls won't voluntarily retell events."

"Yes, but how exactly are memories *recovered*? Do you drag it out of them by shouting questions, or what?"

While Nat asked this, he was tapping on his notebook with a pen. He jotted down, *drugged by mom*, then circled it three times in blue biro. Spokes radiated up from these circles with: *undressed, raped by Dad & others, dog killed*. Words hung on each spoke, as if they'd been impaled. *Memories recovered, hypnosis, truth serum, voice stress analyser*. This next circle of words was impaled on separate spokes.

Greiner chewed the end of the pen and tried to focus on the mind map, trying to connect the dots as Birgit continued her explanation.

"We questioned the girls until we got to the truth. Then followed up with more and more questions until they spilt their guts with all the details."

"You have tapes of the girls for court?"

"Their therapy's not taped," then Birgit added, "because I need to build trust. They have to trust me before they'll talk about intimate things."

"Ah-huh," Nat said.

"Yeah, I know it is slow, but it works. When I think they're ready, we have a session before witnesses, as we just did. These sessions we tape as evidence."

Hackman had heard enough. He resumed his escape, pausing just briefly at the door for a parting shot.

"It's up to you, Nat. Reconstruct the crime. Do whatever you've gotta do. Get some hard evidence at the McKinley place."

CHAPTER 6. **DUNCAN**

Do not enter into an alliance with neighbours until you are acquainted with their designs.

Sun Tzü, *The Art of War*, 512 BC

The phone rang. Three shrill rings before I reached it. The insurance adjuster's on the line with questions at the ready. When I explained the situation he was apoplectic: "You've done what?"

"Removed the carcass — I've burnt it."

"Has it been examined?"

"Of course. Police were here. Didn't you get their report?"

"Says the horse was killed by person or persons unknown. Case is still open."

"Well, the horse is dead, so I'm making a claim."

"We can't pay until this case is solved. It's highly irregular. Should have left the animal for our examination."

"I notified you of his death. Hey, I couldn't leave him in the barn. The carcass was rotting for Chrissake. What was I supposed to do?"

"Could have buried it."

"Hell no, ground's frozen. Have to burn a carcass in winter."

"We'll need that necropsy report, soon as possible."

"What necropsy? There's no forensic and no necropsy. The horse was killed with an *axe* for Chrissake."

"In that case we'll wait for something more definitive from the police."

In response I took a deep breath and tried to stay calm. This was the guy who would pay my claim, I needed to stroke him.

"The police don't know who did it. Look, I'm the one in distress here."

"You'll have to wait until the investigation's complete."

He hung up and I made a pot of real coffee, starting from scratch, grinding fresh beans and filling the percolator with cold water. I like the caramel taste you get with percolation. Flavanoids are released from the beans at 70 degrees and they're damaged at boiling point, which gives coffee a burnt taste. A percolator increases pressure and yields more flavour, at higher temperatures, without burning. Of course an Italian espresso machine can do this, at many times barometric pressure, and produces the very best coffee. The trick is to drink it within seconds of brewing, for flavour departs with the steam.

In Canada they don't know how to make good coffee. Canadians are not quite civilised, not in the way of Europeans; here in restaurants they brew the cheap *robustus* beans, then leave the slug stewing on a hot plate all day until it's stale and burnt.

If there is one thing coffee has to be, it's *fresh*.

After coffee I went to feed the horses, stopping when I entered the barn. Had that eerie feeling you get when you're being watched. I looked around, saw nothing, then moved through the barn checking the horses. When I reached the stallion's box, I caught quick movement and a flash. Thought I'd been shot, then recognised the flash for what it was.

A man stepped out, a gnome in a cardigan, with a middle-aged paunch. I almost hit him in a spasm of anger; instead I dropped into that bent-kneed, martial-arts stance, half-remembered from a lifetime ago.

"Hey man, take it easy. I'm with the *Star.*"

He must have read my face. It went with the stance.

"Piss off," I said, at my articulate best. "Jesus, how did you get in?"

"Walked in from the road, didn't want to bother you."

"No shit," I said, furious, "GET OUT!"

"I'd like an interview, to get the whole story."

"There's no story, no interview, a horse killed is all. Ask the police."

"Already done that. So what about the satanic slant?"

"There's NO satanic slant."

"The sign on the wall?"

"What about it?"

"It's the mark of Cain. Work of the devil."

"I don't know about that."

"Satanists are antichrist; they turn religion on its head. Reciting the Lord's Prayer backwards, stuff like that. Take it from me — that's an upside down cross."

"Well, why put it in my barn?

"Who knows? There's a lot of this ritual shit — it's all over."

"Thought that only happened in California."

"Hell no. There's a case right here over in Saint Catharine's."

That floored me. Could that be right?

"Let me ask you," he said, "Are you Wiccan?"

"Am I what?"

"Wiccan, you know — witches, occult, pagan shit, stuff like that?"

"Get outta here."

Then I took a step towards him. Must have looked threatening for he sidled past my anger and scuttled down the drive while I stood and watched until he left. He'd have never made it past *Tuff* that's for sure. Sometimes I liked animals more than people. Animals don't betray you.

Afterwards I had the nagging feeling that I'd handled it badly. He could write whatever he liked about *Satanic Worship in the wilds of Hillsborough* and probably would. Wished I'd had the presence of mind to strip the film from his camera.

The story never ran in the *Star*. My friend Guy phoned to say he'd seen a bizarre piece in the *National Tattler.* He read it to me on the phone, a beat up of satanic cults, group sex and animal sacrifice. Pictures of my dead horse, naked girls, a photo of me looking like a stunned bunny, and of course that sign in blood.

The piece read as if it all happened right here on my farm. The reporter connected it to every satanic incident known to mankind: animal sacrifice and sexual abuse were apparently reaching the proportions of an epidemic. This stuff was hard to swallow, dished up by bottom feeders like the *Tattler* — last rung of the tabloid press.

I repaired to my office to lick my wounds and stop the bleeding for a few hours, until I had to get horses back in the barn for the night. Through leafless birch outside the window, I watched the horses play for a while in the snow, then scanned the woods through the lens and saw nothing but trees.

Beyond doubt I was the worst kind of fool, for buying a French horse, as if I could afford the risk. As if I was made of money. Christ. I'd even quarantined *Alaric* in England for six months to meet the import regs, then paid freight to Toronto.

That had been real money, more than I had, more than I could afford.

There were no foals on the ground.

I'd gambled on a single hand, gambled everything.

Then lost on the first card.

We went to Yorkville on Giselle's birthday, later in the afternoon. All love has its ups and downs and our marriage had its fair share. It hadn't been the same since Jenny was born. I'd been warned that a woman's love shifts with the birth of a child. What I hadn't known, what I hadn't been warned of, was that her love might never return.

We haven't produced another child for thirteen years and that disappointed the woman deep inside her. Her clock keeps ticking. She's never said anything; don't think she's thought it. It's not something she'd talk about. It's a secret knowledge that I have. Even while thinking such thoughts, it felt good to be celebrating, to leave our anxieties at home. We surged along in the Blazer, singing with the radio, belting out John Lennon's *Imagine*. The impossible dream, a dream we thought could be when I was young, a time when everything seemed possible.

Jenny wandered in and out of tune, which sounded kind of sweet. I wished that we were young again. Giselle looked at me and smiled, as if divining my thoughts.

Yorkville is Toronto's answer to Greenwich Village, though now trendily boutique. We had dinner at the Bellaire Café. Giselle was in good form — tipsy on the wine. What had taken us down this road — where had we lost our way?

With Jenny in her role as the family clown, doing her little mime of walking against the wind, we walked to Aurora Gallery on Prince Arthur

Avenue. We spent hours browsing Inuit carvings, inviting to the touch. The proprietor frowned at Jenny caressing the soapstone. Life-size pieces, the ones I loved, were absurdly expensive. They were for those with a different life. I was failing her in not being able to afford them.

Giselle seized an exquisite carving, a hunter with his spear poised at a seal surfacing at its breathing hole in the ice. It caught an isolated, primal moment — perfect. Jenny bought some flowers for her mother and gave them with a laugh. Giselle clutched Jenny to her in a fierce hug while I folded my arms around them both and held them tight. A moment to hold forever.

On the drive home my vision distorted, signalling the onslaught of another migraine. Giselle took the wheel and I lay on the back seat watching her in the rear-view mirror, watching the teardrop pendant at her neck bounce with every bump in the road. I got more and more distressed as we drove on through the night. A dark band tightening around my head. I felt like shit.

What I wanted was to hold her, put my arms around her and make her safe. I wanted to love her. Wanted to make love, slowly until we both came with a rush. It was not to be. When we reached the farm I was deep in the gnarled embrace of migraine: I stumbled from the truck, vomited then staggered incoherent, to bed.

Giselle came close and I put my arms around her, tried to kiss her on the lips. She twisted her mouth away.

"Damnit Duncan, can't you do something *right*, just once?"

I'd forgotten about the vomit. That night I was not her lover.

I closed my eyes and died of shame.

In the morning I awoke with a migraine hangover. Giselle had already left for work and Jenny had caught the bus to school. When Greiner's Chevy roared up the drive, with its wheels spinning on the ice, I was already aboard Murray's filly. She jumped with fright at the revving car, so I slipped off and walked back to see him. It was not so cold that day and I'd dressed lightly: jeans, chaps, sweater and a blue nylon parka. The filly jerked her head and pulled each time the parka crackled as I walked. She hung back, eyeing the car with her head down, snorting — ready to run.

Greiner lent out the window he'd cranked down.

"Got results on your dog."

"Was hoping you'd find something."

"*Acepromasine* in ground beef."

"*Tuff* would have wolfed it down."

"Yeah, dog like that, they'd be stupid to get outta the car."

"Well, it tells us they planned it. They *knew* there was a serious dog."

"It does," Greiner allowed and stepped out, "seen any strange cars about?"

The filly snorted and backed up, legs splayed. Greiner's move had frightened her.

"Well, no."

"Thought not," he said looking at the horse, then squinting off in the distance as if he was trying hard to remember something. He shifted his gaze and looked me in the eye.

"You been to college, right?"

"Yes," I said wondering what he was getting at, "Edinburgh — ancient history. Taught there awhile."

"So, what brings you here?"

"Teaching's too hard; you keep giving and you get almost nothing back. That's why we're here."

What I didn't say was that I love the outdoors, I love nature, animals and the farm. Here above the snow-line it reminds Giselle of her homeland along the Baltic. I wanted to breed horses here, the best in the world—Thoroughbred horses.

"Ah huh. You study chemistry?"

"Sure, physics, chemistry and math before realising that *I did it because I could*, not because I really wanted a scientific career. Truth is I'm more interested in people and horses than in things. But I do know about *Ace*. It's a sedative for horses. I keep some in the Blazer at all times — just in case."

"Yeah well, there's enough in the bait to kill an elephant, but that's *not* how he died."

"Oh?"

"Knifed in the right ventricle. After they knocked him down with the drug."

"Why'd they do that?" I said mystified.

He looked right at me.

"Filed for that insurance yet?"

"Matter of fact I have."

My precarious finances were becoming central to this affair. I slid my eyes to the mares cropping dry grass where they'd pawed through the snow. Greiner followed my gaze.

"Yours?"

"A few of them."

"Insured?"

"No. Insuring mares is way too expensive. Death cover's no use anyway. With mares infertility's much more threatening."

"I see. Was your stallion ... you know like — fertile?"

"Far as we knew. He test bred a couple of mares in England. One still pregnant at ninety days — standard procedure."

"One out of two doesn't sound good?"

"Doesn't mean that much either. Have to do the stats on a full season to nail it. He could do the deed and sperm motility was normal — good enough for me."

"Okay. So, he was fertile. You think of anyone who'd do this?"

"Sounds like that satanic thing. The mark on the wall."

"It might be at that."

"Can't think of anything else."

Greiner meditated for so long I got the impression he was choosing his words carefully. Too carefully, now I was worried about what was coming.

"A couple a kids, other side of Guelph. They claim there was a witches coven — right here at your farm."

"The hell you say."

"Know anything about it?"

"Hell *No*. Why would they say *that*?"

"They didn't say *why* exactly. I went through the transcripts." He waited for me to say something and when I didn't he went on: "Pretty girls — pretty convincing. Lotta' detail. Parents deny it of course. As parents do. Something's wrong though, I can feel it."

"What happens next?" I said.

"RCMP want the girls here Monday."

"Why do the Mounties want them here?"

"To reconstruct the crime."

"All right," I said, "It's still hard to believe."

"Believe it."

He got out of the car and I waited, thinking that he'd add something more. Instead, he turned and walked across the yard as if I wasn't there.

"Mind if I check the woods?" he flung back over his shoulder.

"Fine," I said, and drew the filly to a rock I used as a mounting block.

Without another word I heaved myself into the saddle as *Jet Stream* danced forward. She reefed at the bit when I picked up the reins, snapping the leather through my fingers. The filly pranced and skipped into a canter now and then as I set off on my snowploughed circuit, standing in the stirrups. She bounded under me, bouncing, stretching and coiling her powerful muscles. The filly was wound tight, ready to explode.

Detective Greiner was by then a remote black form in a white world, slogging through the knee-deep snow, to the grove of beech on the hill.

CHAPTER 7

In warfare, first lay plans which will ensure victory, then lead your army to battle…

Sun Tzü, *The Art of War*, 512 BC

Murray's party was champagne in flutes, elegant women and large, gnarled black-suited men.

"Sköl," Giselle said and looked into my eyes from across the table. I raised my glass, nodded and sipped the wine holding her gaze, delighting in her Nordic beauty. We set our flutes on the table with a clink of glass on wood in unison. A fine woman, my wife.

"Estonian," she said to a query from Murray's wife about her surname. "*Thorne* is a river in the far north. A medieval name in lapland." Julia looked blank so Giselle added, "My parents migrated, well *escaped* from communism in Estonia, when I was a child. They sailed the Baltic at night across the busy shipping lanes to Sweden."

"Sounds dangerous. You must have been scared?"

"I was too young to be scared. Of course my parents knew these waters, though you are right, it was dangerous."

"You got away?" Julia said.

"Yes, to a tiny island in the Archipelago. We hid overnight, then sailed to the isle of Gotland. We lived for a while in Visby, the last walled city in Europe."

"Were you old enough to remember?" Julia asked.

"It is the story my mother told me. I remember being seasick into a plastic bag, more terrified of staining my Sunday dress than anything else."

Julia laughed and conversation withered as we attacked the entrée.

"Then you were raised in Sweden?" Julia said.

"Yes, my father taught school there in Umeo. It reminded him of home."

She looked around, a little embarrassed and fingered the turquoise pendant at her neck, which emphasised her otherness. In Canada many of us, indeed almost all of us around this table, were from somewhere else.

When Giselle spoke again, it broke the silence: "I was the son my father never had. He taught me to shoot: wild duck in spring and *Älg* in the fall," she said.

"You mean *Elk?*" Julia asked.

"No they're *Moose*," I said, "although the Swedish sounds like *Elk*."

Giselle looked relieved; I don't think she knew the English word for the species. At the talk of shooting Murray's colleague perked up. A tall man with a Caribbean tan, a tan that marked him as privileged at this time of year.

"Tell Professor Stanford what happened to your horse," Murray said and introduced Stanford's wife, a seductive presence with cleavage half-exposed. Giselle caught my eye and raised an eyebrow. Her pendant centred at that delicate flute between her collarbones.

"Please do," she said.

So I told the whole story adding the pure fiction of the *Tattler* along with Detective Greiner's planned reconstruction of the crime.

"Do you believe the girls accusations?" Mrs Stanford asked.

"It's hard to accept — a *coven* for Chrissake. We were only away the evening."

"Until two am," Giselle said, correcting me with maddening Germanic precision. With that, the chatter around us ceased; we now had everyone's attention.

"Okay then, we were absent for all of six hours."

"A horse was slaughtered, that alone needs explanation," Stanford said.

"Yes, the insurance company is holding out on us."

"You must have heard of the satanic hysteria sweeping the country?"

"Police said something about Ottawa and Kingston, but aren't they rumours?"

"They are real, though *I think* of them as urban myths," said Stanford with a smile. He was enjoying the attention.

"So they are *not* real?" said Giselle.

"There are far too many cases to be believable."

"People are making it up then?" Julia said, passing another entrée.

"No, no" Stanford said. "They are not making it up. The victims *do* believe their experience of Satanism, but I'm disturbed by some weird, recurring aspects."

"What weird aspects?" I asked.

"Sexual — incest is often invoked."

"Was that in the news?"

"Such allegations are made by girls. And since pubescents find it hard to distinguish between fantasy and reality, they are often ignored."

Stanford looked around the table, appraising his audience.

"Does that not apply to *all* teenagers?" Giselle said.

"No, not at all. Some are sensibly grounded, as much as any teenager ever is," Stanford responded with the voice of authority.

I glanced at Jennifer seated with the neighbours teens at the end of the table and immediately classified her as sensibly grounded. Giselle obviously did not.

"Their rituals are crammed with sacred symbols. And the girls are inevitably from religious families," Stanford continued.

"We're talking *Satanists* here — right?" I asked.

"Not at all. We're talking your everyday church-going *Christians*."

"I see," I said. Not seeing at all where this was heading.

"There is rarely any *physical* evidence," Stanford said. He was on a roll and enjoying the limelight. "So it's hard to verify rituals ever took place."

"Ah, but there is a slaughtered horse in my case."

"Yes, and that does make it unusual."

"And there is that sign in blood," Giselle reminded us with polite formality.

"Question is: Are dead animals and cryptic signs evidence of Satanic rituals?" Stanford asked.

"Police seem to think so," I said.

"Yes, they do and that's a worry."

"Are they wrong?"

"Police assume too much. They assume memories are simply buried. That they lie within the mind — intact. This point is critical."

"Critical to the legal system?" I said.

"Precisely. Truth is we don't ever recall events in exactly the way they happened." Stanford looked around the table for challengers.

"I hear some therapists specialise in recovering memories," Julia said.

"The old amnesia ploy," Giselle said, placing her fork by the plate.

"*Precisely*," said Stanford again, "beloved by movie directors. It's hard to tell if a memory is genuine, or if it's imagined? Perhaps it is instead what the *therapist* imagined."

He paused to finish the next entrée, nutty things in little balls of minced meat. We ate in silence. The silence stretched until we became aware of brittle steel on bone china.

Stanford filled the gap: "Accusers are invariably teens, paired with counsellors specialising in recovered-memory methods. That alone is a worry."

"Really?" said Julia.

She gathered the plates for another round as we took a drink to clean the palate. Stanford carried on encouraged by his audience.

"Yes, a major worry because memories are *not* videos. Memories distort with use — they change."

"I don't know about that," said Julia who obviously thought the whole thing rubbish.

"*Absolutely*," Stanford looked irritated to have met any resistance — however slight. "Incidents not consistent with our self image are warped to fit. Think of staggeringly different eyewitness reports of the same crime."

"You're saying we believe our memories, because they fit with what we know?" Giselle asked.

"No, we believe our memories because they fit with *who we are*," Stanford said.

We tucked into Julia's delicious venison casserole with wild rice from native wetland grasses the local Indians gather around here. While eating I considered what Stanford had said. Could the satanic thing be a lie?

Were the girls falsely accusing their parents? It sounded way out to me.

Dessert came as old-fashioned English trifle. Whipped custard, cream, sherry, fruit and cake. A lush confection. Cholesterol be damned. We were gasping by the time we'd finished. Surreptitiously I slipped my hands under the table and let my belt out a notch.

"Murray tells me you're training his filly," Stanford's wife said.

"Yes, *Jet Stream* will race as a three-year old this summer. Murray didn't want her raced at two."

"You'll race at Woodbine?"

"Well, I broke her and she'll be fit by spring. Tom Roberts will put her through the gates and keep her for the season, he has stables at the track."

"So you're a horse breaker then. How romantic." She smiled.

Giselle stopped eating and looked across at us. "Not as romantic as it sounds — not in winter," she said.

"No, I don't imagine it is. You know Murray from England then?"

"We met here at the Hunt Club in Caledon."

"He's the only breaker with any class," Murray said, raising his wine glass to salute us across the table, "only one who can quote Xenophon." He said this as if it was self-explanatory.

"Who on earth is *Xenophon*?" Julia asked.

"Ancient Greek; contemporary of Aristotle I believe. That right Duncan?"

"Socrates actually. Xenophon wrote a letter in defence of Socrates, but the case was lost. Xenophon was an accomplished man with an almost modern view of horsemanship."

"Ah yes," said Professor Stanford. "We studied *Anabasis* in Classics. One thing I do remember: *to change your life you must begin by first changing yourself*." I squirmed at his existentialism while contemplating the truth ,of it. Stanford carried on, "I recall that only officers were mounted in *Anabasis*."

"The officers were murdered when their Persian allies turned on them. And obviously the Persians of Iran are still duplicitous," I said, "Xenophon was elected by the men as their commander. He led ten-thousand men home to Athens, fighting every inch of the way."

"What did Xenophon have to say about horses?" asked Stanford's wife.

"Horses then were hi-tech weapons of war. Xenophon thought young men should practise their warrior skills rather than to spend their valuable time horse breaking."

"And you agree?"

"Absolutely. It is specialised work. That's my niche in racing."

"That's his God-given talent," Murray says, "Duncan has an affinity for horses. An extraordinary empathy that gives him an edge."

Giselle broke in to rescue the guests. "Come now, I'm sure you don't want to talk horses all night."

"Not at all," said Stanford's wife blinking her dark lashes in the candlelight, "I'm *fascinated*."

We talked instead of politics over coffee at the end of the meal. Julia served a distinctive Colombian espresso. She made a good brew, even if she lacked in the play of politics. In Canada politics are especially intractable. The French have not taken kindly to General Wolfe's victory, with the help of my clansmen the Highland Frasers, back in 1759. For a while in the heady political turbulence of the 1960-70s, there was a terrorist campaign of murderous bombings and kidnappings that has left a nasty taste of bitterness and a linguistic apartheid in Quebec. A complication to French ambitions is that there are five native nations living there, who also form distinct societies: The *Cree*, *Huron*, *Iroquois* and *Innu*. Indeed they have filed land claims to three-quarters of the provence! To a man these native Americans do *not* want to secede from Canada. Despite this, in Ottawa the Québécois are again demanding concessions from Parliament to forestall their perennial threat of secession. Intractable non?

We left late, strolling to the truck in a starry night filled with the reality of bitter cold. Politics as always, lay unresolved. I turned the heat up in the Blazer when the motor was warming and Jenny went to sleep on the back seat before we made it out the driveway. Giselle dozed for a while, slumped against the door, soothed by the pulsating motor. Something must have bumped Giselle back to consciousness.

"You and that damn shrink monopolised the conversation. Must you dominate absolutely *everything*?"

"What *is* the matter, Giselle? I thought you enjoyed yourself."

"All you ever talk about is *horses*. I am sick to death of *horses*."

"But *Alaric* was special," I said, more than a little shocked.

"He was just a horse."

"Jeez, that's harsh. You know I like some horses more than people."

"More than you like me?"

"Damnit, Giselle you're drunk. And you can be a mean drunk at that."

She maintained a wounded silence while I drove us home, keeping a careful distance from the treacherous soft snow that lay along the edge.

It was late the next day, after I had forgotten Greiner, that he arrived. This was announced by the sound of cars tackling our driveway with a burst of revs in low gear. Greiner got out when the engine died and he slogged through the snow to the barn.

"Hi," he said reaching to shake hands. "We'll take the girls to the woods and look around, if you don't mind."

"Sure, I'll be right here in the barn."

He rejoined the others, a Polaroid bumping on a strap across one shoulder. As the girls broke out of the black & white I caught a burst of static from the radio, watching as they and their minders crossed the field, high stepping towards the woods.

The feed truck I was waiting for arrived with a crunch of gears and a throaty roar. I hauled the fodder to the feed room, carrying hundredweight sacks on my shoulder. By the time Greiner returned the truck had departed. By then I was rank and sweaty since I'd stripped to my T-shirt and was pitching bales from the loft down to the feed room when they turned up.

Greiner introduced me to Hackman from the RCMP. I didn't know what to make of this pipe-smoking Mountie until he spoke to the girls, then I pegged him as a psychologist. The dragon lady in uniform had to be the minder. She stepped forward and crossed her arms; the girls had to move around her to see me.

The girls were bursting with health the way teenagers are. The eldest had fair hair, reaching halfway down her back: sisters. The younger still had that androgynous body of pre-pubescence. The older had aspects of an overt sexuality my Jenny had yet to acquire.

"You know this man?" Greiner asked them.

The girls said nothing. The eldest flared her nostrils then chewed her bottom lip. I pictured myself as they would have seen me: torn shirt, a tad worn and decidedly weather beaten, pumped and sweaty from the work. I must have looked a bit feral. Anger came out of nowhere that I struggled to control.

The girls took in the pitchfork, scanned my sweating face and stepped back.

"No," they said in unison looking down and exchanging glances, their hair swished forward like curtains that closed their faces. The older girl flicked her hair, held my eyes and smiled—triumphant. No one saw her in that moment they were all looking at me.

"We've crime-taped a clearing in the woods that's been trampled."

Greiner spoke slowly as if I was a mentally retarded and slightly deaf child. "You know anything about that?"

"No, of course not."

"Don't go inside the tape, it's an official crime scene."

The girls refused to meet my eyes. Their minder glared.

"What crime?" I said, resolving to do precisely that, when he left. "Deer lie in the sun on top of that hill. They'll go right through the tape."

"Is that a fact," Greiner said as he turned away.

With a nod to the Mountie, and with entourage in tow, he headed for the car.

"Stay away from there..." he flung at me over his shoulder.

The starter motor ground over and over in the cold. Greiner looked grim. He tried again and again until the car at last got a grip and coughed into life.

CHAPTER 8

There are five pitfalls for a Commander:
Recklessness, leading to destruction.
Cowardice, leading to capture.
A hot temper, prone to provocation.
A delicacy of honour, leading to shame.
Over concern for his men, leading to trouble.

Sun Tzü, *The Art of War*, 512 BC

We met our friend Guy in the *Bookshop Café*. One of my favourite places, one of my favourite people. Guy lives on the other side of Guelph at Elmira among the Mennonites. Giselle was already there, having come straight from work. As I made my way through the book shelves, I spied her leaning forward to hear what Guy was saying. So close their heads almost touching. The distinctive shape of Perrier on the table. No vices, she won't get fat on that — she'll have salad, no dessert and de-caff herbal tea. Giselle didn't drink during the week, though she'd been known to binge at weekends.

"Ah," Guy said when he noticed me, "Marlboro man."

He was wearing a red bandana around his neck, an affectation I took as some remnant of his being French.

"Hullo Duncan." Giselle's face lit up as I leaned across to kiss her on the mouth. "I've ordered salad. What'll you have?" Her mouth was wet and salty.

"Beef nachos," I said to the waitress as she hovered.

"No salad?" Giselle asked. As if reminding me of my excesses, would protect me from them.

"Make mine beef, if you can kill it, I'll eat it."

Giselle wrinkled her nose.

"Giselle's been telling me about the drama of your horse."

"That's not the half of it; police think a satanic cult killed him."

"A cult? *Incredible.* What do you think?"

"I don't know what to think. I'm losing clients while the bank manager is getting nervous about our loan." I pulled back a chair so I could squeeze in. "Insurance isn't paying. Just as well Giselle's working," I said, flashing her a smile — declaring a truce.

"Did you meet the girls," Giselle asked.

"Police took them to identify the place — and they did! How could they have been there without us knowing?"

"You're not there all the time. Stranger things 'ave 'appened," Guy said, in his French-Canadian accent. He sounded like Peter Sellers in the Pink Panther although he'd lived here in Ontario for years. He wore a black-faced *TagHeuer,* which he now consulted to give him time to think.

"Well... Girls were scared shitless when I met them. The eldest looked at me and smiled, kinda sizing me up and defiant at the same time."

"You are intimidating," said Giselle.

"Intimidating? All I did was stand there."

"That's all it takes, you can look as mean as dirt without moving a muscle, like Clint Eastwood's stare."

"No way."

"Oh yes," said Guy, "you can look hard, even if we know you're not."

It was then I wondered if he really knew me as well as he thought.

"*Mon ami,* do you know them, perhaps from somewhere else?" Guy reached for the bread rolls in a wicker basket on the table.

"Hell no. Never seen them before. Though I think they're screwed in the head by religion and their parents," I paused. "Though not necessarily in that order."

"Are the police convinced?"

"Yes, they are, and that's a worry."

"Perhaps there is another reason our horse was killed," Giselle said as the waitress brought her salad. She has a hamburger for Guy, with a

Canadian flag stuck to a toothpick in the bun.

"*Magnifique*," he says and raises the flag in a salute.

The waitress came back with my meal. Her scent wafted over me — gently disturbing — I paused distracted.

"*Macho nachos*," she said, "cheese, ground beef, pinto beans, chopped tomatoes and jalapeno peppers with avocado."

My mouth burned when I bit into the fresh peppers. I took a draught of Perrier. Giselle ordered Camomile tea.

"Guy, I need to figure out what to do. Police might be on the wrong track. You've been in the force, what's the next step?"

"Whoa — in the force, an MP temporarily. I'm no detective."

"I can't just sit on my hands. Thing is, I don't know what to do."

"You'd better do something or police will tie you to it, that's for sure."

"What about *your* clients? Think they'd know anything?"

"Maybe. I'll ask around."

Guy worked with leather. He now made custom holsters for cops *and robbers*. He cut and moulded wet leather on to the piece for a slick fit. An odd way to make a living, I always thought. I changed the subject.

"Heard from Troy lately?"

"Not for a while. Alison wants me to take him this summer. He gets bored at my place. She's going to England with her live-in lawyer. Troy would cramp their style."

Guy had come to Elmira after Vietnam because of the peace and the Mennonites — one of Canada's religious minorities: fundamentalists who drive horses and run their life and farms in a traditional way. Well, whatever was traditional for the good Protestant burgers of Switzerland in the 1500s. The Amish in Pennsylvania are a stricter offshoot of these *Plain Folk*.

Guy's interest was horses. He figured Mennonites would teach him something about horses. After serving in Vietnam, he was attracted to the rural life — he liked quiet. He'd married Alison a fair-haired girl from town. Guy soon realised that *Plain Folks* horse lore was limited. He had not met a single one who could ride. They had Standardbreds that hadn't made the grade at the track: bought 'em cheap and drove them till they dropped, like we'd drive a clapped out car into the ground.

Alison left him before the year was done and took along his son.

Guy's interest in the community withered after that. She'd left him for a corporate lawyer, which made it worse. Someone with a proper job.

Horses were what we had in common. We both rode to hounds when the hunt was in full cry. At one time, in a bout of togetherness, I conveyed my feelings about hunting to Giselle. She was not impressed.

"Riding to hounds can be as exciting as sex," I'd said.

"And it's probably just as dangerous," was her response.

As a distraction I turned to Guy. "Going to the Derby?"

"*Absolument*."

Betting on the races was Guy's drug of choice. After biting his nails through one race, he'd be looking for the next hit. He was an oracle on pedigrees, having memorised bloodlines of Thoroughbreds on four continents. Guy made an annual pilgrimage to Woodbine. He also went to the Triple Crown: Kentucky Derby, Belmont Stakes and the Preakness. I've gone too. Last season we also went to Florida with a couple of horses for the spring racing, along with Giselle.

Well, I didn't know how much he won or lost over the years. I do know he'd bought his farm from winnings of the one really good horse he'd owned.

We discussed horses for awhile, then Giselle started yawning, so we left. My arm went around her waist as we walked to the cars. She was comforted at first and leaned into me, sharing intimacy, then she straightened when we reached her car, as if she'd come to her senses, and shook me off.

I headed home in my truck.

Next day I took *Jet Stream* down to Woodbine. At daybreak the sun was too weak to break through the clouds and it was cold — damn cold. Giselle was in the shower and Jennifer had already caught the bus for school. I plugged in the block heater of the Blazer, to warm it enough over breakfast to get it started.

On the road, black ice caught the four track in a quick slide, and I fought to keep my foot off the brake. The trailer swerved and clanked at the hitch with the sudden shift in weight. It reminded me to slow down.

I'd arranged to meet Murray after dropping the runner at the track. Murray didn't have surgery Fridays, so he had time between consultations, enough time for me to tool over to Toronto Western and called on him.

Murray was intense as he often is, with a handshake that told me he had something important to say:

"Pathologist found something, traces of *diacetylmorphine*."

"Diacetyl what?"

"Heroin."

"Really. Hmmm, that does change things."

"Yes, it does. Drugs make sense — smuggling drugs," Murray said.

"Is there any other explanation?" I said.

"Not that I know of. No scientific explanation anyway."

"Hmmm, with tranquillisers they'd get kilos of the stuff into a horse. *Alaric* came through quarantine, the day before."

"Do horses regurgitate?" Murray asked.

"No, they don't, they're not ruminants like cattle. They do have a huge gut capacity though, from evolving on the fibrous steppe grasses of Central Asia."

"Central Asia?"

"Afghanistan, Uzbekistan, *Kebabistan*: all those god-awful, dry-as-chips places."

"Hmmm. Then drugs would definitely be worthwhile," Murray said.

"And someone got them out of *Alaric* at my farm."

"They'd have had a vet at the other end — they didn't have one here. Here the gang bangers had to kill him to get the drugs out."

"Bastards."

"Precisely," Murray said. "Sorry to rush, but I have patients. My secretary will take you to Doctor Wharton. He'll fill you in."

Wharton was reluctant to talk to me, though he eventually loosened up enough to explain what he'd found.

"Contaminants. You mean they cut the stuff?" I asked.

"No, it's uncut. It's pure heroin, almost *no contaminants*. Ran it through the spectro-photometer. A trace of *acetyl-codeine*, none of the usual junk."

"So?" I said.

"A commercial lab. It's not made in a backyard like most of this stuff."

"What sort of company makes heroin?"

"Pharmaceutical companies make morphine for prescription. Heroin is an even better painkiller. Better for cancers or AIDS. *Kaiser's Pharmacea* in France is most likely."

"You can tell that from the sample?"

"No," he said. "It's because that's the only place that makes medical opiates legally. There are none in North America."

"I see," I said, trying to get a grip on it. "How come you know this stuff?"

"Worked for the Government Labs in Ottawa."

"Ah."

"That's before they restructured the place and downsized to a skeleton admin staff. We chemists became redundant with the advent of new technology."

"Can you narrow it down to a particular lab?"

"I'm betting it was Europe. The resin is probably from Afghanistan, since they supply most of it. It's not Tasmanian poppy."

"How do you know that?"

"Not a guess this time. Tasmanian product has acetyl-oripavine."

"Oh," I said distracted, "No, I meant about Afghanistan. How do you know it's not poppy from somewhere else?"

"I couldn't swear, but it's from somewhere in Central Asia, that's a statistical guess."

"Based on?"

"Most compounds exist in two forms. The three-dimensional structure is oriented one way in some of its molecules. Others form its mirror image — molecules rotated the opposite way."

"Yes," I said, "left- and right-handed compounds."

"It's mostly the left-handed *levo* form that is biologically active — most of this sample in fact. Ratio of *dexter* right-handed form, tells us its source."

"Great," I said, "cops will check it out."

Wharton was agitated. He exhaled with what sounded like *Phwoar*.

"No they can't. Used the entire sample in the assay; police won't be able to verify it. There's none left, since you've apparently burnt the remains."

"That's right, but what exactly is your problem?"

"Look, Murray has put me in an awkward position. I did him a favour, thinking the sample was from a private patient. I did the analysis with hospital facilities. Now it turns out to be a police case. I can't admit to it. Hell, not with three kids and a mortgage I can't. Christ, I just bought a three-hundred-thousand dollar house!"

"Ah, come on. You must be able to say something."

"Hell no. And I'll deny it if you tell them. Thing is you don't need me. You already have the information — act on it. Go and do anything you want to the bad guys. Just don't expect me to testify."

"Okay," I said, "thanks anyway, we haven't caught them, so there's no need for an expert witness — yet."

I went in search of Murray.

Greiner was waiting for me when I got home. The forensic van was on the track where I'd cleared the snow. They'd been in the woods.

"Find anything?" I asked when I went to meet him.

Greiner looked grim. He came close with his head tilted forward like a bull — so close I felt his breath.

"We have. The area is trampled like she said. We're taking samples."

"It's a deer yard. Deer go there in winter. Take shelter among trees, then graze in fields at dawn. They like lying on the north slope, in the sun."

He ignored me.

"The girls identified this site. They're now wards of the state, it's out of their parents hands."

"There's something ..." I started to say.

He cut me off. I don't think he heard.

"Thing is, the girls were scared. Scared of you. Don't know what you're up to, but I am going to find out."

"Wait on — it was *my* horse."

"Your horse or not, I'll find out what's going on."

"Look," I said, spreading my hands in supplication. "I've had samples run at a hospital. They found heroin in his gut for Chrissake. Someone used the horse to smuggle drugs."

"Why didn't you tell us?"

"I *am* telling you, right now."

"Okay, so who did this assay?"

"I can't tell you that; the guy did it as a favour."

"Could have been contaminated. Heroin from another case. Maybe they got the stuff all over the lab."

"No way. They don't have heroin there." I said it automatically in my defence, but what did I know? I'd underestimated Greiner. Contamination was a distinct possibility.

"Good grief man, evidence won't hold up in court if it doesn't have a certified provenance, if analysis wasn't done by a police lab."

"Well, can't verify it now, I've burnt the carcass."

"You're shitting me. You've got no evidence at all."

Greiner voice was flat, stalled in neutral.

"I'm telling you straight: the girls didn't kill my horse, someone else did."

"We'll see about that. I'm on your case. One wrong move and you're gone."

After that outburst I didn't mention any of the details I'd gleaned from the pathologist. I'd had enough of Greiner by then and didn't care if he believed me or not. I turned my back and went to the barn.

An eighteen wheeler crunched up the drive and I caught a glimpse of a tall, chrome grill as a transporter went by the window with a diesel growl on its way to the barn. It stopped with a belch of air brakes; the horses on board lurched against their railings and scrambled to find their legs.

One horse set up a rhythmic kick on the side of the van as the driver climbed down from the cab. A little guy built like a brick. He banged the side, kicking stopped as the horses inside froze, straining to hear.

"Got a pick up," he said, "*Selous Scout*."

Damn! The best horse in the barn, a stakes winner.

"They're pulling him out? Hang about," I said, "while I phone the owners. Come in out of the cold."

He declined and I couldn't get through to the owner. No one answered. I did check the invoice, on my trusty Mac. They'd paid the bill.

"Sorry man," he said, when I walked back outside. "Gotta take him."

He'd done it all before.

A Kenyan blend percolated on the stove. Pouring the strong brew, I slipped in some raw sugar and cream, sipped it for a few minutes while gathering my thoughts, savouring the scent before dialling. Guy was stunned when

I told him about the heroin.

"*Fantastique.*" Guy resorts to French every now and again when you least expect it.

"They'd have cut one to taste it," he said, "maybe spilled some. They trust no one."

"Sounds about right," I said, "seen that on TV too."

"You know, I had an undercover cop drop by to fit an ankle holster. He said something about a case. *Street kids* he called them. Was cut up about it, as if he cared. A cop that's different. Think he'd talk to you."

"He wants an *ankle* holster?"

"*Absolument.* Hard to hide a gun if you're wearing only jeans and a T-shirt."

"Okay. What'd he say?"

"Hell of a lot of *Horse* on the street. A new shipment."

"Horse?"

"*Horse, H, smack — heroin*. Good God Duncan, where have you been?"

"When was this?"

"There's an epidemic. *The Star* ran it right after your horse was hit. Don't you remember?"

"Vaguely, didn't connect it with *Alaric*. I'd like to meet your man though."

"The narc?"

"Yeah, the cop that's different."

"He'll be here around noon. I'll let him know you're coming, these guys don't like surprises. I'll keep him talking till you show."

"I'll be there."

CHAPTER 9

Activity may be likened to the bending of a bow; decision the release of the arrow.

Sun Tzü, *The Art of War*, 512 BC

A line of denuded poplars amplified my loneliness as I drove up Guy's driveway. The wind blew a white fringe off a ridge of snow in a plume. God it was desolate. The fields were vast, white and so Ontario. He was as oblivious to his surroundings as I was sensitive to them. Guy had a towed a trailer home to where the old farm house had been — before it had burned. A stone chimney stood dangerously poised over the trailer.

Guy now used a part of an old barn behind it as his workshop. He'd shored the logs with five-ply inside and had a potbelly stove to make it marginally tolerable in winter, it kept his stuff from freezing. A new *Eagle* 4WD was parked at a careless angle by the trailer, alongside Guy's forest-green *Cherokee*. A set of fresh tire tracks in the snow tracked the *Eagle*. That would be the cop.

I found them both out back. It looked like a hunter's den inside Guy's workshop. Rifles and a shotgun on a rack. Moose, wapiti and white-tailed deer mounted on a wall that sprouted antlers. Leather off-cuts, cutting tools and racing magazines were strewn on a workbench that stretched the length of the workshop under a window. A dog-eared copy of *The Shooter's Bible* lay on the bench where he'd last consulted it, alongside an out-of-date copy of British *Timeform*.

Guy's treasure was a magnificent birch bark canoe. Its pale skin was cradled along the back wall in leather-lined brackets. It was made by an Ojibwa in Northern Ontario, a man Guy had hunted with. Guy had a photo of the man blown up and blue-tacked to the wall. The Ojibwa had a face etched in mahogany, staring out of the image into the distance, his face so lined he might have been a hundred. A serious man. The birch canoe was a work of art and Guy valued it so much I had never known him to use it.

The Ojibwa called themselves *Anishinabe* — the First People. They saw themselves as human, while strangers were definitely not. The French voyageurs named them *Chippewa* for their engraved birch-bark scrolls, the French at the time were transient, interested only in furs. This name corrupted in the tongue of later English settlers to *Ojibwa*.

The cop that's different, the one I had come to meet, was sitting on a stool at the workbench when I came through the door. While I stomped the snow off my boots, he was trying a holster strapped to his shin. Only after Guy spoke to me did he take his hand off the butt of the pistol. Nervous. He smiled fleetingly, pulled down the cuff of his jeans to cover the gun, then stood and shook my hand.

"Ah Duncan, heard you were with the Regiment."

Saying nothing, I just nodded. *What on earth had Guy told him?*

"Is that plastic?" I said, "looks like a toy,"

"No, not a toy. Latest issue, made of carbon polymer. A *Glock* compact, light, fast and a full nine-mill."

"Police issue?"

"Hell no, army mates. You need a backup that can't be traced."

Guy must have told him about the heroin, for the cop asked:"You're sure about the narcotics?"

Belfast, a North Irish accent. I prided myself at having a good ear.

"Sure, high grade heroin from a commercial lab. Pathologist analysed it. He used to work for customs in Ottawa. There's no mistake."

"He won't testify in court?"

"No. He did the assay for a friend as a favour. He shouldn't have done outside work."

"Well, what's the point ..." the cop said, flaring at some inner angst.

"Come on, Jesus you two, let's quit this pissing contest," Guy said.

"Yeah," we both said.

The cop sat back down on the stool and looked at me.

"Guess we don't need a witness. Not until we've got a suspect anyway."

The cop was a young man. Confident as young men are. Could have been thirty, maybe older, his ponytail and slim build might have made him look younger. I let him ask the questions, answering as honestly as I could, letting him get comfortable with the to and fro. Trying to build a little credit before I asked a few of my own. A silence grew as he realised I knew no more than I'd revealed already. For a while I let the silence build.

"Let me tell you what I know," the cop said. "Had a call at the weekend to a house on Elkington. Two women, no not really *women*, they were still *girls*. Anyways students no more than seventeen, slim with brown hair that reached way down their backs. As it was, their thick hair was spread over their naked bodies like a blanket. So alike they could have been twins."

"Coffee?" Guy asked as a fresh wind dashed snow against the window with a rattle of a machine gun. He had a navy-blue bandana on today, a strange French affectation that struck me as fey, though in Quebec it was all the rage.

Guy half-stood and reached across the mess on the bench to plug in the kettle. We ignored him. The cop carried on.

"In another life they'd have been pretty — maybe even beautiful in that way all young girls *are* beautiful. Did ya ever see what *smack* does to you?"

I was confused by this and shook my head. Guy was clanging through some cans on the shelf looking for coffee.

The cop continued: "Strips the fat from you is what it does. The last place to lose fat is ya face. Take enough smack, it digs out your face, so ya skin becomes all angles, creases and cavities. In the beauty stakes it's hardly value for money, but hey they'd stopped counting the cost."

I didn't know what to say. Guy filled the gap by flourishing a can of *International Blend* and we nodded: "So how the hell...?"

"A guy called it in — anonymous. Must have been big enough to survive the dose himself. When he came out of it, he covers the girls as best he can and leaves."

The cop paused, looking at me, wondering what effect the story had.

Guy checked his *TagHeuer* and the cop stood up now in agitation with his memories of what he was recounting.

"They were stone dead. Skin was frozen solid. Touching it was like touching metal. Been lying there for hours. Curled up together, hugging each other for warmth, as if in great pain," he shifted uncomfortably on the stool. "I suppose they were ..." he said with his face unnaturally still, "they were also somebody's daughters."

A noise came from the window again as the rising storm threw another burst of snow. I turned to stare through the window at the barren landscape. The rumbling of the kettle rose to a high-pitched scream as the water heated then quietened for a moment before bursting into a furious bubbling. No one spoke.

Then Guy leaned over and flicked the switch. Noise from the kettle ceased. The cop stared at me until I met his eyes. I got the feeling he wanted to tell me something.

"One girl couldn't get the needle in her vein," he said, "a long time user. Blood on her arms, between her toes, even her armpits where she'd tried. She knew the sites — she'd used them before. Veins collapsed with dehydration. This time she slammed the needle into her eyeball to get a hit."

"Jesus," I said, in the stillness.

The cop kept on.

"Syringe sticking out of her eyeball when I found her. Fluid of the eye had run down the side of her face."

"*Phwoar*," I said.

Guy stared at the cop with a kind of silent fascination.

"Coroner found high levels of heroin. It was pure with none of the usual contaminants. Does that sound familiar?"

"Absolutely, exceptional purity, a factory product."

"She had semen on her thighs. The other girl had it in her mouth. They'd sold themselves for the smack. That's what happened to the stuff picked up at your place."

He had raised his voice by now — almost shouting. He was indeed a cop that was different.

"Why do they do it?" I said in the breach.

"In my sister's case," the cop said, "she was fleeing life — just running."

His face composed in reflection and his voice dropped an octave, "at the core was her stultifying loneliness, a hopeless resignation to all the things she couldn't face. She used drugs to fill the void."

Now here indeed was a cop that was different.

"Have a teenage daughter myself," I said, "if some bastard got her, it would make me want to kill."

Guy got up and rattled the instant coffee into some chipped enamel mugs and poured. We watched in silence as he sloshed hot water into the mugs.

"Someone has to stand up and be counted, someone has to make it stop," Guy said.

Steam rose with the scent of coffee filling the space. Another beat of silence.

"Where was your horse loaded?" The cop asked.

We all took a tentative sip of Guy's instant coffee.

"Heathrow."

"We'll have to pass it back to the Brits then," he said.

"Won't *you* be able to follow it up?"

"*Not our jurisdiction*. It's out of my hands. Not an official case, not in Ontario. There's no evidence a crime's been committed. No evidence at all. Except for those girls, well their corpses, but we get that every day. *All I have is supposition*. Although I believe it, and you believe it, no-one else will."

"No," I said, "I don't think Detective Greiner did."

We took another slurp of heart starter.

"You could," he said.

"I could what?"

"You could follow it up."

"In England?"

"Yes, of course, in England. You'd better find out where it came from and who the hell put it there. Damnit man, right now you're fucked. Police are on your case. They'll have you for insurance fraud; not to mention those ditzy pyjama girls and Satanic rituals."

"Whoa. I'm innocent man, they can't do that."

He smiled and I felt distinctly queasy.

"Police will dig up evidence of some kind, bank on it. They need to close this case. Sure as shooting, you'll go to jail. Your *only* chance is an official investigation in England." The cop paused and took another swig of Guy's disgusting coffee. "I was in the service: Fourteen Company — intelligence."

He looked at me when he said it, as if it was supposed to mean something. It meant nothing to me. The cop went on: "In Northern Ireland, the Army depended on intelligence. MI5 couldn't supply operational stuff. Their on-ground intel was piss poor. Out of date by the time the squaddies needed it. They couldn't tell us if Mick the Knee-capper was going out to wreak havoc, or if he was going t' pub for fish 'n chips."

I went to take another sip from the mug to warm my bones. The burnt smell of coffee stopped me, so I reached for the sugar instead.

The cop forged into the breach: "Army formed a covert unit, trained us for infiltration and surveillance. Called us *Operators*."

I had the presence of mind to nod again as if I understood, as if it were a secret between us, a secret that I cherished and would keep safe.

"My sister died when I was on active service in Ireland," the cop said. "An overdose. She was seventeen. Sweet Jesus, seventeen on the game and supporting a habit. *That's why I'm a cop*. Why I'm in narcotics — despite not being suited to it."

"Oh," I said, "really, how are you not suited?"

"I've figured it out from talking to shrinks; I'm damaged from working undercover. You have to be careful in their world — forever vigilant. You have to hang on to that fragile sense of who you are. Have to fight your instincts; make yourself wait until you're sure it's the right move."

Now I leant forward fascinated, trying to imagine what that was like. Guy reached for the bowl and added another spoon of white-death to his brew.

The cop went on. "You're always afraid of the unexpected — hyper vigilant. And there are *always* shocks. You can make a move that'll save your life, or make the wrong move and you're dead."

"You made the wrong move," I said. It wasn't a question.

"Just once." His eyes slide off to the right.

"Someone died, didn't they. Someone close to you?"

The cop was startled and drew back. "Yes," he said, "she did." He paused looked at both of us, eyes now brimming with hurt. "They put women soldiers undercover, they had to make it look natural in civilian surveillance. I blew my cover trying to save her. Tried to stop them doing her." Guy and I remained silently appalled. "I was mustered out after that, rather that than going back to the line. Came to Canada instead."

I could see by his face, a twitch in the jaw, that a decision had been made.

"I have a friend in London, an Irishman Tom Finley. A builder, renovations that sort of thing. We were in the service together in Ireland. He married my kid sister back home."

I reached again for more sugar to combat the bitterness of the instant coffee. Guy downed the last of his brew. The cop left his mug untouched while he spoke. "Tom will get an investigation going through Scotland Yard if you'll go there to start it. If you're up to it. He's a good man. He'll want to see you though."

"I've got to do *something,*" I said, coming to a decision, "can't just sit on my hands if cops are going to stitch me up. I need that insurance. And now these girls: I'm a father too, I feel so sorry for their parents."

The young cop put his mug down on the bench, his face gaining animation as he spoke. He was pleased to see me take an incisive step.

"Good, I'll phone you with Tom's details when I get back."

Guy looked at me quizzically when the cop left. We listened to the car door slam. Waited till the *Eagle* coughed to life. Heard it idling like a tractor until the cop warmed it with a burst of revs and took off.

"*Merde,* a hell of a thing. What are you going to do?" said Guy.

"Well... he'll report the heroin, even if Greiner doesn't. The least I can do is get an investigation going. It's also my best shot at getting the insurance paid. After that nugget of misery, I really want to nail the bastards."

For a moment I stopped, reflecting again on what the cop had said.

"What was that all about then: the Operators?"

Guy checked his *TagHeuer* then looked at the snow pelting the window as he spoke. "British Army in Northern Ireland, Fourteen Company intelligence. They ran interference on the knee-cappers in the IRA."

"Why haven't I heard of it."

"It's *classified* for Chrissake. Of course you haven't heard of it."

"So, how do *you* know?"

"You get to know things in the Army, things you shouldn't."

"What did you tell him about me?"

"You know these guys. Told him you were in the Regiment."

"Jesus Guy, that's the SAS: Did you have to do that?"

"Yeah, well it worked."

"He didn't give us his name."

"Course not. He wouldn't give his real name anyway. That *Eagle* he was driving. It isn't his. A new car like that's the easiest way to tag someone. He would have got it from a dealer. Somebody owed him."

"Yes," I said, "no doubt they did."

Now I felt like I owed somebody's daughters.

Discussing my plan with Giselle was a diplomatic move, since I'd already made up my mind to go. I'd convinced myself already that I had to find a replacement for *Alaric*, so I called my usual stand in, Kirsten. She was due for spring vacation and agreed to look after the farm. She'd worked for me the past two summers. Giselle didn't want me to go, until finally, when I explained, she saw the sense in it.

I had the feeling that she thought I couldn't pull it off on my own. She wanted Guy to go with me. At the last minute, when she realised that wasn't going to happen, she decided to tag along herself. My refusal made her angry and she flounced off to bed, moggies trailing in her wake.

That night I didn't go to bed. I couldn't sleep. Instead I went to my office down the hall. Being an attic and having no direct heating, it was colder than the rest of the house. Instead of turning on the light, I sat by the window and looked out in the moonlight. The cold seeped through the glass and chilled me. Twigs of birch scraped against the pane. Snow covered the fields, more drifted against the fence until only the top rail showed. White and frozen dunes on a forsaken moonscape.

The thought of those girls selling themselves for drugs was so sad. Selling themselves for heroin that was smuggled inside my horse. I'd have to do something about it, I had to get an investigation going. I had to go to England.

Thinking of preparing for whatever lay ahead, I looked around the room, then focussed on my bookcase, at all the wisdom contained therein. One book stood out in the moonlight. A slim volume, a paperback in translation: *The Art of War* by *Sun Tzü*. A book I'd glanced at once then put down. Gold lettering reflected light from the burnt-red spine. I took it now from the shelf. The book lay lifeless in my hands, cold to the touch. On the cover a stylised Chinese warrior stood on a swatch of black. When I opened the ancient text *Sun Tzü's* first lines reached out and seized me by the throat.

> *The art of war is a matter of life or death, a road either to safety or to ruin. Hence it is a subject of inquiry, which can on no account be neglected.*

He was writing about my situation. He was writing about me. I would face them and I would fight. If I let it go, and instead relied on the thin blue line of the law, and they failed — what then?

I stood to lose everything: my horses, wife, daughter, and my good name.

I stood to lose my life.

CHAPTER 10. **GREINER**

On the day you take command, block the frontiers, destroy official tallies and stop the passage of emissaries.

Sun Tzü, *The Art of War*, 512 BC

Detective Greiner sat at his desk at the end of a long cold day, going through his in tray, tossing most of it in the bin. He reached for a mug of coffee and the scent of stale cappuccino assailed him. Nat put down the frothy muck and glanced at the postmark on the envelope in the tray, *Quantico*. That made him sit up. He snapped a flick knife he'd confiscated from some young punk and cut through the flap.

The mail came to him because he was the designated Guelph Police contact. And that was only because his superiors wanted to pass on the paper work to someone else. Reports from the FBI at *Quantico* came every month or so, and many of them called for some response. Someone had to do it. Most of this administrative guff didn't interest Nat. He'd just read 'em and forget 'em. This one was different.

INVESTIGATION REPORT

Allegations of "ritual" child abuse

Special Agent Kenneth Burkhardt
FEDERAL BUREAU OF INVESTIGATION

Since 1981 I have been assigned to the Behavioral Science Unit at the FBI Academy in Quantico. When I first heard about cases of satanic rituals and the sexual abuse of children, I believed them. As a psychologist I had been dealing with bizarre, deviant and criminal behavior for many years and had long since realised that almost everything is possible. Just when you think you've heard it all, along comes another case with a different and more shocking twist.

The idea that there are some evil individuals killing people in some satanic ritual is certainly within the realm of human possibility. But as we investigated these reports over the years the number of cases just grew and grew. We finished up with thousands of victims alleging sexual abuse. Because there so many allegations and so little physical evidence, it was difficult to proceed with their prosecution.

That there were so many allegations, so many references to sexual and religious aspects has now caused me to question their reality. Why is it that victims allege similar things, that on examination, don't seem to be true?

The first step in solving this puzzle is to admit that at least some of what the victims describe may not have happened. The ritual context could be a personal or religious interpretation of an otherwise shocking experience of sexual awakening.

Some law enforcement officers are unwilling to consider this possibility; they know from experience that the young girls they interview are not lying. Indeed, these children are not lying, for they really do believe these things.

There are alternative explanations. Some of what the victims allege is often true. Some of it is certainly not. Indeed some recollections are strangely distorted. Satanic allegations are too often steeped in religious symbolism. Some allegations are obviously contaminated by the victim's version of reality — their fantasies. The problem for law enforcement is to determine which is which.

Most of the children alleging "ritual abuse" are undoubtedly victims of some form of trauma. Though their particular trauma may not necessarily be criminal. So law enforcement has the difficult job of determining what actually happened.

Therapists are also interested in what happened. When to confront a patient with skepticism is difficult. It may not be in the patient's best interest for them to learn the truth, whatever that is, if they cannot cope with it.

A legal evaluation of "ritual abuse" cannot ignore the lack of physical evidence. It cannot ignore the fact that such a large-scale, secret and co-ordinated conspiracy is extremely unlikely. Since human nature is so self-serving, there are bound to be internal conflicts to split any group sooner or later; especially something packing such an emotional wallop as sexual exploitation and human sacrifice.

If members of any cult commit murders or kidnap victims they are bound to slip up now and again; they are bound to leave some evidence, forensic traces, boast about their exploits, or breakdown under interrogation. This has not happened.

Media attention, the church's concern with satanic cults, and therapists using recovered memories can create an environment where victims are rewarded, comforted and forgiven in proportion to the severity of their allegations. The whole process encourages traumatized children to tell more and more outrageous tales? The question is: are we encouraging antisocial, histrionic, borderline or otherwise unstable personalities to be drawn to Satanism by publicizing it?

The incidence of "ritual child abuse" in this country depends on how you define it. One example is the murder at White Bear Lake last year. The horror of this case had nothing to do with spiritual beliefs. It has everything to do with the sadistic, sexual perversions of the perpetrator.

Because America has such a huge population, it means statistically, that many children each year are traumatized psychologically, sexually and physically by angry, sadistic and mentally incompetent adults. This abuse is not all perpetrated by cults of Satanists, if indeed any of them are. The fact is that almost all of these families reporting abuse are pious Christians.

On reading this, Greiner's thoughts went into overdrive — *mainstream Christians!* He thought of the Anderson girls, the bizarre ritual and their tale of incest. Had they made it up? He'd seen a lot of people lie, and thought he knew when they did. If the girls were making it up, they were among the best he'd seen — they were pros. He didn't think they were lying. They were kids for Chrissake. He shook his head, muttering as he returned to the verbal diarrhoea of the report, then heading instead straight to the conclusions.

> ...The truth is that for the past eight years American law enforcement has aggressively investigated allegations of ritual abuse; they have turned up no real evidence of bizarre practices like human sacrifice and other satanic atrocities. If the guilty are to be prosecuted, if the innocent are to be exonerated, if children are to be protected, there has to be better ways of evaluating ritual abuse. Until this is done, the satanic controversy will cast a shadow over the genuine and widespread reality of child abuse, which lies at the heart of the problem.

When he finished, Greiner swore and reached for the phone. He couldn't get onto Kenneth Burkhardt at Quantico, so he left a message with his machine. God he hated those things. He set up a meeting with the prosecutor's office for the morning and faxed through the report he'd just read. The chief wasn't in. Nat went ahead anyway. He called Hackman and Birgit the therapist.

Birgit sounded pleased to be consulted and he left her with no idea of the bombshell he planned to drop. He called the Medical school in Toronto and was referred to Professor Stanford, his secretary. Nat faxed them all the FBI report, all except Birgit. He didn't want to warn her — he wanted her guts. He dropped the report on the in-tray of the Chief's desk and headed for the door.

Greiner adjusted the shoulder holster as he put on his coat. He was going to get to the bottom of this. He had no intention of losing out on promotion just because no-one could agree on this satanic shit. Damnit, they could *all* consent to the next move, whatever that was going to be. Mrs Greiner's boy wasn't carrying the can by himself any longer.

Nat got the phone call the next day as he was responding to a domestic at Rockwood. He hated domestics. You never know which way they'd go. A woman had shot her husband. Son-of-a-bitch had beaten her, raped her, or both. Greiner couldn't quite figure it out on the phone. He'd put on his coat and switched a half-eaten sandwich to his left hand to field the call on his way out.

"Detective Greiner."

"Sandler — forensic. Have something on that satanic case."

"Really."

Christ, just when he was getting somewhere, here comes a spoke in the works.

"Tracks of two adults on the hill, male from their stride. Overlaid on deer tracks and the spoor of a wolf. Got photos to send you — of the tracks."

"Two *adult males*. Are you sure?"

"What were you expecting?"

"Blood, children's bare feet," said Greiner.

"Hell no. It's below freezing out there; God knows what it's like at night. You'd lose toes without a good pair of boots. Hmmm, one of the tracks is foreshortened, it's not a child—too deep. Maybe Mukluks."

"Mukluks?"

"Caribou boots. Ones that Inuit wear."

"*Jesus H Christ* — Inuits! What the fuck next? Yeah, fax it pronto will ya."

Nat slammed out the door trying to make sense of what he'd heard. One thing for sure, that dammed séance hadn't taken place at McKinley's.

He'd caught those ditzy girls in a lie.

The Chief was there when Nat arrived. The provincial attorney and Professor Stanford were conversing as they served themselves coffee from an urn on the sideboard. Hackman was late and burst in with Birgit in tow. Nat grabbed a biscuit with the coffee — breakfast on the run.

They sat around the boardroom table. Greiner glanced at the copy of Burkhardt's report placed in front of each chair. He watched Birgit scan the first page as the lawyer introduced everyone. Birgit's face took on a brittle pallor as she read it, then it changed to a blushing red.

"You've all read the report," the Chief asked. "Thank you detective Greiner."

Birgit sat stony-faced. Stanford gave them all a single page with his bio as an expert witness, then outlined with a meticulous precision, his perspective on memories and their distortion.

"Christ," the Chief said after Stanford finished, "where does that leave us?"

He looked across at the State Attorney who hefted the report in both hands and took up the challenge.

"It leaves us up the proverbial creek without a paddle," he said. "This makes the Anderson case a nightmare. We'll be lucky to get out of it without being sued for false arrest. And we've got that Upton case in Saint Catharines."

He glared at Birgit.

"What the hell were you thinking?" he asked.

"Hey, I'm doing my job. Interviewed the girls and filed what they said. *You* mounted the prosecution."

"Based on *your* evidence. Evidence *you* planted by suggestion."

He was almost shouting, glaring back at her.

"Christ," the Chief said again. "Hackman?"

He was looking at Hackman filling his pipe, inviting him to speak.

"I've had doubts about those girls all along," Hackman said. "Angela can talk for hours about herself. Although some fragments do sound coherent, at the end I don't have a clue what she's saying. In my opinion she has Borderline Personality Disorder."

"Which is?" said Greiner.

He was getting impatient with the perfect hindsight of his colleague. Damned Mounties were full of it.

"Borderliners can be charismatic and attractive, they walk a constant tightrope between madness and sanity. An unstable personality: impulsive, manipulative, adoring and needy."

The Chief looked at Greiner who said nothing.

"Carry on," he said nodding to Hackman, "this is something we need to know."

"Borderliners are incapable of insight. They're never free of a deep sense of rage and worthlessness that spills over into self destruction."

"She's mad then," said Greiner.

"No, she's not mad, she's dysfunctional, that's her personality, she is just... well... different. Borderliners have a chaotic internal turmoil that sours all their relationships, with parents, siblings, colleagues and sexual partners."

"So that's where this girl's at," Greiner says, scribbling madly with his ballpoint, try to get it to write.

"They're not *psychotic*," said Hackman, "though they can have psychotic episodes, they almost haemorrhage *emotions*. Rejection, loss or minor slights can trigger severe depression, rage, suicide or even murder. That's when they act out, that's when they come up against the law."

"Borderliners are mortally afraid of abandonment," Stanford said, not wanting to be left out. "They have dissociative episodes, their personality shifts from deep and intimately personal to distant and detached. Their precious cache of emotional memories flips away — out of reach. With it goes their sense of self, their *me-ness* evaporates, leaving them feeling hollow and empty inside."

Hackman nodded as his thoughts turned inward as if consulting a patient long remembered. "An endless well of emptiness that no one can ever fill."

Greiner was getting tired of their psycho-babble, his pen wouldn't write and they weren't making much sense.

"So she made it up?" he said.

"No," Stanford said, "it's as real to her as our thoughts are to us."

"She didn't make it up," Hackman allowed, "her perception is just so distorted she *believes* her story is real. Borderliners will typically embrace religion, charismatics, anyone that will give their lives purpose and structure. Anyone that will fill that vast, unfillable emptiness inside."

Stanford joined the chorus again: "When they're up they can be fine, until that next binge of self destruction. What they can't do, is *change*."

"What about her sister?" Greiner was tired of this psycho shit.

"She is dominated by the eldest. You should have seen them separately."

They all looked at Birgit, her head down, fidgeting with the report in front of her. Stanford surprised them with a question.

"Is there any physical evidence that a crime has been committed?"

Greiner thought about that for a moment.

"We have a slaughtered horse and that mark on the wall. And insurance fraud." Greiner didn't mention his conversation with McKinley when he read from his notes. "Forensics has no blood in the woods. Deer and tracks of two men. Girls lied about the farm. Think they lied about everything."

"Anything on the girls?" the lawyer asked Nat.

"There's no record. We didn't get a physical examination until they came into care. They didn't report the abuse for weeks." Nat glared at Birgit as he said it.

"Well, they have been examined," Birgit said in her defence, "the eldest had a gynaecological exam at the shelter."

That made Nat sit up.

"A bit late," Nat said, "it's weeks after the fact."

"She's perfectly normal. No complications."

"What do you mean, *complications*?"

"Pregnancy complications."

"Pregnancy! She's pregnant and you didn't tell us." Birgit smiled back at him sweetly, "I'm telling you now. Only got the report yesterday. About six weeks gone. I wouldn't discount their story altogether."

"Ah," said Stanford, "she has a repressed religious upbringing, then gets pregnant. She has to come up with an explanation, even to herself, which leaves her blameless for what's occurred."

"So," said Hackman, "she distorts reality to deny her own complicity."

The attorney drummed his figures on the table and they turned to him.

"The most germane legal point is this: Who is the father?"

Birgit again smiled, savouring the moment.

"She says it's her father."

"Ah, then we'll press charges of incest and statutory rape."

The meeting ground to a halt with a scrape of chairs. They stood to leave.

"Nat," the Chief said, "clear up this mess. And do it quick. Publicity is going to kill us."

"I'm on it."

Like what the hell did they expect — a Goddamned miracle?

As he drove back to Guelph, Greiner ground his teeth at the bitch and her complications. What was going on? How could the Chief expect him to solve this without resources. He thought of McKinley's tale of heroin in the horse. He hadn't paid much attention to him. It was a bit far out, a bit too convenient. It depended on who was telling the truth.

The mess that was the Anderson case, that was something that didn't bear thinking about. Heroin on the other hand, that was real, that fitted with the stuff flooding the streets. It fitted with the overdoses in Toronto, it fitted with what he knew. Smack was down to ten bucks a cap on the street, there was so much of it.

He'd sure as hell chase that one up with McKinley.

CHAPTER 11. **DUNCAN**

In war, practise dissimulation ... move only if there is a real advantage to be gained.

Sun Tzü, *The Art of War*, 512 BC

Heathrow was cold on a day that was so typically English. It wasn't home, though home felt nearer. A short dash to the border and I'd be among aunts and uncles I couldn't remember, children who wouldn't want to know me. I was staying with my sister in Knightsbridge where she had a town house and perfect family: a yuppie husband, one boy of ten and a fair-haired girl, a child I hadn't seen since she was seven.

My dad had lived in Edinburgh. In his seventies the last time we'd met, he'd died soon after. I'd call, but it wasn't satisfactory; his hearing was destroyed in the Eighth Gunnery, beating back the Hun. Well, that and shooting grouse and deer before ear protectors were invented. This was my first time in Britain without seeing him.

Dad was an advocate of the manly arts. He'd got me into fencing, boxing and *jujitsu* at an impressionable age, well before I knew about more civilised sports. The fencing was romantic and the clash of steel was loads of fun, the boxing less so. I hated to be hit in the face. Ah, but *jujitsu* had it all, derring do and bags of dirty tricks: breaking fingers, gouging eyes, dislocating shoulders, choking opponents to unconsciousness and other nasty stuff. I loved it. Our master, a wizened old codger named Jack, had been an unarmed-combat and bayonet instructor in wartime. I don't recall the moves in any great detail for it was years ago, I don't even know if it really was *jujitsu,* but I do remember that every sequence ended with the same rasped instruction from Jack, "*...then kick the bugger in the balls.*"

In those days, when I was growing up, the war was still vivid. Not only in our minds, but on the street in the rubble, in the uncertain way people looked forward to the future, and in the way they saw the world. To maim and kill was normal then, for most men had been soldiers and many women too. So many returned to Blighty with empty sleeves, scars inside and out, crutches, prosthetics or a limp, some of them with all of the above — those were other times, hard times that we as children never felt as odd.

It was my genteel mother who made the mistake of buying me a pony and taking me out hunting. Once I'd ridden to hounds, I never saw life in quite the same way again. Among a hundred horses galloping across country in a racket of hooves, harsh collective breathing, the baying of hounds and human cries, tackling hedgerows and stonewalls in our path. The danger and delight were palpable in equal measure. It was *exhilarating* and it made my world sing. Pursuit of the fox was irrelevant — that's what opponents of hunting fail to comprehend. On my pony I had power, the power to run with the pack as good as any man, the power to risk all in the mad rush of hot pursuit. On that lionhearted pony I was king.

Taking a taxi to Shepherd's Bush to meet Tom Finley was a good move; the buses were hard to figure and I was disinclined to tackle the Tube. The taxi wipers were beating a steady tattoo against the rain when I asked the driver to wait. I found Tom renovating an Edwardian Town House. The heritage front was untouched while the inside was being gutted for the new. A couple of Irish lads in their slickers fitted joists and beams into place. They lifted a beam, tacked it with a nail, then cut it to fit with a brief scream from the power saw. They nailed the crosspiece to every joist along its length with a wild beat of hammers.

The sound from Tom's men was too much, so he waved me outside to the minuscule porch at the front. After checking my passport, we spoke away from the noise and rain.

"Need to get an investigation going," I said after explaining the situation. "Can't do it on my own."

The cop must have briefed Tom, because he queried me on the death of my horse.

"Rod passed on the drug connection," Tom waited for me to volunteer something, when I didn't he went on. "That red-haired git is on to something."

"What?" I said puzzled, "he's not a red-head."

"Hmm. Yes, well, you passed *that* test now, didn't ya boyo. We'll get an investigation rolling with an Operator."

"An Operator?"

"He's with the Yard. Brits don't have much to go on, so they're hanging fire. I'll put you in touch. You take it from there." With his thick carpenter's pencil he wrote on a scrap of paper retrieved from a pocket of his overalls.

In the back of the taxi heading for Knightsbridge, I smoothed the wrinkled paper on my knee. He'd written a single word with digits that I took to be a phone number: Mungo 7420-3806. What was I getting into? What sort of name was *Mungo* for Chrissake?

I met Mungo McGowan at a local pub he'd nominated when I'd phoned. *The Cricketer's Arms* was a bit decrepit with its dark wood, a dartboard askew on the wall, a pool table among the stools and beer-stained benches with layabouts sloshing down a few pints. Despite its depressing ambience, it was so typically English it cheered me.

Mungo recognised my foreignness and raised his hand in a desultory greeting. He completed the gesture by smoothing his greying hair.

"Hullo Duncan, sit down. I'll get you an ale."

With ale secured I told Mungo of my problems. He watched me carefully with narrowed eyes as I spoke. He asked about evidence, for the source of heroin being Afghani, and about its processing in France.

"You have names?" he asked.

"Apparently the only firm that makes medicinal heroin is *Kaiser's Pharmacea*."

"I see. And the names of those involved?"

"That's why I'm here, to get an investigation going. I know they used my horse. What I don't know is where to start?"

"We aren't able to launch an official investigation without hard evidence. Although, your contact does believe you. I've seen the memo."

He was careful not to give up Rod's name casually, the way Tom had.

"RCMP has not made an official inquiry you understand, just a memo. No evidence of an international crime, old boy."

"My horse is dead."

"All right. Now as a civilian, there is nothing to stop you from nosing around. I'll give you the name of the vet at Newmarket who quarantined your horse."

"Sure, I'd like to see where *Alaric* was stabled."

"Splendid. I've phoned the vet. He insists the horse was kept on the premises. Their only security, as far as I can tell, are the stable hands."

"Lets them off the hook," I said. "What did *you* tell them about my horse?"

"Told him it had died on arrival — cause unknown."

"Good, I'll say it's an infection. A lie I won't have to answer for."

"Hmmm, take this with you. You might get something useful."

He passed a small device across the table, a voice-activated *Sony* dictaphone, the kind that journalists and policemen use.

I was on the train to Newmarket next morning. Cold seeped into the carriage, a poison gas — moist and chilling. Dressed lightly in a pullover, I shivered miserably on that trip to the heart of British racing.

The town of Newmarket dates from the time of the great plague. Frightened townsmen in the fourteenth century insisted that *outlanders* stay outside their walls. So travellers set out their wares at a new market some miles hence. Travellers remained in quarantine where they stayed for 40 days, though perhaps rats and fleas may not have observed the same niceties.

Everyone looked well enough when I arrived. No sign of plague. Newmarket is a town frequented by small, wiry men in brown jodhpurs. With a khaki photographer's vest over my pullover, and a trusty Nikon hanging from a lanyard around my neck, I fitted right in. Horses abound in that town. Growling horse-trucks bolted through the main street at intervals.

It rained that day as it does almost every day in England. First getting directions at the next pub I came too, *The Eclipse*, I walked in the cold with my umbrella to the Government Quarantine Station at the edge of town to meet Professor Sloan.

The research centre was several redbrick buildings. One contained a high-speed Swedish treadmill where a horse was galloping when I arrived. The vast rolling noise from the machine, rattling hooves and high-pitched whine of an industrial fan was overwhelming. I was amazed the horse put up with it. A digital readout on the wall flicked out the seconds and horse's heartbeat in dramatic numerals.

The air was wet with sweat and the smell of horses. The sight of the horse galloping close up was magnificent. A lean chestnut filly ran on the treadmill flat chat, flared nostrils, muscles pumping, its mane flying in the air stream of the screaming fan. She reminded me of my own *Intrepid Red*.

Sloan was pointed out to me as the tall guy with greying hair, in a lab coat, drawing blood into a syringe from the jugular. The needle remained taped into the vein as the horse ran. Sloan took samples as fast he could by reaching under the side rail to attach a syringe. Every so often he clipped the filled syringe barrels into a rack by feel, without looking — keeping his eyes on the clock, he reach for the next syringe in a smooth practised movement.

The chestnut galloped as if wolves were after it — ears pinned back, eyes wild, mane and tail streaming. I threw up my camera and bathed the scene in a flash. Sloan looked up sharply, seeing me for the first time and scowled.

The treadmill slowed and the horse changed down to a canter, then a flashy trot, like one changes gears in a car. The treadmill stopped with the push of a button, the horse stood — heaving. The fan wound down and steam arose from the animal's body like a fog. The horse shifted weight and the machine clanked. Sweat flowed in rivers down the horse's heaving girth and along its flanks. The bed of the treadmill ran with sweat as if it had been hosed. His blood collection continued while I watched. Sloan never looked up, not once, he never missed a beat.

We were introduced when a groom backed the horse off the treadmill and led it away to be washed. Sloan gave me a run-down on his current project, something about blood buffers. He was experimenting with bicarbonate to see what effect it had. He'd taken his lab coat off and now stood incongruous, dressed in a silk shirt and Saville Row suit talking about squirting baking soda into horses. They tested drugs here to stay ahead of the game.

"A predator and prey relationship," he explained. "An arms race. Bookmakers are the predators of racing, the rest of us: punters, owners, stewards and vets are their innocent prey."

An interesting way of looking at it, but then I knew I wasn't innocent and I didn't like being the prey.

So then I asked Sloan about *Alaric*.

"Of course I remember the horse, passed him myself."

"Passed him fit you mean?"

"Fit for stud and free of disease."

"Oh, well he died the day after arrival in Canada."

"Did he now. Travel sickness?"

"No, they suspect something infectious," I said, staring at him keeping my face still.

He stared back, considering the situation before answering.

"Horses die of all kinds of things. After a long flight, they are prone to travel sickness. Pneumococci can flare up and dehydration can be severe enough to kill a horse."

Sloan was choosing his words carefully, too carefully.

"He didn't die of a travel sickness," I said.

"Well, I know he didn't die of anything infectious."

"How can you say that?"

"He was negative for any known equine disease. Ran the tests myself."

"Well, the horse is dead."

"Not from a contagion. He quarantined here for three months."

"Are you sure? I mean, what about new strains?"

"Look, we've got a small army of people working here—that's why. Most of them are studying microscopic predators of horses. They're with Cambridge, a section of the vet school — we all are. We don't make those kinds of mistakes."

He invited me to tea at that point. It struck me as a peace offering. We crossed the yard to the Professor's office. You are invited to tea in England everywhere, hardly ever to lunch. He stopped at a sleek new Jag in the parking lot to retrieve a leather briefcase.

"Nice car," I offered.

"An exceptional car, quite extraordinary. Goes like the clappers."

He caressed the curve of the hood with his hand.

Sloan's office had that old world look, pictures of his young wife and kiddies on the heavy desk. Frames of a manor house taken at various angles and seasons were on the walls, along with several prints of thoroughbreds as lean as greyhounds. Sloan's wife beamed from one frame, an elegant young woman in pearls and twin set. No doubt real pearls and real Angora wool, an expensive looking woman. Their three chubby moppets starred in their private-school uniforms.

What sort of man has only one photo of his wife and children, yet so many of his possessions? A dozen shots of that beloved house and all his racehorses.

One tiny window brought light high up, not enough light for my taste. I flung my Nikon case down on a spare chair clicking open the flap. He used the phone to order tea while I flicked on the dictaphone.

"Charming," I said, indicating the pictures. "Your family's?"

"Oh the house is mine. Bought it some years ago."

"And the horses?"

"I've raced more than a few in my time."

"Ah, I'm into breeding — until my stallion died."

Sloan remained silent. His hands formed a steeple as he regarded me steadily in the poor light. This was not going to be easy.

"Perhaps *Alaric* was poisoned," I said, steeling myself for confrontation and taking a fresh tack. "Can they detect something like that?"

"Mister McKinley, you have come a long way to see me. You obviously came here for something. What is it you want?"

He looked at me hard and I realised this man was threatened by my being here. I decided to be direct.

"*Alaric* was in good health when he left here. He is now dead and I want to know who killed him."

"I've already explained there are many possible causes."

"No. You see I do know *what* killed him. I want to know *who*. He was killed with an axe for Chrissake."

"With an *axe*?"

His eyebrows shot up in genuine surprise.

"Yes, bloodily and unmistakably. I want to know who stuffed the horse with heroin before he was shipped. Who got to him?"

"Here? You're saying we put heroin in the horse? Ridiculous, it could not have been here."

"You said yourself there is no security to speak of. After this they'd be faced with airport security. They'd have needed a vet. They did it here," I said with a growing conviction.

"Clients come and go every day. We have no reason to guard horses in quarantine."

"Precisely."

"Now look here, are you accusing me?"

"I'm not accusing anyone — not yet. I only want to know if you had suspicions. Did anyone take a particular interest in the horse? Anyone in financial straits?"

"No, and I don't like your insinuations. *Good day Sir*."

Sloan stood with that salvo and glared. I was being dismissed, without the tea and biscuits.

After hoofing it back to town with my umbrella, I grabbed a table at the teahouse for a round of pie and peas. Truth is I longed for home and the aroma of a good Kenyan blend; I was missing Giselle, missing Jennifer, and most of all missing my horses. In this neat stitch of the world I missed the vast wildness that is Canada.

On my way to the station, I noticed a dealer with a royal-blue clone of Sloan's car in the showroom window, along with a Range Rover in forest green. I went in and inquired the price from a pinstriped salesman. His greying hair and RAF moustache were just the right touch for the job. He took in my wet clothes and decided I was a tire kicker. He put his hand on the bonnet to claim ownership — as if to fend me off.

"Seventy-two with all the options," he said, in answer to my question.

"Seventy-two *thousand*. Is that pounds?"

"Of course it's pounds. That's about a hundred and forty-thousand dollars."

He was interested once he thought me a foreigner; he hadn't caught my residual accent. To be dressed without a suit and tie, from an Englishman's point of view I guess, is normal for Americans abroad.

How could Sloan afford that expensive car? Shivering my way back to Knightsbridge on the train, I went over my meeting with Sloan. Why hadn't he acknowledged knowing *Alaric* was dead? He knew that already from McGowan. He must have wanted to find out what I knew. Sloan had been surprised the horse had been axed, though not about the smuggled heroin. If slaughter was not their plan, then killing the horse made no sense.

That new Jaguar, the mansion and those expensive racehorses, not to mention a trophy wife and private schools, the man couldn't do it on a Professor's salary. I knew what my Dad had earned and how he'd lived as a Professor of Chemistry. I'd discuss it with McGowan when he heard the tape.

Perhaps Mungo could find out if Sloan was involved in *Alaric's* death. Greed seemed a slight motive, but men have done much worse when prompted by far less. A man with an expensive wife, a manor house and a taste for the good life. A man who couldn't bear to live below his self-appointed station in life. It seemed like enough to me.

I met Mungo the next day at the same pub and passed over the dictaphone. McGowan listened to my analysis while ensconced in a far booth with our Guinness and ale, listening to the recording. He didn't argue or encourage me with leading questions; he did it like an expert, offering empathy and long silences for me to fill. He neither confirmed nor denied my assessment. He offered nothing more, except an assurance he'd make further inquiries about the life and times of Professor Sloan.

"Enough to start an official inquiry?" I asked.

"No evidence of criminal activity, old son."

"Ah, it does tell us something though. That's why you're still interested."

"It may lead to something interesting."

That was as much as I could get out of him, despite more probing.

"Perhaps you should go to Chantilly," he said clicking the switch on the dictaphone on and off like the ticking of a clock. "You see, without an official investigation we cannot send a man to a foreign country to investigate."

I took another sip and breathed out in a sigh.

"However, if you were to visit France and look up a certain Professor Guignard, that would be kosher. He vetted your horse there."

"Well, I am planning to go to France to buy another stallion."

"Splendid. I'll get back to you with particulars."

"What about *Kaiser's Pharmacea*? Did you check them?"

"I'll make some inquiries."

He took down my phone number and where I was staying, then wrote his office number on a page torn from a notebook. He neglected to include his name on the sheet.

I left him hunched over another pint, frowning as he replayed the tape.

CHAPTER 12

In war there are some roads which must not be followed, armies which must not be attacked ...

Sun Tzü, *The Art of War*, 512 BC

I stayed with my sister again in Knightsbridge. In the deep of night she woke me from a restless sleep.

"Phone, Duncan — Canada."

Reaching out my hand from under the covers, I took the cordless phone, still groggy with sleep.

"Duncan here."

"Better get on home and look after your old lady."

The voice was nasal, a halftone off French Canadian.

"Why? What's happened?"

Silence.

"Duncan."

Giselle's strangled voice said it all, just this side of hysteria.

"Come home — I'm scared. Don't call anyone. Not the cops. Not Guy. Not anyone — PLEASE. Do as they say Duncan, catch a plane home okay?"

"WHO...?" I yelled into the phone.

The other voice came back over muffled sounds in the background.

"Come home hero. Fuck with us and we'll take a knife to her. Leave it alone, alright?"

"LEAVE WHAT ALONE?"

"Don't fuck with us. Come back and fuckin' stay home. Stop it with that horse. Goddamn it."

CLICK. The phone bled that ominous burr of a dead line.

Despite Giselle's plea, I tried calling Guy, he was closer and a hell of a lot tougher than anyone, but he wasn't answering. I was on a plane within the hour. Gail's hubby drove me to Heathrow.

A seat on Air France *le Concorde*. Supersonic to New York was better than a direct flight to Toronto on regular schedule. I was worried about calling Guy. Tried again from the airport — nothing. Should I call the cops? Giselle's fear stopped me: *Don't call anyone. Not the cops. Not Guy. Not anyone — PLEASE.*

She was afraid. I didn't want to screw up. I replayed the conversation in my head. What were they doing to Giselle?

"Anything to drink sir?"

The stewardess touched a thought in my head.

"Your accent," I said, "where are you from?"

"France monsieur."

When I continued to look at her in silence, she added.

"From Basque country."

She had the same accent as the man who'd threatened me.

We hit La Guardia and I scrambled to change planes. In Toronto I could barely wait while they taxied into position. Phoned Guy again from the terminal. The phone rang ten times then stopped. I ransomed the Blazer from long-term parking. Despite having three or four tiny bottles of airport liquors to blunt anxiety, I was close to panic by the time we touched down. I drove fast, too fast. I had to save Giselle from a nameless fate.

Every light in the house was lit when I slammed on the brakes and ran to the door. Slipping through the hallway, I stopped to listen — nothing.

"Giselle," I called.

A cry from upstairs. I flew up them panting heavily by the time I reached the landing. Again I hesitated. She was lying on top of the bed, naked in a sheen of sweat, limbs stretched, a kid playing angels in the snow. Her wrists and ankles tied to the bedposts. Her knickers lay soaked beside her face, with scrunched pantyhose she'd bitten through.

"Jesus! Giselle, are you alright?"

"Oh Duncan."

Her white skin was laid open down her chest, from the notch at the top of her sternum to the brush of her pubis. Blood had blackened and coagulated in the wound — had dribbled down her flanks. Her eyes wide. Giselle, who's always in control, now could not turn away. I stared at her stunning body, at the thatch of her sex. Heard my sharp intake of breath, then I held her head with one hand against my chest and tore at the knots.

"Giselle, I'm so sorry. Sorry I wasn't here."

Giselle tried to sit when I tore the knot undone. She tried but couldn't for the knots at her ankles held her. I enclosed her in my arms, rocking as if comforting a child just awakened from a nightmare. Her breath caught as she dragged it in — not crying, but close. She shook when I wrestled with the cord across her body at her other wrist. When I did so, a foreign scent of men registered: raw and sweaty with a whiff of tobacco — disgusting.

"You were not here. Not here to stop them."

"Oh God, Giselle I'm sorry ..."

While I stroked her hair I couldn't drag my eyes away from the cut between her breasts. A wound that tore down her torso. Almost heaved at the thought of how close they had come to gutting her — a feeling that left me helpless.

"You weren't here," she said.

"What happened? Who did this...?"

"Get off me," she said and pushed with both hands on my chest.

When I undid her ankles she sat up, drawing her knees to her chin. Bent forward and leant her head on her knees, massaging her legs. She looked a fragile, damaged child.

"Where's Jenny?"

"She is all right," Giselle said this without looking at me, "she is with the Pony Clubbers — Murray's daughter."

"Should phone the police."

"NO!"

She started to retch. Her belly heaved once, twice and then stopped. I touched her forehead, held her again in my arms. Smelled the disgusting scent of men in her hair.

"How are you feeling?"

"I want to be sick. How do you expect me to feel?"

"Who ..."

"Get out," she shot at me through clenched teeth.

In the kitchen brewing fresh coffee, I heard the shower running upstairs. Looking out the window, I saw exhaust smoke condensing behind the truck and realised that I'd left the motor running, and ran out to turn it off.

At the breakfast table playing with my third coffee, I replayed the scene when Giselle came down, dressed and freshly showered. She had taken an age. Her blonde hair now wetly dark hung down her back. It pulled her skin tight on her face giving her an older, damaged look. He pendant was again around her neck like a talisman.

"Do you want to tell me about it?"

I'd poured her a fresh cup before Giselle spoke.

"They were here. Sitting in ambush, when I came in the kitchen door. Silent in the dark. I got a shock when I turned the light on. Asked what they were doing. They stood up and said nothing. You don't realise how scary it is when someone won't speak."

I reached across the table and held her hands in mine.

"One caught my arm as I turned to run, kicked my legs out from under me. So fast I didn't know it. Other held me down while they tore my clothes off — everything. They cut my knickers away with a razor. All I could do was scream."

"Jesus, Giselle did they...?"

"Did they what? Rape me. That's what you want to know? They tied me up and stared. Like you did just then. You liked me like that," she said, "it turned you on."

"Stop it. At least you were spared."

"Spared! You are such an arsehole. Can you imagine the horror of being in their power — helpless, totally in their control. They could do anything. And they did. They touched me with their filthy hands."

"It's all right Giselle, they're gone."

"They *cut* me! Like an animal, slashed me with a razor. Do you know what that's like — look at me for Chrissake!"

She tugged her gown open and I saw the ugly wound, running the length of her torso. I couldn't bear to look at it. I already had the first aid kit on the kitchen table and now opened it.

"I'm sorry Giselle — Jeez."

"Sorry! Sorry doesn't cut it. You weren't here when I needed you. Weren't here to protect me."

Indeed, I was not: truth was I felt guilty, no matter how irrational that feeling was. I had failed to protect her. I wanted to tell her that it was all right — to take her in my arms, to love her. Instead, I said:

"I didn't know you were in danger."

"You should have thought of me — protected me."

"Yes, I should have — I'm sorry. Let me tape the wound."

She opened her nightgown and straightened drawing the cut tight. A superficial cut through the outer layers of skin, though no less scary for that.

"They had guns. Would have shot you anyway, if you had been."

"Yes," I said, pulling the edges of skin together, affixing it with a line of butterfly strips. "Suppose they would have."

Why kept ringing in my head. I had touched somebody's nerve with this investigation.

"They made me walk upstairs at gunpoint, me naked ahead of them. They tied me to the bed and called you. The two of them took off after that. Don't remember hearing a car."

"Must have parked down the road."

"Hmm, maybe why I did not know they were here."

"What did they say?"

"Said you had better stop messing in other people's business. *Stop it or we'll gut you next time*," is what they said. "Made me repeat it back, to be sure I got it right."

She shivered, folded her arms across her breasts and looked down. I leant forward, reaching to put my arms around her. Giselle shrunk from me. She got up and headed for the stairs. The phone rang just as she'd turned away. I had opened my mouth to speak. Spoke to the phone instead.

"Hullo."

"Find 'er?" Same voice, alien and flat.

"I'LL GET YOU. YOU SICK BASTARDS..."

"Shut the fuck up and listen. Did ya see the cut? We'll do the same to her as we did ya horse — we'll gut her. Think about it. Leave it alone."

CLICK.

"What did they say?"

I repeated some of it to her, leaving out the worst bits.

"Are you going to do as they say?"

Three beats of silence while I thought. I had to resolve the situation. Had to keep my family intact. She waited with one foot on the stairs. My hesitation distressed her. She said it again with a rising note in her voice.

"Duncan, for our sakes — for me."

"Yes," I said. "Yes, I'll stop. I'll get the police on it."

"DUNCAN NO!"

"Why? Why not call them?"

"I cannot face it. Not now, not ever. No police. I feel so... so degraded."

"All right Giselle," I said defeated, "no police."

"I am going to bed," she said, "alone — feeling sick."

At that moment I felt tired — a falling in the soup kind of tired, my brain shutting down as it also does with migraine. I reached out and stroked her cheek. She looked down refusing my eyes.

"Okay Giselle, but I do want to be with you ..."

Right then I wanted to fold her in my arms, to murmur in her ear, to join with her, to reclaim her as my own and yes — to love her.

She glared at me. "You don't understand anything. I want to be alone. Please, can you please sleep on the couch."

Damn. I swallowed the hurt and ground my teeth as she climbed the stairs. I was so tense one of my molars gave way with a spasm of pain and an alarming crack.

The next day I stayed home, the molar packed with cloves to kill the pain. I worked the horses and mucked out while Giselle fled to work. The temperature stayed around zero and wind picked up through the day. My mind wouldn't stop. What the hell was I going to do? Had to back off for fear of what they'd do to Giselle. Had to find out who *they* were. Nothing less would deliver us. Certainly not the police.

That night Giselle went to bed ahead of me. She didn't say goodnight. She didn't say a word. We'd been sitting together on the couch. Jenny was still with her friends. I hadn't realised Giselle had gone until a commercial break came on TV. I'd been half watching while talking with her, thought she'd gone to the kitchen. The last of the cats stretched, then yawned and slipped off the couch to search.

Later I went up the stairs. Worried about her. Worried about us. The door was shut, though not locked. Giselle had pulled the curtains and affected sleep. Her reading light on and a book lay face down on the bedside table.

"Hi," I said to her back, "you awake," as I got under the covers.

That night I longed to hold her, to tell her she was safe. Though Giselle was again dressed for bed in full armour: panties and nightgown. I stroked her arm and she stirred, then turned on her belly away from me. Again I massaged her back for a while. She lay unspeaking, her muscles tense. I stroked her delicious derriere, but she cringed away from me as if I was unclean.

"NO," she said, now gripping my wrist with both hands, so hard it hurt. "Not now, not tonight."

"Jesus Giselle, take it easy," I said, as if my just saying her name would make it right. Reaching now to put my arms around her.

"Not now. What is it about *no* you don't understand?"

With that I rolled away from her and my erection receded, as if I'd been hit with freezing water. I lay in the dark, staring at the curled outline of her back. Sadness seeped into my soul, a sadness for what they'd done to us. They had come into this room, our room and damaged her. I had been helpless to stop them. Impotent, as I'd been since they had killed *Alaric*. I wanted to lash out. I wanted to hurt them. I wanted to kill. I reached for Sun Tzü, my ancient manual of war.

At that point belatedly realising that I was changing from a civilised man into something else. Something reprehensible. I was crossing the border into their don't-give-a-damn territory — to a place where anything goes. There I felt like a predator, and let me tell you it felt good. I growled under my breath, a wolf on the prowl. I growled again louder this time. I would fight whoever these bastards were.

What I needed were friends and allies: Guy, Mungo and the undercover cop.

I was already up to my neck in cold, dark waters of revenge — way out of depth.

I needed the counsel of Sun Tzü.

CHAPTER 13

He who wishes to fight must first count the cost.

Sun Tzü, *The Art of War*, 512 BC

Jennifer came home on the bus, her backpack filled with books and clothes from her stay-over with friends. I'd already saddled her horse *Shandy* and *Jet Stream*, leaving them cross-tied in the barn. I'd put on martingales, drop-nosebands and jumping saddles. I'd learned to insist on the right gear for control. You never knew when you'd need it. And when you did, it had to be there. Today we would gallop on the snow-covered verge.

The thing is that I wanted to talk with Jennifer, to make contact after so much had happened. I wanted to keep her safe. A vague plan formed in my head.

While I was waiting in the kitchen sipping coffee and scoffing the last of the brie I heard the bus, then the crunch of her footsteps on hard snow.

"Hi Jenny. Want to ride while there's still light."

She looked across at me; I could tell she didn't.

"Sure," she shrugged, "if you want." She made it sound nonchalant as teenagers are wont to do.

Retrieving my boots from the floor, I hauled on my leather chaps to keep out the cold. Our dirt road had good footing in the packed snow, where snowploughs scraped it bare. We trotted a few clicks then galloped a steep hill. The gallop brought exhilaration, along with a touch of anxiety as we neared the brow, worrying if a car was coming the other way — on the wrong side.

Jenny stayed there, walking her horse watching for cars. I trotted down and galloped up twice more on the racer. We walked to let the filly recover, shaking her head, blowing clouds of steam from her nostrils, nervous — hyped from the run.

The trees at the side of the road almost covered us with their branches. The light was fading. The world had that grey winter's cast. Grey sky merged with the landscape as if there was no boundary.

"I'm going to France soon, to look for a new stallion." I paused, considered her reaction before going on. "We need to buy another horse."

"Plenty of *Northern Dancer's* stock around here."

"We need an outcross. Although I've claimed insurance on *Alaric,* I can't wait for payment or we'll miss the season."

"Yeah, well we do need *money* now Dad."

"I'm selling alfalfa that's in the barn down to Florida. They're paying fifteen bucks a bale at Hialeah. Maybe more when it gets there — enough after I split it with the trucker."

"What are we going to do for hay?"

"Hope for an early spring."

A battered Ford pickup came hurtling out of nowhere, sweeping past in a spray of gravel and wet snow — frightening the horses. We let them move forward then reined them in.

"Pasquale brothers," I said nodding at two men in the cab with rifles held between their knees, barrels pointed at the roof. Their long black hair fell down around their faces like hoods. "Hunting wolves for their winter pelts."

"They take deer too," Jenny said.

"Yeah, probably."

The Pasquales were oblivious to land ownership and hunted all over this county. Claimed they were Native Americans when I'd challenged them for being on my land. No bows & arrows for these Indians. Theirs was hi-tech hunting, scoped rifles, radios, dogs and four-by-fours co-ordinating the slaughter. We had an uneasy truce. So I left them alone, afraid for my horses.

"Giselle might come with me. It's romantic in Paris," I said.

Jennifer looked unimpressed. Like most kids, she never considered her parents as being even remotely romantic.

"Don't like to think of you having wrinkly sex," she'd once confided to Giselle.

"Want me to look after the horses?" She said.

"I'll get Guy to do that. Thought we'd go in the March break. You could stay with Aunt Gail in London."

She looked aghast for a moment, then the thought passed. Jennifer had an openness about her that some retain as teenagers. She had not yet learned to conceal her feelings. It made her vulnerable.

"Can't I come to Paris with you?"

"Not this time. It's fiendishly expensive. We'll only stay the week. All the time we'll need to see the horses our agent lines up."

We came cantering over a knoll to see the Pasquales' truck on the verge, the two brothers mushing across the snow in snowshoes. Our horses propped and snorted at the truck. *Jet Stream* swung away sensing something — something unseen in ambush. Her frantic hooves clacked on the gravel. Nothing moves as quick as a frightened horse. I stayed with her.

One of the hunters flung himself down and sighted on the far side of the ridge as we watched. I couldn't see game, just a few birds rising in the sky. They must have spotted something a long way off. A shot rang out. The shrill crack of a high-velocity round. Both horses jumped.

"Sounds like it'd knock down a deer," I offered.

"Or a man." Jenny looked apprehensive as she said it.

I said nothing more. The Pasquales looked good as suspects, they were certainly feral. I let it lie, I didn't want to go too far down that road — not with Jenny. The men stood, slung their rifles and mushed into the fog.

We trotted to keep warm with Jenny going ahead. She half-halted, sat for a few strides, her back swaying with the horse, then did some credible steps of shoulder-in with his neck curved, softly on the bit. Jenny straightened the horse into a complete halt, though this he resisted with a stiffened neck at the last moment.

"Good boy," she said, leaning forward and stroking his neck.

"Nice," I said. "A few more times. Get it right on that side before you start him on the other. Horses don't relate one side to the other as we do."

"His halt's a bit shabby," she said.

"Yes it is, be patient and give him one more step to complete it. When training you use all the tools you've got. *Shandy* knows *words*. He knows *And halt* from your lunging. Say, *Annnd* drawing it out, after straightening your back with legs on in a half-halt. Then a step or two later apply them again for a walk, shorten the walk on the next step and complete it with legs-on for a solid *Haaalt*. Always walk into the halt until he has acquired sufficient balance to stop dead from the trot."

"We're not permitted to speak in the test, Dad."

She said this as if I'm a complete and senile ignoramus.

"Right," I said. "That's why you speak *after* the leg aids, *before* pressure on the bit. *Shandy* will respond and soften his halt." She turned her head as if listening. Suspecting that I'm deluded about her interest in what I have to say, I continued anyway: "He'll gradually learn the aids and halt without resisting, then later you won't have to say anything."

She moved off without a word, as if I hadn't just given her priceless advice. The elder Pasquale roared past in his beat up truck. A brace of dogs were threshing around in back with the thrill of the chase. Our horses jumped away and scattered.

I'd have to flesh out a plan to nail those bastards whoever they were. But I needed money to survive. What else could I sell? I couldn't stand by and do nothing. I'd lose my horses. Nor could I bear to think of their vengeance on my wife and daughter if I failed. By the time I persuaded my nervous horse to a walk, I felt my face had curled into a snarl.

Guy came to dinner that night. Giselle had prepared her cholesterol-challenging, Estonian casserole: pork, onions, apple and cream. She'd cooked it the night before as the moggies looked on, deeply impressed by the smell.

Guy reined in his Cherokee as Giselle lifted the casserole from the oven. He was late as usual, a habit we allowed for in our friendship. We'd delayed putting the meal in the oven for a full half-hour after his call.

We sat together at the dining table and cracked a burgundy while Giselle whipped cream in the kitchen. A clatter of stainless steel on ceramics and an occasional hissing *scat* to her cats.

Then I told Guy what had happened.

"*Morbleu,*" he said, "they came here to the farm?"

"Yes."

"Ah, they didn't do anything *sauvage* — you know, *sexual*?"

He said sexual in a French way, as if he has a lisp.

"No, they didn't," I said, but I looked away.

"So, is Giselle all right?"

"They scared the bejesus out of her. She hasn't been herself since."

"You can expect that. Still, she's strong Duncan, she'll get over it."

"She's not *that* strong," I said, "I'd like her to get counselling. She won't talk about it — not to me, not to anyone."

"Have you gone to the cops?"

"Police? Hell no. Giselle's so humiliated she won't let me. They think we're into satanic abuse. If we call the police, those bastards will come back. God knows what they'll do to Giselle. Or to Jennifer."

"You'll have to find them."

"How am I going to do that?"

Guy was silent. He checked his watch, then glanced around as if casting a net.

"I don't know how, but you're going to have to do something," he said, in macho mode again.

Giselle interrupted us with the casserole and Jennifer clattered down the stairs to join us. She must have been following kitchen sounds from upstairs. Sometimes it was hard to get her out of her room once she'd settled in with ghastly music and endless phone calls to her friends.

We discussed the latest outrageous demands of *Québécois*. To include Jenny in the conversation, we switched to discussing threatening *Gestapo* at her school. A decree by the Principal had upset her, a direction that girls should wear no jewellery, necklaces, rings or earrings. Jennifer was incensed. It seemed sensible to me; I kept that thought to myself.

In short, we discussed everything but the appalling violation in our own house — in our own bed. We kept the attack from Jennifer, at Giselle's insistence. Both Guy and I were reluctant to discuss it. Reluctant to acknowledge that ugly word that lay still in our minds — *rape*.

Guy agreed to feed and care for our horses while we were away in France.

"Stay here in our house," I said, "just in case." We all knew what I meant. "I'll send *Jet Stream* to the track, and the mares and weanlings are easy to look after."

"Sure," said Guy, looking from me to Giselle waiting for a sign. Some indication that we could say what was on all our minds. It didn't come.

"Jennifer will come as far as London. She's staying with Gail in Knightsbridge."

Jenny looked up, her face at once defiant.

"I don't want to go with you."

"What? We've already discussed it. You agreed."

"No Dad, *you* discussed it, *I* listened. It's what you always do."

"What is wrong?" Giselle asked.

"I don't want to go that's all. I'll stay here with Guy."

Jennifer glared at us and pushed her chair back to get up—it fell with a crash. She disappeared through the door to the stairs. Giselle went after her.

Now we were alone I discussed my vague plan with Guy.

For dessert we had wafers, dipped in whipped cream and a touch of *Cointreau*, with a pot of fresh coffee. Now with Jennifer upstairs I wanted to discuss the situation, but Giselle avoided my eyes and started to clear things away. Guy soon got the message and took to his feet. He kissed Giselle chastely on the cheek, shook my hand with his tradesman's paw and promised to call again. Then went outside in the cold and fired up his Jeep.

When I went to the barn to check the horses Giselle repaired to the bathroom. She came to bed late, clothed again in that ubiquitous nightgown. I was reading my manual of instruction — *The Art of War.* Her scent hung the air as she turned off the light and got into bed. We lay side by side for a while — miles apart.

"You okay?" I said.

"Can't stop thinking about them coming back?" she said. "It is not good for me. I need to have control."

"Do you want to talk about it?" I said.

"No, I do not even want to think about it."

I stroked her hair, then her face, moving my hand across her chest to her belly, it brushed her breast in passing. She stiffened and turned her head away.

"Okay," I said, "you don't want a cuddle?"

"No, I do not."

"You don't have the same needs as me — for body contact."

"And you resent it," she said.

"Yes," I said before I could stop myself, pausing for a beat, "yes I do, I feel bereft."

Turning my back, I reached for some tablets I kept in the bedside drawer, looking for something that would help me sleep.

When I pulled the Blazer up behind the Banque Royale in Quebec Street it felt warmer. There's less snow in Guelph than on tenth line. In these parts, they call roads *lines* or *concessions*: as in lines on a map. What there was of the white stuff lay in dirty mounds of the city's snowplough. The ground now had that mushy feel after wet snow.

Since I was early, I picked up some photos from the booth and bought flowers for Giselle. She felt the stress of our precarious finances more than I did and I was trying to placate her. The fact is I was trying so damn hard to be successful for her sake, to give her the life she wanted. To please her. Perhaps irises would cheer her. Then I stopped at the Bookshop Café for a cappuccino and time to collect my thoughts. I had to come up with a coherent argument, before facing the Bank Manager.

The manager was a big man with a square Germanic face. He crushed my hand before I sat in front of his desk. His trouble was that he was slow; he didn't have the normal neural processing speed. To compensate he blustered and left it to policy to get him through.

"Having trouble raising the mortgage payment this quarter," I said.

"Oh, only in this quarter, or is it incompetence."

"You mean *continuing*," I said. "No, it's a one off, a cash flow problem."

By then I knew enough to use a banker's words when talking to him.

"Someone killed the stallion we imported from France."

"I have the report. We have an exposure of a hundred thousand. Now you're saying you can't pay the mortgage?"

"Look, I made a claim on Alliance. I'm sure they'll pay, but not sure when. Anyway, have a tax refund due that will go close to the mortgage." I said it despite the uncertainty. "And I'm sending the remaining lucerne hay to Florida."

"Now see here. You can sell all your livestock to clear the debt."

He looked at me as if I'd forgotten something valuable and he'd miraculously reminded me of it.

"Except they're brood mares and about to foal. I'd get far less now, than when they drop the foals. Ten times more for them as yearlings."

"You have yearlings?"

"I do. Auctions are late in the summer and in fall."

"Well then," he said.

He leaned back in his chair and clasped his hands behind his head, like we'd completed discussions after reaching an obvious conclusion. This wasn't going anywhere. I decided on a new tack.

"Need to buy a replacement. Will my insurance do as collateral?"

"Certainly not! The claim will be paid to us anyway as holders of the loan. And we have no assurance it will be paid."

"I'd like to apply for a new loan then, to buy a replacement stallion"

"I'll check the claim right now. If we know you'll be paid, then we could consider it. At a higher rate I might add, rates have risen three points since."

He picked up the phone and after asking his secretary for the number, by yelling through the door, he managed to get the call dialled. After a bit of to-ing and fro-ing he put down the receiver.

"You know, Mister McKinley: Alliance have rejected your claim."

"Really, on what grounds?" It was news to me.

"A lack of security at your stables. Shouldn't be telling you this, but you are under investigation for a fraudulent claim."

"The hell you say."

"Yes, that's right. Under the circumstances, we can hardly offer a new loan. Your debt is a hundred and fifteen thousand, eight hundred and seventy-three dollars — with interest. The mortgage is now over due. If you cannot pay sir, we will be forced to foreclose. It might serve you well to sell up yourself."

"Oh, when is the deadline?"

"We can call in our loan at any time, since your collateral no longer exists. The mortgage is due March thirty-first."

At that I wanted urgently was to leap the desk and throttle him. Instead, I restrained myself, and didn't blow that fuse, not then anyway.

"Yeah right," I said getting up to leave.

Pressure building again, a migraine kicking in. My body was paying the price for suppressing my anger. That telltale constricting pain in the frontal lobes. Street sounds were impinging, loud enough to make me flinch. Visual distortions came next in bright auras. I needed to go home. I needed a bed in a dark room before it became a full-blown episode. Needed to get home while I could still drive.

Giselle brought me breakfast before she left for work. She loved the flowers I'd left and kissed me lightly on the cheek. She had a different view on the value of things. To me people and animals were important, material things meant next to nothing.

I fed my horses and rode *Jet Stream*, with the remnants of migraine sloshing around in my head. It was noon by the time I'd finished the chores. I'd made a sandwich from *cavanossi* we had in the fridge, with a cup of Java to warm my battered soul.

If I couldn't sell the hay soon I'd have to make some hard decisions on raising money. I knew Bernie, a neighbour, coveted my three-horse *Rice* trailer. Apart from my remaining hay in the barn, that trailer was the only thing readily convertible to cash. Would he buy it? Now *that* would carry the mortgage.

The mares were walking the fence in single file behind big *Red*, when I reached for the phone to call Bernie. As I reached across the desk, my eye lit on the envelope from Taxation. I hadn't looked at the mail when it came in. Hated bills. I'd open them only when I could no longer avoid it. The refund had arrived. Could hardly bear to look at the figure, knowing with absolute certainty that I'd be disappointed. The check was over five grand. Thank God, now we had our mortgage. The world did look brighter.

Now I had to get cracking: find a new stallion and find those bastards. With money in hand it came down to France or the mortgage. To be safe or bold. Maybe I could borrow money for a new stallion elsewhere.

I should discuss it with Giselle, but an image of that intellectually-challenged bank manager flashed inside my head. I'd risk a default on the mortgage by throwing the dice once again.

So then I hunted through the mail, and when I found the envelope, withdrew the prints. Leafed through them and looked at the shots of Giselle and Jennifer on the ski slopes. From the collage on the desktop a spectacular image of the mares galloping in the field popped out. A shot of mist and flying snow. A photo I'd taken from this window.

Something about the last print made me hesitate. It was a snap of the woods across the road. The shot I'd clicked off accidentally. That's when I'd looked across to the woods, when I noticed movement. Like the vision of most predators, the human eye seeks movement. I saw something again when moving my eyes across the surface glaze. Something small and indistinct: a man in the woods, dark clothes with a hood. I was certain of it.

Oh my God, he is holding a rifle!

CHAPTER 14

The natural terrain of the country is the soldier's best ally…

Sun Tzü, *The Art of War*, 512 BC

The Jumbo took off at noon. The collective noise of massive engines drilled into my skull. Out over the choppy waters of Lake Ontario I looked down at white caps breaking. A speedboat was cutting a white V on a heading due south across the border. A drug runner — well at least a merchant banker; who else could afford a hundred grand for craft like that and time for an all-day run?

From this perspective I was fascinated by houses fast receding, marvelling at the deep mystery of flight. Sure, I knew the physics of turbulent flow, relative air pressures, even the basics of aerodynamics — as everyone does. It was the deeper mystery of flight that amazed me — the heaving, double-storied building, whooshing-through-the-air-magic of it. A tremble in the aluminium skin reached me through the upholstered seat. Then a powerful kick of turbines as the pilot opened the throttle and eased the flaps. I loved it.

Jennifer watched the flight attendant go though her paces on seat belts, oxygen masks and emergency landings. Jenny looked like she had thrown on her clothes that morning in a mishmash of colour as teenagers do. It looked too as if basic black had the inside running, with garish coming up on the outside.

She had a dyed purple streak across her fringe, and mascara as if she was auditioning as a clown. Puberty was catching up. Perhaps this was to show us she was making her own choices. I shuddered at my daughter, the gypsy.

Giselle pulled out her copy of *Fancy That*, a drop-dead gorgeous model on the cover: soft brown hair, white even teeth and a great tan. It was the latest thing on crocheting. Why couldn't Jenny choose to look like that? They sat immune to the wonder of flight, while I gazed entranced through the window.

When lunch came, I chatted with Giselle over the remains of an airline omelette while I sipped a Chardonnay. I had already declined the airline coffee, for I could not abide the industrial version of my addiction. Jenny had walked up the aisle to get a coke. Her reaction to the trip, at dinner with Guy, had been because of a boyfriend she hadn't wanted to leave.

"Boyfriend," I had said to Giselle, "what boyfriend?"

"She *is* fourteen Duncan. A boy from school. Don't embarrass her, it is a big thing at her age."

"Didn't realise she had a boyfriend. Hadn't thought about those hormones kicking in."

"No, you wouldn't Duncan. He is not her first either, she's growing up."

In a show of acceptance, I gave my gypsy a smile as she returned to her seat, with a copy of *Vogue* in hand. Maybe she'd get some fashion tips.

Relaxing came hard for me I had to think. I *had* to find out who was behind the attack. I had to protect my horses and my family. The police in England were on the case, even if the OPP had gone off on a satanic tangent in Canada. I wanted to enlist police help for the invasion of our home. Giselle was so humiliated she wouldn't condone it, wouldn't speak to me about it. I felt airsick just thinking of vengeance, of retribution. I wanted to kill.

With this murderous thought in mind I wondered about that man in the woods. Was there something familiar in the image? Was it the way he stood? Was I reading something into it that wasn't there? I'd dropped the negative off that day in Toronto to get it blown up to poster size. Perhaps I'd recognise him from the blow up.

I'd also left behind that dramatic shot of the mares with *Red* in the lead galloping in the snow. The way I'd framed the photo, tight on the mares, had obscured any signs of civilisation. Something primal in the shot stirred my soul. They could be a herd of wild horses, far from the hand of man — galloping from pursuing wolves far out across the tundra. I felt an affinity with them.

Gail and her perfect family met us at Heathrow. After a brief chat, we said good-bye to Jenny. Gail looked at me hard when I took her hubby aside and told him man-to-man that we'd had a 'home invasion' that had scared the hell out of us. Jenny wasn't told, so as not to frighten her. Told him we were afraid for her.

"For God's sake, don't let her go out with *anyone* you don't know."

Richard looked at me strangely. Gail gave me a sisterly hug and whispered. "Take care of Giselle; she needs you, now more than ever."

"I'm not sure that she does — that's the problem."

"Have a great time in Paris. We'll look after Jenny."

"Yes, I know you will. We've had a problem at the farm. I'm worried about her — about her safety. Don't let her out of your sight — okay."

"Oh?"

"Richard will tell you about it."

The loudspeaker announced our flight for boarding in French, but airports being what they are, it sounded like Swahili.

"Gotta go."

Then I gave Jennifer such a hug that words caught in my throat. I didn't want to let her go. In such a state I found myself trembling in her embrace.

"Take care," was all I got out. "Be careful Jenny — don't go out alone."

"Take care yourself," she answered.

Jenny was squirming, wanting to get away, reacting to a closeness she'd grown away from. An aeons old process of breaking away. I knew that teenagers distancing themselves from parents was normal. While I was expecting it, her distance still hurt. I kissed her when we parted — suddenly afraid.

When we landed I called Mungo from the airport. He wasn't in, so I left a message with the duty officer. Walking with Giselle along the causeway to our flight, I put my arm around her waist and nuzzled her ear. Strands of her hair caught on my tongue. It felt great, embarking on a new adventure. Her scent was enough to restore my humour. It doesn't take much for me to feel good with Giselle.

"Let's make it romantic," I said, "Paris in the springtime."

"Oh Duncan that is lovely, but how can you think about romance at a time like this?"

"I'd like to forget that stuff for a while. I want us to be close."

"Yes," she said, "let us make it romantic."

Our adventure in Paris began the moment we landed. Everything that could go wrong did. Our own personal proof of Murphy's Law. It drove the wedge between us deeper. Our luggage didn't turn up for one thing, then when I phoned the hotel they had no record of our booking, "We are already full, *monsieur*." After ringing around and getting a place to take us, we went outside to look for a cab.

After struggling in my English and Giselle's schoolgirl French the driver of the only cab refused to understand where we wanted to go. I'd taken the precaution of writing the address down while on the phone, even that didn't work. He shouted something incomprehensible that sounded ugly — something Giselle wouldn't translate. He got out of the cab to cool down, turned on his heel, then with a Gallic shrug, got back in the cab and sat staring stoically ahead.

More cabs arrived and we managed to persuade one to take us, sans luggage. I finally realised what the problem was, apart from not speaking French. The hotel was only a short distance from the airport. Small beer for the cabby.

We went to bed in the city of love — exhausted.

CHAPTER 15. RAOUL

On the point of marching, begin by seizing something which your opponent holds dear...

Sun Tzü, *The Art of War*, 512 BC

A meeting took place that same day, a meeting that would change my life, although at the time I didn't know it. At Grenoble in the French Alps, a big man took a call at the reception desk of hotel Préfecture. He listened intently for a moment then spoke.

"Then cut the bastard's legs off. Christ! Quote them below cost. Do what you have to. AND DO IT NOW."

He slammed the phone down at the desk, towering over the concierge and scowled. He switched on a smile like a beacon when he caught sight of his lovely wife. She walked across the lobby of the chalet towards him, light and bouncy in her skintight ski suit.

"Business again, Wolf?"

She asked in French, her native language, though she was from the mountains of the Basque, an identity she thought of only when Basque terrorists were in the news. They wore matching navy Lycra with white trim, making it obvious to anyone that they were partners. The big man nodded and maintained an expansive grin as she threw her arms around him. They linked hands as they walked to the lift.

"Chantel back?"

"No. She's still on the slopes."

"Ah then, let's go up to our room."

Bernard was always somewhere close. The big man was aware of Bernard moving to his side in three quick steps. He turned and glimpsed three suits walking towards him. He recognised the prick of a lawyer in the lead.

"Armand. Good to see you." He said in English. His features displaying no pleasure to go with the words. He glanced at the grim faced accountants from the office. "I see you're here for a meeting, let's go up to my suite."

He turned to her and shrugged apologetically. "Darling, you'd better go along by yourself, I'm going to be busy. I'll join you for dinner with the Deminenkos."

He waited until they were secure in the lift before asking Armand. "What's this about?"

"At nine tomorrow morning Congress will block Reagan's supply bill."

He assimilated this in silence for a few moments, sorting through the implications.

"So? What's your take on the time frame to sort it out?"

"Here's the thing," said Armand as he stepped into the lift. "Reagan has a serious rift with Congress. Our man doesn't see this resolving any time soon. Senator Cartwright is mad as hell over Reagan's stonewalling."

"What did they expect, electing an actor as the president, for Chrissake?" The lift stopped and they all waited for him to get out first. "What does it mean for our deal?"

They moved into the hotel suite and took seats by the window. One suit sat on the bed, there were only three chairs. Bernard, the watchdog, remained standing.

"A drink?" The big man asked.

Two suits requested a whiskey and Bernard moved to pour them.

"One for me, Bernard," the big man said.

"What this means," said Armand, "is that payments are being held indefinitely until this is straightened out."

"Indefinitely! Christ almighty, hope you're talking days not weeks?"

"Way I read it and I do have inside information," Armand glanced at the man sitting awkwardly on the bed, "we're talking weeks, perhaps months. Army and civil Government will be paralysed from tomorrow morning, when the funding of current accounts cuts out."

Bernard found the ice cubes and handled the drinks. Wolf took a sip with a clink of ice. "I take it this is a major problem?"

"Oh, yes. We've supplied those parts on thirty days from the date of last shipment. To the tune of… let me see... of what André?"

André stood and opened the folder in his hands. "Three point eight million in total including ..."

"So when's that due?"

"Friday week. Of course, with supply blocked, it won't be paid. And it includes three hundred thou ..."

"Yeah alright. What's our legal position?" said the big man.

"Not good. We may be able to sue, though doubt any court will uphold it. As foreign suppliers, we are not about to win damages from the US Government. We're bound by their courts in the contract."

"We can't force payment for material already delivered?"

"No we can't. They don't have the money to pay, even if they wanted to."

"We have any leverage?" They all knew what he meant. Armand glanced again at André.

"Not this time," Armand said.

The big man's face darkened as if the whiskey had flooded his brain.

"Haven't we paid off enough of those greedy bastards? Fortier's wife fucked Colonel Hackett's ass off to get that tender. Mind, she'd 've fucked the entire army if we'd given her a chance — eh André."

André squirmed in his position on the bed, turning bright red. He looked down, shaking with anger while the suits laughed.

"Shut the fuck up, you bastards," he said, getting to his feet.

The big man stared at him for a second, as if he would strike, then his gaze resolved and he collected himself.

"Bernard, take our friend André downstairs to the bar."

"Eh, Boss ..."

"NOW — DO IT."

The room was silent until the door closed behind their resentment. Neither Armand nor the suit looked at each other, they stared at the rooftop view out the window.

"Let's discuss the Canadian deal without André. Where's that at?"

"It's looking good," Armand said refocusing. "We've taken over the

Ames factory at Kitchener. We've started small scale production to sort things out."

"There is one critical problem," the accountant interjected.

"What. Can't you guys keep things straight? Christ, what am I paying you for?"

"Canadian Government is demanding another three and a half million in guarantees from us by the end of April."

"More guarantees! "What the hell's going on?"

"They've taken fright at Congress blocking supply. They too, have inside information. They want us to show we've got the financial clout to meet the Canadian supply contract, independent of American finance."

"Jesus. I take it you've already failed to get credit."

"That's about it. Banks know payments are held up. That it could crash."

"Hmmm. We'll have to raise cash. Divest some property. We have saleable assets and I do have funds coming in from another operation. We've got cash coming in, so listen, this is what we're gonna do..."

The big man Wolf, with his wife and niece, were seated beside the Deminenkos for dinner, at a table by the window overlooking the slopes. Floodlights lit a path down the mountain in a surreal yellow glare. Their eyes sought the skiers banking and turning in their strange dance down the slope, just as you stare at a campfire. Wolf stroked his wife's thigh under the table, running his hand up under her dress. At the same time, he rubbed his leg against Chantel's knee on his other side. Gorgeous women. He had it all.

They ordered enough to feed a small village in Bangladesh. So much that their empty plates and half-filled bottles occupied another table beside them. A waiter hovered in the background, ready to step forward if anyone at the table raised their head. They had eaten well with a shrimp salad for an entrée, followed by the richest German cooking.

The remains of the food lay in plates scattered on the table. They were busy dissecting the remains of a Swiss strudel, except for the big man and Deminenko's chubby wife. They had chosen the Bavarian chocolate cake topped with lashings of whipped cream. They spoke in French, despite the big man's disdain for the colonial accents of the Deminenkos.

"We have an option on a new sire. Been racing him in partnership in France," said Frank Deminenko. "*Danski*, Group one winner, son of *Danzig*. He won *Les Enfants Prix* at Longchamp last year. Broke down in training this season: flexor tendon. My racing syndicate's not into breeding — not here in Quebec. Are you interested?"

"Might be. What's the Dam?"

"A stakes winner, *Vagerio*, a daughter of *Vaguely Noble*, solid black-type."

"What are we talking?"

"Two fifty for half."

"Hmmm. I'm leery of first season sires. Been caught before. Question is: Is he fertile?" The big man smiled across the table.

"We can make it conditional. Test breed the horse straight away."

"I'd want a vet check before I put up money. Call me Monday."

They took coffee, port and after dinner mints when the lights on the slope went out, plunging the countryside into darkness. As their eyes adapted they could see stars in the clear sky hidden before by reflected light. It reminded Deminenko of summer night hunting in the far North.

"Since you'll be in Canada this spring, why don't you join us for hunting at the cabin? Do ya good to get away for a week. Great guide, best in the business. Elk and bighorn sheep too. You might even bag a bear."

Wolf's wife draped herself around him, disinhibited by wine and his attention.

"Hey, bring your wife and lovely niece too," he said, leering at Chantel.

Hunting deer didn't interest the big man, but getting a bear in his sights, and a week of Chantel. That could be something.

"Hmmm. Maybe possible, where is it?"

"We get a float plane to Val-d'Or right to the cabin. No way in except the lake, has to be summer when it's clear of ice. This is deep north woods." He leant back in his chair and lit a cigar as a fleet of waiters came to their table for the dregs. "Course if bear is what you want, there's the Rockies. Ski a few days at Banff then fly into the Stikine."

After dinner he took his wife and Chantel to his suite, poured three lines of coke on the coffee table, snorted a line and felt better. It kicked right in and he felt the bright electric glow expand in his brain — anything was possible. He watched as the women sniffed, their eyes wide, their heads snapping up as they finish. Chantel seemed to float through the connecting door to her suite.

Now they were alone, he selected a video from the hotel cable and flicked the remote. A porno film started with an orgy, a scene of every imaginable combination of tits and arse. Skins with hues from black to white and cool California tans. The camera zoomed in on two women with enormous breasts kissing and stroking each other. One strapped on a dildo, the other dropped to her knees and took the enormous phallus in her mouth and sucked it while looking up at her lover.

Wolf became aware of his wife shivering. He tore his eyes away from the scene and removed her underwear — slowly. He unhitched her bra, freeing her firm breasts, sliding her lace panties down from her waist over her thighs, barely touching her skin. She shivered again, anticipating his hands.

"Turn around," he said. She did so until she's now facing away.

"Bend over."

She did so unwillingly, her legs straight, placing the flat of her hands against the floor, presenting herself to him, like a bitch in heat. She felt his hands sliding, fingering her.

"Oooh," she said as the sensation fills her.

"Down," he growls as if to a dog.

She crouched, knowing what was to come. He removed his fingers, swung his leather belt and struck her once, then once again — hard. She whimpered and bit her lip, drawing blood. The white skin of her rump burnt red in twisted angry stripes as thick as rope.

He threaded his belt around her neck pulling it hard to the buckle. Then he moved in front of her. She knows what she has to do. She slid his trousers down and over his feet one at a time. His erection was now unrestrained. He pulled her to him with the belt around her neck. She opened her mouth and took him in — while looking up to him for approval.

"On the bed," he said after a few sucks, wrenching her forward with the belt.

Then he took her from behind, cupping her breast with one hand while holding her hard by the neck. He kneaded her breasts as he drove his hugely swollen erection into her from behind.

"Yes, oh yes, fuck me — don't stop."

The connecting door opened then with a creak. She looked back frantically at the sound. She lived in uncertainty; she never knew what he would do. He had the power to corrupt anyone, everyone: man, woman or child. Chantel slipped into the room in the half-light, his wife breathed a sigh of relief. It is friend not foe.

"I heard you," she said as she unfastened her nightie and lets it fall with a rustle at her feet. She stepped out of the silken splash of hardly anything, and joined them on the bed. "Didn't want you to finish without me."

Her tawny body is flawless, with taut muscles like a cat, no fat. A body etched with youth. She kissed him on the mouth, licked his face with her quick tongue then lay on the bed beside them both, on her back.

"Kiss me," she said reaching for his wife, who was straining to remain on all fours against the man's weight.

She leaned over and kissed Chantel, running her tongue inside her wet mouth. Chantel bites her lip. He pulled away seeing this — throbbing. It excited him on to see the women together. His wife pushed her breast into Chantel's mouth, climbed on her and covered her with her naked body. The big man moved over them both and slid into the young woman. Chantel arched her back. A few strokes and he's back to his wife for more, then to Chantel — teasing.

When he was in her, she reached out and fingered Chantel, he thrust in time to her increasing rhythm. Chantel's excitement rose until she threw them off. She reached for herself with both hands. She threw back her head and came with a violent arch of her back and long drawn out whimpers. God, it's good to see a woman come, he thought.

Wolf was on the brink. When his wife's fingers touched him he came too; his creamy spawn falling on the women, marking them — claiming ownership. Chantel reached for his stickiness and rubbed it into her taut belly. The steamy scent of sex embraced them all.

Wolf's wife was now frantic and climbed astride him, and with a groan impaled herself on his shaft and moved urgently — riding him. Her long red hair obscured her face as she threw her head about in a chaotic swirl with her rising agitation. He pinched her nipples suddenly against his thumbnails until she cried out. But still she kept moving in a progressive rhythm of need. Then shrieked while still contracting, pressing down hard to keep the sensation going, to slump spent against his chest.

CHAPTER 16. **DUNCAN**

There are five ways of attacking with fire. The first is to throw fire and burn soldiers in their camp...

Sun Tzü, *The Art of War*, 512 BC

I rented a car and held my breath while they ran my credit card and made that inevitable and worrying call. This was the French equivalent of Rent-a-Wreck. We pulled an off-white Citroën with small holes in the doors, and rust patches in odd spots: patched, not painted. It made me think it was a police vehicle in a former life. A strange car the Citroën — so French, so chic and not at all muscular. It had the odd trait of adjustable height and suspension settings. This would have been fun, except with this particular car the suspension was stuck in just one position, inches from the ground.

We took the Survilliers exit off the Paris A1 and headed for Chantilly. I wound the car up to 160 clicks on the Autobahn, or whatever they call it in French. I dropped the window down, while farmland whipped by and turned the radio on full blast. I felt good. We had made love last night, long and slow in a new affirmation of life.

Giselle's silk scarf floated out her window, a pale, blue flag in the slipstream. The colour matched her pendant. Her blonde hair whipped across her face — stunning. I glanced at her and laughed. She looked back and smiled, then began tapping her feet to the sound of Cat Stevens. She swayed to the music as he sang, *A hard-headed woman*. I sang along and Giselle joined me in the chorus.

We found Le Professeur inspecting a horse. One of the flunkies hobbled it out on three legs from the stall. When they unwrapped the bandages I could see the horse had a bowed tendon. The flexor tendons of a front leg were torn internally from hard racing.

Evolution shaped horses with spindly legs. Their muscles are located high, powering the legs through long tendons, hence their fragile legs. Further distortion of the wild horse occurred in the process of its domestication. We've spent five thousand years breeding horses that are stronger and faster, though inevitably more fragile, than those in the wild.

The horse the vet attended was a strong-looking bay, except for a swollen leg. Muscles bulged through its gleaming coat as it walked, the outline of each muscle etched by lines moving with the hide dividing them. It is recognised by breeders that soft tissue injuries are not genetic weaknesses, whereas lameness due to broken, or deformed bones, is taken to be inherited.

"Don't think he'll race again," I said.

"Maybe not," the Professor said. "In this case we tried something new."

"Oh, what is that?"

"Heard of a split tendon operation?"

I had to confess, that I had not.

"An operation to split the fibres longitudinally. We are implanting filaments of carbon to guide tendon regeneration."

It was impressive, if it worked. And perhaps it might. I'd seen horses crippled with tendon damage. Few ever made it back to the track. None that I'd seen had raced again. Still it was worth a shot.

"Phoned you about a horse called *Alaric*?"

"Yes of course. A good horse. You have him still?"

"No," I said, "he died soon after arrival."

"Oh, from what, monsieur?"

At that I hesitated, thinking of rabbiting on about infectious disease as I had with Sloan. The cause of death was already known to whoever did this: they were aware of it by now. So I said instead:

"He was killed with an axe."

" *Morbleu*! Killed, but why?"

"Yes, I wondered about that too, until we found heroin in him."

"Heroin? Oh, ingenious, yes? Frightful waste of a horse."

"I was hoping you might know if anyone had access to the horse."

He pointed out *Alaric* was in quarantine in England for three months and that he was sent to Canada from there. I didn't say the heroin was refined in France, or that I suspected it was smuggled from here. Despite his reluctance, I pressed him into giving me the name of *Alaric's* trainer, and directions to Montrose, where the horse was bred.

"Could have been anyone monsieur. I know these people. England is more likely. He was sent from there, no?"

"Yes he was, I checked in Newmarket — nothing."

This time it was I who gave a devastating shrug.

"You should go to the gendarmes," he said, "it is criminal, yes."

"Perhaps, but I have no evidence. What do you think they'd say?"

"They'll say the horse was shipped from England, that it has nothing to do with them."

"Precisely."

Giselle had drifted away from the conversation and was idly watching the bay being put away. He got a cold hosing of that deformed leg.

"A good horse?" I asked, for I knew such operations cost thousands — that's dollars, not measly French francs.

"Quite good." He said, "Horse won a Group one from three starts at two. Broke down this year. Might have run better at three, then again maybe not."

"And his sire?"

"Danzig."

"Ah," I said, "an exceptional horse."

Giselle was looking out across the back to the marvellous green turf of the racetrack at Chantilly. Her gaze took in a castle that dominated the course.

"What is that building, a palace?" she asked him.

"Palace? Oh," he said, "No, they are stables, built three hundred years ago, though it looks a palace *non*, fit for a king."

"Yes, indeed. Which king's horses were there?"

"He was actually. Ah, how do you say — a prince yes, Prince de Conde. They have stalls for more than two hundred and forty horses. Way before they had racing here. Stables were for cavalry and coach. Racing began here at Chantilly a good hundred years after that."

"May we see inside?"

"No Madam, it is not permitted. Though you may visit the Grand Chateau of Conde, his lavish mansion, near the railway station. It is worth the trip."

We drove to the training track at Chantilly, into thousands of acres of forested grounds. Miles of unfenced dark red, wood chip tracks wound through groves of oak, birch, and other varieties I couldn't identify. The lush grounds filled me with a spiritual feeling for these woods.

The grass manicured to a fine even height with broad-leafed trees here and there gave it a more a parkland feel than a forest. A man in a blue beret rode on a mower, putt, putting across the green expanse. In the distance, a pair of riders cantered horses stride for stride. They drew nearer and went by with clicking hooves, breathing in a harsh synchronous unison and flicking heat and sweat from their hides. We could hear their riders shouting to each other, though what they said we couldn't tell. I fell in love with the place. I could've stayed forever. Giselle was anxious to visit the chateau.

We searched for Monsieur Olivier, *Alaric's* former trainer. Giselle asked for him in her stilted French. She's a good-looking woman and it ensured a certain civility from the hangers on. I was not accorded the same respect. The trainer was away at a race meeting. He would not be around until the morning — early morning.

"At what time?" I asked in English and met another Gallic shrug.

We did meet our man from the British Thoroughbred Agency. He'd organised an inspection of a couple of horses in training. They might be useful to race this season then put to stud on retirement. J B Kennet was exactly how I pictured a bloodstock agent. A Yorkshire man, well dressed in a brown suit with the porkpie hat that is *de rigueur* for that generation in racing. He was a small man, small enough to be a jockey in his youth. Kennet was impressive in his encyclopaedic knowledge of bloodlines, of French and English horses, and those of America, Canada, Australia, Japan, South Africa and the Argentine.

We inspected a lanky Chestnut racer by *Arctic Tern* and a sprinter by *Forli*, while a few grooms stood about and watched us. Neither horse impressed me with their conformation. It's not a good start to breed from a sire that is not mechanically correct — especially in the straightness of its forelegs. Though established farms will risk it, they'll breed anything to anything, if the horses can gallop. These forelegs were not straight — far from it. The defects were especially noticeable when we had the groom trot the horses for us.

JB, as he wished to be called, agreed with me in a mumble that sounded like a heavy smoker clearing his throat. Despite my assessment, JB pointed out that the breeding of each horse was impeccable, both outcrosses to *Northern Dancer's* line. He thought them possibilities, if not hot prospects, should we find nothing better. I did not.

Giselle loved the chateau, though it looked to me like a giant wedding cake; a cake made by chefs who couldn't quite make up their minds. The grounds were magnificent: lakes, fountains, canals and a marvellous assortment of trees. Green with splashes of coloured flowers. Inside a museum with delicate furnishings, mediaeval *manuscriptus*, gilded bric-a-brac and paintings by Raphael. They demanded a month's pay for us to see it. I paid like a faithful retainer, while Giselle walked in the door, a Duchess.

Ah, the good life. How many peasants worked here in poverty to keep this luxury afloat for so long ago? No wonder they had a revolution! I dragged Giselle away, when it closed at five. On the way out we passed an arboretum with a marble statue of naked lovers entwined in a passionate embrace. I glanced at Giselle and caught her looking at it. I smiled and looked away. We headed back to our lodgings with separate thoughts.

An image of Giselle lying naked on the bed had flashed hot in my brain, her legs spread, her hands tied tight to the bedposts. The razor cut running the length of her chest in a thin red line. And when I arrived she bit down hard on her lip and her eyes blazed into mine.

When the alarm clanged, I arose and left Giselle asleep. She didn't want to go to the track at this ungodly hour, so I had suggested she stay at the hotel until I returned. I didn't want her to be out on her own. Didn't want her to be afraid. She turned over in the bed, pulled the duvet over her head and muttered something I didn't catch.

"See you," I said touching her cheek lightly, "back at noon or thereabouts."

That's how I came to be driving in the predawn, lights ablaze, the countryside whipping by while remaining intent on where I was going, intent on the thoughts swirling inside my head. This time I *was* focussed.

The forest at Chantilly at dawn was splendid, as I imagined it would be. A mist hung over the park at daybreak creating an enchanted forest. Breathing in the magic I found a place by the track to view the gallops. Horses came by me working in twos, threes or fours galloping through the mist.

Rounding a barn I found Monsieur Olivier talking to a knot of people. So I waited, watching horses come and go until they had all dispersed.

"Nice horse," I said in English, nodding at a sleek two-year old jogging off the track covered with a creamy foam. A mist arose as if it had just taken a bath. It danced for a moment on the spot in a piaffe while the trainer spoke to the rider.

Olivier was a thin man, tanned and with a watchful eye for horses. He wore a denim Mao cap with a red star, which gave him a revolutionary air. I apologised for not speaking French. He agreed that *Alaric* was a fine horse. Professor Guignard was right, Olivier spoke English well.

"Who was *Alaric's* groom?" I asked, after we ran out of banalities.

"Nadim."

"Nadim, eh. I'd like to speak with him if I could."

"No, monsieur."

"No?"

"Nadim does not speak English. He is Afghani. Apart from his native Pashtu, he speaks only French and that badly."

"Ah," I said, and looked again at Olivier. With his dark skin and sharp features, he could well have been Afghan too.

"Perhaps you could translate?"

"No monsieur, Nadim is no longer here."

"I'm disappointed. *Alaric* is a tough horse. Near took my arm off first time I went in his stall. Nadim might know a few things. Where can I find him?"

"I do not know monsieur," he said. He must have seen the look of disbelief on my face, for then he said, "He has gone to the country."

"You know where?"

"No," he said, "we did not part friends."

"Oh, why is that?"

He ignored my question, asking instead one of his own, one that startled me.

"You still have the horse?"

"No," I admitted, "he had a misadventure."

"*Misadventure*. What is that?"

"Well, this misadventure was a steel axe embedded in his head."

Olivier stared at me as if I was mad, perhaps he misunderstood my English.

"Ah," he said, looking away.

He'd caught sight of a petite woman coming our way. She wore a dress the colour of the sky. A filmy dress that moved like a breeze around her as she walked. Olivier waved, his eyes sliding over her as she strode towards us.

"This is Missus Kelemann, the owner of the black colt you admired."

"Hullo," I said, and glimpsed her disturbing green eyes.

A young woman in her twenties with a skin unaffected by the sun. After introducing us, Olivier monopolised the woman by drawing her aside with a hand on her arm. I could hear him rabbiting on about the horse, in a trainer's argot that is used the world over. They turned and looked to where the horse was being unsaddled then hosed down.

Trainers go on about the horse showing a lot of promise, how one day he'll be a champion, though right now of course, he's not quite ready, he needs more time, perhaps an easy sprint first up, or words to that effect. This time it was in French. I didn't understand a word of it. I didn't need to. I already knew what he was telling her.

While he was chatting, I studied this stylish woman. She was willowy and casually pretty in a way that Giselle was not. She had a slim taut body with pert young breasts and fashionably sleek hips, that dazzled in a flowing summer concoction of blue silk. Her heart-shaped face had an amazing symmetry, her cat's eyes exotic with auburn hair flowing down her back in a chestnut mane. The mouth was freshly wet and a tad too large, unsullied by lipstick. There was confidence in every tilt of her head and every Gallic gesture. She wore a straw hat with a blue scarf tied around the crown. She held it now with one hand while her sunglasses pushed up in her hair caught flashes of the sun. Then she replaced the hat, held the sunglasses in one hand, looked up from under the brim and spoke to Olivier. Sunlight played softly on her face.

This vision reminded me of Claudia, a schoolgirl vixen who had taught me, with her ripening body, about lust. I had lost her to a college man five years my senior. For a long while afterwards, long past my teens, I had looked for her in other women. Sometimes deep wounds take a long while to heal. I saw here an image of my long lost Claudia in all her sensuous vitality in the form of Mrs Kelemann. I was smitten.

Though drawn to her in a primal way, I had no thought of being unfaithful. I also had no thought either of a Mister Kelemann, whoever he was. I wanted only to know this creature, to be among her friends, to occupy some planetary orbit of her space. We are drawn to people who offer promise and avoid those we sense will fail us. The enchanting Mrs Kelemann glanced my way, half smiled and blinked her feline eyes. Olivier glared at me, as men do in such circumstances.

"Where are you from?" she said, as we walked together to the car park.

"Canada," I said, "Southern Ontario."

"Oh, you have no French?"

"My excuse is that I'm Scottish."

"We have a house in Montreal. We go there when my husband is on business."

"Though you do live here in France, Missus Kelemann?"

"Oh please, call me Simmone." She pronounced her name in the soft French way. "But of course. Yes, we live in France — when we're not travelling. What is it you are doing here?" She asked of me.

"Looking for a new stallion."

"At Chantilly?"

"Actually right now I'm looking for my stallion's groom, Nadim. Olivier trained *Alaric* before I bought him."

"Oh yes," she said, "the big chestnut. Nadim went to work at Montrose. We too have some horses there."

"Good, I'm planning to go there tomorrow. They have a two colts I want to see."

She refused me her phone number and while laughing at my advance granted me *adieu*. I swallowed my rejection, as men do.

"Oh," she said softening her refusal. "Where are you... in Paris?"

I told her the hotel and gave her my card. The one I'd printed on my trusty Mac. She headed for a sports car the shocking colour of arterial blood.

Subdued, not knowing what to think, I sauntered over to the bullet-holed Citroën and got in. As I did so, I leaned out to straighten the rear vision mirror. I noticed the same man in a dark suit I'd seen earlier at the track. He'd been around yesterday too, when we were looking at prospects with JB, our man from British Thoroughbreds. Suits are out of place at a racetrack this early in the morning.

He was getting into an Audi way back in the lot.

CHAPTER 17

Of all those in the army close to the commander none is closer than the spy; of all rewards none more liberal than those given to spies; of all matters none is more important than secret operations.

Sun Tzü, *The Art of War*, 512 BC

Giselle came with me to Montrose the next day. From Paris we took the road to Loches, via Saumur. They had some potential sires at Montrose, though I didn't fancy their breeding, except for a *Sea Bird* colt.

As I drove chatting with Giselle, with one part of my brain I was trying to think of a line of questioning of Nadim, something more effective than what I'd been doing. What I needed was information. What I needed was to know my enemy; what I really needed was someone in the enemy camp; what I needed was a spy. The more I thought about it, the more I thought Nadim was a distinct possibility. I recalled a snippet from Sun Tzü I'd read the night before.

What enables a man to strike and conquer, and achieve things beyond the reach of ordinary men is foreknowledge. Foreknowledge cannot be obtained from previous experience nor by deduction from what has gone before. Knowledge of the enemy can only be obtained from other men.

Saumur was where the Fulton family had bred *Alaric*. The yearling sales at Deauville are a big event in this resort town; it is famous for the horses and racy crowd attached to them. Many horse studs are right here in Normandy, the land of Norsemen who swept down by sea a thousand years ago, ferocious men who had made this rich farming land their home.

Giselle was quiet, staring at her reflection in the mirror. She didn't respond to the radio, or to my optimism, an optimism I was finding harder to maintain. We drove through Saumur to Montrose, a mansion that was more a castle than a country house. Giselle was aguish with the ambience of grandeur.

Bertrand Fulton showed us the horses for sale. We saw two mediocre racehorses that had been retired to stud and a half brother to *Alaric*. This stallion had not raced, due to an early injury. It is a huge gamble with a sire that has never raced. I was not inclined to take it, even if he was by *Sassafras*. A Group-one winner is what I needed, so I shook my head at that offering.

They showed me the colt by *Sea Bird* preparing for racing at three. He'd won stakes his first year and he'd be racing again within weeks. He was brilliant: tall, straight-legged, muscled and lean-bellied, the way horses get when they're galloped.

The asking price was a half million — in dollars. Why did they want to sell him right now at the start of the season? This was of course a gamble that I'd enjoy, if I had the bread. The horse could be syndicated then put to stud, but there wasn't time for that, they were in a hurry to sell him.

"A bit rich for my blood," I said, "who's the owner?"

"*Compagnie Fabriquante SA*."

This horse was way out of my league, but before we left I asked after *Alaric's* groom, the elusive Nadim.

"Why yes," Bertrand said, "Nadim, perhaps it is he? He led out that *Sassafras* colt for you. I'll send a boy to fetch him, yes."

Giselle translated for me when Nadim arrived. A young and wiry man with jet-black hair and a brown Afghan face — prominent nose. I asked Nadim about handling *Alaric* as if I was having a lot of trouble with the horse. He knew *Alaric* could be vicious.

"*Sauvage* with mares," he said, "you 'ave a man each side of him. He bites the mares hard to draw blood on ... how you say it?"

"*Wither*," I volunteered.

"Just so, the wither."

Then it was I asked him in English, what had made him leave Chantilly. Nadim looked away towards the fields and picked his teeth with a fingernail.

"I like the countryside," he said with care, "it is beautiful, *non*."

And of course I did agree that it was beautiful, but then so was Chantilly. He was less than convincing and I wasn't getting anywhere. Sun Tzü's advice about employing spies buzzed in my head. Hmmm, how did it go? Nadim was a potential spy all right, he knew something, but how was I to recruit him?

Although he was wearing the same jacket and boots as the other grooms, I was aware that Nadim looked sharper. He was well fed, sleek and wiry. He also wore a Rolex that if genuine, was worth a thousand bucks. He had a gold chain with a medallion around his neck. Men wear such jewellery in France. It looked like solid gold. The styled hair and manicured fingernails were out of place for a stablehand. Someone had paid him well.

He might be in the enemy camp, he might have the information I needed, but for the life of me, I could not think how to approach him. I decided to press him instead. Even then, remaining civil, I put it to him gently: "Did you have a disagreement with Olivier?" He glared at me and shrugged. "Well did you?" I said.

"Fuck you," he said in English and moved away, glancing back once as he walked to the barn. I could think of nothing in reply.

We drove for a few miles back the way we had come, discussing Nadim and the death of *Alaric*. We didn't come up with anything more practical than pulling Nadim's fingernails out one by one until he told us his contacts. "How much does he know anyway?" I said, "If I had hired him, I'd have made damn sure he didn't know who I was."

"If it were Guy, he would have terrified the kid; we would have an answer by now."

"We can't do that," I said. "We can't go around frightening people."

Though of course that was exactly what he would have done. Guy would have intimidated the bejesus out of the lad. Nadim knew something we did not, something we needed. There was too much at stake for me to be a wimp. Morality and an innate adherence to the strictures of civilisation had held me back.

Saumur is not the most attractive town. It is famous for the ancient cavalry school, and that's why we were here. I'd been looking forward to it. The town has a fortress at its centre with octagonal towers and a strange assortment of roofing. Some of it must have been destroyed. The Cavalry School on Rue Beaurepaire is home to the *Cadre Noir* with ancient traditions in the fine art of classical horsemanship. Grand exhibitions are held here in summer, then International Horse Trials were held later in the fall.

By the time we got to the academy there was no equestrian action. The riders had been and gone. A lethargic horse was being lunged in a Chambon by a cadet. The young man gave a command and flicked the whip. The horse cantered. Dust from the arena kicked up in a fine mist, which showered us — so we left.

We learned, from a chap who showed us around, that the school was established in 1763. The last military action was less than fifty years ago. Cadets from the school delayed an overwhelming force of Germans in 1940 at the bridge over the Lorie into Saumur. The cavalry put up such stiff opposition it stopped the German column. Only after hours of German shelling were those gallant cadets forced to surrender. That's how the castle lost its roof.

After the Cavalry School, we stopped for a late lunch at a roadside café late in the afternoon. We shared a Chardonnay, some desultory conversation and local fare before climbing into the Citroën and heading back to Paris.

It is at times when one is unprepared that dangerous things happen. Times when you are tired, angry or distracted. This was as quick as a shying colt. In a heartbeat a van loomed up to overtake us — CRASH.

The van hit with a screech of metal. The car rolled before I blinked. Over and over again. My head bumping the roof, bouncing off the door. We hung in our seat belts from the roof — upside down. The horn blaring, motor running, the wheels spinning, scraping on metal — a sound that was damaging.

My head ached. Giselle hung by her belt, white-faced and silent. Fuel drenched my head and chest. I inhaled petrol fumes and panicked, then clutched at the winder to crank the window. Jammed.

"GET OUT," I shouted.

I don't know if she heard me over the blare of the horn.

Somehow I mashed the belt catch and fell upside down, catching my right shoulder on the steering. My head hit the dashboard. Shit!

"GISELLE. ARE YOU ALRIGHT?"

Giselle muttered something I couldn't make out. Supporting her weight I released her seat belt and eased her down — BLARE, BLARE, BLARE.

"VAN RAN US OFF THE ROAD," I said, a touch short of hysterical.

"WHO?" Giselle shouted, "I didn't see anyone."

Blood dripped down her face like a scarlet curtain and I wiped it off with my sleeve. The blood kept flowing. It was then I saw it was my own blood, from a cut over my eyes. Giselle too had a laceration where the wire frame of her reading glasses had cut her forehead.

"GET OUT BEFORE IT CATCHES FIRE."

Reaching for the keys I switched off the ignition — at least that stopped the horn. Stillness, followed by a ticking as the motor cooled. I broke glass with my boots and we scrambled out.

We'd only crawled a short way when the fumes found the hot exhaust. A flash lit the engine compartment with a HUMPH that blew in a spectacular whoosh of orange flame and a shock wave that hurled itself against us.

The explosion brought the Gendarmes. They'd have seen it from way off. They arrived within minutes and proceeded in a rapid French that even Giselle couldn't answer. One tried his English and we were able to handle that. The flap of skin hanging loose from a cut down my face was enough to get their attention. The copious bloodflow impressed them sufficiently to call an ambulance.

"No, I didn't see what kind of van. A dark one."

"You say monsieur, the van hit you deliberately?"

"Yes, it was overtaking then swerved and collided."

"Ah, a dog? A drunk perhaps?"

He leaned close to sniff my breath.

"No, no dog, nothing on the road," I said.

"Who would do such a thing, monsieur?"

"Because..." I drew breath and told them everything. Well, not quite everything; I told them about my horse being slaughtered and gave a synopsis of what had happened in France. Not all that much when you reduced it to a few hard facts. It sounded paranoid as I said it, even to me.

Perhaps he smelled that chardonnay. He scribbled something in his notebook.

"We will report to your statement." He said in mangled English and checked my passport that I had produced from my jacket. Giselle's handbag with her passport and money had gone up in flames. So had the papers for the car. Though luckily, of all the details I had in my mind, one essential thing remained — the name of the rental company.

The ambulance took us to a nearby hospital. After being x-rayed then lying around on a gurney for hours, we were examined, treated and discharged. We both sported micro stitches on our faces, care of France's finest. The waiting gave me time to think. All I came up with was my brilliant foresight in ticking the comprehensive insurance box on the car rental slip. Giselle asked me in a quiet moment, why I'd shouted at her in the car when we crashed.

"*Shouted*? I was calm, besides the horn was blaring."

"It sounded like you were shouting," she said. "You scared me. It didn't sound like you."

Perhaps I had. I certainly felt like shouting: shouting for her to love me.

The doctors wanted us to stay around, to check for concussion or internal bleeding before they let us go. By the time they discharged us the sun was sending slivers of light through the canyons of the city. When we got back to our hotel, we crashed into clean sheets and slept through the day.

That evening I phoned Mungo at New Scotland Yard. He was intrigued that someone had tried to kill us, until he realised I couldn't describe the van: not its colour, make, nor license plate. I did manage to give him Olivier's full name and Nadim's. Then I gave him Bertrand Fulton's to run through the system.

"Did you get anything on Sloan?" I asked.

"Sloan won the Oaks with a good mare. He won enough for that Jag."

"Oh," I said. "What about the manor, public schools, his expensive wife?"

McGowan didn't respond.

"Anything else you remember," he asked. Transatlantic static filled the line like a question mark.

"One thing," I said, "*Compagnie Fabriquante* is selling a top horse that's now in training."

"So?"

"It's not unknown to sell a good horse. It happens when owners have to dissolve a partnership, or if they are desperate for cash. Perhaps the company is desperate enough to trade in drugs."

"How do you spell that?"

"Spell what?"

"*Compagnie* ... whatever old boy."

"Well, *F-a-b-r-i-q-u-a-n-t-e*." I tried the pronunciation a few times without the Tee. "Point is, no one sells a really good racehorse unless they have to."

"Why not, if they need the cash?"

"Because a good horse could potentially win a million, tax free — if you backed it."

"Hmmm," he said.

"Company name rang a bell, though I didn't immediately recognise it."

"And now you do?"

"It's on *Alaric's* papers, but I'd never heard it pronounced before."

"I'll look into it," he said and hung up.

As soon as I put the phone down it rang. It was Simmone.

"Duncan," she said, "I need to see you. Have something to tell you. You must meet me — you must."

She sounded on the verge of hysteria. I knew then I should step back, but I didn't. I think then she knew I couldn't.

"Okay fine. Let's meet tonight," I said, wondering what this was all about.

"Café Le Marquis, Rue Faubourg," she said.

We set a time. What on earth would I say to Giselle?

Giselle in her practical way had booked for the *Ballet de Paris*. She knew I didn't appreciate the artifice, and since my presence spoiled the illusion, she decided to go alone. Have to say that I found ballet fey, artificial and constrained. It's the opposite of theatre where the story is explicit. I'd prefer a wild gypsy dancing barefoot, to the cold, white sterility of ballet. Giselle knew it, we had already been over that ground.

"Fine," I said when she told me, "I'll stay here and read."

John Le Carré's latest and greatest, *The Little Drummer Girl,* lay on my bedside table. I felt guilty lying to my wife, as men do, but the need was unequivocal. An appeal for protection is something men respond to instinctively. Simmone had pushed my damsel-in-distress button. The feeling I had for this woman was different to what I had with Giselle. It was as if they inhabited parallel lives.

I met Simmone at the café. She looked stunning in a flimsy yellow dress with a vague floral pattern. The colourful effect was heightened by her chestnut mane. The magnificent symmetry of her face completed the picture. She had a natural beauty, the sort of breathtaking appeal that a lack of make up did not dilute: this set her apart from other women.

"Duncan," she said, "I am cursed by being able to see things."

"Seeing the future, do you mean?"

She was one of those women whose emotions range over their features in full view. It makes them vulnerable. I didn't believe in the mumbo-jumbo of the paranormal. At least I didn't then.

"I have premonitions," she said, searching my face for a sign. "I see things and they happen, precisely as I've seen them."

"Ya, right Simmone: What have you seen?"

With a touch of anxiety I reached for her as I said it. She seized both my hands and held them to her breast.

"Please, you must protect me from ... my husband."

She glanced around, never quiet — distraught.

"What is the matter?"

Muscles of her face danced and fought under the skin around her jawline.

"He hurts me. He will hurt me bad."

"Then leave him Simmone."

"You don't understand," she said. "He is not like other men. He will never let me leave him — never. He will kill me first."

"He plans to kill you?"

"It is not that."

Her accent was amplified by her distress, it entranced me. We ate and drank a little wine, so that the strain of my own situation drained away, it paled in comparison. Simmone conversed in unfiltered chaotic thoughts of her crisis with her brute of a husband.

"'*E* attacked me," she said, dropping her French aitch's. "You cannot imagine what he does, 'e is crazy jealous."

Emotion flicked across a fresh bruise on her delicate cheek as she spoke. She lifted her auburn mane and showed me purple bruising with a yellowed centre like a starburst. There were also fresh deep bite marks on her neck.

"He has done this?" I said, appalled.

"I am frightened — like a child."

Although I didn't know it then, the fear she had of him was justified. At the time, despite the bruising, I thought she was being overly dramatic. Mistakenly I interpreted her desperation as manipulation.

"You have no idea of the things he is capable..."

"What things?"

The fact is I shocked myself saying it, realising at once that I was titillated by imagining things sexual. I assumed, as men do, that she wanted me to solve her problem. Looking back, she just wanted to talk, to share the emotional process, as women do. Share it with me because she sensed me as someone who might care for her. Perhaps she truly did sense the future. Though I doubt it. The truth is, as I see it now in hindsight, she never really thought me strong enough to rescue her.

"A wolf traps me in the dark, deep in a dungeon," she said. "I am a child and his fangs tear at my body until I am nothing."

"That's your premonition?"

"There is more." As we talked an emotional charge was building: my brain awash with primal thoughts, the sort of feelings men can't ignore. "He cuts a white angel in her chest with a knife; she runs with blood. Red streams run down her body."

"A white angel. A bleeding white angel. This is what you dreamt."

"White skin, white hair, white everything — red blood."

To calm her I touched her face, stroked her cheek there in the café, as if we were alone. She put my fingers to her lips and kissed them, licking my fingers to the tip, then sucking my thumb: drawing it into her mouth. Her sucking electrified me, her face melted and her eyes slid up as if she was hypnotised. I withdrew my thumb and kissed her on the lips, sliding my tongue deep inside her moist cavity, hugging her, savouring the moment — blocking out the world. Simmone's her hair fell across my face, heavy with the scent of lust. The sheer erotic scent of her. Pillowed breasts lay soft against my chest. I knew I shouldn't, but God it was delicious: she felt sooo good.

"Let's go," she said.

"Where? We..."

"NOW," she said and stood.

Staggering to my feet I pulled on my coat, feeling macho like that cowboy in the Marlboro ad. We stumbled out and I paid the bill as we left. At the desk they took all I had left in my wallet and fished for change in my straining jeans. To hell with the tip.

"Stay with me," she said, looking straight ahead through the windscreen when we got into her car.

"You mean tonight?"

She turned her head and looked at me intensely, "I mean *forever*."

"What the..." I manage to stammer and leaned towards her.

"Love me — love me right now. Don't leave me, not ever. I cannot be alone."

She started to cry when I pulled away to gain perspective.

"I can't, I'm sorry. I have to be there for Giselle."

"Giselle: You have a wife?"

"Yes, of course I have a wife, just as you have a husband." That brilliant line from Zorba the Greek came to mind and I was stupid enough to repeat it: "Married? Of course I'm married: Am I not a man? Are not all men stupid? Wife, children the whole catastrophe!"

Simmone stopped the car, her foot jammed hard on the brake. The seat belt clawed at my shoulder and my head hit the side window with a CRACK. She screamed then slammed into my chest with her fists, clawing with her nails. Her talons caught a flap of skin across my temple and I felt the first sticky flow. I clicked the door open and she accelerated with a roar, I was half out the car door, making an escape. When she took off I tumbled all the way and hit the gravel.

Aware now, after blacking out, that I was lying on my back winded, looking up at a dark sky. Aware that the gravel had cut my hands and my back hurt something fierce.

Crazy bitch.

I caught a taxi back to my hotel.

CHAPTER 18

Warfare is based on deception. When able to attack we must seem unable; when near to the enemy we must seem far away...

Sun Tzü, *The Art of War*, 512 BC

My angst festered like a sore now that I was crossing a great divide. I didn't know where it would take me, I only knew there was no going back. I hired a van from the same Rent-a-Wreck company with peeling paint and disaffected staff. Just as well, they didn't give a damn. If they were on the ball they wouldn't have given me a replacement. After filling out the paperwork and making sure to tick that insurance box they signed the docket. This new van was an '84 Ford cargo model in matt black. What I liked was that it had windows only in the front. The rest was closed in. For what I had in mind that suited me just fine.

On the main street I found a hardware store and pointed to a garden hose and some nylon cord. Giselle was dizzy this morning and had taken *Gravol* to calm her vertigo. I'd left her sleeping in a sumptuous bed.

From one of those spartan but chic excuses for a phone box I phoned Simmone. I was relieved when she agreed to take the call, since she was after all, the only one I knew who spoke French. I had to see her again, had to figure out what the hell was going on. Like who the fuck is her husband anyway? And apart from all this psycho shit, why is she so frightened of him?

She was cool on the phone. Adamant that she wasn't about to see me again any time soon. I still hadn't told her of my slaughtered horse and decided to keep it that way.

"I need to speak with Nadim about how he handled my horse *Alaric*. Can you please call him and refer to me as a wealthy client, and at least *imply* that you'll be there." I figured that a call from Simmone would bring any red-blooded male on his hands and knees.

"Why should I do this thing for you?"

"Because damnit, I thought there was something between us. I thought you wanted my help."

"So did *I* Duncan. So did I."

"Well, let's start again shall we. Start afresh."

"How do you know this man, Nadim?" she asked.

"We met at Montrose where he works. Please Simmone."

"Okay Duncan, for *you* I do it," she said. "And you will owe me," then she hung up.

Now it was me with premonitions, for I knew that I would pay for this favour in the future and pay dearly. Simmone did as agreed and arranged the meeting in the same café, set in a Bohemian district of students, artists, writers and freaks. When she phoned back it was done.

Cooking spiced the air like it does in the back streets of Morocco. The day was closing. Time to eat. I got there early, after fobbing off Giselle with another excuse. I didn't tell her of my plan; she would have been horrified.

While waiting I sat in the dark trying to doze. Rhodopsin levels build in the dark, improving my night vision, preparing me for battle — following the lore of Sun Tzü. When it was also dark outside I strolled to the café. Waiting on the opposite side of the street, I looked into a store window where the café was reflected. Then I leaned against a lamp post to wait in the urban jungle — prepared for war.

Nadim appeared some forty minutes after I had long tired of waiting. He was not alone. He'd brought a friend with him, a big man who looked a hell of a lot stronger than Nadim. Damn! This was a huge complication; one I hadn't planned on. Still I wasn't going back now, so I crossed the road going after them. Once inside Nadim took a seat facing the door while I waited, hands in pockets — too high on adrenaline to heed the night chill.

People feel the call of nature when they turn to food. Unlike women, men tend to go alone. So I waited, a hunter alert for that moment when prey is vulnerable. An Inuit on the polar ice, spear poised, waiting for a seal to rise — a predator. Being the hunter makes you brave.

After a short while Nadim's companion rose to leave. At that moment a woman swept past me with her escort towards the café. I followed their scent and strolled in on their heels as if I belonged. Nadim looked away after a cursory glance at the arrivals. Then I moved past them to his table when they took off their coats, unhurried as if to go by. He saw me at the last and half rose from the chair. By then I was beside him, prodding the hose into his side, from within my coat pocket.

"Come," I said in his ear, invading his space, leaning over him, so close he could smell me. "*Now*, or I'll blow your fuckin' head off."

That did the trick; he bolted for the door. I went with him around the corner into the alley, sliding my arm around his shoulder and getting a grip on his sleeve.

"Arsehole," I hissed.

He hesitated in the dark so I shoved the hose in his back. Another corner and I had him beside the van. Then he hit me — a vicious sneaky elbow in the gut that took the wind out. Kneed me in the jaw with a crash when I doubled up, snapping my teeth shut with stunning pain. He was fast. Faster than me and a hell of a lot stronger than I'd counted on.

Now I was on my knees gasping for air, one hand still caught on his jacket. Braced myself against the van and went for him. *Hard and fast* I remembered from my old instructor, do as much damage as you can: face, eyes, throat, solar plexus and groin. So I rammed him in the solar plexus with my head, with all my weight behind it. He fell back over garbage cans clattering with an awful noise. I went after him like a sewer rat: head first, all teeth and claws. He put his hands up when I went for his throat and I caught his fingers in a jujitsu hold bearing down hard on his little finger. It gave with a sharp CRACK. A cry came from him as a sob.

That's when I let the moves come, as they had years ago. Leaping back to my feet I found my balance and slammed the heel of my boot hard into his solar plexus, the air left him with a *WHUFF*. Another boot strike to his face when he jerked forward, which smashed the bridge of his nose. I could feel it give under my sole. Blood and tissue flew from the blow like a sneeze. A painful sneeze at that.

The fight went out of him. Nadim lay on his back with his hands to his face. I stood like a wolf over his prey — willing him to move. Wanting to make a kill. The feeling shocked me. I'd awakened the warrior inside, the one I'd repressed all those years. So long ago I'd forgotten it was there.

As I reached out with my left hand to help him to his feet, his hand flopped to the cobbles and he snaked a knife from his boot with an ominous CLICK. I leapt back. *Shit.*

He was on his feet again, light and balanced, blood flowing redly down his face — watchful. He pulled his lips back in a snarl and a flick of his eyes told me he was coming. My body kicked into gear with a rush and I focused on the blade. Stepped back and looked for a weapon — anything, any weapon. My night vision is what saved me. I made out some garbage cans and what looked like a broom.

Two steps and I was on the broom and caught the sound of a single footfall as a sledgehammer slammed into the back of my neck. A massive blow that knocked me to the ground. I flashed on a monster over me. Nadim's mate!

Damn. I was still aware — though barely. I lashed out at him with my heel, at his leg — full force. I aimed below the knee, on the outside, at that point where the peroneal nerve crosses the fibula. 'Dead-man's leg,' it's called when the nerve is crushed. I missed the spot, but hurt him all the same, if his howl of pain was anything to go by.

Then I managed to get a foot to the ground, half rising to one knee, when he moved in for the kill, lashing out again with my remaining strength. This time his fibula broke with a *SNAP* like a fresh carrot. A demented scream came from him as he hit the ground.

Nadim was back on his feet and lunged at me with the knife. I managed to roll away with a frantic jerk and the blade clicked on stone. Then I'm back on my feet in a movement inspired by self preservation. He closed again and the blade ripped through my jacket and shirt and bit into a layer of skin across my ribs in an upward sweep. *Jesus.*

I stepped back fast, onto a garbage lid that flipped up and banged into the back of my knee. Reaching down for it with my left hand as he charged, I swung the lid up as a shield and he hit it with a CLANG. I snared his jacket with my free hand, and acting on instinct, rolled on my back, planted my feet in his belly and heaved him in an overhand throw. He hit the stones on his back with an scary wet sound.

As I staggered back to my feet Nadim too scrabbled upright again with that damn knife. *Find a weapon — any weapon*. The words of my *jujitsu* instructor came back from boyhood. I seized the broom and swung it hard against the wall; the head smashed off, leaving a long, jagged spear.

He stopped when he saw it, so I went for him, the moves coming from ingrained training long, long ago. I faked a quick overhand blow to his head like a club, and when he raised his arms, I dropped the point in a classic fencing move, plunging the splintered point with a lunge deep into his chest.

He went down with a scream. Struggled again to his knees, then my instincts took over: that phantom instructor yelling in my ears, *kick the bugger in the balls*. I landed a hard, driving punt to the testes. He dropped with a high-pitched yelp like a struck puppy.

Damn. This was serious. I ditched the bloodied spear and kicked his knife under the van. The big man writhing on the ground stared up at me. I remembered then why I had trapped Nadim. Somehow reason returned.

Somehow I expected people to come rushing because of the noise. Nothing. If anyone had heard, they'd ignored it. I ripped off Nadim's shirt, packed his sucking wound with it and strapped it tight with his belt.

Two teenagers in baggy pants with caps askew turned into the alley and went by on the other side of the van. I froze — watching. The bigger lad picked up my blood-tipped spear and held it poised. They were silent. One of the teenagers kicked a tin can that had fallen from the garbage; they raced for it as if they were on the soccer field. They went yelling and whooping down the alley away from us, dribbling down field.

When they were out of earshot I hefted Nadim into the van. He watched me with fear from where he lay, eyes beseeching — he said nothing. I checked inside his elbows, half-healed tracks and some ugly bruising. Pink bubbles came through gaps in his shirt on his chest.

Before I took off, I stepped over to the man on the ground, who was trying with his hands to stem the blood flowing from the wound in his leg. A wound where the fresh white bone of his fibula had broken the skin.

"Don't say a word." I growled in a gangster voice. "I know you. I know where you live. I'll come after you and I'll *kill* you, if you even look at a gendarme."

Back in the van, cranking the starter I was shaking so much I could barely hold the map. I planned a route to the nearest hospital and dropped the clutch. I had to stay with him, intimidate him so he wouldn't call the gendarmes. As soon as I saw a phone box I called an ambulance and gave directions in broken French, to the street where the man lay with his broken leg. I checked with them, as a friend would, as to which hospital they'd take him: to make sure we went to another.

After x-rays they strapped his chest and left Nadim and I in a room by ourselves. I'd passed myself off as his friend. Explaining that he'd been mugged while I'd panicked and ran away. I told them he was allergic to morphine, codeine or indeed to any opiates. It seemed quite plausible, they were busy and didn't object to my waiting.

Before this I had planned to hold him in the van while he went through withdrawal cold turkey — to get the truth out of him. Now I'd do it here in the hospital. Maybe if I frightened him enough, promised him the syringe, I could still win. I'd told him the syringe held morphine, in fact I'd filled it from the tap.

There was nothing else to do but to stay with him overnight. I'd found a sign, what I took to be a *Do not Disturb* sign in French, so hung it on the door. I phoned Giselle from a phone down the hall and told her I had Nadim, then hung up when she started interrogating. Nadim became more frightened as the night wore on, his eyes never leaving me. He couldn't sleep with the fear. I was silent, deliberately letting the silence build. First he filled the air with threats, then followed eventually by pleadings for a hit. I made no response.

Sweat broke out, above the plaster on his nose and he started a tirade of cursing in every language he knew. There seemed to be quite a few. It was impressive to a mono-linguist. His voice was rising to just short of a shriek, so I went to him and held my hand across his mouth. Held the syringe high now, showing it to him.

"Call out and I'll kill you, you stupid fuck."

He stopped struggling, his eyes clicked on the syringe.

"Tell me about *Alaric*. Tell me about the drugs. It was you held him with a twitch, while they stuffed the smack inside and stitched him. I need to know who *they* are." He tore against his restraints and his eyes swivelled around the room like gun barrels. "Then and only then will you get the morphine. Hold out and I'll kill you with a needle in the heart."

I ripped the pillow out from under his head when I said it. He stared at the pillow in my hands then up at me. I think a light went on in his brain. I had taped his mouth with a swatch of surgical tape when I'd strapped his wrists to the gurney. Now I tore the tape off his mouth. It must have hurt.

It took until four in the morning, until all his courage had drained, until withdrawal had driven him to an animal level, striking out with his legs and heaving against the restraints. I held the syringe up and squirted fluid through the needle.

"*Names,* you dopey fucker. I need names."

Ripping the plaster off his mouth again I stared him down. Nothing. In a rush of anger I reached for the tubes draining his chest and ripped them out — tissue, blood and plastic — the lot. He gasped horrified as liquid poured from his wound and pooled on the sheets. A fetid smell arose at once. I was aghast myself and about to call the nurse when he blurted into the silence:

"*Campagnie Fabriquante*."

"I know that already damnit. I want *their* names."

"Fortier," he said, licking his lips and eying the syringe. I tensed my thumb on the plunger and another drop oozed from the tip and ran down the needle. He followed the precious fluid with his eyes, appalled at the loss.

"Please."

I ignored the plea.

"Where can I find him?"

"I don't know where he lives. I swear it. He arranged everything."

"More names."

He was sweating now in rivulets, his skin a dirty white under his tan.

"A vet. I don't know — silver hair. I swear. Never saw him before."

"The vet, an English accent?"

"Yes, *Anglais*."

I raised the syringe and eased out another drop.

"NO PLEASE. Don't ask me names, it is best not to know."

"You'd better tell me what's going on?"

"They'll kill me..."

"So will I," I snarled, squirting more fluid in a shocking careless arc from the syringe, "And I'll do it right now, right here. Where'd the stuff come from?"

"Afghanistan," he said, "from Mahjadeen. Hard men they... they'll kill me. And they'll cut your balls off."

The door squeaked open and a freshly starched nurse came in with a tray of medications held with both hands. It broke the moment. I could see in his eyes he thought that he was saved.

"*Qui êtes-vous*?" She demanded in French taking in with one glance the torn out tubes and my syringe. She moved in, positioning herself between me and Nadim, protecting him while medications tilted in their paper cups with her agitation. This woman was going to be trouble. What little French I had, I recalled now.

"*Pardonnez moi, mon ami*," I said, looking past her at Nadim, "*s'il vous plaît, excusez moi*." I dropped the syringe on her tray and moved without haste to the door. I had what I wanted — I was gone.

Giselle wasn't there when I got back to the hotel. She'd left a note:

> *Duncan, do not know where you are? I'll be in the Eiffel restaurant at the top from noon. Spoke to Guy on the phone — everything is fine at home.*
>
> *Giselle.*

How like Giselle, efficient, without a trace of warmth or panic at my absence. She had not signed it with love. I wondered about that, and I wondered if she was safe. Thinking about it made me anxious. Would they track us here? I scribbled a reply in case I missed her, then ran *Campagine Fabriquante* to ground in the Yellow Pages. Then managed an appointment with a Monsieur Fortier that afternoon under cover of negotiating a deal on the colt.

Eventually I found the Eiffel, via the subway with the aid of the hotel map, and paid my ransom at the entrance. We creaked up the archaic lift in the guts of the tower. I looked out over the city that is Paris. Didn't like the height and when I got out on the balcony, I noticed the pronounced sway of this rickety Meccano set. I managed by force of will to free my hands from the rail, long enough to get a shot with my trusty Nikon.

Since I hadn't spotted Giselle I went to the restaurant and ordered *Le Hamburger* with *pommes frites*. I doubted their coffee, so ordered tea instead. The waiter took the order with a sneer he likely reserved for the British. A Scottish accent is so persistent in émigrés.

Giselle entered and I watched her for a moment before she saw me. A Viking striding among the tables, parting the stunted French like Moses crossing the Red Sea. For a moment she seemed a stranger. I saw her not as my wife but as a fascinating woman to whom I felt an immediate attraction, a feeling of what might have been. The moment evaporated and I steeled myself for conflict.

"Where did you get to Duncan?"

"I got to Nadim," I said, and waited until she sat down. "I got a name: Fortier, an executive with *Compagnie Fabriquante*."

The waiter came with my burger. Giselle wrinkled her nose and ordered a salad.

"I've an appointment with Fortier at three."

"How did you do it, Duncan? How did you get names from Nadim?"

"I rented a van ..." I confessed, and related the rest of the debacle.

"My God. What were you thinking? You could end up in jail."

"I'm desperate. We weren't getting anywhere being nice. It's done now — damnit."

I'd thought she'd be pleased.

"What if he goes to the police?"

"I doubt he'll do that. He's in a brutal withdrawal right now."

Fussing with my burger I waited for Giselle's order.

"Do you mind? It's getting cold."

Giselle frowned. I bit into the bun.

"What are you going to say at this meeting?" she said.

"Don't know, not exactly. I want to meet him. Want to see what I'm up against. I'll pass it on to McGowan, tell him the stuff's from Afghanistan."

"They'll come after us. You know they will. My God, what they threatened on the phone. Threatened Jennifer too." I squirmed in my seat. "God," she said, "what will they do to us."

"They'll do nothing," I said unconvinced. "We'll go as soon as we've seen Fortier. Go to Deauville to find a sire. They won't know where we are."

"*You* have to go, not me. I don't feel safe. Don't ever want to go there again." She shivered, pausing for a moment, watching my reaction like a bird of prey. "I am going home. I will be safe with Guy."

"You'll be safe with Guy, but not with me?"

"Oh Duncan, I'm not going down that road."

She started on the salad and we ate the meal in silence. My burger and chips tasted like chaff. We rode the elevator down together.

"You could take Jenny home. She'll want to get back to her horse."

"I will call her from the hotel," Giselle said, "right now I am going with you."

"To *Compagnie Fabriquante*?"

"I want to look Fortier in the eye — I want to face my fear."

We went on the subway and I tried to call McGowan from a phone box on the way. The phone rang forever and stopped unanswered. It should have been answered by the duty officer. It should have been a warning. I guessed he was out, figured I'd call later.

Compagnie Fabriquante occupied an entire floor of an elegant building on Rue Pont Neuf. There was nothing I could discern about the nature of their business. A striking white and blue abstract hung in the anteroom where we sat and waited on a fine-grained leather couch. A gilded secretary guarded the entrance to his office, her nails raking the white keys of the typewriter like spots of blood.

We were buzzed into Fortier's office with a mindless smile from the secretary. Giselle frowned. A handsome man in a dark three-piece suit rose to greet us from behind the desk. Giselle glared at him.

"You are interested in the *Danzig* colt, yes?"

"Precisely. May I ask why he is up for sale? "

"Certainly you may ask." Though he failed to continue so I filled the pause. "Is there something we should know about the horse?"

"No, not at all. He is sound. We... that is the company, has decided to divest itself of all its racing stock."

Yeah, right. I glanced around the room to see if I could catch a hint of their business. A fabulous Ken Stubbs of the great racehorse *Eclipse* and a photograph of *Arctic Tern* winning the *Prix Arc de Triumph* hung on the wall. He was a racing aficionado. As if divining my thoughts Fortier said:

"We make military *matériel* — we keep a low profile in this newly sensitive milieu."

"Oh. I'm interested in racing the horse in partnership. Would you come at two hundred for half?"

I'd said two hundred because when dealing with thoroughbred horses you talk in thousands. I'd taken a chance; after all he might've taken me up on the offer.

Fortier shook his head. "No partnership. It is a genuine sale. He is a good prospect. We will get our price."

"You know, we did buy a horse from you once before."

"Oh?"

"*Alaric*. Your company raced him at two and at three."

"Ah, yes *Alaric*. A good horse. How is he?"

"He's dead."

"Dead. How is that?" He leaned forward — interested.

"Someone killed him with an axe."

"An axe!" He looked puzzled, "Who would do such a thing?"

"A smuggler. The horse had heroin in its gut."

"Ah, narcotics. Have they been apprehended?"

"No," I said, "Interpol traced them to France."

Giselle shot me a warning glance. Her pendant flashed when she turned her head. Fortier caught it. I could see the cogs meshing in his brain as his eyes darted from one of us to the other."

"You are enjoying Paris, Missus McKinley?"

Giselle stared at him for a full minute before she spoke. What the hell she was doing? The silence stretched until I wondered if she would speak at all.

"You know they attacked me."

"Le contrebandier?"

"Yes," she said, "the psycho fuckin' smugglers you miserable bastard. YOU POOR FUCKIN' EXCUSE FOR A MAN!"

She sprang at him then, and in her ballistic rage she almost made it over the desk. I say *almost* for he stood up and warded her off with a stiff arm. Papers flew, like you'd see in a cartoon. I got hold of the waistband on her skirt and hauled her down. Fortier had seen her coming. He'd snatched a letter-opener and leaped out of his chair — *en garde*. His chair tipped and fell with a thud on the carpet.

Giselle strained, caught in my arms, shaking. She'd used up her anger. Hitched her skirt up and squirmed, wanting to get away. I went with her. In the elevator, she leaned over and whispered, "He did not know about *Alaric*."

"No, but he wanted to know if they'd been caught. No one has done that."

"Bastard," she spat and kicked at the panel under the controls. I put my arms around her. She went stiff and stepped back suddenly, panicked, as if I was a stranger.

"No Duncan. Not now."

"Alright, damnit." I turned away and watched the numbers flicking on the indicator above the door, as we passed each floor.

At our hotel I helped Giselle pack. She couldn't get it together in her overwhelming agitation. I wanted to hold her, wanted to kiss her mouth. I wanted to make love to her before she left, wanted to make her mine again. Giselle turned and shrugged me off when I wrapped her in my arms.

"Duncan don't... not now."

Jenny didn't want to go home when we spoke on the phone. She wanted to stay with Gail in England. I arranged to meet her after Deauville. I'd pick her up from my sister's on my way home. Giselle phoned home and spoke to Guy in her soft voice.

"How are the mares?" I said, when she put me on the line. "How is *Red*?"

"No, foals. Mares are fine. *Red's* belly has dropped. No strangers in the night though, so that's a plus."

"Good. I've got a lead here that I'm following."

"Go to the police, Duncan, if it's solid."

Solid indeed. I decided not to tell him what I'd done to Nadim.

"How is Giselle holding up? She sounded kinda strained."

Giselle was walking toward the bathroom so I waited for her to close the door before I answered.

"Not good. We went to see this fellow at *Compagnie Fabriquante*. Giselle went berserk. We didn't get much out of him. He was surprised to hear *Alaric* was dead. He wasn't surprised to hear about the drugs. The crash we had has unnerved Giselle. You'll be meeting her at the airport?"

"Of course. She will be all right here. How about you?"

"My main worry is paying my hotel bill."

"Can't help you there. When do you get back?"

"Have to go to Deauville to see some likely prospects. I'll meet Jenny Friday and be back in Toronto by Tuesday, I expect."

"Take care and don't go out at night if you can help it."

We went to Charles de Gaulle on the airport bus.

"Don't worry," Giselle said, "I will call Guy if I need to."

"Yes, I know. I'm still worried. I don't like us being apart."

"For God's sake Duncan, don't be childish. Above all, do not let Jenny out of your sight."

"Goodbye," I said to her back as she turned without touching and stepped through the barrier.

I watched Giselle as she put her bag on that dinky conveyer they have for x-ray, then she walked through the magnetometers. I waited a while in the foyer overlooking the takeoff runway and spotted her plane taxiing to the end in the queue. It gunned its engines down the tarmac, a roaring whoosh of acceleration, with the stink of kerosene, until it launched into space, then clawed itself up through the lower, dense layers of air. A two-storied building flying on sheer thrust, I watched it recede to the size of a child's toy, then I remained until it became a speck in the sky.

An overwhelming feeling of fatigue came over me.

A feeling that I was in enemy country,

alone in a hostile place.

CHAPTER 19

In the art of war... it is better to capture an entire army than to destroy it ...

Sun Tzü, *The Art of War*, 512 BC

The sun shone as we hurtled through Normandy, the throaty exhaust of the Beemer trailed behind us like background music. We had the top down and Simmone looked magnificent, her face alight with her hair streaming, a red banner in the wind. Simmone leant forward in her seat belt and hit the radio; the plaintive sounds of Joni Mitchell washed over us. She had let me drive her car and I was loving it. Apparently she was representing her husband at the sale of one of their horses at this auction. I'd persuaded her to let me drive down with her. I'm sure her husband didn't know, not that I gave a damn in the throes of sexual obsession. But the thought lingered: who the hell was this guy? And why was he so scary?

Driving a good car is like riding a fine horse — an infinite pleasure. I reined it back in difficult corners, flicking through the gears, balancing it with a burst of acceleration and let it have its head on the straight. I drove like I rode, way too fast.

We stopped for lunch at an outdoor café in Rouen. The Beemer stood in the parking lot, pawing the ground. I savoured a café latte while Simmone had a pot of herbal tea that smelled of liquorice. We had a ploughman's lunch with crispy bread, several cheeses and grapes, white and red. I could get used to this.

"Wonder what the poor people are doing today," I said to Simmone.

She looked at me not comprehending, so I tried again. "It's good to be alive, to be in France, to be with such a gorgeous woman."

"Ah," she said, "it is lovely — though it is also daring."

"Daring?"

"To seduce the wife of a powerful man is daring. Yes? Perhaps dangerous."

"Ah," again feeling queasy now she had brought it up.

"What does the lucky Mister Kelemann do?"

"Ah, luck has nothing to do with it. He is a businessman. That is all. It is best you do not know details."

What the hell had I gotten into? Was he some drug lord who'd cut my balls off if he caught me with his woman? Her natural pheromones and her inclination to reveal no more overcame my doubts and better judgement. I changed the subject instead of pursuing it.

"You know," I said, "there's an ancient monastery near Toulouse, where William the Conqueror lived with his sister. Well almost ... his first cousin, brought up together, so it was decidedly incestuous."

"Incestuous," she said, savouring the sound, searching in her head for its meaning. "Ah, naughty. You know there are always men like Guillaume who do what they want."

"Hmmm," I said, thinking of whoever killed my horse. Someone was doing precisely what he wanted. "Guess you're right. There are some who get away with it."

She looked at me as you would look at a naïve child. Her lips twitched into a wicked smile. She sipped her herbal tea.

We spent the night in Rouen at a Bed & Breakfast run by a middle-aged couple who were quite taken with Simmone. I couldn't afford a hotel. Prices were appalling and my Visa Card was already at full stretch. She'd arched an eyebrow and gave me that wicked look again when I asked the proprietor for one room and signed as Mr & Mrs McKinley.

Simmone was a woman who loved men, I discovered. Loved men in a way some women love chocolate. She loved the sound, smell and feel of a man. She said that she felt hollow inside. I filled her, returning her affection with passion. If I'd known then what I know now, then perhaps

I'd have not have stayed that night, never dared to touch her, never risked the devastating obsession she came to be. But of course, we cannot change the past.

No... I would have loved her, even if I'd known. A sexual obsession is akin to madness, it's something that cannot be resisted. The brain slips into automatic and testosterone takes over.

I'd already seen signs that my intuition was trying hard to warn me. I could no more have turned away from her that night, than a hungry lion could turn from an antelope with a limp. And I was hungry. She was the sort of woman for whom a man will risk everything. Those words of Zorba reverberated in my head: *Am I not a man. Are not all men stupid?* I realised much later the universal truth of them.

It was a short trip to Deauville. We left early despite our desire to linger in the afterglow. I met JB Kennet of the BTA, while Simmone went shopping down town. She didn't want us to be seen together. I had instructions to behave myself with her in public.

Kennet and I inspected two sires who'd passed the cull on performance and breeding. This was a sale of racehorses, brood mares and stallions. We discussed their merits and I had to listen hard to catch JB's broad Yorkshire accent. His enthusiasm helped me maintain my courage. A lot was riding on this decision — my entire financial future.

The first horse was a muscular grey, *Rougeford* by *Grey Sovereign* who'd won a Group-I as a two-year-old, over a metric mile in Longchamp. He'd broken down in his third year and looked out of condition after being laid off with injury. He snorted and reared at something fleeting and, being so strong, damned near lifted the groom off the ground at the end of the lead rope.

In his favour was the fact he had early speed. On the Dam's side, he had black type, which meant they were stakes winners. This entitled it to a bold font in the catalogue. He'd had only the one win from six starts, but that was enough to demonstrate his class. The agent and I chatted for a while about bloodlines as we waited for the British vet to appear. Kennet had arranged the vet especially for me; he didn't trust the frogs. We couldn't test breed *Rougeford* of course nor obtain semen. Though the vet, when he showed up, did palpate the testicles, inspect his sheath and evaluate his skeletal conformation. He pointed out a knee that wasn't quite straight and a resulting cannon alignment that required correction by the farrier.

"Perhaps that's why that tendon failed," the vet said.

"Though don't be put off too much," Kennet added. "There're horses like *Vaguely Noble* with crooked front legs and still ran like hell and sired champions."

A test for lameness was pointless. What I wanted to avoid was a bleeder, a genetic weakness common in thoroughbreds and certain to be passed on. I wanted the vet to scope the horse. We had permission to lunge and scope the horse and did so in one of the unused action rings. Certainly JB was making the right moves to make a sale.

The groom lunged the horse at a steady trot, until the dry sand formed a cloud of choking dust. He held *Rougeford* while the vet plugged in his scope with an extension cord and threaded the fibre optics through his left nostril and down into his lungs. The agent and I held our collective breaths for a result. This might be the horse I mortgage my life for. The vet ignored us until he'd finished sterilising, and rewinding, his gear.

"A good horse for stud use," he said, "no sign of bleeding."

Good enough. I'd have liked a full work up on Sloan's high-speed treadmill and the time for a test breeding, or at least a sperm motility count. An infertile sire would break me. So many ways to fail. Auctions were not like that, you couldn't check the stock. One of the reasons I disliked them.

"You pays your money and takes your chances," Kennet said. "And big money too — that's the name of the game."

We went together to inspect the last of the horses, a bay Kennet picked from the catalogue. The groom clipped on the lead and led him out. As soon as that horse saw daylight, he snapped to the end of the lead as if he hadn't been out before. He looked so fit you'd think he'd run forever. He bucked and played like a two-year old, although he was now four.

The horse was still in training, sound and entered for a Group-II at Deauville, Wednesday week. A rangy, light-boned horse by *Riverman*. A classic racehorse. All legs and neck, when he'd stand still long enough for you to see him properly. He looked fit with a Greyhound fineness to his belly, bulging gaskins and rippling muscles in his rump.

"I checked with the Jockey Club," Kennet said. "Neither horse is a bleeder."

Bleeders had to be reported by the trainer whenever it happened. When a blood vessel burst after a hard run, blood streamed from the nostrils and there'd be no mistake. Bleed twice and they're banned for life as unsafe to race. A horse can fall when it bleeds for they can't breath through the mouth, so they collapse when the lungs flood. Small bleeds do occur after training and a trainer might wipe blood away with a rag to hide it. They still breed 'em though, even if they are banned from racing.

The vet examined him. We had no permission for the scope, so all he could do was palpate the wedding tackle and evaluate his conformation. I checked his entry in the catalogue again, some black type in the Dam's line, though sparse. He'd won nothing as a two year old, once at three and he'd placed in a Group II as a four-year-old a month ago. Not a lot to show for two seasons of racing and three early races this spring. It was hardly rational, but I liked him.

"What's his name?"

"*Kikkuli*."

"That's the one I want."

"He's not won a Group race."

"If I'm going to take a great risk, then I'll take it on an outstanding athletic horse, a horse I really like." I saw him as a perfect match for *Intrepid Red*. "This one has the pedigree. He's a classic racehorse with arrow-straight legs. An outcross for all those *Northern Dancer* mares."

"Aye, he's that. He's also later to mature. You'd do better with the grey."

"Fair enough. Hear what you're saying. I still want this horse."

JB had seen customers do this before and he had the sense to realise when to shut up. Most horses are bought and sold on half-felt hunches. In the face of uncertainty, going with intuition is as good a way as any to make a decision — after you've narrowed the odds.

"I'll race him here, then ship him home for the breeding season."

"Can you afford that?" He had arranged my finances for this through Barclay's and knew my precarious position.

"No, of course I can't afford it. I'm doing it anyway."

We fixed a limit of a hundred grand, the same as the Barclay's line of credit. JB shook his head.

"You won't get him for that Duncan. The grey comes up first in the catalogue, will we go to the same amount on him?"

"No," I said, "I'll only bid on the bay. If we're outbid then I'll let you know."

Now I did know that I'd have to pay ten percent on the fall of the hammer. You could arrange to pay the balance within a reasonable time frame if credit was guaranteed by a reputable bank. You couldn't take the horse from Deauville until you'd done so.

"Will they give us ten days on the balance until he races?" He shook his head again. "I was hoping BTA will pull its weight."

"I'll see what I can do Mister McKinley. I'll try and get him for ye."

He'd seen the challenge and was ready to do battle. I was wracking my brains to think of what I could sell at home to raise the extra cash.

The sale started with a rambling preamble from the auctioneer, while I found a place to sit in the stands. I watched, saying nothing, sitting alone until Simmone arrived and spotted me. Her husband was selling a colt — way outside my price range. Her scent engulfed me when she sat down; it was all I could do to stop from wrapping my arms around her.

"Hullo Mister McKinley," she said when she'd reached me.

The auctioneer spoke a rapid French and through an electronic scoreboard the crowd kept track of the bidding. JB was bidding for a client and I marvelled that he made his moves before the bids were updated on the board.

It is an advantage to have an agent bid for you. So people won't know who they're bidding against. Many people get to know you in the racing game and they're not all friendly. Some are wealthy enough to run the price up on horses in the ring just to cause you grief. Auctions bring out the very worst in people.

The fast grey came and went for $180,000 in American dollars. I was staggered by the price. I wouldn't have got him anyway. I was playing a game out of my depth, where I didn't have enough chips. They'd crush me. When it came to the crunch, I'd have to settle for some runt because it was all I could afford.

"This one," I said to Simmone. "Lot two ninety eight."

She read through his rap sheet.

"Why do you want this horse? He's only won two races."

"Because he's the type I want, with stamina and speed, and he's ready to run. I'm taking a chance, but he's a great looking horse, he's one I'm willing to take a chance on."

"You should buy our colt," she said.

"Jeez, can't afford an *Arctic Tern*. Wish I could. Besides the bay might win the race, then I'd have him for nothing."

"Do you know the racing odds on him?" A good question and I should have known the answer. "No. His last win was three weeks ago."

"Hmmm," she said, "they may have thought it a fluke and entered him for this sale. The race entry will ensure a good price."

Her saying it annoyed me, for I'd thought of the same possibility when she'd asked about his odds. I had an awful feeling I'd find out he's a 100 to one long shot for the race.

Lot 298 charged into the ring full of bounce, tugging at the end of his lead. My agent joined the bidding early, to what translated to $95,000 in my head.

"Jeez," I said out loud.

But then I realised that by firing the opening shot he was trying to discourage opposition, those who were looking for a cheap horse. His bid was topped to $100,000. When he looked across at me, I nodded.

So I translated the figures on the board to our bid at $110,000. It flashed to $120,000. I shook my head. The beautiful bay was knocked down on the next bid at $130,000. It felt like a blow to the head. I stood up without a word and made my way through the crowd to Kennet.

"Thanks for the try," I said laying a hand on his brown-suited shoulder.

"No wait," he said, as I turned to go. I turned back and he leaned forward.

"The people who bought him. They're really after another colt at the end of the sale. They discussed it with me beforehand. They've risked the horse they want by losing their nerve, buying *Kikkuli* was their fallback."

"So?" I said, not thinking it through.

"So, they're American, they'll make a deal. Make them an offer. Offer to buy him, then they can get the horse they really want if they're pushed over their limit."

"Hmmm. That sounds good. Oh, no."

"What?"

"I can't offer the full price they paid for *Kikkuli*."

"Well damnit, offer them the hundred for a two-third share. To stand at your place."

"Done," I said, "you've got my authority. Go for it."

He'd not done this out of friendship. He stood to make a commission on this sale, of course. Something else occurred to me.

"Which horse are they on JB? And what's their limit?"

"Hey, Duncan you know I can't tell you that."

He thought for a moment, casually turning the pages of his catalogue to fold it back at number 364 and wrote $300k in the margin. The numbers burned a brand in my head as I headed back to my seat.

Simmone sold her husband's horse, it reached the reserve, so she wasn't consulted. Horse sales, they can be way up or way down — by thousands. Almost never what you expect. So many factors in the economy affect disposable income, the sort of money that's available for gambling on horses. It's not just the local economy, Japanese, Arabian, English and American buyers dominate the market, to the exclusion of almost everyone else. Old money, oil money, money for jam. Kennet resumed his seat near the pillar, caught my eye and flicked his catalogue. I took it to mean the deal was done.

The auctioneer called Lot 364, a sleek black by *Storm Bird*. As he pranced in the ring, the bidding rose swiftly to $280,000 then stalled. The bidding was against JB. The equivalent of "going, going...," droned the auctioneer. Kennet's stone face revealed nothing. He frowned. I took a breath and raised my hand. A spotter caught the sign and the board flashed $290,000 in equivalent francs. Simmone swung around.

"Duncan..." was all she said.

My hands shook and I couldn't look at her. Sweat formed on my brow and my face glowed beet red. I kept staring straight ahead. Heads turned to us as they spotted the bidder. I waited feeling trapped in my colossal stupidity, wondering what to do. Could I say it was a mistake if it's knocked down to me?

The board went to $300,000 as the auctioneer's voice rang out again. Another bidder went to $310,000 where it stopped. Kennet smiled. I let out my breath, then wiped the sweat from my hands down my trousered thighs.

"Got him," I said, to Simmone's astonished face.

"No, no you didn't ..." she started to say.

"No, not this one, the lovely bay — lot 298, *Kikkuli*. We made a deal; I've bought him."

"You did? What about this horse you just bid on?

"Forget it," I said, standing up and smiling. It felt sooo good. I spoke to the grinning JB Kennet who was going right now to sign the papers. He'd authorise my line of credit to be paid to my new partners. He'd drawn a blank agreement from his briefcase that covered our transaction and I signed with a flourish.

"Who are they?" I said.

"The Benjamin brothers from Ohio. They've agreed for you to stand him at stud. You're the majority owner."

"Fine," I said and left.

Later I collected Simmone from the stands by walking past her and waiting until she saw me. We went back to look at my new purchase by moonlight. I opened the top half of the door and looked in on him, an animal that I'd bet my livelihood on — maybe my life. In the shadow of the stable I took Simmone in my arms and kissed her hard on the mouth. She took my hand and led me inside her bra.

Being with Simmone was like being on a roller coaster, not knowing what to expect, being savaged by her soaring changes. She was up one moment, then down when frightened the next. Just this side of chaotic. What I neglected to foresee was that it would eventually prove disastrous.

We spent the night in Deauville at the Maison Medard-Bourgault on Rue de Gasp Oest, this time on Simmone's *Visa* with her BMW safely in the lock up garage. We repaired to the suite for a night of lovemaking that left me depleted and in a severe sleep deficit.

"When will I see you again?" I asked, when we'd dressed and were ready to leave.

"Duncan please stay. Stay with me. Stay forever."

"I can't Simmone. Not now."

"Not ever." she said.

"Don't say that. I do want to see you. We'll work something out."

"Will we?" She looked dejected.

I'm sure that I'm not the first lover to be struck by a fleeting glimpse of the enormous gap between his beloved's modest estimation of her worth, and the sublime and delicious reality of her being. A distance that is as far apart as reverence and contempt.

We parted in an embrace that left my mouth tasting of her, tasting her saltiness — the saliva of her mouth. Her nails dug into my arms, so deep they hurt. She clung as if in torment, as if she were afraid, as if I were her last chance of redemption.

"Don't leave me," she whispered, "don't ever leave me."

"Simmone."

"I am afraid," she said.

Then I broke from her by turning and picked up my bags.

When I looked back, she was gone. Though her scent clung, so that I caught a whiff of her in snatches through the day. And when I did, she came rushing back.

CHAPTER 20

It is a rule of war: If your forces are five to one — attack ...

Sun Tzü, *The Art of War*, 512 BC

The ferry arrived at Dover on crossing the channel. After the chop of open water I had several cups of railway tea, hoping the sugar would settle my gut, then boarded the train to London in a kind of tannin shock.

Gail and Jenny picked me up at the station. I didn't notice her car pull up at first, until Jennifer came over. She put her hands on my shoulders to stop me from being effusive in public and gave me a peck on the cheek. She looked so young with those long legs, like a two-year old filly.

"Hi Dad. How's Mum?"

"Fine. She went home Wednesday. Everything okay?"

"Oh yes, of course. Did you buy yourself a horse?"

"A classic racehorse by *Riverman*. He's running next week."

"Racing — where?"

"Deauville: *Prix Kergorlay*."

"You won't be there to see it?"

"No. I have to get back — Guy's been looking after the place. And you have to get back to school."

Gail smiled as I settled in the front seat. For the first time in a long while I felt guilty, for I now had secrets to keep.

"Hullo Duncan, good to see you again."

She wrenched the gears with a crunch and we joined the traffic at the exit. Her children were at school. I told them about the trip to France, more or less, dwelling on the car accident, the Eiffel and the auction. I had to be selective about what I told them. After that fiasco with Nadim, I felt like I had a criminal past.

We dined with Gail's family that night. A fine feeling to be there, to be in a family again, even if the kids did get into a slanging match about whose turn it was to do the dishes.

The children went to bed early and I had a cognac with Richard, my brother in law, discussing the things that interested him most — cars. With most men you can discuss women and aspects of their never-knowing mystery or sports. With most of my male friends we'd discuss horses or war stories — anecdotes of pain, surprise and conquest. With him it was cars. I guess there's not much else if you're an accountant. British cars were the topic to be precise, as he deemed those the only ones worth talking about. Don't think my Blazer got a mention. He drove a Rover 3500 and you can imagine how riveting that was! I tried to get Gail into the conversation but she busied herself with the kitchen — she'd heard it all before. Jenny was on the phone most of the night or messing with the kids in their rooms. Why is it Dads have such trouble talking with their daughters?

Alone in this cold bed Simmone came to me, naked and with great need, as she had the night before. I missed the scent of her, missed her buoyant breasts, missed the nipples she had thrust in my mouth, the thin undulating line of her taut belly, her musk scented sex, her mass of auburn hair and the perfect symmetry of her face. I missed her.

Sexual obsession is something I would not wish on anyone. Though what a wasted life if you never know it, never taste it. Such a waste to live through the years of your passing without knowing that heroic joy and to feel that vast abyss of mystery that can lie between a man and a woman. Lying there I felt an overwhelming desire for her. I longed for her. I lusted for her. I could feel her lips on mine, could taste the tang of her in my mouth. In an empty bed, I was devastated. Alone I touched myself until I came.

A fog of isolation engulfed me, along with sneaking tendrils of anxiety and yes — fear. A deep felt sense of loss and a gnawing depression that, by degrees, dampened my senses. I lost sight of her. No longer felt her.

Lost the vision of her face and sense of her body that moments before lay firm within my mind. I was alone.

After that I must have drifted into sleep for I awoke with a sweaty anxiety from a dream. A dream of our last conversation. It raised two questions:

Who the hell is her husband? And why is she so afraid of him?

Giselle would be back in our farmhouse by now with big, competent and gung-ho, Guy. He'd protect her with his life if need be. Would that be enough? Was there more than friendship? I tried not to think of it.

That despicable assault now occupied my mind. What could I say to Giselle to ease her pain? I felt impotent for not being there to protect her, not being there when she needed me. A shadow flitted into my dream and would not be stilled. It was the shadow of death. I played with it, enjoyed it and felt sullied by the thoughts. I spent a restless night and awoke sweating, bedsheets soaked, my mind ablaze with possibilities of vengeance.

I phoned Giselle as soon as I woke and told her Jenny was all right. She was cool on the line, told me the horses were fine, waiting for me to fill the silence. I did not.

"Dawn already has a foal — chestnut filly. Two are due to pop in the next day or so." All was well.

"Bought us a stallion at Deauville."

"Oh. How deep are we in over that?"

"The full ton, a hundred thousand."

A brief pause on the phone while she took that in.

"Duncan, what are you doing? We haven't got *Alaric's* insurance yet."

"Can't wait, the season will be over. Anyway, it's done now. I'll ship him to UK for quarantine after he races here Wednesday."

"He is racing?"

"Yes, a Group One over a lot of distance. He's a stayer, it suits him. If he does win we'll get him for free."

"What odds are they taking?"

By this time, I had looked up the betting in a French newspaper and learned the awful truth.

"Eighteen to one."

"A long shot, Duncan. Christ, he hasn't a prayer. Did you put money on him?"

"Every last franc I had — to win. They're underrating him."

"You are hopeless."

"I'm flying back today with Jenny. I'll be there around four. How's Guy?" Again she paused.

"Okay," she said, "I'll pick you up at the airport."

I reached McGowan by phone. He was on his way out when he took the call, or so he told me.

"Cricketer's Arms at noon," he said, "same pub. You know the one?"

"I'll be there."

I reached the pub at noon. My eyes again took some time to get used to the dim light. The long bar, dartboard on the wall, pool table and smell of beer and piss were still there, the louts had gone. The bartender stood behind the bar wiping glasses with a cloth.

Mungo was the only customer. He was sitting again in a wooden booth by the window and raised one hand off the table a few inches in greeting. His dark eyes tracked me to the booth and held me when I sat. He had two glasses of brew in front of him and pushed one across to me.

"Cheers," he said, taking a sip of Guinness, "made a few inquiries. Kaiser Pharmacea runs a tight ship. I don't to see how it could come from there."

"A tight ship. You mean they're beyond reproach?"

McGowan looked at me coldly. I realised then he didn't like being queried, didn't like giving out details.

"A public audit is done each year by law. The reagents going in are compared with those out, and the products packaged and sold. We have the auditors' report. They agree to the gram. There are no discrepancies. Trust me on this, the heroin was processed elsewhere."

"Damn, I was counting on it. Counting on this being the source."

McGowan went to the bar again and got another Guinness. I stayed with my ale. Mungo had a taste for the Irish brew. Though if he'd once lived in Ireland, his voice had no trace of it now.

He had a great capacity for reflection. He'd sometimes pause and reflect in mid sentence. He did so now as he stared into the depths of the darkly mysterious brew. When he made up his mind, he looked up.

"On the other hand, *Compagnie Fabriquante* is interesting. They paid Sloan a hefty consulting fee on *Alaric*. Paid after they sold him."

"Ah, Sloan took the drugs from *Alaric* when he was imported to England. Then replaced them before shipping the horse to Canada."

"Looks that way."

"What else have you on *Compagnie Fabriquante*?"

His face told me he didn't like being interrogated.

"They're in the business of manufacturing and procuring matériel. Guns for those who need them, from those who don't. Buyers are mostly third-world despots and their political sponsors."

"And?"

"They're legitimate, if that's what you mean. Though there are anomalies. Rumours of how ruthless they've been in securing contracts."

"Oh, like what?"

"Ah, bribery, corruption, blackmail, intimidation; the usual way of doing business in places where you can't drink the water."

"They're not third world for Chrissake — they're French."

"That's what makes them interesting."

"Hmmm," I said, "I understand their racing interest. The directors are into the finer things in life. Racing is up market, it's exciting and the company writes it off as advertising. It gives hard-to-get credibility for a company that's on the edge of respectability. They'll meet more people in business and government through racing than they will otherwise."

While I took a sip of ale I thought of that fine colt for sale at Montrose.

"They're cashing some of their bloodstock. Maybe they are hurting?"

"Not that we know of, though it's hard to tell. They have a habit of forming separate companies, even consortiums with their competitors, when competing for large tenders."

"One of their spin-offs could be in urgent need of cash?"

"Yes, it's worth following up." He swallowed a draught of his Guinness and wiped his mouth with the back of his hand. "Now, what else do you have for me?"

"I spoke with Nadim. Opium resin is coming from Afghanistan."

"Nadim told you that?"

"Not willingly. I tried to be civil, I tried being reasonable. The lad's excitable and well, we finished up fighting. Had to take him to hospital. I spoke to him there."

"Hospital? Christ what did you do to him?"

"He got hurt, a chest wound."

Truth is I was trying to be casual, playing it down. It seemed extreme when described aloud, even to me.

"A *chest* wound. You must have had a hell of a fight?"

"He had a knife."

Mungo looked at me as if reassessing my nature, as well he might. I had just finished reassessing it myself.

"Do you know what you're doing, old son?" he said.

"Only meant to scare him. Christ, there were two guys. I was lucky to get out of there alive. It got out of hand — alright."

"A chest wound is definitely out of hand. What happened? You shoot him?"

"No, hell no: he ran into a broom handle." McGowan said nothing. He waited for me to go on. "He had a knife and was coming at me." This was not coming out well. "Nadim told me the resin's coming in from Afghanistan, and to *Compagnie Fabriquante*."

"If you threatened him, what makes you think he told you the truth?"

A good point; one I hadn't considered. I considered it now.

"Because I offered him heroin. He's an addict and by that time desperate. He offered the company's name in exchange for a hit. I assume they have the capacity to process it. They do have chemical facilities?"

"They manufacture metals and plastics — they must have."

"Alert the gendarmes then and search the place?"

"No."

"No. Just like that — No. Why the hell not?"

"We want it all Duncan. We don't just want the peons. We don't want them aware of our interest and clearing out. We want everything, the whole shooting match: lock, stock and smoking barrel. We want it all before we show our hand."

"How British."

"Be that as it may. You get names from Nadim?"

"André Fortier, company director. We went to see him."

"We?"

"Giselle too. We talked about a racehorse they had for sale."

"And?"

"He wasn't surprised about the drugs smuggled in *Alaric*. He wanted to know if the desperadoes had been caught."

"And have they?"

"No. Not as far as I know. Aren't you kept informed at the Yard?"

"Yes, of course. Been out of touch with the office of late. Anything else."

"Fortier was surprised at *Alaric's* death. And at the attack on Giselle."

"Anything else on Nadim?"

"A nurse came in and scuttled the conversation."

"Nothing more you wish to add?" I looked blank so he added, "like you kicking the bugger in the nuts."

"Might have done."

"Hmmm. Ruptured his left testicle. Rather painful I hear, what."

"Oh."

"You surprise me lad."

"Surprised myself at being so harsh when needs be."

McGowan glanced at his watch then got up to leave. He put his hand out to stop me.

"Give me five."

"Huh? Okay sure."

This was spooky.

"One more thing. How did you *find* Nadim? How did you get him to talk?"

"He'd been sent to the country, to keep him out of trouble. They couldn't have known I'd go to Montrose. That was a fluke. When I did see him, we arranged to meet again in Paris. He came back there to score. You heard the rest. In the hospital he was hurting, you could see it in his face. I promised him a hit and he talked."

"Did you give him the hit?"

"Hell no. I was bluffing." It sounded weak even to me.

"Maybe he didn't tell you everything."

"Oh, why do you say that?"

"Because he died last night of an overdose. Check it out." He dropped the Herald Tribune on the table with a thump, turned and left, leaving me in the booth twiddling my glass. This time it was me who was frowning.

Jenny and I flew to Toronto the next day. Giselle came to meet us. We kissed and I held her close, soaking up her warmth. I asked about *Red* and if she'd foaled: she hadn't. We piled into the Blazer and drove out of town via Woodbine to catch *Jet Stream's* first race. *Jet Stream* blitzed the field in the back straight and was first to round the turn into the home stretch, only to die in the last few strides, pulling up third.

"She'll do better on the next run," I said.

Murray took us around to the barns to see how she'd pulled up. She'd been hosed down and had ceased blowing from the run, long before. She looked so fresh you'd have thought she had not raced at all. As usual I'd backed her to win. Murray, being Murray had a bet each way and won, so he was feeling expansive. We left him with the filly munching lucerne, while we took off for the farm. As we drove, I thought of Simmone and of her strange dream.

It came to her as she slept. From far, far away in the depths of a primal forest. Dark shapes flitting through the trees, surrounding her, engulfing her. A shape at her side, protecting her, then it twisted and split. Blood ran from a ragged line in his breast. She could see the men now, and they were men, as they ranged closer. She wanted to run, but could not. She wanted to scream. From out of the trees came a rain of arrows that struck men down. They lay where they were struck, their life's blood draining into the fine deep covering of forest litter. She woke, sat up in bed. Awoke from the sound of screaming; it did not stop until she realised, realised that the screaming was hers.

On the first day back, I fielded her phone call. Long distance blips broke the static followed by Simmone's erotic and breathless voice.

"Duncan, we are coming to Montreal for the summer. I must see you."

Everything is a crisis for Simmone. Nothing in her life is simple — ever.

"Of course. When will you be there?"

"April twenty until the end of July — two months. I must see you. I have to get away."

"Can I contact you?"

"No. Not here — I'll phone you. My husband will be away in May. I need you *now*."

"Okay. Right now is not a good time, just don't do anything precipitous."

We chatted in an intimate sexual way, as you do when stoking the fires of lust with salacious language. She hung up, leaving me feeling as lonely and emotionally entangled in her plight as ever.

CHAPTER 21. **GREINER**

So in war, the way is to avoid what is strong and to strike at what is weak.

Sun Tzü, *The Art of War*, 512 BC

Detective Greiner took the call at home while watching Hill Street Blues. The phone rang just as Furillo's wife was again giving him heaps. Furillo had found her sitting in his office having a nervous breakdown, when he'd come back from a wretch of a case. What a bitch — no man deserves a wife like that. He tried to keep track of the TV dialogue as he fielded the phone. Greiner's wife looked up and turned her face towards him — listening. He bent to kiss her. Noreen the dispatcher was on the line.

"Nat, we've got a Hit and Run in Kitchener. Can you make it pronto?"

"Yeah," his attention switched to the phone, then back. "Where's it at?"

"King and Highway Eight, close to four-oh-one. Donavon will meet'cha."

"Right. Got it."

He put down the phone and glanced at his wife. Her head was again bent over the books in her lap, her hair falling over her eyes. She was marking school papers. She looked up at him in that exasperated way some women reserve for their husband.

Nat said, "Sorry darl, gotta go: Hit and Run."

He was putting his arm through the holster rig before she answered.

"It's okay. I know it's your job. It's just that I miss you though, when you're away."

He crossed to her and kissed her forehead. Then grabbed his coat off the rack. The back door slammed as he went out.

A wet residue reflected the lights off the tarmac. Greiner could see a pack of vehicles in the flickering neon sign of *Alfa Laval*: hyenas gathered at the kill. He pulled off the highway and joined them. The local cops were putting up crime-scene tape. Their headlights lit the battered cladding of the factory, lighting a bag of clothes on the ground. He could see an arm and a leg poking out of it. An ambulance was waiting: waiting for Greiner's okay. The driver and his buddy were sitting in the cab smoking. They had the engine running, keeping the heater going.

Donavon lumbered up as he cut the engine. Nat smelt his beery breath.

"Hey Nat, got a genuine mystery for ya here," Donavon said, as he led the way to where the body lay. A faecal smell surrounded them as they drew near, along with the unmistakable odour of blood, a combination that in Nat's modest experience meant death.

The body lay with blood pooled under it, coagulated blood from the nose and gaping mouth. The head lay distorted, face squished to one side where the truck hit. Nat decided he'd been struck in the pelvis, about bumper height for a four track or light truck. The bag of clothes that had been somebody was wrapped in an Armani suit, Nat could tell from the label, dark grey with a long-waisted European cut. A suit that Nat himself could not afford.

"Have you moved him?"

"Nope. Thought you'd want to see it."

"Yup. Who called it in?"

"Young guy going to his girlfriend's down the road. He's over there. I've got notes. Be in tomorrow to make a statement."

"He didn't see a vehicle?" Greiner asked.

"Nope."

"Skid marks?"

"None at all. There's blood on the wall — paint too. Some rubber though where he backed up."

Greiner studied the streaks then glanced at the wall. Black marks again, at waist height. A crumpled gash along the aluminium cladding.

"Christ," Nat said, looking sharp at Donavon.

"Yeah, looks like it to me too. You want to call it in, or will I, eh?"

"Need a name."

He leant across the body, to the swell of a wallet in a trouser pocket, took out a driver's license and business card, emptied the rest into a baggie. Punched in his call sign in the patrol car and got an earful of static.

"We have a homicide here Noreen: Fortier, André F. He's the Chief Executive Officer of *Canadian Precision*, or he was. Married, no children. None on his medical least ways. Start a file will you, and search the name. Leave the file and printout on my desk? And call me straight away if there's anything in the database."

A Ford Capri pulled in and a man climbed out with camera and notebook in hand. Nat recognised the local reporter and went over. It might help if readers of the *Guelph Advocate* had seen a truck in the vicinity.

"No pictures," he said, as the reporter pointed his camera at the body. "The guy's a mess. I'll give you the story, and be sure to put my number in, as an appeal for help."

The uniforms waited for crime-scene forensics, while Donavon instructed them on a search within and a broader scan outside the taped area. Then he piled into Nat's car. They'd go check out the address on the license and break the news to his wife.

They drove in the dark towards Elora on Highway six, stopping every now and again to check letterboxes with a flashlight. Nat turned in the driveway of an Ontario farmhouse: austere, straight sided, double-storey, brick. Maples draped in ice formed an eerie canopy, reflecting their headlights as they drove to the house. The door remained shut as they skidded to a stop in the snow, got out and walked towards it.

Nat could see a figure at the window, backlit by the light inside. She didn't open the door when they knocked, so Nat held his badge to the window in a puddle of light where she could see it. He mouthed words through the double glazing when she drew the curtain.

Nat could see she was nervous. Of course, what does the presence of police ever mean, except bad news. What could he say to this woman that would ease her pain. Nothing. He took a deep breath and played it straight.

"Afraid we have bad news."

"What...?" she said. "What is it?"

She had a soft French accent — European. Not the harsh vowels of Quebec.

God, he hated this part of the job.

"Your husband, André. He's been in an accident." Nat paused for a second or two while she took this in, "I'm afraid he's dead."

"Oh," she said, sitting down. He saw the fright in her eyes, the flare of anger. She was good he thought. Controlled, didn't give much away.

"You have someone who'd come stay over: friends?"

"No," she said, "I have no friends."

Nat became acutely aware of how attractive this woman was.

"Nat, let's get Noreen over here," Donavon said. "Get a constable to fill in her job. Let's say it's for witness protection until we know what's going on."

Nat was relieved, he nodded assent as Donavon moved to the phone.

"What is going on?" she said, "what sort of accident?"

"André was hit by a truck: hit and run. I'm sure it was quick," Nat lied. "Did your husband have enemies?"

"Enemies who would *kill* him?"

"Well ... yes."

"No."

"You're sure about that?"

"He has *not* enemies," she said in English that was a touch off the mark.

He noticed the present tense, but didn't correct her.

They got nothing more from her in the next twenty minutes other than coffee and her name — Juliet. It suited her. Nat watched her taut figure and long legs in that swish dress as she brewed coffee at the kitchen bench; they both did. He studied the swell of her breasts, the way her hips flared from the waist and the rich mane of brown hair. There was something uneasy about her as she felt their gaze then she softened and revelled in it. She turned her full gaze upon them, tossed her hair with a flick and smiled. She had a conspicuous sexuality that only some women possess and fewer are comfortable with. She filled the room with her girly scent and full-bodied femininity. She made them aware of her, make them feel uncomfortable. Her presence made them feel so damned male.

They left when the uniformed Noreen arrived in her typical take-charge style. Nat planned to drive Donavon back to his car at the scene, before heading home for the night.

"Hell of a woman," Donavon said, when they clipped their seat belts and turned onto the highway with a change of gears and a throaty growl from the V8. Nat knew instantly which woman he meant.

"Yeah ..."

"Yeah, *what*? There's a *what* in there Nat. I can hear it."

"She wasn't all that broken up was she? Shocked, but not surprised."

"Ya ask me, he had enemies alright. *She's gorgeous*. Anyone sticking his missus is a distinct possibility."

"Maybe."

"Jesus Nat, you've got the hots for her yourself — that look on your face."

"What look?"

"Fascination, Nat. *Fascination*."

Next morning Nat called immigration and got the word on Fortier. Apparently he'd been in the country only a month.

"How'd he make such deep fuckin' enemies in that time?" he'd asked Donavon.

"*Has* to be someone fucking her."

"Either that or he's skimming money outta' the till."

Greiner called the company and spoke to the comptroller, telling him about Fortier's death. He arranged with them to interview staff. He was silent on the end of the phone for a while listening, then turned to Donavon.

"You know what they're making in that factory?"

"No, but I've got a feeling I'm going to find out."

"They make the C-seven. Canadian version of the M-16 — America's infantry rifle."

"Ah, big money there. *Government contracts*, that's enough right there to kill for."

"Companies are your end of it, Bill. Get on it, we need to find out what's going on."

Nat downed the last of his tepid Tim Horton's coffee and grimaced at the bitter grounds. He tossed the crumpled plastic cup in the bin, watched as it hit the lip, bounced to the floor and rebounded. Donavon caught the rebound in his paw and netted it in one easy motion. Nat grinned.

The team headed for the door.

The factory entrance was on King Street. A few doors from where they'd found the body outside Alfa Laval. A large building. It covered the entire block to the next road.

They met the manager, interviewed the office staff and spent most of the morning going through Fortier's files. No financial discrepancies that Donavon could discover, nothing out of the ordinary. The company supplied rifles and spare-parts each month to the Canadian Government on a fixed contract, a contract they'd won through open tender. Component parts were sold on a separate contract to a US supplier, Brown & Fleming, for all versions of the M-16. What conflict of interest could there be? If there was, it wasn't obvious.

There was nothing out of the ordinary in Fortier's diary. Nothing to connect with his death. Fortier's secretary in her shit-kicking Doc Martins brought them both coffee on a tray with croissants. A warm, eager-to-please woman just out of her teens. She had that healthy vibrance only the young and very fit have. Greiner went through Fortier's diary and the day's phone calls with her.

Fortier had stayed late that day, until well after six, according to the security tape. The secretary herself had left at five. Rodwell, down the hall, had left at about 5:30 pm. That left Fortier here alone for a half an hour. Late enough so that it was dark when he left.

Greiner got Bell Canada to fax a list of yesterday's calls to the office. That's when he hit pay dirt. A call of a minute-and-a-half came in at 4:27. The secretary swore she didn't answer it. They said nothing and stared at her. She looked at them over the tops of her glasses.

"Well, I might have been away from my desk for a few minutes. I did go to the toilet around then."

"So," Nat said slowly, thinking it through. "Fortier answered that call himself. Arranged to meet someone. Had to be someone he knew, someone who kept him here till after the others had left."

"See if you can find out who called," Nat said to Donavon handing him the list. "Be surprised if you do. That call was made from a pay phone."

Donavon nodded and took a sip of fresh coffee the secretary had brought and bit into a warm, buttered croissant.

"Stay and finish here," Nat said. "I'm going to the prosecutor's office, get a phone tap on Missus Fortier. I can argue reasonable cause. If the lovely Madam does have an illicit affair we'll soon find out."

Two days later Nat was waiting at the Wellington County Court at eight am when he got a phone call. He was due to testify on an arrest made weeks before. The caller was Kleinhardt, insurance investigator.

"Been trying to track you down."

The insurance guy wanted Nat to drive in to Woodbine, for Chrissakes! He'd been bugging Greiner about that dead horse of Duncan McKinley's.

"Got a situation here Nat, like McKinley's case," he'd said, "I want ya to see it."

Jeez, these insurance guys see conspiracy everywhere. They must be recruited on some sort of paranoia scale.

Nat testified and managed to get away soon after. Instead of being obliged to hang around, he'd got away on the basis of this other urgent investigation at Woodbine. Now as he drove down the 401, he realised that he was no better off. He still wasn't getting through the logjam of paper on his desk, or getting anything on that hit and run of Fortier.

The satanic stuff was driving him nuts. The local police, the RCMP and many in the FBI were convinced there was a rash of satanic crime, while Professor Stanford at Toronto University and Burkhardt at Quantico thought it was something different, something they called false memories. Fallacious recall aroused by church counsellors in needy girls.

If those so-called experts couldn't get their act together, how could he be expected to get his end sorted? Meanwhile the prosecutor was gung-ho to cut the guy off at the knees. The prosecution was going ahead for an arraignment on incest charges against the girls' father in the satanic case. The case was a mess and the insurance company weren't having any. They weren't about to pay out on a horse with this satanic nonsense.

"That's bullshit," Kleinhardt had said.

Hardly a logically compelling analysis, though intuitively it was hard to fault. The company were determined to pin it on insurance fraud. Could McKinley have killed his own horse? Nat shook his head as if answering himself. He couldn't see it. Though he reflected, stranger things have happened, he could think of quite a few right now.

Greiner flashed his badge at Woodbine and was directed to barn seven. He spotted Kleinhardt in a brown suit as he climbed out the car. A groom led two horses that shied with a clatter of hoofs and a curse. Kleinhardt led him to a stall and Greiner looked inside. A bay stood against the back wall, foreleg lifted with the shin swinging, showing a jagged edge of bone.

"What the hell happened here?"

The investigator unlatched the door and stepped in. The horse turned towards him with a loud snort and reared. The front leg flailing, held only by a strip of its hide. Blood flecked them in a fine spray. They retreated from the stall tripping in their haste.

"Jesus."

"Wanted you to see it," Kleinhardt said, "just like McKinley's huh?"

"Break's in the same leg, but McKinley's horse was gutted. What's the story here?"

"Groom found the horse this morning. We stand to pay out two hundred grand on this one. I'll get the vet to put it down now."

"You left it in pain until I saw it?"

"I want you to take action against McKinley. Want to see what he's capable of."

"Alright, get the vet, for Chrissake."

Kleinhardt spoke to the groom while Nat stood outside the stall feeling sick and trying to decide what to make of it. The shock of that horse alive in the stall was worse than the corpses he dealt with: at least they were dead. Kleinhardt joined him and they stood for a moment watching the occasional horse being led by. Nat felt himself shaking.

"You telling me this is *not* the first?" Greiner said.

"Five or six we know of in the past two years. Total payout more than three million Yankee dollars. Equine insurance is payable only on the death of a horse. A broken leg is one injury there's no cure for, ya have to put the horse down."

"So, if a horse gets hurt and lives, insurance won't pay?"

"That's about it."

"With a broken leg, the vet puts it down, and insurance pays."

"Yeah. There's a rumour of a guy doing this at ten grand a pop. They call him Doctor Death: Two cases in Ocala last year. One in Ohio, though that could be genuine. McKinley's horse, and now there's one at Woodbine. Another horse in Chantilly when McKinley was there two weeks ago."

"*Chantilly*?"

"*France*: Racecourse outta Paris."

"You *know* he was there?"

"We *saw* him. Caught his name on a flight manifest. Called our man. He spotted McKinley; saw him run off the road. Our man called the gendarmes."

"*McKinley* is Doctor Death? Is that what you're saying?"

"I *know* it."

"You have evidence?"

"Circumstantial." Kleinhardt was an ex cop. Greiner remembered him from his days when he was in uniform down at Mississauga. "The incidents have all occurred when McKinley's been in the vicinity."

Greiner raised his eyebrows at that. "Was he *here* yesterday?"

"Gatekeeper's records prove it."

"A lot of people were here yesterday," Greiner said, wondering how it fitted together. "McKinley's horse was gutted. Hardly the same MO."

"Don't be so sure. If ya did your own horse, wouldn't you do it different, so the cops wouldn't twig? Leg's the same, the rest's irrelevant."

"Jeez, that's devious. Okay get me the records, find out where he's been. I'll need a statement from you. My office tomorrow, first thing."

"I'll be there."

"And Kleinhardt," the insurance guy turned to him. "For God's sake, put that horse out of its misery."

The call came through on the radio as he drove back to Guelph. He was driving west on the 401, now humming with cars and laden trucks — the curse of Canadian highways. Noreen, now back on duty at dispatch, patched the call through.

"McLeod here, RCMP." A deep resonant voice boomed out of the radio filling the car with its presence. It sounded like the cartoon voice of Dudley DoRight that could have been the sound track of a movie. "We have an Interpol inquiry from France."

"A monsieur Fortier?" Nat asked.

"Ah, no. A Duncan McKinley. Believe you're handling the case."

"Well, yeah," said Greiner. He was still thinking of the stricken horse and his conversation at the track. What sort of man could do that? His mind switched gears as he registered the Mountie breathing into the microphone awaiting his reply. He didn't want to give too much away. "Looking at insurance fraud — not much evidence. What've the French got?"

"He's a suspect in the homicide of one Nadim Shabouh at Montrose. The gendarmes want to interview your Duncan McKinley."

CHAPTER 22

Appear at places which the enemy must hasten to defend; march swiftly to places where you are least expected.

Sun Tzü, *The Art of War*, 512 BC

McKinley a suspect in a homicide? Nat sat up. The French want to interview him. No doubt they'd like to clip his testicles to electrodes and crank up the voltage. Meanwhile, because of the niceties of jurisdiction they'd fax a list of questions for the OPP to ask. Then they'd send a man over to interrogate McKinley after they'd studied his answers. Perhaps they'd get a confession out of him — perhaps not. Nat had seen it work before. First have a man give a detailed account of himself, then armed with his statement and its contradictions, interrogate him nonstop until he finally gave it up.

Nat would be delighted to bring McKinley in for questioning. He'd arrange it as soon as he got back. Now the day looked brighter. He pressed on the gas until the speedo hit 140, he flicked past a cowered Ford, ahead of a long line of Japanese toys sticking religiously to the limit.

Noreen had returned to dispatch after the night with Juliet Fortier. She had that burnt out look about her, Nat noticed. She'd said the duty was uneventful — boring. He couldn't imagine that. He figured Noreen hadn't liked Juliet, hadn't gotten along with her. Mrs Fortier was the sort of woman who makes few female friends. Juliet had indeed made some calls last night. Noreen said she'd asked about them, but all she got out of Juliet was that she'd called her relatives.

Greiner finally got his wiretap; it took until the next day, mid-afternoon at that. Now a day late he saw the transcripts on his desk. Nat read through the transcripts — nothing: expressions of sympathy, a poignant call to France to tell his mother of her son's death. A call to Guelph for the funeral arrangements. God this was tedious. Another call to Guelph for a flight. A call from France, Fortier's brother by the look of it.

What? *A flight*, where? Ah, *Washington*. Date? Damn, left today. A hotel: which hotel? *Marriott*, two nights. The question is: *Who did she meet?*

Crossing the border to give chase wasn't on. You had to be in hot pursuit of a felon for that, even then you were supposed to hand it to NYPD right at the border. Not every case was a mad pursuit. Mostly you just followed, to see where they went, what they did, who they met.

If you got permission for funds, you could fly down and ask for co-operation from the locals on a surveillance detail, but that was unlikely. In this case, with their precipitous funding, he'd have to pass it to his superintendent. Hey, let them decide if they wanted to ask another favour of the Americans.

The superintendent wasn't in — as usual. Nat gathered the transcripts and headed for the phone. He'd have to call ahead, then drive to Burlington to petition the District Commissioner.

"Jesus, it's a wonder we catch anyone in this goddamned system," Nat muttered to the room at large. No one took any notice.

In the end he managed to make the call. He asked the local cops over the border for a list of the people Juliet Fortier had seen in Washington. It wasn't *surveillance*, since it was after the fact. More like backtracking, an assignment for some uniformed wannabe. He was on his way out the door when the phone rang. He turned back for it.

"Jacques Ganong, I should like to speak with Detective Greiner?"

Not a request, more like a command — French accent.

"Speaking."

"I am replacing André Fortier as CEO of Canadian Precision. I need to discuss your inquiries into this unfortunate business. Do you have a suspect?"

"Not as such, so far there's not much to...," Greiner said, then something snagged his attention, not *snagged* precisely, it was something he couldn't quite put his finger on it: "Yes, let's meet," he said, "tomorrow, your office, ten am."

Where the hell was Donavon?

Greiner had a bad feeling about his impending meeting with Sheila the Crown Prosecutor, a control freak who masqueraded as a lawyer. The feeling wasn't helped by Sheila keeping him waiting, while she pretended to read at her desk. Her short blonde hair showed dark roots as she hunched over the papers. Her suit sported shoulder pads and a pair of boots, that she could wear on any construction site, completed the effect. Lesbian chic he thought.

Nat coughed then coughed again, waited. She ignored him. He started whistling.

"You get anything out of McKinley's interview?" she said, exasperated.

"Didn't expect to *break* him exactly."

"Then what *did* you expect, Detective?" What a ball breaker, he thought. "I expected to find how he will answer charges when he's dragged into court. That *is* where you're going with this one isn't it?" Nat said.

"Of course that's where we're going. The father raped his little girls for Chrissake, at McKinley's farm."

Nat took a deep breath, this was not going well.

"Don't think you should take it to court. The case is a mess."

"Get a law degree, did you Nat?"

Jeez, Nat thought, she is a right bastard, born to the silk.

"I'll let you know if we get anything," he said.

He stood up to mark the end of it and turned to go. Sheila rocked back in her chair.

"*No* Nat, you'll do more than that — *you'll break* the father," she said.

"Christ, what with, an iron bar? There's nothing on him, except the girl's testimony. It's his word and their mother's against their own bizarre tale."

Sheila grinned at that, the grin of a cat that's eaten the last of the cream.

"Wrong again. It's *his* word against *all* of them. Wife has now confirmed her daughter's version of events."

"She did! When?"

"Yesterday, while you were out getting tips at the track. For Chrissake, what does it take to get your full attention?"

He wanted to leap the desk and throttle the woman.

"I resent that remark. I was out there on the street following leads."

"Resent it all you like. You missed the fact that Jennifer McKinley goes to the same school as those ditzy girls — McClure Ross." She looked at him as if he were an insect — a stick insect, one that's eaten its mate.

"A lot of kids do ..." he said, then realising she was baiting him, "that significant?"

"They knew each other, Detective. Jennifer McKinley told them she was a witch. She told them of a coven. She told them about Satanic rites at the McKinley place. It's in their statements."

"That's kids' stuff. You know kids say outrageous things."

"No, *I don't* Nat. What I want you to do is to stop being a psychologist. You're police. I want you to get a confession out of the father — one that'll stand up in court. And find out where the hell McKinley fits into this?"

She held up her left hand and started to check off on her fingers the points she'd made, as if he was a schoolboy.

"He's involved in *fraud*. The girls *recognised* him."

Two fingers went down.

"There's *evidence* of his horse's slaughter," another finger down. "Forensic evidence on the dog *fits* the girl's description of its death."

Her hand had now closed to a fist. Greiner resisted the impulse to give her a stab of his middle finger as he walked out the door.

"I've cleared it with the Superintendent — you're in charge of this case only as long as you're making headway. So for Chrissake, get on it."

He made it almost to the door before this last salvo with both barrels hit him in the back. What a bitch. He hoped she'd go down for the count at this hearing.

Donavon waved a sheet of paper when Greiner came in.

"Pay dirt, Nat. She saw a guy in Washington."

It caught him by surprise; he was still seething from Sheila's attack.

"You just got a fax from New York. Juliet Fortier saw a Colonel Hackett of the US Army — at the Pentagon."

"Whoa, that's a bit close to hubby's business."

"Yeah, especially with Hackett being in armament procurement. With an inside track on those tenders, eh."

"Ah, maybe she's representing the firm: Canadian Precision?"

They looked at each other for a second while they processed the thought.

"Nah," they said in unison.

"Anything else?" said Nat.

"He used his Amex card on food and wine at the Marriott, same date."

"Since this is Juliet Fortier we're talking about, that's near enough to conclusive evidence."

"Absolutely, Nat — absolutely."

Later I came back to the house after mucking out and working horses. I was tired, the colt I'd ridden had been fractious with the high wind spooking it. *Intrepid Red* was looking kind of anxious. Better sleep in the barn tonight, to look after the mare if she did foal. Not that I'd miss much by being out there. I was bitter at Giselle's continued criticisms and above all her rejection. God, I was missing Simmone.

By then I'd run out of energy, depleted of an inner resistance, caving in to the chill. Loneliness overwhelmed me when I walked indoors. A fluff-haired moggie on the bench ignored me. The refrigerator motor clicked off, the only sound an eerie shrieking of the wind. I shucked my felt-lined boots, made toast, ground coffee and sat the percolator on the stove. The phone rang. Greiner came down the line: "We need to talk with you. Girls' case is going to trial — preliminary hearing, be here by two."

Just what I needed.

"I'll be there if you really do need me," I said, cursing myself for being so amenable. Though I suppose if I didn't agree to it they would get a court order. He'd already disconnected. The percolator erupted like Mount Vesuvius, and when it subsided I poured myself a full-bodied mug of Java. We are such primal creatures — now with something in my belly and the scent of coffee, the world looked brighter.

It was past two when I made it to Guelph. Greiner left me to cool my heels in one of those bare interview rooms for a while. Grey metal furniture and no windows. Donavon, his sidekick, read me the conditions of interview. After the preliminaries, they sat for a moment staring at me as if rehearsing in their heads what to say. Perhaps they were waiting for me to speak. At last Greiner started.

"The girls described the woods at your farm, *before* we took them there."

"I don't know what they described — whatever it was, it wasn't my place. Damnit, they're nuts." The detectives sat waiting, letting the silence build. "Can't you see that?" I added. "Jeez, get a lie detector or something."

"We did — they passed."

"Oh... well. If they were there, and it's a big *if*, it must have been at night. Otherwise how could I have missed it."

"How would you *know*, if you were asleep?"

"My dog. He'd have raised hell."

"Your dog starred in the saga. They claim he was drugged then stabbed."

"Claim? We know he *was*, you told me."

"Yes, but the *girls* didn't know." I shook my head.

"Can you answer verbally for the tape?"

"Well... I don't know. Horses make a noise if something frightens them."

"Would you hear them if you were asleep?"

"Usually do, if something disturbs them."

"But you wouldn't *know*, if it *didn't* arouse you."

"Guess not."

"Did you ever meet the girls, *before* we took them to your place?"

"I'd never seen them before, not until you brought them to my barn."

Another beat of silence.

"Thing is, *they recognised you*. They were *afraid* of you."

"Who knows what they think? Ditzy flakes the both of them. They need a psychiatrist."

"Got 'em that too. He'll testify that they're telling the truth."

"The *truth* — Jeez. Truth is that no one knows what happened."

They went on for hours. First one, then the other. Greiner and Donavon took turns bashing me about the head with the same blunt instrument. It got us nowhere.

"I've had enough. I'm leaving. Have you forgotten? I'm the victim here."

"If you leave right now, we'll be forced to arrest you."

"*Arrest me* — on what charge?

"Fraud — insurance fraud."

"What, back to that again. You think I killed my own horse?"

"You tell me."

"NO GODDAMNIT."

"Ah," Greiner said, "Touched a nerve did we?"

"I'm pissed off that you don't believe the bleeding obvious."

"Obvious to you."

"Obvious to anyone with half a brain. I breed horses. I stay up all night to help mares foal. I don't hurt them, I don't kill them. I have an affinity with horses."

"It has happened before. Six times this year, to be precise."

"What's happened? You said you'd never heard of a case like this?"

"Hadn't until I checked it out. Horses in Florida, Ohio, Woodbine and one at your farm. All of them broke a foreleg."

"Well, what do you make of it then — drugs?"

"No. Not drugs, plain ol' insurance fraud."

"What about my gutted horse?"

"Ah, in that *you're* unique."

"What are you talking about?"

"In other cases the horses weren't gutted, only their forelegs were broken."

"So they're not the same."

"Not *exactly* the same," Nat said, "thing is, gate records place you at these places *and* Chantilly."

"It's *Chaun-tilly* not *Chant-tilly* —*Jesus!* I was looking to buy a stallion, a replacement, that's no secret."

"What about Florida, Ohio and Woodbine?"

"You kidding, Florida is the heart of southern racing. I go to Hialeah for the sales every year. Go to Woodbine too, to watch 'em run."

"What about Ohio, Doctor Death? Were you at Beulah Park on April ten?"

"Where exactly?

"Columbus for Chrissake! Expect me to believe you don't know where it's at.

"I *was* there, in Columbus, but not Beulah Park. I interviewed for an equine appointment at the vet school. I didn't go near the races."

"Sure of yourself *boy-oh*," Donavon said.

"No, I'm terrified. Terrified that I'll miss the season. Terrified I'll default on my debts, go bankrupt and lose my farm. Hey, what's with this Doctor Death shit anyway?"

"You don't know?"

"No. And I should get a lawyer right now. You're setting me up."

"Oh yes, you'd better call your lawyer alright."

"Well, fact is I don't actually have a lawyer."

"Better find one and quick. One that's fluent in French."

"What — why French?"

"Because the frogs have some questions for you concerning the murder of one Nadim Shabouh, late of Montrose — France."

"*Murder!* Fuck you," I said. Articulate as ever, and at once frightened by this turn of events. "I'm leaving right now, do what you will." I stood up, despite them both leaning over me. Greiner and Donavon exchanged glances as I pushed past.

Donavon said something I didn't catch.

Greiner nodded and smiled as I left.

Later when alone, I called Simmone. She was in Toronto with Raoul on business. There I asked the Four Seasons to page Mrs Atarmon — a sign we'd arranged. Simmone came to the phone breathless, as if she'd been running. Her girly voice was filled with a sexual promise.

"I must see you. PLEASE. Raoul is threatening me."

"I can't see you here. Toronto's too risky — my wife and Raoul are both here. We agreed to talk only on the phone."

"If you love me you will come. You promised to be there for me?"

"Where could we meet and not be seen?"

She must have thought about it beforehand for she said immediately.

"The Royal York. Raoul is away on business."

"Royal York?" I said, wanting to give myself time to think. "What is it, a hotel?"

"An old one on Front Street by the train station. In the lounge, shall we say an hour?"

God I felt young again, a hormone charged adolescent. I padded up the stairs on the thick carpet and saw her, a moment before she spotted me. She was a beautiful stranger, a star in a movie, wearing one of those filmy dresses like a model. Her marvellous face and those breathtaking breasts had an effect that every man knows. Lust kicked into high gear — I was hers.

When we kissed, she clung to me as if I was her only hope. Her saviour. Through the dizzy scent and hormonal fog of sex, I figured we'd better go in and eat, than be so conspicuous by drooling over each other out here.

"Where are they going?"

Leaning close I whispered in her ear when we'd corralled a table and sat over cappuccino and some sticky buns.

"Spatsizi Plateau. I traced a map from Raoul's briefcase."

She passed me a crudely pencilled map on onionskin paper. Simmone reached over and pointed with a blood-red nail.

"A tributary of the Stikine then by boat from Gladys Lake. They'll be outside the park. There is a lot of grizzlies — wolves too."

It's much easier to travel by boat than pushing through a tangle of thickets and trees at the edge of a lake. We'll need a canoe.

"Okay," I said. "When will they get to the lake?"

"They leave at the end of the week. They are staying in Banff for three days to ski if the weather holds. They'll fly in by floatplane. I'm going with him to Banff. Staying there until they get back."

Now I had a spy in the enemy's camp.

"How many?"

"Three. Raoul's niece is staying in Banff with me. There'll be a guide at the lake to meet them."

She placed a photo on the table, a big man with a rifle in his hand standing beside a guy with a wolf over his shoulder. "You'll need this," she said, "to identify him. Raoul is in the safari suit."

"So, that's your husband. Who is the guide?"

"I don't know," she said, thinking about it. "No wait, Raoul was talking about an outfitter ... maybe Wankel, something like that — definitely German."

She pronounced it with a vee the German way and I made a mental note to find out who Herr Wankel was.

"How are they armed?"

"I do not know, it's not the sort of thing I can ask."

"Okay," I said, "I have to go."

"Duncan," she said, looking up at me with those big green eyes. "Raoul is a wolf — a rabid wolf. You must kill him."

Jeez that sounded ugly. I glanced round to see if anyone heard; no one paid any attention, except for the waiter who came over when he saw me.

"Check please."

My stomach churned at the ordeal to come.

We took a room and made love with an electrifying intensity, until we were satiated, well after noon. We had double servings of coitus, fellatio, cunnilingus, coffee, liquor and chocolates. Somewhere in there I discovered she never wore knickers and a nightdress was something alien to her. While exploring her body I found a maniacal criss-cross of scars on her inner thigh.

"How did you get these?" I said, running my fingers across the scars.

Her answer was to reach for me, hold me in both hands and pull me into her; we fucked until all was forgotten. We dragged ourselves out of bed and parted at the back entrance to the hotel. Simmone kissed me with such passion, it went through me like I'd been struck with a knife.

"Please Duncan. Come back. Don't ever leave me."

Now I was so bonded to this woman I was barely able to walk away. I turned every few strides to see her standing, like someone's lost daughter, a waif dwarfed by the hotel's massive doors.

CHAPTER 23. DUNCAN

It is a military axiom not to advance uphill against an enemy, nor to oppose him when he comes downhill.

Sun Tzü, *The Art of War*, 512 BC

Light filtered through the curtains and lit the ceiling in indistinct patterns. All night I had lain awake, sick with apprehension. The race at Deauville was being run while I feigned sleep. I'd had a long night of anxious insomnia. Getting up, lying down, raiding the fridge, watching *I love Lucy* in the dark, eating a frozen dinner. I drifted in and out of consciousness, going over all the options — on edge.

Would *Kikkuli* win? I needed a sign, an omen of things to come. Was I backing another loser with my life savings — my life's *borrowings* in this case? Could I save my family. Would I win back Giselle.

Giselle lay on her side of the bed, encased in her night gown and underwear, deeply asleep — oblivious. Her blonde hair spilled prettily over the pillow and she was breathing through her mouth with a kind of purr. I watched while she slept. Her vulnerability made me think of a child, a beautiful child at that. No sound from Jenny's room.

In the office I dialled the operator, a terse exchange, a few clicks, then the trainer's voice, high and slurred.

"Oui monsieur."

"Hullo," I said, "McKinley: how did my horse go — *Kikkuli*?"

"Excellent indeed."

"Excellent?"

"*Oui*, he finished second to *Royal Tern* — hundred-thousand francs."

"That's great." A quick calculation returned thirty thousand dollars. "Terrific. Did you back him?"

"*Oui, le totalisateur*: 'e got fives in the end."

As usual I had bet only to win.

"Ah, then someone made a killing. Did he pull up well?"

"A killing, *monsieur*? Pull up?"

"Was he injured in the race?"

"*Oui*, 'e overreached, a fetlock nicked. 'E be okay."

Never mind. Now he had the credentials to stand at stud.

"*Merci*. I'll get BTA to ship the horse to Newmarket."

Waking Giselle first with a kiss, I told her the good news. She felt delicious so I kissed her again. Sometimes when I am half-asleep, I imagine that I can taste her on my lips. She smiled in a sexy way and climbed out of bed.

"How much will be left ... of all those francs?"

She was forever the realist, a sobering check on my optimism.

"Covers costs. We'll get him here for the season. We've turned a corner Giselle — we'll make it."

She stood with a half-smile on her lips and locked the door, silhouetted in the glow through the curtains. Her nightgown dropped with a rustle of silk. The razor scar pulsed tense and angry. I tried hard not to let my mind go there — bastards. She slid her panties past the curve of her hips and they dropped to the floor. She stood at the foot of the bed, then leant forward. Her breasts swung free — perfect.

While I stroked her stunning body, she lay beside me quivering. I slid my hand between her legs massaging her labia until she took up the rhythm. Then I knelt to stroke her plump derriere. She said something muffled into the pillow then raised her gorgeous rump towards me in an unmistakable gesture.

From behind I gripped her neck hard and entered her slow at first, then harder, pushing, driving myself inside her, finding the rhythm, until she collapsed on the bed. Coming then in a shuddering pulse, I bit her neck then held her in my teeth like a stallion on a mare. Giselle shivered, turned without a word and opened herself to me like a flower, letting me lick her rapidly to climax. Her head thrashing now, her body arched to hold herself hard against me to keep the feeling going.

It was the last time we made love.

Jenny flounced down the stairs barely awake. She sat across from where I was pouring coffee. Giselle was taking a shower. She took ages in the morning, getting ready to greet the day.

"Thanks Dad," Jennifer said, pushing an empty mug across for me to fill it.

"Didn't realise you drank coffee."

"As long as there's cream and sugar."

"Connoisseurs drink coffee black," I said.

Jenny pulled her usual face at my archaic advice and sipped, after adding cream, watching me over the rim. I didn't take aficionados seriously either. So I added a dollop of cream and a teaspoon of dark brown sugar. Okay so I liked to vary my addiction.

"Jenny," I said, "the police told me the Anderson girls go to your school."

She nodded and looked bored. A practised look.

"So?"

"So, why didn't you *tell* me?" I went on, not wanting her to embarrass herself, by lying. "*They* said they were friends of yours."

Jenny opened her mouth in surprise.

"They're *not* friends! They're dweebs."

"You do know them."

"Sort of. They're not in the same class. They're wannabes, they hang around our group. We rip them."

"*Rip* them?"

"Tell them stupid things. They're such try-hards they'll believe anything — they're lezzos," she adds to deter me.

"Jenny for Chrissake. What did you tell them?"

"Nothing."

"*Nothing?* Come on: Did you tell them about our farm?"

"I might have laid it on a bit thick, about our champion stallion and mares."

"What about *witchcraft*?"

"Where'd you get that?"

"From the *Police*. It's in the girls' statements. It ties them to us. Damnit, they didn't kill *Alaric*, but they've complicated the hell out of it."

"*That's-for-sure*," she said, in a single word.

She stuffed toast and marmalade into her mouth, avoided my eyes and gathered up her books. "Gotta go, Dad — see ya," she said, as she leapt for the door. She'd spotted the bus moving slowly up the road along the fence line.

When Giselle came home I was seasoning my not-so-famous Irish stew. She was immaculate in her navy business suit, set off by the jade clip and turquoise pendant. I wanted to take her in my arms. I wanted to kiss her. I wanted to drench myself in her scent. She brushed past to remove her coat, scrunching her nose at the stew. The last time I'd cooked it, it had a decidedly lumpy texture. Its remains had gone solid in the fridge overnight.

"Hey, got it right this time," I said.

"I was in Toronto today," she said.

Giselle handed me posters she'd picked up, rolled and shrink-wrapped. We leaned over them as I unrolled the first poster on the kitchen table. The visual image of the mares galloping in the snow leapt at us. We saw raw power in the mare's movement, as I had seen it that day as *Red* took off in the lead. I scanned the image for flaws, nothing except a fleck in the foreground. We were awe-struck. It was the sort of shot you get just once a lifetime, and only if you're lucky.

"*God*, that is beautiful," Giselle breathed, "Such a magnificently *wild* feeling."

Giselle reached for the other roll and we unravelled it together across the table, fighting its desire to curl. A dark photograph, blurred with no movement, not surprising since I had clicked off the shot while scanning the woods with the telephoto lens. I heard a quick intake of breath from Giselle as she stared at a patch of indistinct pixels among the cedars.

"That's Guy," she said.

"Think so?" I leant over, peering closely, "maybe — hard to tell if it's a person at all."

"And if it is: what the hell's he *doing* there?"

"Ask him."

"Ask him? You mean just come right out and ask him?"

"Sure, if he was there, he was there for a reason."

"Okay fine, I'll go see him about it."

Greiner arrived Friday. A pale morning. I had been working a colt on the track. The colt was still blowing hard even after walking back from the field. My unwelcome visitor had company, as well as his Irish sidekick.

A man spilled out of the back of the car, as I kicked my feet out of the stirrups and slid off the horse. The colt snorted and pulled to the buckle. The man was tall, square shouldered and moved with the co-ordination of a skilled boxer, not too tall, or too thin — maybe a fencer. He wore an impeccable suit and still managed to look uncomfortable in his tanned and battered mask of a face. He looked like a dangerous man. I could see no good coming of his presence.

"Bonjour. Inspecteur Dessaix, Direction de la Surveillance du Territore," he disclosed when introduced.

The best defence is attack I recalled from Sun Tzü. The great debacle of French Sécurité flared in my mind — I ripped a lunge with a verbal riposte.

"Ah, the brave Rainbow Warriors?" I said.

"*Non monsieur*," he said, on the back foot and parrying. "*Non*, that disaster was *Sécurité*. It was *we* who investigated those duplicitous ... Ah, how you say — *bastards*."

He stopped then, smiled and looked at me closely. It appeared Inspecteur Dessaix realised I'd reached him in a vulnerable spot. He saw now, that I too might be dangerous. Not quite the rustic Canuck he had taken me for.

"Chrissakes McKinley, he's *French* police. Got a problem with that?" Donavon snapped.

"He's *not* police," I said. I didn't know who or what he was: I only knew he wasn't an ordinary plod.

"We'd like a word with you?" Greiner asked.

The way he said it, it didn't sound like a question.

"Sure, come in the barn, while I finish with the colt."

A grunt was all I got from Greiner. Still I led the way with the flighty colt in tow. Inspecteur Dessaix made it plain in his excellent, though accented English, that he knew I'd been to Chantilly and Montrose.

"And when did you last see Nadim Shabouh?" he asked.

"Nadim. At Montrose on the twenty-ninth."

"And what did you want of him?"

"I went there to see some promising stallions. Nadim worked there. He'd been *Alaric's* groom when he raced in France — way before I bought him."

"Ah, yes I see."

"The horse was savage — hard to manage. I asked Nadim how he'd handled the horse." As I said this, I ran my hand down the colt's neck, undid the girth and stripped the saddle off. Then picked up a brush to wipe away the sweat. The colt stamped a hoof and skittered away from the stiff bristles.

"Ah, *sauvage*. I see, is that *all* you discussed?"

"Yes, that's all."

"Ah, then explain to me *s'il vous plait*. Please, I do not comprehend — perhaps it is my *Anglais*."

"What is there to comprehend?"

"The horse was already *dead* monsieur, when you saw Nadim."

He had me there. I too had misjudged him.

"Alright," I said with a shrug and leaned against the nervous horse, "I asked him if he knew anything about *Alaric's* death. It is curious, you must admit."

"We at DST admit nothing *monsieur*. Did Nadim know about the horse's death?"

"No."

"And you believed him?"

"I guess so. It was a shot in the dark."

"Ah, a *shot into the dark* — I see. That is good, very good. I like that. How you say — a metaphor. Quite. It is apt for our line of work, *non*?"

"*Yours* perhaps, not mine — I'm a horseman."

"Yes, *now* you are a horseman, but it is not always so *monsieur*. Did you see Nadim later, at the hospital perhaps?"

"No, of course not, we, my wife and I, were in hospital ourselves, we were both injured in the crashed van."

The colt skittered around again and swung his rump towards them, ears flat against his neck, he was cranky and ready to fire. His steel shoes clattered on the concrete floor, scattering the spectators. All except for

Inspecteur Dessaix, he stood his ground unafraid and uttered something soothing to the colt in French.

"*NO*," I scolded the colt, then turned my back on them and brushed away the sweat with short quick strokes while the colt arched his back in a reflexive response.

"No matter, I have a witness description that fits you precisely," he said to my back.

I turned again to face him.

"Look, my wife and I were injured. You must know we had an accident, that some bastard ran us off the road."

"*Merci monsieur*, we know this. That impressive gash on your forehead?"

"Yes."

Then he said, "Did you know Nadim was murdered?"

"Your friend, Detective Greiner, told me," I answered.

Dessaix sniffed at the reference to Greiner as his friend. The French have an eloquent body language.

"Did you supply him drugs?"

"Drugs? *NO*, absolutely not."

"Nadim died of an overdose," said the Inspector, "but then perhaps you knew this already."

"*No* I didn't. And I'm sorry for Nadim, I really am. Does his death have anything to do with *Alaric*?"

"Not for me to say *monsieur*."

Greiner shrugged when I looked at him.

Donavon answered in a voice that none of us believed: "No — no connection whatever."

It was then I realised what the inspector had done so cleverly. Why he was being so amiable. By interviewing me here, he had come inside *my* territory, to where I'd feel least threatened. Least likely to demand a lawyer, least likely to complicate my answers with evasions, legalistic or otherwise. The French couldn't care less if what I said to them held up in court or not — they just wanted the truth. They wanted to know who *I* was; they wanted to know about *me*. Was I delusional? Was I a full-blown predator — a dangerous psychopath? Was I the sort of man who would have overdosed Nadim? No doubt they already had a psychological profile of their killer. When he saw that I was not antisocial or discernibly odd, when he saw me take care of the misbehaving colt calmly, and deal with their visit in a reasonable way, then he was satisfied. He could look me in the eye and see that I had *empathy*. And he knew that psychopaths do not. This short-circuited at least one of the unanswered questions in his investigation. He now knew what sort of man I was. Inspecteur Dessaix and his team could move on.

That's what made Greiner and his sidekick so unhappy. The OPP wanted to nail me as Doctor Death. Where on earth had that come from? They'd brought the Inspector to interrogate me, to put me under pressure, and for Greiner it had all turned to mush.

As they got in their car to leave, Dessaix turned towards me for a moment, his hand still on the door.

"You saw André Fortier I believe, in Paris."

"Yes, my wife and I saw him together."

"And may I ask your business with *monsieur* Fortier?"

"We made an offer on a horse his company had for sale," the Inspector nodded waiting, expecting more, "he refused our offer," I added.

"Fortuitous," he said, "your *Kikkuli*, the horse you did buy, had a splendid race."

"Yes he did," I said and smiled.

"He was examined *thoroughly* by *our* vet on export. We had to know, you see."

"Indeed."

What was he saying? That the horse was checked and cleared of drugs? Did he also mean I had been cleared of suspicion? The car door slammed before I could clarify his statement. I let it go. Greiner scowled as he looked across at Donavon, when he backed up the car to turn in the driveway. He reefed the wheel around with the heel of his hand to affect a wheel-spinning turn of the Chevrolet in the rough gravel.

Why is it that women so complicate one's life? I'd gone back inside after putting the horses out and repairing a panel of fencing. The coffee had just percolated with an explosive whoosh when the phone rang. A frantic call from Simmone that caught me unprepared. The vulnerability in her voice taped into a primal response with a rush.

"Duncan *help me*. I have to get away."

"Get away. You mean *from him* — now?"

"Yes, *now*. Where can I go?"

"Can't you find a hotel and just do it?"

She answered in a small voice like a child.

"It is not so simple. I am afraid. You don't know what he's like. You don't know what he's capable ... "

"What do you want *me* to do?"

"Come here. Take me away ..."

"Simmone, I can't leave at a moment's notice — what would I say to Giselle. Get a flight out to Toronto. I could book a place and meet you."

"I have no *real* money," she said, "only credit cards, only what he gives me. He'll find me if I use them." She hesitated and I listened to her pregnant silence on the wire. "I could wait until he goes away."

"Look, draw cash on the card. Book a flight to France via New York, on your Amex," I said. "It'll look like you've gone home. You can bail out in New York and catch a Greyhound bus back to Niagara. We could meet there."

"Yes," her voice was still off key.

My mind snagged on something she'd said.

"What do you mean *wait* until he goes away? He's going hunting *now*?"

"Yes, he's leaving on Thursday."

"Can't you wait until he's gone, then make your move?"

"No. I'm afraid of him. Deathly afraid."

"Afraid of what?"

"I 'ad another premonition."

"And ..."

"It's preposterous, a nightmare, I don't know what it means. *These men ... men in the forest lying dead on the ground, their eyes picked out by crows*."

"Good God Simmone: Your husband, what are you afraid he will do?"

"I am afraid he will *kill* me," she said, her voice by now a whisper.

In the background I heard a sound, like a door closing; the phone clicked off with an ominous burrrrr.

Much later I reached the duty officer, who for once, patched me through to McGowan.

"Mungo, the DST were just here: an Inspecteur Dessaix."

"Where are you calling from?"

"Home. I'm at home — why?"

"*Direction de la Surveillance du Territore* is like the French FBI. More secret service actually, it's complicated, *Sécurité* is a mess. It means you're targeted. As of now assume your phone is tapped."

"Should I call from a phone box?" A short pause.

"One that's well away from your house. But not now, I'm on my way out."

"I'm worried for Missus Kelemann. She's terrified her husband will kill her."

"Well now, that's a distinct possibility. He is a right bastard. And there is something you should know about *your* Missus Kelemann."

My Missus Kelemann. I wasn't going to like what was coming next.

"And what's that?"

"Her husband Raoul is the head of *Campagine Fabriquante*."

"You sure?" I said, "I just spoke to her."

"Course I'm sure, that's our man: *Raoul the Wolf*. Oh, and while you're at it, while you're so well placed to find out what he's up to. *Do let us know*."

"Yes, but... Ah."

"Oh, Duncan do be careful, old son. This particular villain *kills* people."

He clicked off.

My hands shook as I hung up the phone.

CHAPTER 24. GREINER

And so in war, do not pursue an enemy who pretends to flee...

Sun Tzü, *The Art of War*, 512 BC

"**Detective Greiner**," he said to the receptionist, "... to see Monsieur Ganong."

Jacques got up fast and bounded around the desk with his hand extended in greeting, "*Bonjour.*"

The office had been redecorated since Nat was here raiding files. It now had an old world feel to it, a fine table replacing the desk, and a glass-fronted bookcase was lined with colour-coded binders. An artistic image of an attractive brunette and two lovely children beamed out of a frame on the desk.

Greiner looked around, the previous metal filing cabinets had gone from the room. The feature window looked out on the car park and Jacques was momentarily distracted by something outside, he frowned while looking past the detective through the glass. Greiner turned and was rewarded only with a Buick backing out fast from between parked cars. A secretary brought them coffee. A younger woman, a woman Nat didn't recognise.

"Is André's secretary around?" he asked.

Ganong hesitated for a split second.

"No. No sorry she isn't. She left soon after his death."

"Oh," Nat said, "that's a pity. She was very helpful, when we looked at the files."

"Yes, I imagine she was. And certainly I will do all I can to help, if you have any further questions."

Ganong asked how the investigation was going, but police are trained not to give anything away. They fenced back and forth for a bit. Greiner got the distinct impression he was losing traction in this conversation. The man's English was as good as his own and he was very interested in where the investigation was heading.

"Understand you're manufacturing the M16 rifle. Is that right?" Nat asked.

"We've retooled the design and are now fabricating a modified version of it here under license for the Canadian Government. We have separate contracts in the US for their M16 parts."

"A modified version. Why *modified*?"

"Short answer is that it's colder here. Alaska, Yukon and North West Territories are close to the Soviet Union and China, and in the event of war the North-West might be the front line. We need *matériel* in these conditions to remain operational down to minus fifty Celsius."

"That's damned cold."

"Yes, there's that and our experience in Vietnam identified a need for a wider tolerance of moving parts."

"Ah, so the rifle won't jam in the cold?"

"Precisely."

"Why wasn't that done from the start?"

"More explosive gases escape from the breech with wider tolerances, so accuracy, range and stopping power's way down — it's a trade off."

"So it's not as good a weapon."

"Actually it's better. It won't jam as easily in the mud and snow for one thing. Besides, accuracy and power are vastly overrated when it comes to military use."

"Thought you'd want *maximum* killing power."

"No, not at all. Kill a man outright and you've taken one soldier out. Wound him, and you take two or three out of the field. You're rid of those who remove him from the line, and those who transport and care for him."

"Well, don't ya have to hit what you're aiming at?"

"Most infantry rounds are *not* aimed, so accuracy is hardly an issue —

except for snipers. But then they use a separate rifle in the larger NATO calibre."

"You obviously know this business Mister Ganong."

"I'm a military engineer. I saw service in Algeria. Saw far too much in Algeria. Left at the first opportunity and got into management."

"That was in France right?"

"Yes, Campagine Fabriquante."

"Now I'm confused — *Campagine Fabriquante*?"

"The parent company. We supply management and engineering to this independent Canadian company."

"I see. You were appointed to this position by the parent company. Might I ask who made the decision exactly?"

"The *Chief* of course, Raoul Kelemann."

"And when was that?"

"Ah… let me see, yes April fourteen, the day André Fortier died."

"Just like that. He didn't wait to confirm André's death. He didn't wait to consider alternatives before making an important decision?"

"You don't *know* Kelemann. He is a man of action. A man of quick decisions. He was my Colonel when I served in Algiers."

"Ah, so he is military too? Was André Fortier?"

"Was André what?"

"Was he also military?"

"Not at all. He was an accountant, an MBA. Fortier was never in the army. I didn't know him well."

"Okay, then tell me about Colonel Kelemann."

"A good soldier."

This was followed by a silence that extended to an awkward interval.

"Is that it?"

"Did you know he was captured in Algiers."

"No," Greiner said. "I don't know him at all. Fill me in?"

"He was tortured in Algeria. All prisoners were. He was crammed into a cell with so many, that in the forty-degree heat many died. They gouged and clawed each other for space to lie down, for scraps of food and water.

He knew what his fate would be; it was to be hung upside down like a side of beef, from a hook through his Achilles tendons, while blood drained from the jugular — blood for direct transfusion of injured rebels.

Prisoners were kept there until needed; they were blood on the hoof."

Greiner was feeling queasy. This was a nasty tale. Ganong continued:

"Without refrigeration Algerians improvised in the sickening heat of Africa. Raoul knew what they would do. He'd seen it himself, they were like animals. That's why he was so stoic and took such appalling risks to escape."

"How?"

"Our unit overran a rebel field hospital once in battle — appalling conditions. That is how he knew."

"No, I mean how did he escape?"

"His jeep had hit a mine. Crushed his legs when it overturned. Raoul couldn't stand or walk by the time the rebels reached him. In the cells, when they took him prisoner, they raped him. Held him down between them, beat him to the edge of death itself. They knew he could not walk, could not defend himself, could not hold them off.

Raoul was young then and he was very strong. What they didn't know was that he was also unbelievably tough. A very determined man. He worked his body in the cell, and nurtured it, slowly regaining strength. He bullied the others with his strong arms to get the water he needed, and the lion's share of food. He got tidbits for the guards.

His legs gradually healed in response to this harsh regime and his better nutrition. He never let on to them for a second, that he was getting better. *Never*. Not when they beat him, not when they sodomised him — never. They kept him for weeks, held him there in the cells for weeks while other prisoners were being sent to the battlefield to be drained for their life's blood. They were sent to their doom while Raoul remained. He was their favourite. Their nightly plaything.

Raoul gradually built up his strength and awaited his chance. When he at last seized it, he had the advantage of surprise. He broke the neck of his jailer with his bare hands, bit through the windpipe of another with his teeth. Not all that difficult for a young and well trained commando. He finished off the rest of the guard squad with a grenade and the jailer's machine pistol. Then absconded in a jeep."

"Wow," Greiner said. Somehow he felt sullied from the telling. "That's a hell of a tale. Hell of a *savauge* tale." Ganong shrugged extravagantly, as only the French can without looking ridiculous. "One thing, though perhaps I should *not* tell you: I do so only because I am deeply disturbed by what 'as happened to André. You see I need this crime to be resolved. I personally need to know what happened."

"Oh, and what is it you need to tell me?"

"When Raoul escaped in Algeria he took no one with him. He left his fellow prisoners, even men from his own regiment. He left them there in the desert to die of thirst, or be killed by rebels. He is a smart and cunning man. He knew he could get away on his own, he knew the weak will and sickness of others would be a burden. You see there is some part of him, some indefinably human aspect of his mind, a connection most of us have with others, that is completely missing."

"Jesus!" Nat left, puzzled by Ganong's motive for telling the story. It sounded like a warning. He wondered about Ganong's rapid appointment, about what part he might have played in Raoul's story. It seems odd for the company to have had a replacement ready at such short notice, a man so obviously suited to the post. And if Ganong was so suitable, why wasn't he appointed in the first place? It made more sense than sending Fortier over here, an ineffectual accountant for Chrissake, with no military or engineering background. Still he couldn't figure why Ganong denied any knowledge of Hackett — so obviously a key player in the parts contract?

The only thing that Detective Greiner could figure was why Ganong was so worried about Raoul's ruthlessness. Did he suspect Raoul of Fortier's murder, knowing full well that Raoul Kelemann was capable of ordering it, or indeed of accomplishing it personally. Perhaps now that Ganong was in Fortier's job, it troubled him; he might be next in the firing line, that is if anything else were to go wrong.

In the event, it was Donavon who flew to Washington to interview Colonel Hackett, the man Juliet Fortier had gone to meet. Nat wasn't available, for he'd been informed, with another imperious call from Sheila, that he was needed at the hearing of the Anderson girls' father.

In the courthouse Nat listened as the prosecutor, Sheila Biannaca, addressed the jury with her opening comments.

"The evidence you are about to hear will be disturbing. So disturbing, the court expects you to put aside your emotional reaction and be objective."

The jury squirmed in their seats as she said it, not wanting to hear what was coming. Again the girls recounted their bizarre story at the not-so-subtle prompting of Sheila, the older girl on the stand first. At one point she buried her pretty face in her hands. He golden hair spilled over her. The jury squirmed some more.

"I'm sorry," she said. Tears poured down her cheeks when she lifted her head. "This is really hard. I'm so embarrassed."

She paused for a moment to collect herself, took a deep breath.

"I screamed when they raped me. I implored them to stop, no one did."

Listening to her narrate events, Nat was again willing to believe it was true despite being as sure as you ever can be, that they were lying. A doctor was called who said she examined the girls. She had determined the oldest was sexually experienced and indeed pregnant.

However, the defence pointed out, this was not done immediately after the event, for the girls did not come forward with their accusations until later. Nat took the stand and attested to the circumstances surrounding the girl's statement. He was questioned about the physical evidence: slaughtered horse, Doberman, trampled snow in the clearing at McKinley's farm. The clincher came with the girl's mother who confirmed their story. Stating under oath she was present at the ritual.

She plunged ahead with her version of events. "... a disgusting rite ... my husband forced us to attend ... forced us at knife point on pain of death." Her voice had a staccato quality, the narrative was hesitant as if she was ashamed. She glanced at the defendant — her husband, then turned from the man's shocked countenance.

What a flake, Greiner thought — *what a fuckin' dangerous flake*.

The defence called Professor Stanford. The professor walked to the stand as if he were on show, and was duly sworn in. The defence set the stage.

"Professor, please tell us in your own words, about your understanding of memory. Does the mind record events as they actually happened?"

"No, we all have our own perspective, and our minds rewrite reality. Memories reflect our last retrieval of them rather than a precise account of the original event."

He looked at the judge then, to make sure she was listening.

"We do this to remain consistent with the image we have of ourselves.

Memories are a blend of fact and fiction. We all have our own reality. Distortion derives from our selective perceptions of experience. Within the context of our self-image, memory is more a narrative a writer might evolve, through a bit of judicious editing."

"You have evidence for this?"

"I cite a recent study at the University of Utah by Kirkwell and Everingham. There are other experiments: At Utah they deduced people are not objective observers like we think we are."

The judge yawned and tried to stifle it.

"Our minds reconstruct memories. And if our perceptions of ourselves are faulty, we continue in a damaged way within this self image."

"Could you explain that in plain English?" asked the defence counsel.

"Hmmm, let's see. Okay, how can we know if we are good parents? Good sons? Good lovers? Do we know if we are doing the right things to achieve our personal needs and life goals? No, of course we don't."

The jury looked as if they did.

"Such questions take on a mercurial aspect when we realise how fallible perceptions are. Memories can even be altered by subsequent events. Emotions can implant false memories of things that never happened. People may believe they did happen. That is why memory is unreliable."

The defence interrupted, "You're saying children have difficulty telling reality from their fantasies."

"Precisely, memory implanting is a technique some religions, cults and therapists routinely use. Most don't do it maliciously; some don't know they're doing it at all — nor how destructive it can be. It's known as Recovered Memory Therapy."

"Do you agree that this is an acceptable treatment?" asked the defence counsel.

"No, definitely not. Though it is popular among Christian counsellors."

"Ah Professor, and you are medically trained are you not?"

"Yes, I am."

"Yes, you are. Of course you are. So, how is it Professor, that you can tell us about a treatment you personally have not *ever* used?"

"This therapy may be used with the best intentions, but because of a religious bias, children's sexual fantasies are seen as evil, and are cast as the work of the devil. A harmless fantasy to a child can too easily become a false memory, with satanic ritual abuse, in the hands of the therapist."

"Objection, this calls for conjecture," from the defence counsel.

"Sustained. Please rephrase your testimony."

"Hmmm, let me put it this way, false memories of incest are common to this therapy. Such an accusation can ruin people's lives; it can disrupt a family beyond repair, even if it is not true."

"Ah, but *do* children lie about such things, Professor?" The defence asked.

"Children don't usually lie about sexual or physical abuse. But if coerced they might disclose fantasies of things that never happened. Adults too can be induced to do so within a cult or religion."

"Objection: calls for speculation."

"Sustained."

"Let me put that another way: people can be cajoled into voicing false memories by having correct answers accepted and praised by the interrogator. Wrong answers are ridiculed. After countless humiliations, they will realise they're getting it wrong. Subconsciously, they'll create a story that will satisfy the therapist. It's like the Patty Hearst syndrome."

The judge interrupted, "Are you saying these girls have come to believe their own fantasies?"

"I have examined both the girls. In my opinion they are not wilfully lying, but truth is subjective, it can only be what we know, we construct our own reality. Their version of events has evolved and gotten richer with each telling. It has been shaped by the therapist's suggestions and during their police interrogation."

The defence demolished Nat's testimony. They threw the lack of forensics at the jury, then the mother's ditzy story. And that damned deer trampling the site in the woods after the event. It was enough for the jury to discount him.

Donavon took the bus into Washington from the airport. After picking up his counterpart, one very black and portly detective with a wicked sense of humour, they grabbed a taxi and tooled over to the Colonel's place in Georgetown. They wanted to catch Hackett at home, relaxed after he'd had dinner and a drink or two with wifey.

Indeed they did. The Colonel was in an expansive mood when they arrived and invited them in straight away. Apparently they'd had a break-in next door that same evening, so he was expecting the police. They got that straightened out first, when seated in the den and had popped a Bud apiece.

"This here's Detective Donavon from the Ontario Provincial Police."

"Ontario? What the hell has that ..."

"He's investigating a homicide in Kitchener. Guy by the name of André Fortier. Foreigner — a French national."

"Yes, I see. That's too bad. It's true, I did know André."

He was quiet for a moment squirmed and picked at a thread on the chair.

"A homicide you say. How did it happen?"

Hackett's eyes slid from one to the other. He didn't know what was coming next, but he was a good poker player.

"Hit and run. Supposed to look like an accident. An amateur job, but they nailed him alright. We have good forensics, so I have no doubt we'll close this one. Now to come to the point Colonel, I must ask you: Where were you between six and seven pm on the night of April fourteenth?"

"Ah, that's when ... ?"

"A week ago Tuesday."

"Believe I was working late that evening, usual thing on Tuesdays, don't get home till eight."

That shouldn't be too hard to check. Donavon made a note to do so. He noticed the way Hackett had handled the question. He knew it was coming. Donavon then went through the Colonel's dealings with *Campagine Fabriquer*. It took them a half-hour or so. Having studied accountancy at night school for three years, he was able to see that the business sounded kosher. Still he had this nagging feeling the Colonel was hiding something.

"And Missus Fortier, did you know her too."

"Yes of course— Juliet. Is she ..."

"She's okay — fine. I believe she came here to see you."

He opened his eyes at that one and started to bluster.

"No, of course not. Where did you get that...?"

"We have her here on the seventeenth, staying at the Marriott with you Colonel." He got up and closed the door so they could not be heard.

"Now see here."

The American detective broke in, "Don't give us that shit. We have your Amex receipts. Pretty wife of yours will hear about it if you don't shape up."

Hackett sat down and slumped forward. He spoke in a whisper.

"Okay, I saw Juliet. She came here because she was upset by André's death, that's understandable. It's true, I had an affair. My God, what red-blooded man wouldn't. Have you met her, detective?"

"Oh, yes."

"Then you know what I mean. I didn't know what to do — my wife and all. Juliet kept saying *they killed him* — that they would *kill her*. So I asked who *they* were and that's when she went ballistic. She was terrified they'd come after her."

"Why?" Donavon broke in. "Why would they come after her?"

"She said it was best I didn't know. We had a disagreement after that. She spent a few days at the hotel — then she left."

"So, what was this fight about, eh?"

"I said disagreement."

"Fight, disagreement — whatever."

"She wanted to go back to France. She wanted me to drop everything and go there with her. She wanted me to be her saviour."

"You didn't obviously."

"Hell no, I couldn't — not without fucking my own life up completely. When I told her that, we had a hell of a row about it."

"So, she went to France alone. To where exactly?"

"Marseilles, that's where she's from. I assume it's where she went. Haven't heard from her again. Hey, what could I do? I've got a wife, kids, the military, a career — Jesus."

Donavon and the local detective looked at each other. The American raised his eyebrows, Donavon shrugged. She had checked out of the Marriott on the twentieth. There was no record of an airline flight that day with Juliet on it, nor at any time after that.

They'd come up blank.

CHAPTER 25. RAOUL

... we must guard against ambush and spys who may lie covert, seeking our weaknesses and overhearing instructions.

Sun Tzü, *The Art of War*, 512 BC

Simmone's husband knew the *investigateur* was coming and waited for him. Raoul sat in the book-lined den at his home in Montreal, going over his options, toying with them — letting decisions slip and slide through his mind. He was trying them on, wrestling with them one at a time, then flinging them off again. Decisions that took him first in one direction then another. He frowned as he thought these things through.

Raoul let the bell ring three times before indicating through the intercom for Bernard to get the door. He gave his bodyguard time to check the man. After a short interval, he rasped again into the intercom:

"Send him in."

Bernard opened the door and brought a man into the study. A man in his thirties, with one of those sharp-featured faces that is permanently tanned. He had lank black hair and day-old stubble, fashionable among *Québécois*. He carried a leather satchel, not a briefcase. A satchel like those used in First World War films, ones that *aides de camp* and spies carried. Indeed he looked like a spy — without the trench coat. He wore black trousers and a white shirt, now open at the neck. Raoul dismissed Bernard with a wave while the man settled in the chair offered. They spoke French, Raoul in the colourful French of Marseilles that contrasted with the harsh colonial patois of the spy.

"You followed them?"

"*Oui monsieur*, indeed yes. I am sorry, forgive me ... Ah, what you suspected is true."

"You have photographs?"

"*Oui monsieur*."

The man reached into his satchel and produced a manila envelope, tossed it on the coffee table between them. Large prints in black and white spilled out on the lacquered surface. Raoul looked hard at him for a second, then reached for them.

His face changed colour as he rifled through the pack. His hands shook. He could feel a rage boiling as he scanned the blurred image of his naked wife cavorting with a man — *that* man. They'd been caught by the glare of headlights through an open window — like deer in the path of an oncoming car. A dozen shots of them walking together, holding hands, kissing, then fucking *flagrante delecto* in what looked like a stable. Simmone looked absolutely radiant. His eyes narrowed when he looked hard at the leading man.

"How did you get these?"

His voice was barely contained, it came out more like a snarl.

"Infrared film with telephoto lenses. Technology makes it simple, non."

"They did not see you?"

"*Non*, of course not — I am *professional*."

"I want negatives too."

"*Oui monsieur*, of course, they are there also."

Raoul reached into the envelope again and withdrew a smaller packet of negatives. He studied them by holding them up, one by one to the lamp, making sure they were all there. The lamp cast a pool of yellow light in the dim room, illuminating both men's faces as he scanned them. The men were silent. The only sound was the rasp of their breathing and a slap, slap as photos were discarded one by one from Raoul's hand to the tabletop.

"Develop these yourself?"

"*Oui*, my own darkroom. No one see them."

"No one — you're sure."

"*Absolument*."

"You made copies?"

"*Non monsieur*, I may be weak but I am not stupid. Surveillance is my business, confidential business, with men *très sérieux*."

Raoul withdrew an envelope from the drawer of a low table. Dropped it on the desk.

"As agreed," he said.

The man snaked his hand out for it. At the last moment Raoul snatched his wrist and held him in his grip. He bore down on the man hard, to show strength, twisting the spy's wrist back to cause excruciating pain. The man caught his breath and stifled a scream. Raoul looked him in the eye, like a lizard without blinking, making him take the pain.

"Forget this ya hear. Forget it ever happened."

"*Oui monsieur*."

"If you mention it to anyone —anyone at all— you're a dead man."

The spy looked down, drew a painful breath, and let his wrist go slack in submission.

"Understood," he said, his voice high-pitched with pain.

The spy took the wad of bills and grasped them in his shaking hand, when Raoul released him. As he got up to leave his eyes fixed on Raoul, his eyes were mean and small as beads.

"Bernard," Raoul bellowed on the intercom when the spy had left and he heard the front door close. "Get hold of Harry — tonight. A meeting, my office tomorrow morning, first thing, don't ask — *just do it*."

Raoul clicked off, stood up, then roared in anger and lashed his fist at the wall, smashing the plaster into an ugly jagged hole.

Raoul looked hard at the roadmap that was Harry's face, over the coffee and croissants assembled on the desk. "Find McKinley and break his goddamned balls," he said to the guy they call *The Hound*. The sunlight from the window transformed the office into the facsimile of a cosy den. The hole in the plaster now looked barbaric, completely out of place in such refinement.

Harry was like a bloodhound with a lined, baggy face several sizes too large for him. Raoul knew Harry from his army days in Algiers. He used him now and again for many things. He was Raoul's punisher. In one way, and one way only, Harry was like himself, totally ruthless — a natural. "Find the fucker and beat the living crap out of him. Use a bat. Bust his

Goddamn balls, so he'll never have another hard on. I want to see him hurt, and hurt bad. Tell him we've got his daughter, hell tell him anything. Then find the skinny bitch and *break* her."

Raoul's face transfused with blood as he spoke, turning an ugly red in his tirade. "*Twenty large,* Harry. Keep what you get for the girl. Ten now, the rest when job's done."

Harry hesitated, then looked him in the eye: "I'll need another five up front — expenses."

Raoul glowered as if he'd just heard the man utter the most disgusting obscenity. Harry didn't blink. "Fuck you. Goddamned expenses. You'll get damn good money for the virgin. That is if she *is* a virgin." Harry shook his head.

"Another three — that's it," Raoul said.

Harry nodded, took the money and the folded sheet of notepaper Raoul passed him.

"And Harry, one more thing ..."

The man stopped his motion to rise from the chair, to listen to Raoul,

"I want the fucker *alive*. Make him see you *do* her. I want the bastard to suffer."

Half way between sleep and consciousness, I was floating to the surface when the call came. I picked up the bedside phone, not yet sufficiently awake to wonder who was calling at this hour. Not awake enough to care. Birch scraped the windowpane again in the dark.

When I heard that atrocious accent, I knew immediately who it was.

"You stupid fuck. Now it's personal. We're going after your *daughter*."

"YOU STAY AWAY FROM HER."

Shouting down the line I was now bolt upright. Giselle lay wide-eyed beside me.

"Stay away hell. We'll take her and we will *break* her. We'll sell her t' fuckin' niggers in Algiers."

"STAY AWAY FROM HER, YOU BASTARDS. I'll GET THE POLI..."

CLICK, burrrrr and the line went dead.

It took me ages to quieten Giselle. To get her calm enough to talk. To keep her from that catatonic state when she'd sat naked and silent on the side of the bed. Her long hair swaying back and forth across her face like a feral child. She had a warm bath and drank camomile tea, while I stayed with her, talking to her; talking her down from that dark place her mind had been. When she calmed down, I called Greiner. He gave me the third degree on every word that was said in the phone call. There weren't that many when you got right down to it. *Psychotic nutter*, is what he thought. He suggested we send Jennifer to stay far away with relatives for a while. We were way ahead of him. This attack had tipped me over the abyss — now it was *me* who wanted to kill.

Simmone came home late that night from clubbing with Chantel. Too late. She is nervous, knowing how unpredictable Raoul can be.

"Come here bitch," Raoul says from the den.

Simmone walks to the door and nods to Bernard, but her heart sinks. She knows that tone of voice. The way he says it makes her mind freeze. Panic kicks in. She walks, but her legs are already stiff, her bowels already loose; she knows full well she is a prisoner going to her execution. She tries hard to co-ordinate her movements, tries to do the simplest thing — walking.

He kisses her lightly in a feigned civility. She sits at the antique table facing him; the mirrored surface reflects her bright eyes, her face flushed as if in sexual heat. This time it is fear that arouses her. Fear that transforms her face. She is now no longer beautiful.

Raoul says nothing, simply reaches for her right hand with his large left paw, and holds it firmly on the table, staring into her eyes. He lifts his right hand and smashes her across the face, a backhander that tips her chair over with a crash. She sprawls on the floor. He is still holding on to her wrist and she's dangling by one arm.

There is blood, when she lifts her hand to her cheek. She feels the jagged line where his signet ring has cut her flesh. Raoul remains silent. He throws the sheaf of photos at her. One falls on her chest and Simmone holds it up to see what it is. She looks from the photo up at Raoul with wide eyes, in shock, her lipsticked mouth forms a perfect O.

She tries to get her legs under her to stand. Raoul kicks them out again. She falls and screams as he draws his foot back and kicks her with all his force, hard in the belly. The wind goes out of her with an Oomph.

She doubles in pain, whimpers and draws her knees to her chest in a primordial response. A submissive little girl, while daddy kicks her again and again; now in the head, then the back, until she lies broken, bloodied and senseless on the floor.

She wakes in dim light, a basement, lying on a cold concrete floor — naked. A rusted grate is over a drain with a single, inadequate globe flickering overhead. Her head aches and there is blood still flowing from gashes in her forehead and her cheek. The place stinks. It's musty, damp and disused. She realises that she is wet, sitting on the cold cement in a puddle of her own making.

It isn't the same basement, but it might as well have been. The first basement where Daddy beat her senseless, every night for weeks. The basement where Raoul held her, long ago, when she was sixteen, when she'd run away and Raoul had found her homeless in Marseilles.

Raoul had broken her then, like some men break horses, broke her spirit with violence and the threat of more to come. Raoul had made her his own. He had made her his creature. He held her in his grip, told her what to do, what to say, who to fuck, how to do it and when. He'd staged erotic plays where she and others, and there were always others, acted his choreography in plays of ferocious dominance, degradation and submission. These sexual shows, were staged discretely in their house, they became the source of Raoul's wealth, before he graduated to a higher calling.

Her mind flashes on the beatings, the sting of the whip, leather cutting deep into her flesh. She freaks, scampering around the basement floor, bent low — screaming. Now in full cry, she stands scratching at the walls, she is searching, searching for a way out. Nothing. A single window that had existed at one time is now bricked in. She claws at it, gouging at the mortar until her nails break. Blood oozes from her fingertips. An ancient freezer sits along one wall, its big enough to store a body, the rubber seal has perished. She lifts the lid in trepidation of what's inside. Then drops it shut again without looking. In the end she lifts the lid again and looks inside, there is nothing. Nothing but stains leaking from the lid. She slams the lid down with a bang on the red-brown stains of her blood.

A flight of stairs leads to a trapdoor where she must have come in. She dashes up the stairs and belts the door with her fists until the pain forces her to stop. Simmone wipes her knuckles, sucks them to ease the pain. Her blood churns her stomach, it is nauseating. Slumped at the door she screams, sobs, then begs, and finally beseeches Raoul. She falls, collapsing at the head of the stairs — until hope fades.

When she rose again to consciousness, Simmone goes back down the stairs and sits in the furtherest corner, hurting inside her head, inside her heart and in every living pore. A hurt that spreads like a malignancy through her body, overlaid with cold, humiliation, fear and an edge of hunger.

That first time when Raoul locked her in a basement Juliet was there. That other time she had hung on to the deeply scarred and grievously wounded Juliet. The beaten, broken lovely Juliet was her only friend that time when she lay dying. That was the first time Raoul broke her. That time something changed deep within her. Something burst inside in her mind and never healed, something she never recovered from.

The light from that single feeble globe flicked out and died, she is now alone in the dark.

Raoul kicked her awake. She felt pain and a loud crack as a rib gave way. She screamed at the pain of it, then called out in that dim light, "Daddy?"

Simmone cringed on the floor, in foetal position, waiting for what was coming. Raoul hauled her upright and dragged her to the freezer. He forced her left hand into it, lifted the lid, then smashed it down on her hand. She screamed as her fingers snapped. Then he draped her sullen body over the freezer face down. Raped her savagely, then buttoned his coat, letting go his hold on her and she slid to the floor. He said nothing. The light clicked off again when he left.

That's how it went. Over and over, how many times she did not know, she lost count. No place to hide, no one to call, here in this place there is no hope. She lost track of time, of the days, and of the nights. Here there was no day or night. Her days reduced to those short moments when the small globe was switched on. Her nights were the trackless dark. The pain continued. He beat her again and again. He broke the fingers of her other hand, slowly this time, one by one. He raped her when he was drunk and whenever he felt like it. Her tan faded, her gym-toned body was long gone, her muscles were now flaccid, wasted with starvation.

The beatings and rape came and went in an irregular and irrational cycle. He did it whenever it suited him. Whenever he was there. He did to her whatever he wanted in whatever orifice took his fancy. No food. Only water to keep her alive, slopped into a bowl by the trapdoor.

By the time he came for her again for the umpteenth time, she was looking forward to it. Looking forward to the light going on, she was eager to hear his voice, writhing with a breathless need for his touch. She wanted pain. She welcomed it. *Pain was how he touched her*. She yearned for the most primitive of all our needs — human contact. This time she whimpered like a puppy when he entered her.

This is the time he left an open can of dog food upended on the floor. She ate it greedily lapping from the bowl on her knees like a dog; he forbids her to use her broken hands. As the days went by he fits a spiked collar around her neck. He leads her naked around the basement, with a chain clipped to the collar; she follows on all fours on the cold, bare cement. He tells her to sit, to stay, tells her to beg, to roll over, to pant and bark like a dog.

He has her eating dog meat out of his hand, licking the last of it from his fingers, as if it's delicious. It *is* delicious. He does this until she begged him. Begged him to touch her. Begged him to fuck her. Begged him to make her whole, to make her human.

Her screaming stopped. She took to fawning over him whenever the light flicked on and he came down the stairs. He was the one who kept her alive. The only one who looked after her. Only *he* would let her live. There was no room for anyone else. No room for anything. Not the police, not Duncan, not even herself. She had no self, no boundaries, no identity, there was nothing inside her but a void. Nothing outside her but humiliation. There was only Raoul. He was God, Jesus, Christ, Daddy, White Knight, Dark Lover, he was all this wrapped into one; he was her *saviour*. Her mind centred on him, obsessed on him, featured him in that dark basement, and in all her dreams he came to her burning bright, bathed in light.

The cut on her forehead festered to an ugly gash, a greenish-yellow seam of pus, by the time that Raoul retrieved her. Her broken fingers were by now but a dull ache. He hauled her up the stairs and bathed her in tepid water. He let the warmth flow over her raw skin and watched her soften as it eased the bruises that covered her broken body. She loved it, the tension within her died, muscles became even more flaccid until she had no strength left to stand. Such a simple thing. Cool water felt to her an elixir. A magical elixir and Raoul her glorious saviour.

He opened a first-aid kit to dress the wounds on her head, cheek, knees, elbows and buttocks where they were rubbed raw from the rough cement. Raoul taped the dressings and straightened the worst of her fingers and bound them to spatulas, which served as splints. He demanded she swallow antibiotics and vitamins that he shook from bottles into her hand. He let her crawl on the soft carpet, ever so thankfully to his feather bed. And later in the dead of night, Raoul himself came to that great bed. He folded her in his arms and she felt safe.

She felt that it was over.

Felt that she was home.

She felt she was his woman again.

CHAPTER 26. JENNIFER

What enables a man to strike and conquer, and achieve things beyond the reach of ordinary men is foreknowledge.

Sun Tzü, *The Art of War*, 512 BC

Jennifer noticed them hanging about the school. Swarthy men with long hair, black and sinister. Young men, dark, maybe Greek, Italian, Lebanese — whatever. Athletic by the look of them and the way they moved. She never got close enough to see them clearly. They kept well back, way across the street. They'd fade away between parked cars, if she turned to look at them. She wasn't sure they were even the same men, or if they were actually watching her. Sometimes they looked Hispanic. At times there was just one, alone and somehow forlorn, never more than two of them watching her at once.

Jenny wouldn't have noticed them, except that she was fast becoming attuned to the attentions of young men, and these guys were persistent. At first she thought they might be waiting for one of the other girls, but eventually she decided they were not. As the days passed she entertained some wild scenarios: drug dealers, kidnappers, rapists, serial killers, undercover cops. She'd seen it all on TV.

Jenny enlisted her friends in her cause and they kept an eye out for the men after that, reporting various sightings, not only at the school. When nothing happened, despite these strays still turning up from time to time, she noticed them less and less, until eventually she put them out of her mind. Forgot about them. The girls by then were also bored with the game and ceased to bother with strangers in the background after a while.

About the same time she noticed the guy from the end of the road, from tenth line, walking by on his way to work. She didn't know his name, but she'd seen him on the bus. A handsome guy about eighteen or so. An Indian. He had the blackest hair and dark, dark eyes, a supple skin the colour of coffee. He wore a duffle coat like a spy from an old war movie.

He'd say "Hi," and duck his head a little as he went by, polite in that shy way of his. When he smiled his teeth look so bright in the expanse of his high-cheeked handsome face that despite herself, she felt drawn to him.

Her girl friends teased her, of course; he must have sensed it, for when he saw them with her he'd pass by with a singular, formal nod. This day she'd just stepped off the bus and started crossing the road when a car came screaming around the corner, almost knocking her down. A Buick, it spun on some black ice at the intersection and slammed into the curb. The car sat silent for a few seconds. The driver cranked the starter, grinding the car to life. She saw someone with long red hair through the tinted glass — a woman.

Three shots shattered the rear window and it fell to pieces. Jenny dived for a phone box to hide, the sound ringing in her ears. The engine caught and the driver threw the car into gear with a screech, then spun its wheels, leaving two strips of smoking rubber. The panicky howl of a patrol car reached her. Police roared past in pursuit, leaving the reverberation of the screaming motor and wailing siren in its wake.

Two dark men came running towards Jenny. They skidded to a stop when she saw them and looked around, just as the car took off. She could have sworn that one of them was that Indian boy who lived at the end of their road. The two men sauntered back the way they'd come, like nothing had happened, like bad actors in a silent film.

Detective Greiner, stopped in the grove of maples and got out of the car some ways from the house. He took in the pickup truck parked at an angle by the shack. The pickup had more dings in it than an elephant's hide, and in the dusk, had about the same indeterminate colour.

"Hullo," Greiner called out, to what might be a figure in the doorway.

Donavon already had his hand on his holstered gun.

"*Jesus* Tom, *No*," Nat said, "leave it."

He sure as hell didn't want the Pasquales to get the wrong idea and let rip with deer rifles. These guys were hunters.

"Hi boys," he said, with a wave to show he wasn't carrying. The man in the doorway said nothing. "Want to speak with your Dad," Nat added as he walked towards the shack.

The man stepped aside to let the cops enter, a strapping young man, his face handsome like those in the Yucatan — carved in stone. An old Indian sat at the table in the gloom. The long dark hair and copper skin like one of those sepia toned photos you see in a museum looking sternly back at you. The table bore the scattered remains of their evening meal.

Nat pulled out a chair and sat down while Donavon walked across the room and checked the woods outside, through the window. Two Pasquale boys stood across the table from Greiner, with not a trace of emotion registered in their faces, their Indianness unnerving. This was not going to be easy.

"Look guys, I'll give it to ya straight. I don't care what you've got in the freezer. Don't give a damn if you're hunting deer, wolves or whatever. We've got a situation at McKinley's we're trying to figure. We need your help."

Greiner looked around the table at them — silence.

"I know you've been in the woods at McKinley's. Seen your tracks there."

He gestured at the pair of Caribou Mukluks stuffed with newspaper, drying under an overloaded hat rack by the stove. What was it with Indians and hats?

"Thing of it is, McKinley had a horse killed, we don't know the killers, but figure they may come back. Thought you boys might have seen something down that way."

"Heard about the horse," the old man said. His voice shocking them with its resonance in the silence of the cabin.

"So you *have* seen something?"

This time there was no answer. Nat started in again.

"You were at the Johnston place next to McKinley's. We've seen you-all hunting. Aerial photos from the Mounties for Chrissake. Do you really want me to confiscate what ya got in that Goddamned freezer? You going to tell me what's going down or not?"

The old man looked stern and glared at the boys.

"Cessna," the younger said in that flat tone Indians have, "Mounties on tenth line, saw us take deer."

The older man spoke again, "Ahanu was there in the woods on and off. He kept an eye on the place after the killing. He saw something, might be nothing at all."

Greiner looked at the young man who had spoken before.

"Was in the Cedars over the road when I seen a car. Couple a fellas."

"Can you describe them?"

"Nah, too dark."

Silence for a while and Nat resisted the temptation to jump right in and yell at him. He shot a warning glance at Donavon who was by now shifting his feet.

"Why were you there?" Nat asked.

The youth ignored him and continued. "They walked up the road to the house."

"When was that?" Nat asked, "The same night the horse was killed?"

"No, maybe a week later. Might have been Thursday."

"How long were they in the house?"

"Couple a hours. Weren't no one at home when they got there. Then Missus McKinley came home."

"Did ya hear what they said?"

"Nah."

"So, what happened? Did you get a closer look?"

"I might have," he said, looking at his father. The old man nodded. "Snuck up to a window. They was upstairs, couldn't see nothing. Couldn't hear nothing either, double glazed."

"You see what happened after?"

"Nah."

"So, McKinley met with two men. They must have surprised him — turning up like that at night on foot."

"Nah."

"No. What do you mean — no?"

"McKinley wasn't there, nor was Jen. Only the Missus."

Greiner picked it up right away.

"*Jennifer*. You know her name?"

The young man blushed, looked down, said nothing. It suddenly became clear to Greiner why the young buck had been hanging around the McKinley house.

"Christ," Donavon said, speaking for the first time," this is not going anywhere."

"It might," the old man said from the head of the table.

"Oh?"

"Boy saw the car."

Nat swung back to the young man: "Ya get the license plate?"

"Sure," the young man said: "Buick, brown, eighty-three model," he recited the licence plate letter perfect from memory: "GWD -394."

Donavon radioed the details through when they got back to the car. They tooled down tenth line past McKinley's, the place now lit like a Christmas tree. The answer from the bureau came back as they turned onto the county road.

"*Canadian Precision*," the dispatcher said.

"What about them?" Donavon said into the mike.

"The registered owners of the car you tagged."

"*Canadian Precision*. That's the outfit Fortier headed before they bumped him." He signed off. "We could put out an APB right now," Donavon said. Nat thought for a moment.

"I'm sure I saw that car leaving the lot when I was interviewing Ganong. Could be any one of their staff. Though I'll bet that car is unassigned, a run-about for the execs, a car they'd use for a covert meeting, for visiting a mistress, anything that might be dodgy."

"Maybe," said Donavon, "or maybe they're not *that* smart."

"What the hell." Greiner said, "Call it in."

The wanted car turned up next day at Toronto's Pearson airport, parked in the long-term lot. Uniforms opened it. Nothing, except for a whiff of perfume, wrappings from a French deli, glass from a shattered rear window and a bullet lodged in the roof.

"Two shots went through the roof. The one we found was soft point — two-seventy. Not police, no match in our database."

"Hunting calibre."

"Deer rifle. Heaps of them out there."

"The shots went high. Someone on foot."

"Could be."

Greiner made another trip to Ganong's office in Guelph. Apparently monsieur Christobal had left the car at the airport and taken the 6:40 back to Montreal.

"Who the hell is Christobal?" Greiner asked.

"Ah, Bernard Christobal is a personal assistant to the company owner."

"And he is?" but Greiner knew, even as he asked.

"Raoul Kelemann."

CHAPTER 27. DUNCAN

The wise general will use the highest intelligence of the army for spying...

Sun Tzü, *The Art of War*, 512 BC

Giselle came down the stairs to breakfast that morning in a navy suit with a cream silk blouse underneath, her unfettered breasts bouncing their way down the steps, barely contained within her blouse. The colour set off her blonde hair and tanned Viking skin.

"You look gorgeous."

"Why thank you kind sir," she said, smiling.

I'd already fed the horses. Now I brewed some New Guinea Gold that I'd picked up in town. I kissed her, lingered for a minute, wanting more, wanting her — now. She broke the moment. We sat down to toast and coffee. Jennifer had not yet surfaced.

"Have you thought about what we discussed last night?" she asked.

"I've thought about it. I couldn't stop thinking about it."

"And?"

She looked at me across the rim of her cup.

"I don't know," I said. "I don't see how we can."

"I can't stand this. Not after they tried to kidnap Jenny."

"We don't know that. It could have been a stolen car — anything."

"I called the police, Duncan. They were chasing some woman who went ballistic in Katie's Diner. Drove a fork through a guy's hand. Police didn't catch the car."

"So it was an *accident*," I said.

"Jenny claims two men followed her. Police weren't impressed. Young girls get anxious, happens all the time."

"You know what Jenny's been like — hormonal."

"Well, I am terrified it's the same men. That they will kill me or Jenny to get to you."

"I won't let them touch you, Giselle."

"You weren't there for me. You weren't there with Jenny. Why would I think you can protect us? What are you going to do, follow me around all day? Can you protect our daughter too? Hire bodyguards around the clock?"

"The police are working on it. We've told them all we can."

Giselle snorted.

"Duncan, they think you killed *Alaric*. They think you killed horses at the track. They don't know about the attack on me. Don't know about Raoul. God knows what they think about the satanic stuff. Police will do nothing."

"We could tell them about Raoul," I said, trying hard to think.

"Tell them what precisely? A respectable French businessman had your horse gutted and damn near did the same to your naked wife? Not likely."

"There are connections leading to Raoul."

"You can't mention stabbing Nadim — they think you *killed* him."

"There is McGowan at Scotland Yard."

Giselle snorted again.

"Duncan, this is between us and Raoul. We have to finish it."

"*We?* I got the distinct impression you wanted *me* to."

Giselle fixed me with a glare, as only a wife can.

"You can do it. You're a man — if you are really a man. You are the one who has the strength for it, who knows how. Damnit Duncan, talk to Guy. Maybe he will understand your hang ups."

"Guy. How the hell can he help?"

"He knows about this stuff."

"He was so gung-ho he enlisted with the Americans for Chrissake."

"Well, he might be macho and he *is* eccentric, but he's decisive," she said. "He will know what to do."

"Yeah right. *You* think Guy will talk me into it."

Giselle stood up then as we heard Jenny's footsteps on the stairs.

"I have got to go — bye Jenny," she called, her voice rising. "Talk to Guy."

She hurled this over her shoulder at me as she went out the door.

I met Guy for lunch at a touristy place on the main drag of Elora. I had to go that way to get the Blazer serviced. I hung around the garage while they greased the truck, then headed uptown. The café was authentic. Immigrants had done it in a Sicilian style right down to the red and white checked table cloths and bottles of Chianti in wicker baskets on the shelf behind the cash register. The place even smelled Italian: a rich, garlicky smell of meat and pasta hung in the air.

Guy came in and grinned when he saw me at a table facing the door. I had the posters with me in two rolled tubes. When we'd ordered our pasta, I unrolled the first, with horses in the snow. He looked at the poster and smiled.

"Great shot, Duncan — superb."

"Absolutely." I felt the same rush from the picture of those galloping horses. "I swung the lens around after I took it, to see what had startled them. I focused on the cedars across the road, then accidentally clicked the shutter."

That's when I unrolled the second poster dramatically on the table over the first.

"There?" I said, pointing to the blurred features in the woods.

"Who, do ya think?" Guy asked.

"It looks like *you*."

Guy snatched a glance at me, bent over the table and peered at the image.

"Yeah, it does — sorta. The beret anyhow." I was silent. "It's not me Duncan."

He frowned and shook his head as if puzzled.

"Thought you might have been standing guard."

"It occurred to me, but no I didn't."

"Then who… ?"

"A *toque* do you think?"

"Yeah, he is wearing a watch cap. And that's a rifle?"

I pointed with a fingernail to a dark line.

"Could be," said Guy. "Could be a branch."

The waitress came then with our pasta steaming on two plates. She was dark and plump with a faint moustache on her upper lip, Mediterranean — the proprietor's wife. I rolled up the posters as she put the pasta down with a clatter of plates in front of us. The rich smell of braised mince and oregano made me realise how hungry I was.

"I know who killed *Alaric* — who's threatening us," I said. Guy looked at me sharply, but said nothing. Waiting for me to go on, "*Compagnie Fabriquante*. Run by a fellow called Kelemann — Raoul Kelemann."

So then I related the confession of Nadim about opium coming to France from Afghanistan. Told him about my fight with Nadim and how I got his confession.

"*Fantastique* Duncan. I didn't know you had it in you."

"Nor did I. First I got desperate, then I got mad. The scary thing, I realise now, is what a kick I got out of it — the terrific, fuckin' buzz of the fight."

"*Magnifique*, you've found your warrior soul."

"Not the best side of me, I can tell you. You know I wanted to kill him, something fierce, it was all I could do to stop myself."

"So now, oh warrior, where is he?"

"That's the weird part — Nadim's dead. An overdose. The police interviewed me Tuesday — French intelligence: DST."

"Jesus, they came here — to Canada?"

"Guess the drugs made them nervous. Anyway, they said I was in the clear. Though the OPP don't share that opinion."

"Greiner, you mean."

"Yeah, Greiner and his sidekick Donavon. They were both there." Glancing at the door I half rose as a man walked in and sunlight filled the room. Guy saw my look and realised how jumpy I was. "And here's another thing," I said. "Nadim pointed us to an exec, André Fortier. And Fortier was *not* surprised by *Alaric's* demise. He wanted to know if we'd caught the villains!"

"*Merci*, he could be into many things, 'e is a Frenchman *non*?"

"Here's where it gets interesting: André Fortier was French alright, and he was killed in a hit and run at Kitchener last weekend."

"Greiner told you that?"

"They thought I might have something to do with it. But my ignorance was obvious — even to them."

Guy studied me as he digested the two murders in my wake.

"*Mon ami*, there's something else then, isn't there?"

"Yes, the killers phoned me again."

"Again, and what ..."

"They threatened my daughter this time. Threatened Jenny with rape."

"Bastards!"

"I don't know what to do. I did tell police about the phone call, but I haven't told them about Raoul."

"You're right — don't."

"McGowan told me about *Compagnie Fabriquante*. Told me Kelemann is in Montreal for the summer."

Hearing approaching footsteps I flicked a glance at the waitress heading for our table with a latte and a long black. I didn't want Guy to detect the lie. I didn't want to tell him about Simmone — that I had a spy in the enemy camp.

"Kelemann's planning to hunt in the Rockies this month. We're safe for a while."

Guy shook his head, putting his latte back on the saucer.

"If he has sent someone to kill you, then you are far from safe. A hunting trip would be an ideal alibi."

"Oh," I said, "then perhaps we should go away."

"I don't think so."

"Why not?"

"Because you'd be running scared. They'll send a pro. He'll get Jennifer first as bait. Then he'll kill you."

"Jeez! So, what the hell should I do?"

Anxiety made my gut contract. My breathing sounded like a dog panting, even to me. I pictured myself in the cross hairs of a sniper's rifle. The finger-light touch, tightening on the trigger.

"The thing to do is stop running. Go after him — kill the bastard. It would solve everything. A hunting trip — perfect."

"Jesus Guy — kill him? That's murder. *What if we're wrong?*"

"What if you're *not*? You're a threat. You're a threat because he wants to do it again with your next horse. That horse made millions for them. That's why you were warned off by the attack on Giselle. They don't want to kill you, not yet anyway. They want to stuff smack in your next horse as well."

"He's already killed two people I know of. He's threatened Jenny, maybe had a crack at her already in Guelph."

"So, do something about it."

"Well, I don't really *know* anything. I only suspect he had Fortier killed."

"That's to your advantage. He doesn't know, that you know about him. He doesn't know you're going to attack."

"Well, I haven't decided to attack."

"We'd better take Giselle with us, in case he comes after her again."

"Giselle?"

"But of course, you cannot do it alone. You cannot leave her by herself unprotected either. He'll have men with him — armed and dangerous men. He might have already sent men to get you."

"You said *we* Guy, do you want to put yourself in harm's way? Do you want to relive Vietnam?"

"It ain't Nam, Jesus Duncan! I can't let them do this to you. Not without a fight — this is war."

"I don't want to get you involved. I haven't decided what to do yet. Though, whatever I do, I am going to need all the help I can get."

"That's settled then."

"What about Giselle. If Jenny goes to London, Giselle could go with her?"

"We need three for a fire team. *Do it*."

"I need to think, this is serious. Maybe Greiner ..."

"*Mort bleu*. Greiner will do squat. You can't tell him about Nadim."

"No — besides Nadim's dead."

"Damnit Duncan, are you saying you don't have the guts for the job? You're going to let them rape your wife, threaten your daughter and *still* do nothing about it?"

"I can't be absolutely sure that it's Raoul."

"You're making it easy for him, because you can't make up your mind. Because you're not *sure* you're doing the right thing. I'll bet he's made up his mind. He would do you in an instant. Let me tell you Duncan, *in the real world you can never be absolutely sure of anything*."

Guy was laying it on the line, in a way I didn't like, in a way that showed my weakness — a way that stung. I stood up and my chair crashed to the floor adding emphasis — it fuelled my sense of drama. I hauled out my wallet and threw a twenty on the table as the waitress hurried over.

"Fuck you," I said to Guy and stalked out.

When I got it started, I roared away in the Blazer like a rejected teenager. He infuriated me more as I drove toward home and my temper cooled; infuriated me to realise that what he'd said was true.

McGowan flew to Toronto on Thursday. I took his call the same day and he asked me to meet him in the Cabaret bar, downtown Hilton, a request with just a hint of drama. The bar was gloomy when I got there — an hour's drive. Mungo was sitting at a booth in the corner contemplating a pint of dark fluid that could only be Guinness. He looked up as I slid into the seat across from him, my back to the door.

"What's wrong?" I said.

"Good to see you in unblemished health Duncan. I'm only here on a short visit. I needed to see you."

My eyes adjusted to the dim light. He wore his usual dark suit with a nondescript tie, his greying hair brushed back from his temples in defiance of his gradual balding. Mungo looked like any other businessman in the bar. I was out of place in a denim jacket with jeans and boots.

"You have something to tell me?"

He was contemplating his next move, searching perhaps for the right phrase.

"I need to warn you. At a professional level, it is not in our interest for you to come to grievous harm."

"Oh," I said, startled.

"You see old boy, when you commit adultery, if the husband were to find out, you could find yourself confronting his displeasure. Now if he were a man of no moral constraints, like our mutual friend, you could find yourself in dire straights."

"Kelemann knows?"

"Word is you were seen with his wife in France. There's probably a contract out on your life by now.

"*Probably*, you mean you don't know?"

"I'm breaking it to you gently. You're targeted all right, and not on a feeble freelance arrangement, it's a done deal. A deal that's signed, sealed and now awaits delivery."

With that I felt a queasy roil of panic again, deep in my guts, finding it hard to breathe.

"One of our chaps saw you at Deauville. We know that Kelemann keeps tabs on his wife — always. He's a control freak. He knows you were with her — that you have a sexual liaison. We know, from prior experience, that *his* penalty for this is death."

"The hell you say. What do you think I should do?"

"The obvious — break it off."

I catch an image of Simmone rolling away from me, her long hair tangled on a bed. She is coming softly to the surface through auburn strands, in the afterglow. She implores me with her eyes, as if afraid of my leaving. She smiles in satisfaction as I roll my naked self on top of her. Mounting her. Holding her down with my weight, my hands locked on her wrists.

McGowan looks over at me — puzzled. I shake my head to clear it.

"Will that stop Raoul?"

"No, that in itself won't save you — though it is the first step. She's bait in the trap now. You need to let the bait go. You need to go to ground. Get out of here. Take your family. Don't wait to pack, just get out — now."

"Jennifer's going to my sister's in England."

"Better give me her name and address then."

"Sure," I said, unthinking and wrote it down.

"Thing is, I can't go *now*, the horses, our farm, Giselle — Christ, everything."

"He'll crush you Duncan — unless you get him first."

He smiled at the thought, so I asked: "Can you help?"

"Help? What! Help *you* get him. Hell no, I can't help. You're on your own. Personally, I felt it my duty to warn you. Can't have you knocked off your perch by the frog."

He didn't for a moment contemplate that I would try to kill Raoul. He didn't see me as capable of that; he saw me as a civilised amateur in his nasty professional world.

"Can you notify the RCMP?"

Silence.

"Well then, will you enlighten Detective Greiner for Chrissake?"

"Not our way, old son. Not our jurisdiction. We want *you* to do something else."

"Christ I can't run right *now* — I have my horses to look after. And what about Giselle? What will they do to her? If I bolt they've already won." What Mungo had said finally caught up with me and clamoured for attention. "Something else? What else do you want?"

"*We* want to take over your Missus Kelemann, so to speak."

"Take over Simmone, what do you mean?"

"Madam Kelemann has supplied us with information. We don't want to lose that conduit. We appreciate your assistance, believe me. But now you're blown, we need *you* to bow out, and we can't afford to let *her* go."

"Let her go. What the hell *do* you want?"

"We want her to report to one of our chaps."

"One of your chaps. What chap?"

When he said it I looked him in the eye, McGowan stared back, saying nothing. My mind wound around another possibility altogether.

"I want you to give Missus Kelemann this card."

McGowan slid a card across the table face down. Face down, always secretive — that about summed him up.

"Suggest to her that she make contact with us, with our chaps immediately."

Immediately I turned over the card he'd given me and looked up puzzled:

"With *us* — *our chaps*. Who the hell are you McGowan? If that is your real name?"

McGowan was silent. Which told me it wasn't. At least he had the sense not to persist in the pretence of New Scotland Yard.

"You're not with the Yard?" I said, mulling it over, "You're not police at all. MI-six then is it?" McGowan said nothing. "No. Well, perhaps one of the other spooks?" Silence from across the table. "Who the fuck are you? A secret squirrel, that's for sure: Whitehall, Washington, Tel Aviv — which is it?"

McGowan sat unnaturally still. When at last he spoke, he did it so quietly, that it struck me as having a faintly religious tone. I had to lean forward and lower my head like a devoted disciple to hear him.

"It doesn't matter who *I* am, old boy. You don't need to know. It is enough for you to know that I'm one of the good guys."

While I stared at him, trying to connect the dots — a piece clicked into place.

"That's why the French were benign. You'd already told them I *didn't* kill Nadim. DST are building a case against *Compagnie Fabriquante's* guns-for-drugs in Afghanistan. That's why you're after Raoul."

McGowan didn't answer. He turned his head and cast an eye over those in our vicinity. No one looked up. No one even looked in our direction.

"Good luck Duncan," he said.

He extended his hand to me as he stood. I shook it as if to absolve him personally of all responsibility — responsibility for me.

"When it comes right down to it, we're always on our own," I said in a flash of insight. "Even in a civilised world, we have to protect ourselves from the bad guys."

"In a civilised world," McGowan said, the weight of experience ringing weary in his voice, "we never know who the bad guys really are."

He stepped forward, then paused and turned towards me.

"You know the drill, give me five. Oh, and you can still reach me at that number."

Yeah, I nodded and raised my hand for the waiter to fetch another ale, watching as McGowan walked unhurried to the door.

He left me feeling alone and wondering.

Wondering who the bad guys really were.

CHAPTER 28

If you see those who draw water begin their task by drinking water themselves, then you know the army is suffering from thirst.

Sun Tzü, *The Art of War*, 512 BC

Daybreak came and I sat up in bed and through the window grass rippled like the surface of a lake. Trees around the field were flailing, battered by the wind. Giselle stirred with my movement and winced at the light spilling into the room.

"What's the time?"

Her voice croaked in that dry mouthed sort of way you have on waking. Her blonde hair lay strewn over the pillow. An errant strand fell across her face. Her eyes had that scrunched up look of a kitten blocking light.

"Half six. It's Saturday, you don't have to get up," I whispered.

"Thank God for that," she muttered turning over, twisting the duvet around her, leaving me bereft of covers.

Softly I stroked the curve of her back, slid my palm along the delicious dip of her waist and followed a swelling hip to the potent curve of her derriere. Her musk shook the fog of sleep from me like a hit of caffeine. I wanted her with an urgent desperation. What had lain between us now was gone — dissolved in some long forgotten anger. Now was not the time for words.

When we kissed I nuzzled her neck. I kissed her skin, licked her earlobe — her scent hit me with an intensity that kicked my smouldering lust into flame. She rolled onto her belly with a grunt. I bit her neck and stroked her legs, feeling her nether lips against the soft cotton of her panties. Giselle moved, involuntarily picking up the rhythm. I slipped my hand into the elastic of her waistband and felt it snap as she moved away. She flounced up onto all fours in the bed, her hands clawing the sheets, fingers spread like blood tipped talons — a lioness.

"No, not now damnit!"

"What's wrong?"

"You don't know what is wrong? You think being humiliated by them was nothing? You think I can forget being forced... then make love to you, like it never happened?"

Here were words she'd not expressed before.

"*Forced*. What happened Giselle? Were you raped?"

"*Raped*, what is that precisely? I'll tell you what that is: that's being forced to make them come in your mouth? They cut me — cut me anywhere they liked. They did it when I refused them, you saw it yourself. They cut me with a razor down the middle."

"It must have been awful."

"I went ballistic, panicked. I couldn't stop them. I would have done anything to stop them cutting me. ANYTHING. You were not there Duncan, you cannot know what it was like? You weren't there to save me from them."

"Well, at least they didn't..."

"Didn't what, *fuck me*, do you mean? They fucked me like a dog."

"A dog? What the..."

"In the arse, Duncan."

"Oh, Darl," I said, holding her as she sobbed, rocking back and forth. "Why didn't you tell me?" "I felt like a slut for what they made me do." Her voice softened from her strident harangue. "I am so ashamed." She looked me in the eye. "I want you to kill them. And I want to see you do it. I want to be in on the kill. The question is: Are you man enough?"

"I'll kill him," I said, and meant it.

She kissed me on the mouth, her lips full of promise. I held her tight. She got to her feet and headed for the bathroom. I shivered, alone on the bed — deserted.

After feeding *Red* and the others I phoned our neighbour's daughter

Kirsten, and arranged for her to look after the horses at the farm from next Friday. She could use the money, she had plans for college in the fall. I wondered then vaguely about my ability to pay her; my check account had gone into free fall again.

Jenny came down to breakfast while we were still eating. She was dressed in breeches, ready to ride. I could use her help with the horses.

"We are going away again, for a week this time," Giselle told her.

"Again. What's going to happen to me?"

"We will send you to England to stay with Aunt Gail."

Jenny flushed and her mouth formed an Oh. I wondered if Giselle had the money in her own account for the ticket. I sure as hell didn't.

"You will have more time with Malcolm, though you must come home for the last term of school."

"Malcolm?" I said, "Who is Malcolm?"

"A boy in England, Dad — you'd like him."

"I doubt it," I said in a classic reaction to a shift in my daughter's affections.

"You knew about this?" I said to Giselle.

"Jenny is growing up," Giselle said, then turned on that practised look that wives reserve for their husbands.

"Where are you two going?" Jenny asked.

"Eh, camping up north — Algonquin," Giselle improvised.

"Camping? You hate camping mum."

"Duncan convinced me that Algonquin is beautiful this time of year."

"That's so romantic. Come on Dad, let's work those horses."

We were riding the verge. The grass had sprung and the ground soft underfoot. The turf sported an array of daisies. Jennifer was aboard *Shandy* and I was on a new two-year old sent to us. We had trotted about 10 km when we encountered the Pasquale brothers, in a truck sounding like it was internally haemorrhaging. They drew alongside and slowed to keep pace.

"How ya doing?" The youngest in a dark watch cap asked, looking at Jennifer.

Truth is I didn't know what *he* was doing. I sure as hell didn't like the way he was looking at my daughter.

"Fine thanks," she said, then surprised me by adding, "great day, eh."

At that I stopped my horse with a jolt of recognition. The Pasquales stopped too, puzzled.

"*You're* in the photo," I said, "it was *you* in the woods."

They looked for a moment like they might bolt. The older brother shifted the truck into gear with a crunch, but held tight while the young man spoke.

"Yeah," he said, "I saw them."

"You could have told the police."

"Told 'em."

"Do you know who they were?"

"Didn't know them, but gave cops their license tag. They'll git 'em."

"Why were *you* there?" I asked.

"That satanic stuff in the news," he said, glancing at Jenny, "That's nasty, so thought I'd look out for ya. I'm real sorry that happened."

In a flash, as if someone had turned the page, I saw him differently. He looked down and his brother took it as a sign to let in the clutch. The pickup lurched away with gravel scattering from worn treads.

"What were they talking about?" Jenny asked.

Hearing her query made me consider for a moment what had been said. Sitting astride my horse, he moved underneath me snatching at the bit, wanting to be gone. I slipped the reins through my fingers and let him move out in an enthusiastic walk — away from her.

"Nothing," I said, "we were talking about nothing at all."

We went over to Guy's place on Sunday after dropping Jenny off at her friend's. The snow had gone from Guy's fields except for a dirty patch here and there, like someone's washing blown off the line. His trailer lay in the lee of a stand of scraggly spruce, swaying and bending in the wind. This terrain was so bleak and devoid of life, it could well have been the barrens up north. The fields had been ploughed last fall and were rough like Guy's driveway, where the surface was broken into tire ruts and water filled puddles.

We'd brought camping gear in the Blazer and were lugging it over to the trailer when Guy came out of his workshop in the barn.

"Over here," he yelled into the wind.

We changed tack and headed for the barn. Threw the gear on a bench and I started sorting through it, soaking up the warmth from the pot-bellied stove. Giselle stood in awe, staring at the bark canoe, cradled on the wall.

"Like it?" Guy said.

"It is exquisite."

"*Merveilleux,* so fragile the bark is like paper — I can't bring myself to use it," Guy said. "Maybe, someday — someday special."

We piled our sleeping bags on the bench along with the two-man tent I'd bought years ago. It'll keep out the black flies and mosquitoes with its nylon netting. Save us from being eaten alive. The fabric was a deep green, the colour of endless forests of fir.

I had a deer rifle my father gave me: A Finnish *Sako* .270: a bolt-action hunting rifle with open sights. A high-velocity calibre, good for a long shot at deer out on the moors. I'd bought three boxes of ammo years ago and hadn't used them.

My father used to take me out on the moor to hunt stag. We'd leave in the dark and drive to where he'd scouted earlier in the Land Rover. You had to stalk deer over there. We didn't shoot from ambush as they do in America. The treeless moors offered little cover unless you lay among the heather. Deer could disappear in a fold of land in a blink; you had to follow gullies and ridges until you picked them up again.

A stealthy, strenuous activity with violence and death at its end. Not always a long shot either, we'd just as likely creep over a ridge and come face to face with deer. A killing snapshot thrilled my father. He was from an earlier time, a time of hunting, fishing and shooting — a time of war.

Sure, I loved to hunt, though I didn't go much on the kill at the end. Not that I was squeamish. I just didn't want to *kill* animals. I loathed butchering and all that entailed, cutting the meat, chopping joints in a welter of blood. I detested backpacking the meat out to the Land Rover. A tight shot through a camera lens was more my style, but it wasn't an option then.

Guy had already assembled our matériel. A tiny tent of cammo fabric. Cammo shirts for us and sleeping bags. He had a 308 *Remington* semiautomatic, with a four-power telescopic sight and a half-dozen boxes of shells.

"This is for you," he said, handing a pump-action shotgun to Giselle. He rummaged in his pack and came up with four boxes of birdshot for the *Smith & Wesson*. The sort of sawn-off shotgun cops have on TV.

"Shotguns loaded with birdshot were very effective in Nam," Guy said.

He was grinning, enjoying our macho intent, though I felt squeamish with all this death-dealing hardware. Giselle examined the gun then cocked the pump action with an ominous CLACK-CLACK. Her femininity fell away as she sighted along the barrel.

Guy picked up a black contraption with pulleys and strings. It took a second or so before I realised what it was — a compound bow. Guy showed us a matching set of arrows with steel broadheads that clipped on to the frame and looked so sharp you could shave with them.

"Why the bow?"

"It's *silent*, no flash — nothing to give you away at night."

"*At night* — Jesus, we're hunting in the dark?"

"Who knows? Might turn out to be just what's needed."

Now I surely didn't like the idea of sneaking around at night with a bow when *they* had hunting rifles.

"Ah," he said, "I saved the best for last." He pulled up his jacket and revealed a holster. "Glock eighteen," he said, flourishing the black pistol like a magician pulling a rabbit from a hat.

"Military model, polymer frame, our cop had it in Ireland. The only model that's fully automatic."

"Jesus, do you have a license for that thing?" I said.

He looked at me for a second and smiled, shaking his head.

"For Chrissake, we're going to kill a man and you're worried it's not licensed! Ya can't get a license for a full-auto anyway."

"Okay, okay," I said, realising how serious it was, and that thought sobered me. What the hell was I doing?

"We'll break up the guns and ditch them on the way back. Don't want to be pulled over and found with a weapon that's killed someone."

He'd bought us each a puny daypack. "Since we always *fill* a pack, whatever its size, I got small ones, they're all we'll need." He'd half-filled each one with snack food, vitamin tablets and trail mix. Dried chewy food that didn't need cooking. In the side pockets, ammo, first-aid kit, field dressings and insect repellent. Guy had enough water canteens and purifying tablets to hold us for a week, along with a case of *Gatorade*. Guy shoved his share of the food in his pack and palmed a wicked knife.

"Might be useful," he said and looked me in the eye. "Can't be too careful. No fires. Cold tack all the way. No shiny metal, tape it so it doesn't flash in the sun. We're tracking these guys — don't want to give ourselves away."

"These *guys*?" I said, "We're after Raoul."

"Be *all* of them against us in the bush — better believe it. Bullyboy and his buddy minimum — there'll be more. And they'll be armed to the teeth. You can bet on it."

I nodded and looked across at Giselle — her face serious, she nodded in return. She was so intent it was scary. "Got cammo outfits for all of us," Guy said, "and face paint."

"*Face paint!* Jeez, that's a bit over the top."

"This way they won't spot your pale face. Skin has a sheen to it. With paint we'll be camouflaged so well they won't see us, even if they're looking straight at us."

"Okay, right — face paint, check!"

"Oh, and no deodorant, perfume, soap or toothpaste on this trip. Scent lingers, it's a dead giveaway. In Nam the VC tracked our city boys by the scent of their aftershave, and took their lives."

We packed the guns in the Blazer under feed sacks and drove north past Orangeville. Guy took along old cans for targets and we stopped en-route to pick up a half-dozen melons. I pulled onto an unused logging track that Guy knew. We reached a clearing after nearly being bogged in a marsh. Low range in four-wheel drive got us through. The forest was dark, the sort of dark that chills you. It lead to an eerie brooding — it felt right to practice killing here.

Guy set out cans and melons, shoulder height in the trees. Some at the edge of a clearing and more further back in the woods. I could hardly see them in the murk. We waited until he was back before loading. You don't want anyone even *touching* guns when you're down range. Guy showed Giselle the shotgun and how to hold the recoil pad hard to her shoulder. He put his arm around her to show her the grip. I felt a twinge.

"She knows how to shoot Guy. Her Dad taught her."

"Maybe, but I bet she's never killed a man. Nor have you. There is just one way to do it: *shoot first*."

We both scowled. Giselle smoothed her hair.

"What the hell does that mean? "

"Always plan to shoot from ambush. Never give them an even break. Never shout *freeze* as they do on TV. Don't say anything at all. Just get in that first shot, and get it on target."

We were both silent, our perception changed.

"And if they're moving, follow their movement, get their centre of mass in your sights and move through to give them a lead, then squeeze off the shot. Get them *first*, and when you've hit 'em, hit 'em *again* in the chest. A *double-tap* stops them shooting back."

It sounded like something a sergeant yelled at him back in Nam. A gunnery version of the injunction to *kick the bugger in the balls*. Well I did know *that* worked.

Giselle leant forward. A blast filled the silence and vaporised the nearest melon. It morphed into a man's smashed head as it fell. She fired another blast. Another head gone. The last melon further away was unaffected when she fired.

"That's your effective range." Guy said, "Ya need to know that to avoid being killed."

The smell of burnt powder filled the air, as if we'd broken wind in the middle of a war. I'd been stalking deer with my Dad for years. Had used this rifle before, a rifle built to work day in and day out in the cold and mud. I hefted the weight of it and closed the bolt on a round, raised the gun, focussing on the **i** of the front sight. The rifle gave me power.

Raising the gun, I burst a melon viciously with a hollow-point, then struck at the empty cans, working the bolt in a rhythm from a long ago memory. The empty brass flicked out hot, humming with each pass. I missed one shot, slowed my trigger draw for the next, aligned the sights and squeezed off another round: a kick in my shoulder and high-velocity crack and the far can spun to the ground 100 metres away.

Guy's rifle had a loud, hard, sound when he fired. A hard-hitting military calibre. He blasted all but one — the can already toppled from the far stump.

We blazed away together, savages rejoicing in a chaotic binge of sound. Guy urging us to get that first shot in; as fast as we could align a clear shot. He took to yelling which target to go for and we complied.

"Better get used to each other's guns — just in case," Guy said.

We switched weapons and I shot the double-action Glock, without doing much damage. Guy switched the gun to full automatic and showed me how to grip it in both hands. I let rip with the full 17- shot magazine, in one long *Ripriprip...* smashing the stump where the cans had sat. The gun recoiling above my head.

"Boy that felt good," I said, when my ears ceased ringing.

"*Merveilleux!* Take it for backup. You've only got the bolt action. I have the bow and Commando knife as well."

He took the holster off and adjusted it on my belt, then fitted the black knife on his own belt in its place. I blasted away with the shotgun, and Giselle with the Glock.

Between us we fired off ammo in quick time. The reverberation of gunshots rang in our ears, and the sting of cordite stayed with us even on the drive home. We went to a different spot a few days later, then another a week after that. We got faster, and under the tutelage of Guy, our aim sharpened for that critical first shot.

Afterwards I reminded Guy to replace the ammunition and not to touch it with his bare hands. Guy showed us how to strip and clean the weapons. He warned us against using gun oil on the mechanism. Oil attracts dust and mixes with the burnt residue.

"Creates a slurry that jams a gun. It clogs automatic weapons," he said.

Guy used a dry lubricant made for locks; he applied it with a puffer.

"*Molybdenum disulphide*," he said. "Army doesn't use it, because you have to be meticulous. The lube doesn't seep in, like oil does, to places where you haven't thought to put it." It felt like we were in good hands.

Guy got his bow from the Blazer then and put another melon in a tree some 30 metres away. He fitted an arrow, drew and held it, then released with a twang. The arrow pierced the melon passing through up to its fletching. He fired a few more, then went to retrieve them. We watched him stride back towards us exuding confidence, holding the bow in his left hand and with the arrows gripped in his right. I was glad he was on our side.

Giselle put the bow high in the air and drew back as she lowered it as Guy had done. Her hair hung down over her face, shielded one side as she struggled with the pull. She didn't have the strength to pull the bow past mid draw, so after several tries she admitted defeat.

Now I *did* have the strength to draw the bow, as I raised it, but after intense concentration, and all six arrows, still couldn't hit the target. I retrieved the arrows and fired again until I did manage to slice a piece of melon with a glancing blow on the last shot. It was a good place to stop.

"Arrows tear through organs and blood vessels," Guy said, "animals die from haemorrhagic shock — loss of blood."

"Same as a bullet?"

"No, a bullet causes hydraulic shock, adjacent tissue is damaged mechanically by a brutal displacement of tissue fluids."

It sounded like Guy recalled it verbatim from some old army manual.

"You're just as *dead* from an arrow as from an atom bomb," I said.

Then I reflected for a second that we weren't talking about targets, but about our fellow man. Suddenly it felt like I had taken the wrong path.

Truth is I shouldn't have brought her. Shouldn't have promised I'd kill Raoul. Not only Giselle, I had also promised Simmone. Promised I would save her.

Yes, I did see revenge as a kind of wild justice, but what the hell was I thinking!

CHAPTER 29

When an army feeds its horses with grain and kills its cattle for food ...then you know they are determined to fight to the death.

Sun Tzü, *The Art of War*, 512 BC

For months I'd looked forward to the Highland Games at Fergus, a small town in the heartland of Southern Ontario. During the games it's a town that swells with tourists and the sound of massed pipe-bands in a glorious stirring of nostalgia. It wasn't home, but if I half closed my eyes it almost felt as though it could be.

We left the Blazer on Saint Andrew Street and joined the street parade — walking in the wake of a band in a line of swirling kilts and stamping feet, with a militant clash of brass and rousing pipes.

Jennifer had refused to wear the kilt I'd bought her, last year in Toronto. Giselle wore a sensible skirt with flat shoes and of course she looked sensational. Jenny sported high heels and a rather flimsy dress, the sort of dress that clings to the body and flutters in the breeze. The sort of dress only teenagers with well-toned bodies can get away with. I was dressed in black.

People on the sidewalks smiled at us as we walked to the grounds. Though I suspect in our small family it was only me who felt their chest swell with strong ethnic pride at the sight and sound of those highland bands.

At times of great stress, the stress I felt at our predicament, anticipating this day was to return ourselves to what we took as normal. By the time I'd dragged Giselle from one more booth of knitwear and Jenny from the Celtic jewellery it was time to meet Guy. We found him waiting while the arena filled with a mass of colour and sound as the bands assembled. Guy was bored, indifferent to the stirring sounds of yore.

Guy didn't understand the isolation, the loneliness, the siege mentality of being an immigrant far from his Scottish home. He didn't have the need that I had, to reach out and touch the past. He looked so damn French with a red bandana on his brow. He had a white T-shirt and denim jeans, like a misplaced cast member from Grease: sort of an ageing John Travolta.

"Quaint," he said to me, indicating the swirling bands with a nod.

The Black Watch marched in last and halted with a sudden shock of silence.

"You know," I said, "The Black Watch got their name from being first on the field against the French at Fontenoy, fighting to the death."

"Not into this tartan kick of yours, Duncan."

"I enjoy our wealth of history. Thought you might as well."

"In Quebec I was brought up on *Roman de la Rose*. Chivalrous knights, damsels in distress, that sort of thing."

"Ah, I'd forgotten the Gauls were Celtic too."

"King Arthur, Tristan and Iseult. Now *those* are great stories."

"Hmmm," I said distracted, wondering what he meant, then in a moment of insight I realised they were all stories of romantic conquest, in a tradition from long before the birth of Christ. Stories of younger men usurping older warriors — seducing their wives.

The quarrelsome Scots have a fierce reputation. They've upheld this distinction from the days when blue-painted Picts attacked Germanic tribes of Angles, Danes, Saxons and Jutes who'd colonised Britain. Romans had built the huge earthen works of Antonine's Wall across the entire country — in a failed attempt to hold the wild Celtic tribes at bay. Hadrian followed with a stone wall further south, in another vain attempt to contain the marauding Celts. Their fierce reputation continued for thousands of years: Crimea, Boer war, the Great War, World War Two , Korean war, Malaysia, Northern Ireland and now the Falklands.

As a lad, I had read Scottish tales of entire villages battling to the death with double-handed claymores and hand axes over disputed ownership of a ten-acre field. My ancestors on my mother's side, the Fraser clan were fanatical fighters. And of course those tales of Robert the Bruce and the rebel William Wallace, *Braveheart*, who led the Scots in revolt. Perhaps it was scarce resources that drove the fiercely independent clans of proud, incendiary Celts.

Where I stood in the heart of Fergus the mass tartan of the bands left the arena and athletics began. The games are a tradition among the Scots: to select the finest runners as messengers, the strongest for the Chieftain's bodyguard and comely dancing maidens for his bed.

A gunshot punctuated the clamour and we all turned to watch a field of men stride out at the start of the mile. They were thin, their muscles standing out in cords as they swept past like racehorses. Jenny was entranced. Two men broke away on the third lap, running neck and neck in front until the cracking pace broke one and the pack ran him down in the straight. A red-haired boy lean and tough as a greyhound, held on till the tape majestically alone.

The dancers were Jenny's age — teenagers, athletic and attractive, as girls are in the bloom of youth. They looked combative in the stamp of the highland dance. My mind returned to my resolve to hunt Raoul. Jenny went off with her school friends among the dancers. She gathered them with smiles and saw us off with a wave of farewell.

Giselle had brought a picnic lunch in a basket. She picked a spot for our assignation deep among the trees. As we walked into the woods I noticed how quietly Guy moved, as if he was back in the jungle. Aware of those around him, carrying nothing that flashed or jangled, no coins in his pockets to make a noise. He was soft on his feet as if a part of him remained forever in Vietnam.

We sipped French-onion soup with homemade crusty bread. Giselle brought the soup in a thermos and fruit salad in another. She had even brought a jar of clotted cream for the dessert. Giselle hadn't brought coffee, as she knew how much I liked a fresh brew and detested second-rate versions of my addiction. A couple of beers for us and of course a Perrier of pure spring-water for Giselle.

On the checkered picnic rug, I unrolled a map of Western Canada, a map I'd brought with me from the truck. I pointed to a tiny spot on the large-scale map of British Columbia. "They're going to Spatsizi Plateau in the north west, flying first to Calgary, then Banff and on to Prince George. From there to Gladys Lake in a float plane."

"How does McGowan know this?" Guy asked.

Never had I dared tell him about Simmone. I told them again that McGowan had told me. Guy accepted that.

"The Brits want Raoul for arms dealing. I gather *Campagine Fabrique* is selling guns to the IRA. Maybe McGowan has their phones tapped."

"*Mon ami*," Guy said, stroking his stubble, "perhaps he has a spy."

"It's possible," I said, feeling like I was found out. Then carried on: "Banff's the centre of the grizzly population. They'll have to go Gladys Lake to hunt them though. Bears are a protected species within the park."

Giselle looked worried. I fished the photo out of my shirt and flicked it on the map.

"That's Raoul Kelemann, the one in a safari suit."

We leaned forward to stare at his square Germanic face. The image was clear enough to see a receding hairline. He looked like an older Harrison Ford.

"These photos from McGowan too, I take it?" Guy said. "Does he know we're going after Raoul?"

"No, of course not. No one knows."

"Then why tell you of their itinerary?"

A simple question, but it caught me flat footed. I cast around for a convincing answer.

"To let us know that we'll be safe for the time Raoul is away."

Guy grunted. Giselle nodded. They seemed satisfied.

"They're going down this branch of the Stikine," I said, pointing again at a squiggle on the map, "We're going to need a canoe."

"Well, this *is* the right occasion," Guy said. "We'll take mine."

Before I could protest, a family appeared beside us and proceeded with unpacking their picnic basket. We fell silent and continued our soup and bread. The soup was still hot and the bread had that doughy taste you get with homemade. The family was led by a strawberry-blonde with a brown-haired preteen at foot. They wore tartan sashes and wide smiles acknowledging the festivities. The father was dark, perhaps Italian. The girls were plump and didn't look like they were his. He had the strangest face, with baggy cheeks as if he was a sax player. He looked over and reminded me of a bloodhound. I folded the map while we waited for them to go on a safe distance, out of earshot.

"We can take a plane, but that's expensive," I said. "Or take the train and hire a four-track from Jasper. But considering everything it's best to drive all the way."

"No question, we'll take the plane," said Guy.

"Cheaper to drive the Blazer."

"Might be cheaper Duncan, but it's a hell of a long way."

"It's not only the money. It's carrying the damn guns. We don't want records. A plane's too easy to ID us afterwards as hunters in that area."

"And the truck won't?"

"No, there'll be heaps of Chevy's on the Trans-Canada. And at least half of 'em will have canoes strapped to the roof. We'll be anonymous."

"I don't like it. Can't afford the endless time on the road."

"*You* can fly if you want Guy. I'm taking the truck."

"*We*," said Giselle with conviction, "*We* are all going in the truck."

"*Merci*. I hope that heap of junk is up to it."

CHAPTER 30

The art of war is a matter of life or death, a road either to safety or to ruin ...

Sun Tzü, *The Art of War*, 512 BC

Spring came early that year. Snow melted in several days of unseasonable warmth. Green tufts of grass showed through in bare patches and the land acquired that peculiar spongy feel when sodden by groundwater underneath. Ditches along the fields and driveway flooded with the run off, then mud formed in deep wallows at the entrance to the barn.

I'd had the mares under lights in their stalls for three weeks, an artificial lengthening of days that switch the mare's hormones to the spring breeding cycle. It's important to have early foals because two-year-old racing is so lucrative. Since horses are arbitrarily accorded their birthday on January first, it's critical to get it right. Buyers don't spend big on the runts of the litter.

Now that I had no stallion, I injected *Shandy* with testosterone. So *Shandy* became hypersexual, full of raging hormones, a testosterone bomb, primed and ready to explode, just like a teenager. Then I'd tease the mares each morning as I led them past his stall.

When I led an empty mare past *Shandy* he whinnied and arched his neck far over the stall door to touch noses, then sniffed down her back right to her rump as I led her past. She consented by swinging her quarters towards him and lifting her tail. *Shandy* raised his head and rolled his upper lip up in the Flehmen gesture of stallions high on a mare's scent. A mare's pheromones signal her fertile oestrous. *Shandy* screamed in rage when I took the mare away.

I'd used this trick with him before — before I'd got *Alaric*. *Shandy* was difficult for Jennifer to ride in the spring because of it. His frustration and intense interest in the mares made him tough to train. The upside was that he did put on heaps of muscle, ran like a hare and his coat gleamed like a new penny. He looked splendid.

Jennifer planned to enter him for a series of Horse Trials around Caledon and a Three-Day-Event at the Ridgeway in the fall. She had a lot of work to do with the horse for in those days it included steeplechase and roads and tracks as well as the cross-country. Jenny planned to take him to Darien Ford's for a clinic in dressage and jumping as soon as the school term ended. In the morass of my finances, Jenny's extensive plans for her horse caused me yet another dose of anxiety.

The days went by in a flurry, a constant round of feeding, watering and mucking out. *Shandy* teased the mares and we groomed yearlings for the sales. We lunged them every other day in the round yard, so they'd look like racehorses when they went to auction, that alone took hours of patient work.

The vet called by when I needed mares palpated, to detect their ovulation. I trailered mares to Quentin Nash's place, Hindmarsh's, or Winfield's Farm, depending on which stallion owners booked. I watched the pregnant mares, for signs of foaling. Mares are secretive, they often foal at night, they feel safer after dark. After predators have fed.

That evening I called our neighbour Kirsten again and asked for her help at weekends. Jennifer helped too after school. Giselle was a willing, though not an enthusiastic helper in this hectic time. She needed slow weekends to recover from her hectic weeks in the corporate jungle. Throughout the short days and those long, long nights I continued to fret about Raoul's threats and the choice I had to make. I felt more like a harbinger of death than a righteous avenger.

Jennifer left on the Monday. Giselle drove Jenny to the airport and Kirsten came over to the farm. She pulled up in that big Ford pickup of hers and climbed down with her ponytail bobbing like a chestnut filly. So tiny, and with that freckled complexion, it was easy to mistake her for a child, until you saw that intense look in her eye. I showed her what feed and work I was giving the horses and she nodded. My anxiety about leaving my horses dissipated. I focussed instead on the awful task ahead.

Another phone call from Simmone. Her voice flat, though no less urgent. I arranged to meet her the next day in Toronto. I met Simmone at the Michel Café on the first floor of the Eaton Centre. I sat for a moment at an outside table to look at her and revel in her delicate face framed by flames of auburn hair, though still mindful of McGowan's warning about Raoul having her watched. Her hair lay down her back like a russet waterfall. She wore a dress of the most vivid blue, a dress her fluid body was trying to escape. No nickers. I noticed that her left hand was bandaged — even that looked chic.

Simmone was chatting with a young thing in her late teens with brown shiny hair. Simmone's eyes darted around like a deer. She checked the entrance whenever anyone walked in, then turned away. Her companion chattered away with her hands and arms, expressive in the French way. I knew she was French from the way she moved her hands and tossed her head, even from this distance, outside on the terrace.

Men in the café noticed them. Who wouldn't. An older guy in his fifties, grey hair, black casuals, sat facing their table. He was fascinated by them, staring unashamed as he ate foccacio. I ruled him out as a watcher — he never once glanced at the door.

A young guy in a suit sat a few tables away and leaned back against the wall, nursing a coffee. He looked around at the door as if waiting for someone. He took another lingering look at Simmone. Nah. A bodyguard's not going to sit where he has to turn around to see the entrance.

Has to be that middle-aged guy in the navy skivvy facing the door and taking no notice of Simmone or the girl. Just when I decided he was Raoul's spy, a young lady entered. He stood to embrace her, they swept out of the café in a bubble of chatter and a clatter of high heels.

To hell with McGowan. I had no idea who was watching her and I wasn't about to find out by sitting here. I stood up and went inside. Simmone spotted me immediately, leaned forward and said something to the girl. She swung around to appraise me as I walked to their table — a weather-beaten Joe in jeans and crumpled shirt among the silken set. Simmone rose and kissed me chastely on the cheek. It was as clear to me as if she had put her hands on my chest and held me at arm's length.

"Careful," she breathed in my ear.

Careful — careful of what?

"Chantel," she said, introducing me to the young woman.

Ah, Raoul's watcher. Chantel had that androgynous look of a preteen model. Her treacherous hormones were just emerging, but they already signalled a vibrant fertility. I could almost feel the weight of those swollen breasts peeping from her blouse. She leant forward and extended her hand to me, in a way that suggested I kiss it. I shook her hand instead.

Simmone looked delectable in that exotic dress, though she was much thinner than when I'd last seen her, a touch this side of anorexic, with an anxious haunted edge that I found unsettling. Despite her beauty, she looked ill. I was about to ask her about her bandaged hand when there was a sudden crash from the kitchen. Simmone's body spasmed in response to the sound. The muscles along her jaw line a knotted cord with her massive effort of control.

"Oh," she said catching herself a hair this side of panic. I sat down and exchanged pleasantries. A waiter came and I ordered cappuccino. Chantel got up to leave.

"Have to go shopping. I'll leave you guys alone."

"See you here at eleven," Simmone said, Chantel nodded.

I flicked a glance at my watch — a half-hour. What did Simmone have in mind?

"You okay?" I said, leaning towards her.

"No Duncan, I'm not."

She looked for a moment as if she'd cry. Her face changed into her stone face, a mask against the world. Something in her mind must have kicked into gear for she looked at me as if I were a new and dangerous species she had never encountered, a look I'd never seen before — it unnerved me.

"I'm staying with Raoul."

"What! After all this — you're *staying* with him?"

"It's over Duncan. I can't be with you. I can't leave him."

"*Can't leave him!* The last time we spoke you couldn't *stay* with him."

"I needed you then. Needed you to protect me."

"Simmone, for Chrissake, how can I protect you a thousand miles away?"

"Precisely. You weren't there. You'll never be there. I know that now."

Reaching across the table, I took both her hands and looked into those lovely feline, almost almond eyes.

"I loved you then Simmone, and I love you now."

"No Duncan. Love's easy to say. It's what you do that counts — you weren't there. You can't protect me from Raoul. He will always be stronger, you'll never destroy him — it's not in you. He will kill you."

"WHAT THE F..." I shouted at her. Diners turned and focused on us.

"Goddamnit Simmone, he'll destroy you before he's finished."

"HE ALREADY HAS, YOU STUPID FUCK." She screamed this at me as she stood up. Remained standing by the table, trembling with rage, radiating hurt. A rage that frightened me. "YOU DON'T KNOW WHAT HE's LIKE. HE'LL GET YOUR WIFE, HE'LL GET YOUR DAUGHTER, THEN HE'LL FUCKIN' KILL YOU."

Chantel was coming to us from outside on the terrace, a hand to her mouth and a frown across her brow, she moved towards the door to intercept us. I eyed Simmone across the table, not knowing what to say, not wanting her to go either. I wanted something from her. Chantel took her hand and gave her a tug.

"HAVE A GOOD LIFE," she shouted, with just the right touch of irony, it would have been masterful, except it was a thousand decibels too loud.

All I could manage was, "*Jesus!*"

At least I'd followed McGowan's advice. I'd taken the first step to redemption, even if it had been thrust upon me. At that point I remembered Mungo's appeal for me to recruit her. Wanting to maintain the bond between us, however tentative, I fished in my shirt for the card, and slid it across the table to within her grasp.

"Here call this number: there's spooks who will help, if you get into real trouble."

She looked at it then I saw again that ugly side of her. She tore it in half and threw the card in my face. At that moment the waiter brought me the cappuccino I'd ordered. I took the frothing cup, set it down with shaking hands and watched her finely-muscled back as she left arm in arm with Chantel.

Tomorrow was another day.

CHAPTER 31

At first exhibit the coyness of a maiden until the enemy gives you an opening; then be the running hare…

Sun Tzü, *The Art of War*, 512 BC

It was a killing moon. The sort of cloud-free full moon that men chose in times past, to hunt at night. We picked up Guy, stowed packs and weapons in the Blazer and tied his birch-bark canoe to the roof-rack, then covered it with a tarp. We stayed for another of Guy's instant coffees, dry toast and bacon that we ate standing near the stove. I had another panicky crisis of conscience as we headed up Highway Six towards Owen Sound. We'd swing north to join 400, then take the Trans-Canada for our trip west. The radio, a motley selection of tapes, a thermos of *my* coffee with a slab of *brie* and crackers kept us going.

Guy monopolised the conversation at first, talking mostly to Giselle about things of no consequence, speaking over the plaintive sounds of Judy Collins. We soon lapsed into silence, obliterating the six-pack of Molson's in quick time. The Blazer droned on in its motor's roar and vibrating rhythm, while my mind drifted back to Jennifer, horses, always horses, and the farm. I can tell you we all had more than a touch of cabin fever by the time we stopped.

We stayed in Sudbury that night, a post-apocalyptic vision of service stations and fast-food joints. The town is built on the rim of low hills within an asteroid crater, now desolate from heavy-metal pollution of the mines. The mines here extracted nickel from the ground, a mineral that came to us from outer space. Mines spewed certain death to vegetation and uncertain damaged health for the rest of us.

Giselle and I took a room at the Canadiana on Lorne Street with its glassed in porch that walled it off from the fumes. The black and white sign was streaked with a brown veneer of acid rain. We followed Guy's advice: showering without soap and brushing sans toothpaste. Giselle left her perfumed toiletries at home.

Late that night I sat up dry firing the Glock, clicking the trigger while keeping the sights aligned to build in the shooting reflexes for what we had to do. I was now becoming obsessed with killing Raoul. The horses, the farm, even Jennifer faded into the background. Giselle and I slept chastely. Though *sleep* is hardly what I did, more like a meticulous examination of the decrepit ceiling.

Guy slept in the truck.

It took us two more days and a night of hard driving to reach the provincial border. We emerged from the endless forests and lakes of Ontario to the empty prairies of Manitoba, then to that unloved and eerie city of Winnipeg, a city built on the junction of two rivers — trade routes of Indians and *voyageurs* in times past. Flat plains stretched forward to the horizon, broken only by the incongruous skyline.

Downtown we noticed shops were boarded up. Here people live in the suburbs, with their shopping malls, in separate communities. The burbs housed people leading isolated lives. The city was deserted, with no one on the street, except for ferals at night — this city more than most. It disappointed me to see Canada engulfed in the ubiquitous underbelly of America. From the boarded shop fronts, the disenfranchised were a bit stroppy around here — if not downright hostile.

Since we were here in this neck of the woods, I wanted to see the Métis people who arose from Cree and Assiniboine women fraternising with French *voyageurs*, those intrepid men who came in search of furs — 200 years ago. Métis soon occupied the area, living off the vast buffalo herds. They saw themselves as distinct from whites and Indians — with their own identity.

Louis Riel led the Métis in rebellion against Canada in 1869 to protest the sale to settlers of their land. In a diplomatic blunder Métis were not included in treaty talks with the Indians. They were ignored for they saw themselves as neither French nor Indian, certainly not English. And they got angry. Riel and his rebels took Upper Fort Gary by surprise, slaughtering soldiers there. Then the government took the fort back with a mere handful of Mounties.

Canada granted Métis land in Manitoba as a peace offering. What they did not do is forgive Riel the traitor. Things worsened when Riel was elected by Métis votes to the House of Commons, but from this he was barred because of his mutiny. So Louis Riel spent the next sixteen years on the run. The Canadian Government never pursued him. He became a victim of his own paranoia. There were rumours he ended up in a Montana asylum, because of these delusions.

Dissatisfied, Métis mounted another insurrection in 1885. This too was led by Louis Riel. The upshot of this rebellion was that the Métis were overcome in battle and surrendered. Riel was convicted and hung as a traitor. The Métis still harbour resentment to this day.

When we spotted Café Métis on Portage Street, I insisted we stop. Inside the cavernous interior we found a booth to sit while our eyes adjusted to the dim light. A dark eyed waitress spoke to us in a French that even Guy couldn't grasp. When the waitress stepped back looking perplexed, a giant came over. Fully six and a half feet tall, he leant over the table, looked me in the eye and asked in slurred accented English if we had a problem. The guy must have weighed 150 kilos, his arms were tree trunks and his breath stank of garlic. His lank black hair and coffee skin gave him the quaintly feral look of Polynesia. He looked like Riel must have done long ago — a trifle threatening.

"Hey, no problem."

I leaned back and lifted my palms off the table in supplication.

Guy stared at him and put his hands on the tabletop, flashing his *TagHeuer,* ready to rise. Guy's a Doberman — oblivious to size, with no thought of self-preservation. I could almost see the hackles rise on his neck and hear a growl emanate from deep in his throat. Giselle stared at him in awe. I tried to warn Guy with a shake of my head. He didn't look at me. The big fellow ignored him.

"Waitress doesn't understand your English," the giant said.

"Ah, right," I said, wondering what was coming next.

"What do you want?" he growled, and when I leaned forward he said, "Perhaps I can translate." And so he did.

Guy and Giselle shared the driving with me while one of us slept in the back seat as the Blazer charged down the highway. We'd bought a tape of Carly Simon and sang along to *We have no Secrets*. I don't know why we liked that track so much. Guy and Giselle listened with as much intensity as I did. Perhaps it resonated because I had so many secrets myself. Secrets that were tearing me apart. When the song played, my mind turned to Giselle and to what was going on in her head. What had really happened? What scars had formed in her mind? And where the hell was Raoul right now?

As we drove across the emptiness, I was struck by the lack of livestock. The plains looked dead, except for acres of still-green wheat, without fences to hinder the huge combine-harvesters of Agribusiness. Rarely did I see cattle, then just one or two, and there were no bison. Not one.

Herds of Bison had once fed on the great plains of North America, from the Great Slave Lake in the north right down through Texas, west to the Rockies and east to the Atlantic. Plains Indians killed them, ate their meat and used their hides for clothes, bedding and tepees. Even buffalo chips were used for the fire on these treeless plains. I had read accounts of travellers who saw herds of Bison back in 1874.

They rode the prairies when the beasts blackened the land to the horizon.

As they rode forward the bison parted like a vast sea, surrounded the rider, closed up behind, keeping about a half-mile distant at all times ... as far as the eye could reach, south, east and west there was a solid mass of buffalo — thousands upon thousands — steadily moving north as winter retreated.

"Where are the bison?" I asked of the proprietor at a decrepit roadside gas station, a greasy redneck in overalls. He said a rancher close by had four. One had a calf this spring. Four today after some hundred years after they teemed across the plains in fifty millions!

Hunters first came here 12,000 years ago. Men followed the herds through their seasonal migrations. When the last Ice Age ended and the climate warmed, herds migrated northeast out of Asia, grazing the tundra grass into the heartland of the Americas. Men trailed the great herds across the Bering land bridge. Then with the generations, buffalo wandered south in grasslands between the massive glaciers that covered this land.

Indians stalked the herd — trailing them like wolves, covering themselves in wolf pelts to get close, for bison are unafraid of wolves, their constant companions, doctors of the herd — removing the sick and the lame. Men ambushed bison in ravines, or stampeded them over cliffs at places like *Head Smashed In Buffalo Jump*. After a massive kill they cut meat into strips, pounding in fats, currants and herbs, then dried it in the sun — *pemmican* for the winter. Winters are cold in America.

We were wolves, tracking Raoul to his lair. Stalking him to a secret place, a place to become our killing field in a northern forest. Giselle and I were amateurs. I hoped we would be up to the task. I worried that we would fail.

To Giselle's dismay our truck was by now littered with the remains of fast food, hamburgers, fries and chocolate were our major food groups on this trip. We had a clean up here, to get rid of the mess. Still no matter how much we scrubbed the cab reeked of MacDonald's, the scent of rancid fat and dead meat, with more than a hint of body odour.

We took the Trans-Canada again, to Regina and then on to Calgary. I couldn't stop thinking about Raoul and my fears for Jennifer. The Blazer roared on into the night, an angry malevolent spirit, stopping just long enough to feed at bowsers along the way and fuel the occupants with traditional Canadian fare: burgers, cokes and fries.

CHAPTER 32

...the skilful general conducts his army as though he were leading a single man by the hand.

Sun Tzü, *The Art of War*, 512 BC

We camped alongside the highway, Giselle and I in back of the Blazer, Guy in his cammo tent. We hit Calgary in the morning, another city of suburbs that stretched for miles, granite canyons with no heart. When we stopped for coffee, I found a phone and called Simmone at the Banff Springs Hotel. She didn't answer, which made me wonder if she would thwart us. Would she tip off the police, now that she was back with Raoul? I wondered what had happened to her. What was happening to our spy.

On the way we traversed Kananaskis country across foothills with an exhilarating panorama of the Rockies. The high mountains stretched on the horizon for as far as we could see. The sinister role of our mission sobered me and destroyed this otherwise brilliant moment. I said nothing, drove in a moody silence watching the white line, while Giselle exclaimed at the beauty of it all.

Banff is a tourist town. A ring of mountains surrounds it, beautiful, menacing and jagged mountains, like Indians circling a wagon train. A monolith of granite, Mount Rundle towers over this village.

Giselle thumbed through our *Guide to the Lonely Planet* and we settled on the Banff Hostel on Tunnel Mountain, a place with a laundromat, where we washed the clothes we'd slept in. After stopping by the supermarket on Elk Street, Giselle cooked us a meal of real food in the hostel kitchen: steak, mashed potatoes, carrots and peas, instead of those accursed burgers.

That morning I went for a walk and I couldn't stop thinking of death. A migraine frayed the edges of my mind; it enlarged as I walked, like a fast-growing cancer. I called Gail in London from a phone box. I had to know that Jenny was all right. I let the phone ring until it was exhausted. No answer. I tried to call Simmone — same thing.

I wandered in a kind of frantic desperation, trying to justify to myself that what we were doing was a necessity, necessary for Giselle, for Jennifer and for me. I wanted to make it right. What I didn't know then, what I refused to face for long afterward, was that it never would be right again — not ever.

I pictured Giselle in my mind. She is standing in a doorway, smiling as the last of her clothes fall with a rustle to the floor. She steps forward extending her arms towards me. I push against her, feeling her naked body white-hot through my shirt ... The picture fades like the end of a foreign film.

Back at the hostel, I found Giselle and Guy enjoying a late breakfast of bacon and eggs among the backpackers in a crowded cafeteria. They looked up when I came to their table. There I told them I'd phoned McGowan and we'd gone over Raoul's plans. We all looked again at Raoul's photo that I produced, for we wanted to be sure of our man.

"Good work," Guy said, "The Brits must be sticking to him like gum on shoes. Jeez," he said, as the thought struck him, "hope we don't meet his watchers."

What I didn't tell him was that *we* were Raoul's watchers.

"Doubt it," I said, "why would they worry about him out there in the wilderness?"

That night we met a young fellow in the hostel kitchen. He'd spoken to Giselle in Swedish, when he'd seen her white-blonde hair. He had a strange tale to tell.

"Du ar Svensk?" he'd said.

"Nay. Man yah can prater Svensk."

Giselle spoke Swedish from when she lived there as a child and Sven was relieved to find someone who spoke his language. Later we saw him again sitting alone in the communal lounge. Giselle spoke to him and agreed we'd give him a lift to the railway in Jasper on the morrow.

Sven began to talk as we drove the majestic Icefields Parkway, past Lake Louise, then on to Jasper. He'd been in Canada a week. Yesterday he'd gone for a walk alone in the woods. Like many Swedes he was emotionally aloof, self-contained, he hadn't told anyone where he was going. I had trouble focusing on his tale. My mind kept coming back to Raoul and his danger to Jenny. I thought then of *Red* and the broodmares in Kirsten's care. Were they all right?

Sven had been climbing on a trail around a mountain, on his left a sheer rock wall, on his right a drop to a creek far below. As Sven rounded a bend he came face to face with a grizzly heading down hill. He remembered thinking that if the bear wanted to eat him there wasn't a damn thing he could do about it. Nothing had prepared him for this.

The bear charged and Sven had nowhere to go. His mind froze. Then Sven's body responded at the last minute and, suddenly galvanised, he leapt over the edge. A claw tore off the lobe of his ear as the bear went to swipe him, and its paw hit his pack, breaking it clean off at the straps. We all looked at his ear, now encased by a field dressing. Sven stopped rolling, picked himself up and spotted a tall pine on the steep slope and went for it. He'd read that Grizzlies couldn't climb. The way Sven tells it the bear hadn't read the same book. It zoomed up the tree like an axeman in a tree-felling competition.

As Sven hung onto the treetop, the bear stayed lower, not trusting the treetop to take its weight. Still the giant reached for Sven's boots. Sven pulled his legs up and held on, only a few centimetres away from those claws. The bear tried jumping up a bit, a couple of times, then got distracted and after a long while it climbed down. And there it hunkered down at the base of the tree.

Sven wasn't distracted. He was focused. His attention was absolutely riveted on that bear. He stayed in the tree a full hour *after* the bear had trundled away in the woods. When Sven did decide to climb down, his limbs refused to move. His body simply refused to cooperate and obey the directions of his mind. It seemed that the trauma had paralysed him. He stayed in the top of that tree for another hour. When his legs and arms started to cramp in painful fixed contractions he surveyed the problem again. Only then did he recall a ranger's cabin he'd seen, some way down the trail. If only he could get back there, he thought that he'd be safe.

When his foot reached the ground he heard a twig snap. Not daring to look back, he ran in panic, for he could hear the bear plunging down the trail after him. He could already hear the mad panting breath of the bear *gaining* on him. At last Sven saw the log house and without pause tore into the cabin, boots slamming on the floorboards. He swung around to shut the door. *What door?* There was no door! No glass in the windows either. He looked behind him, almost fainting with relief to see — nothing there, nothing chasing him but his own fear.

Sven climbed up through a window onto the roof and stayed there. As the shadows lengthened, he worried more and more about spending the night here alone on the roof, where any bear could get him if it happened to scent his presence. So while it was still light Sven made a break for it and ran back down the mountain, eight kilometres flat out to the hostel. He'd paid the price of his rugged individualism. What you got with that was a side order of loneliness, with no friends, no lovers, no backup, no support, no help from strangers and no kind thoughts from passers by.

Sven had reached the end of his emotional resources. He desperately wanted out: out of the wilderness, out of Canada, out of the wild, wild west. He was going home to Burgsvik, among the well-tilled fields and broad-leafed berried woods, among the blond-haired and civilised pagans of Gota; he was going home to the isle of Gotland alone on the cold Baltic sea.

We left him standing there, a lonely figure with his monstrous pack and its broken straps at his feet, on the station platform at Jasper. We rounded up the Blazer, mounted the worn-out beast and headed into the mountains at a hand gallop, on Highway Sixteen towards Prince Rupert.

> Sven had reminded us of a harsh reality,
> here in this wilderness we are alone.
> And alone is a dangerous place.

CHAPTER 33

... tactics and the fundamental laws of human nature; these are the things that must be studied [in warfare].

Sun Tzü, *The Art of War*, 512 BC

It took another two days of hard driving to reach Gladys Lake in the Spatsizi Plateau Wilderness. The last on Route 37, a gravel road turnoff from a long way out of Prince George. Giselle and I had reached an uneasy truce and Guy had fallen silent. He didn't need people in the same way we did — not even friends. The scenery went by in a blur of firs bordering a thousand swamps and lakes. We saw elk, goats, bighorn sheep and a moose once in the waters of a pristine lake, feeding on the fresh new shoots of reeds. Once at dusk we saw a wolf dash across the road in our headlights. No bears.

The engine poured out a throaty roar, a sound that changed pitch only when logging trucks approached and I slowed. Giselle and Guy put their hands on the glass to dampen the vibration and prevent the windshield cracking from the flying stones. The tarp stretched over the canoe made ominous noises when gravel kicked up from the trucks.

The lake was magnificent. Firs crowded the shore on all sides. Tree covered islands were dotted across the lake as if strewn by some giant's hand. There was no wind and the water was leaden. No one in sight, no cars, no boats, no sign of civilisation. When we stopped the primal smell of the forest, its decay and ancient firs washed over us. Outside the truck we felt a chill.

Guy and I unpacked the canoe, relieved it was undamaged. Guy insisted on spray painting our weapons in black, so there'd be no flash from the sun. Even the stock got streaks and smudges of matt black. He was meticulous, I'll give him that. We left the bits to dry while we drove the Blazer further into the woods. Guy covered it with a net he'd brought, then added small leafy branches as camouflage, aware of the possibility of it being seen from the air.

We dressed in our new cammo gear and Giselle removed her pendant. I stowed our packs and with all aboard, we pushed off from shore. Giselle in the middle, dipping her paddle in black water, uncertain of the stroke. I was in the bow, with Guy at the back, steering with each muscled stroke of his blade. He wore his bandana, this time a black band across his brow. The packs lay with our weapons wrapped in plastic on the floor of the craft. We left our tents behind.

The birch canoe felt light, like a leaf on water. A flight of loons swept low and landed, their webbed feet splayed out, braking on the surface — splashing foam.

We paddled for about an hour along the shore to the river, feeling for the rhythm, settling into it, enjoying the physical effort after being so long in the truck.

"You know," Guy said, "I'll bet they have an outboard."

"Damnit! We never thought of that before. Won't be able to keep up if they do."

"Might be an advantage," Guy said, "they won't hear *us* over their motor. And they won't get too far ahead."

He'd just said it when we heard the drone of a plane coming in from a way off. We paddled like hell for the shore, scrambling to pull the canoe up, after we flung out our gear. We lay half covered in brush when a floatplane skimmed the treetops with a roar and landed with a long plume of spray in the lake. The lurid yellow plane taxied in a hiccupy, staccato rhythm, then turned behind a headland, out of sight.

"What now?"

"Wait to see what we're up against," said Guy.

He fished for a tube in his pack, then applied cream to his face in dark streaks, covering every square inch he could. No magic colours, no ritual patterns, just streaks of dark green to cover skin.

"It'll take off the shine," he said, as he passed it to Giselle. "Do your forearms, inside wrists, neck, ears, cleavage and hair too. You don't want anything to reflect light in the gloom of these woods."

He helped by applying the cream to our hair until we looked disgustingly dirty, beyond all recognition. Guy reached into his pack again and fetched three woollen watch caps of dirty green. We thought he'd finished until he broke small twigs from a bush and stuck them all over his gear, with a heap in the wool of his cap. We did the same. We looked like Dad's Army, but we blended with the bush.

"Now whack the mozzie repellent on top of all that."

"Guy, is this really necessary..."

He cut me off with a scowl: "Hell yes," is all he said, then put his finger to his lips in that universal sign for hush. We lay there in the brush for an hour in excruciating silence. It's amazing how much noise there is in the woods: flies, a breeze through the trees, birdsong and vague rustlings in the bushes that could be anything at all.

We heard their boats first, putt-putting around the headland, before we saw them cruising along the far side. With their sighting our adrenaline kicked in like a wake up punch. I got binoculars on them and saw two hunters in each aluminium hull. A big fellow in the prow of the lead dinghy had a rifle slung in the crook of his arm.

Guy hefted his rifle and lined up the telescopic sight.

"No," I hissed, "not now."

"Just scoping," he shot back.

"Don't know who's there. Might've left a guy with the plane."

"Could you get Raoul from here?" Giselle said, thinking out loud.

"No," I said, "can't be absolutely sure it's him."

Giselle stared at them across the lake. Reality caught up with her. A reality that we were going to confront our enemy, track him down and kill him.

We waited until they were out of sight, then before we left, broke out the ammo and donning cotton gloves, loaded the guns and spare magazines. We didn't want our fingerprints on the brass.

Guy held the canoe while we boarded and he pushed off. This time we were conscious of the noise and strove to be quiet as we paddled close to shore, coasting around each turn. We were going with the current, it would be harder coming back.

The splash of paddles and the pull on our muscles settled into that hypnotic rhythm that paddler's know. We couldn't hear their motors, but we knew they were somewhere ahead. We had to spot them first. I scanned with glasses from time to time studying the river, straining for their sign. This time we were the ones armed and camouflaged. We were the hunters.

We were moving so quietly that on rounding one bend we saw a moose in the water, dead ahead. He stood frozen for a moment in surprise, then flicked a turn and headed for the woods at full stretch. He hurtled through the forest clearing fallen timber in his stride. That's when we heard the shot. A high-velocity crack that reverberated over the water. Another three shots in quick succession. A heavier gun.

"Military calibre," said Guy.

We looked at each other in surprise. Guy looked grim.

"Didn't expect that," he said.

We paddled to the next turn and coasted around the shoreline. Nothing. We went a kilometre down river before we spotted them on the far bank, maybe five or six hundred metres away. We pulled in to the shore screened by a thin growth of reeds.

They had shot a Moose, had already chopped the antlers and slung the trophy in their craft. They were on the far bank cutting meat from its rump, they'd leave the rest to rot. The men rested on the shore as we watched. They had a beer and a sandwich while we fed on beef jerky and granola bars.

We had taken precautions, we carried Gatorade and water in army canteens. Even in paradise you cannot drink from a stream without risking a nasty little parasite — giardia. I took a swig of Gatorade, and with my head back, spotted an eagle, high up with wings outstretched, circling on a thermal in the sky — sensing prey.

A flock of ravens, black as ink, reached a tall tree at their kill, wheeling and squawking as they landed. The big man drew a pistol and fired shots at the birds, which scattered squawking, jinking in mid air into malevolent shapes. Black feathers fluttered to the ground in slow motion.

The men pushed off and drifted in the current for a while before starting the outboards. We waited until they were out of sight, around the next bend, before we followed in our birch canoe.

Again their outboard motors left us way behind. We paddled slow, conserving our strength. Sweat formed on my face, mixed with the cammo paint and dripped a sodden green down my shirt to the crotch. The river narrowed as the day wore on, until the current itself was sufficient to carry us forward. Along the shore, we remained silent, scanning the way ahead.

We heard them before we saw them. Male voices, carrying over the murmur of water, as they yelled and whooped. We climbed ashore and covered the craft with brush, took our bearings from an odd-shaped boulder in the stream, then struck out on foot, picking up a deer trail that ran among the trees along the river. We walked in single file, watching where our feet went to avoid dead wood, almost forgetting to breathe.

We smelled the smoke of their fire before we saw them. The sound of a radio gave us direction. We stalked them. We paused downwind of their campsite. They were on our side of the river at a natural campsite, a glade with boulders against the stream and a beach where they'd hauled their boats. Their guide must have known this spot, and cached supplies here to be ready for them.

Their radio was beaming out a race meeting in a frenetic slew of names as the runners hit the straight. The big man was standing by a log, listening. As we watched, one man moved across to a tree and unhitched a rope that lowered their supplies. He fetched a bottle from it then hauled it up again, out of bear's reach.

They had pitched two *Gore-Tex* tents in jungle green. A ring of stones contained their fire, flickering around the roasting meat. The fire flared now and then, as the fat melted with a tantalising sizzle. The smell of roasting meat prodded our hunger. Our dry snacks, even the chocolate, seemed a hell of a poor substitute for roasted moose.

The large man leaned to turn the roast and I focused the glasses on him. I passed them to Giselle. She studied him, then scanned each man, staring at them for an age.

Guy scoped them with his rifle sight. He gestured for us to withdraw down the path we had come. As we turned Giselle's boot scraped against something on the ground. It sounded explosive in the silence. We froze. Nothing. The radio and the beer had dulled their hearing. We were the hunters. They were prey.

We walked all the way back to our canoe before we felt secure enough to speak. Even then we kept our voices down to a whisper, though the breeze was coming up river.

"Well," I asked Giselle, "did you recognise them?"

"It is Raoul from the photo. One looks like the man who ..." She couldn't quite get it out and paused, "... I cannot be certain."

"How to take out Raoul without the others coming after us?"

"Too risky," Guy said, "kill them all. No witnesses."

"Jesus Guy. We can't do that. Are you kidding? Murder four of them — fuck. We can end it with Raoul. Get Raoul for what he's done to Giselle."

"I am with Guy on this," Giselle said, "I want them all, for what they did to me. Like you said Duncan — it is war."

"Our war is against Raoul. If we kill them all, it makes us like them."

They thought of this in silence. Giselle looked at each of us in turn. Guy looked into the woods as if he heard something. I looked right back at her.

"Which of you is man enough to do it?" she said.

"Jesus Christ — Giselle!"

"We'll both do it," said Guy. "Sink their boats first, so they can't come after us. Then we hit Raoul."

"At night?" I said.

"At dawn." Guy said, "We'll hole their boats, then take out Raoul at first light."

"Sounds like a plan," I said. Giselle nodded.

We settled back against our packs in the brush, chewing a trail mix of almonds, sultanas and pecans with dark chocolate. I savoured the smooth, bitter taste of the nuts and chocolate, waiting for the light to fade.

What would Sun Tzü do?

That is what I thought as I slipped into my sleeping bag. Although it was spring, the cold reached in for us this far north. My gloved hands and booted feet were chilled. I gathered the swag around me. A line from Sun Tzü appeared like a refrain within my mind: *Attack your enemy when he is unprepared, appear where you are not expected.*

The warlord would surprise them. He would have killed the lot of them from ambush, warrior that he was. Guy was a warrior too, he was enjoying this — revelling in the hunt — while I was out of place and felt it. We had scouted the enemy. We had a plan. What could possibly go wrong? That thought and a deep anxiety over Jenny, over *Red* and the rest of my horses, kept me from sleep. I worried so much that I wished we'd never come. Wished that I'd not been so stupid as to bring Giselle with us.

Looking out at the old growth of massive firs and underbrush I listened to noises of night, wind in the high branches, the sounds of scurry as something made its way in the dark. Far off I heard the eerie call of loons. Nearby something in the bush cried out. An owl swept through the air and struck at something on the ground; carried it off, with the thing still screeching, dangling from its talons. An age-old dance of predator and prey.

"Let's go," Guy said close by. I woke up fast. It was still dark as I reached for my trail mix. "Don't," Guy said. "No eating for six hours before ops."

Guy had said it on reflex, a military lesson well learned. Six hours is the time to abstain from food or drink before surgery, so the victim doesn't drown in their own vomit under anaesthesia. You don't fart or burp either when you're stalking on an empty stomach. Guy had said it without thinking, but it did make sense. It reminded me of what we were letting ourselves in for. If any of us were shot, we'd lack all but the most rudimentary first aid. No back up. No chopper with Medics and their hi-tech gear coming in. That's the way it was out here in wilderness. No help at all if one of us were hit right here — today.

Giselle was standing, legs apart like an avenging Amazon in the moonlight. She had her shotgun in hand and a bandolier of cartridges slung across one shoulder. I didn't want her to go. I didn't want to go. I didn't want to leave the one safe place we had in the wilderness. Already it felt familiar. Out there anything could happen. And with what we were planning it would. The only thing we could count on was that something would go wrong.

"Stay here," I said to Giselle, "we need you to look after our canoe."

"I *am* coming," she said.

"No," said Guy, backing me for once on this. "*Merde*, we really do need you to mind our gear. There are bears."

"Leave the packs, take them with you, do whatever. I am coming."

"Damnit, we don't need you at the sharp end Giselle," Guy said. "We need you to stay here."

Guy surprised me. He'd given no previous indication she was here on sufferance. He'd welcomed her presence — until now.

"To hell with this," she said, "I'm going."

With that she turned and walked down the trail. Guy rushed to pass her, to take the lead. I picked up the Sako, the Glock tucked in my belt, bringing up the rear.

A waning moon was blocked by the canopy, so by the time we got to their camp our eyes were well adapted. Guy and I headed for the boats while Giselle positioned herself on the edge of the clearing, to cut them off if they came this way. I suggested in a whisper that she toss a stone to warn us if needs be, something we'd hear without drawing attention to herself.

We moved our way through the trees toward the boats. I followed Guy, moving slow, putting each foot down, testing it before letting it bear my full weight. Feeling our way among the brambles, stopping to listen now and then, trying not to make a sound.

We should have thought of it, we should have taken precautions, because it was exactly the wrong moment when it happened. We heard the scream first — a woman's scream, high pitched and terrified. Giselle's scream cut off with a BOOM in mid cry, a single massive shot. A smashing of branches, of something moving off through the forest, going away. A flash of light. A searching beam of light in the gloom.

"FREEZE."

We froze. A man's voice, loud and excited.

"A fuckin bear! Christ, look'it I found taking a leak."

Another voice now. "Get down ya fool. Bitch won't be alone."

They haven't seen us. We stay absolutely still, not wanting to give our position away. A man has Giselle around the neck. I turn my head, ever so slow, to see where Guy is. He's not there!

I see his dark form on the ground. He must have dropped at the shot. He's better at this stuff than me. He's trained for it. He's learned reflexes that work out here in the bush, from all those dangerous years ago in Nam. He turns his head and his eyes glint in the moonlight. He directs me to a tree with his gaze. A stout tree. I ease behind it and crouch without a sound.

From his prone position Guy can't see above the brush on the ground. Next thing I know he's on his feet, snaking his way up the bare trunk of a sapling. I see Guy's rifle come up in my peripheral vision.

"No," I hiss.

The man with Giselle turns towards us, perhaps he's heard. He crab walks to their fire, holding her in front like a shield.

"What the fuck?" someone says, "Who's there?"

"Down," was all I hear from Guy — just that one urgent command.

I drop. Surely they must have sensed movement, for as I hit the ground, guns go off and rounds smack into the woods above my head. The air explodes with the rattle of automatic weapons. I snatch another frantic look. The man frog-marches Giselle into to the firelight, a pistol at her head.

"*STEP OUT* OR I SHOOT THE BITCH," he booms.

Giselle is struggling, the man holds on. Guy is on his feet. Again he wraps himself around a sapling — a different one this time. I think for a moment he is going to parley. Guy says nothing. He just leans against the tree absolutely still, staring through his telescopic sight. A good scope gathers ambient light, it brightens your vision, makes it easier to see — easier to shoot.

As I watch Giselle ducks and twists in the grip of the man, then bites into his fleshy forearm. Guy fires in that instant, and in that instant the man's head explodes in a pink spray, like our melons. A searchlight reaches out and frames Guy against the night. He stands for a split second, in the beam, then an automatic opens up with a spray of sound that slams Guy on his back. He lies still and they keep firing until they all run dry.

In the lull, when her captor falls, Giselle scoops up her shotgun and runs. I give her covering fire, aiming at where I've last seen their flashes. Giselle hasn't fired, whether out of fear or discipline I don't know. Withholding that shot and scooting out of there has saved her; otherwise they'd have mowed her down. As it was they are more concerned with shots coming from me and they return fire.

Shots with long-reaching flashes from a heavy calibre come back at me. They are joined by the rattle and supersonic crack of a light automatic.

Their searchlight sweep resumes. I fire but the spotlight moves and they switch it off. I can't see them any more, but I can hear them moving relentlessly toward us, spread out through the underbrush.

With a sudden insight I pull the Glock and fire a clip on full-auto in a blast of reverberating sound. That scares the bejesus out of 'em. Now they hit the ground and hold their fire; they must think we have a machine gun.

I am in the dirt, crawling back to where I've last seen Giselle. I make it as far as the river before their rounds resume and reach the brush around me like a deadly sprinkler. The trail angles down towards the water and I can hear Giselle crashing through the underbrush on my right. At least I hope like hell it's her.

"*Giselle*," I call softly. Lead cracks through the trees ahead of me and I hit the dirt again. I wait until she reaches me, running hard, out of breath, the shotgun firm in her hands.

"Duncan," she says in relief, "where is Guy?"

"*Canoe*," I say to her, "*let's go, right now*," and we run.

"*Here*," I say when I see the boulder in the creek. Sweat pours off my face, and the panic builds. I fight to keep it down. We find our canoe, resurrect it and throw our packs in the bow. Giselle steadies the craft to step in.

"*Where is Guy?*" Giselle says again, perhaps sensing what is coming.

"He didn't make it, Giselle."

"*What?* What are you saying?"

"He's dead. They shot him."

We hear voices, then they fall silent. The men are wary of ambush, walking the trail in our direction, calling to each other — coming our way.

"Go, Go, Go."

We plunge our paddles in deep and pull with all our strength, with hardly any splash. We make it to the next headland along the shoreline, without a shot being fired, stroking with the ferocity of an Iroquois war party.

We keep a cracking pace with fear at our backs. I can see Giselle's muscles ahead of me contracting, straining in the moonlight as she strokes the water. The cammo dye is now streaked with sweat into intricate patterns on her hair and skin at the back of her neck. I knew we'd out pace them in the canoe; they are afoot.

"They'll go back to their boats and come after us," I say.

We stop, exhausted from paddling against the current, our paddles across the gunnels in front of us, sucking the air in ragged gulps. They will take us on the river with their outboards, so we'll have to hide. We hadn't a chance against military weapons if they catch us. We'll have to ditch the canoe, strike out in the bush and hide. I wave Giselle to the bank and we pull hard to shore, manoeuvring behind a fallen tree half in the water. Another tree looms over us, an inch from falling.

"Hide the canoe. That's our marker," I say pointing to the leaning tree. "They'll catch us for sure on the water."

We step in the murk, into cold water and throw our packs on shore. I scoop a couple of decent rocks inside, push down and slip water over the gunnels until it sinks.

Slipping my pack on and picking up the bow in one hand and my *Sako* in the other I step onto the game trail. "Let's get out of here."

After a brief trot we ignore the game trail and made our way deep in the bush, crossing fallen trees and crackling underbrush of brambles. It's slow going and we've only gone a short way when we hear the sound of their outboard. We stop and lie shivering under a fallen tree.

Giselle's mouth is now swollen from insect bites. Her hair has lost its sheen with mud and sweat. I've cut my cheek on a twig and my ungloved hand is scratched from when I crawled through the brush. I slip my gloves on again, against the chill and wipe the blood away. "What happened?" I ask.

"A bear. It was sooo big. I mean *huge*. I screamed, I know. Couldn't help myself."

"Must have come to their fresh meat. Should have thought of it. They grabbed you, huh?"

"He had a gun, Duncan. I didn't know he was there. I am *so* sorry."

We are both silent, thinking what her scream has caused.

"Guy's dead?" Giselle asks again.

"Yes, we're on our own — outnumbered and outgunned. They've got all the aces, a platoon of men, military weapons, outboard motors, and floatplanes, along with scads of supplies and ammo."

"What *happened* to Guy?"

"They picked him up with the searchlight, firing automatic rifles. He was lifted off his feet by the force of it, and slammed over on his back."

"We do not *know* for sure he *is* dead. How could we?"

"My God Giselle, I saw him: He was hit."

"What if he is *not* dead?"

"He didn't move. He was still on the ground."

"We cannot leave him. We have to know."

"I don't see how."

"You can go back."

"The hell I can. There's no way back. We've got to get *all* of them now."

Despite Giselle, I feel utterly alone. Guy has been our rock. The macho man we could count on. The only one with the training, personality and will to pull this off. What will happen to us now? We are a couple of duffers running around hiding in the bush. They are army trained, hell they could be battle-hardened veterans of the French Foreign Legion for all I know.

We gave up our recriminations because we ultimately lacked the energy to continue. Guy's death finally sinks in. We are too afraid to grieve. If we hadn't been so tired, if we hadn't stopped arguing, lying there staring out at the night, we wouldn't have noticed it. A movement along the bank. A darker shadow on the trail. I put my finger to her lips.

The man out there is at home in the forest, a creature of the woods. He is stopping every few minutes to listen, looking back now then, looking under the branches towards the river. Bobbing his torso every now and again, so no one can get a clear shot at him. I am hoping he can't see where water has dripped from our wet clothes, across the trail.

He looks down at the ground in front of him. *Shit*. The Glock is now empty and I need a spare magazine to snap into place. Can't do it now, the sound will give us away. Working the bolt for a fresh round in the rifle will also be noisy. The guy moves like a hunter; if he hears us, if he smells us, if he even senses our breathing, we're dead. I make a mental note to reload, if we ever make it out of here.

Now I become aware of the bow forming a nice comforting curve in my left hand — perfect. I'll take him with stealth, in silence, the others won't know. I move slow and as he straightens and walks further along the trail, I fit a broadhead to the string. When he stops, I draw the bow to its full extent locking my arm and back muscles against its tension, sighting along the arrow to his deep shadow.

In the moonlight I hold the razor point to the middle of his back. Waiting to loose it in that Zen moment of the hunter, the moment that feels right. The shadow moves his head to the front, and that is when I ease the arrow's release. The soft *whack* and sting of the bowstring against my forearm sounds horribly loud in the dark.

BLAM. A blast of his gun as he turns. Buckshot rips through the brush, off to our right. There's a tiny splash as my arrow hits the water. I remain absolutely still, resisting the urge to dive for cover. I suppose it isn't surprising that I missed, *but I am surprised*, I thought I had him cold.

With a CLACK-CLACK he works the pump action and reloads. He turns back to the river, and seeing nothing, moves on. Giselle has not made a sound. I think she's stopped breathing altogether.

A stab of light comes from their craft and flicks over us. Their boat chugs on through the murk upriver. The light goes out, and their craft is hailed by the man on the bank. They exchange something rapidly in French, something I don't catch. Now they are out of sight, all we hear is the throb of a motor and a wink of light as they take their man on board.

Scrambling in my cargo pockets I find the box of pistol rounds and recharge the Glock. Then I slip five rounds into the *Sako* magazine and an extra one in the breech, click the safety on. Giselle still hasn't fired a shot.

"Must be *two* in the boat," I whisper to Giselle. "Guy's killed one and there's that hunter that missed us on the trail. He'll be back in the boat by now. That means they've left no one back at camp."

"So?"

I am turning it over in my mind, trying to get a grip on what it means, what edge do we have? What are the risks? What must we do to survive?

"*Sooo*," I say slowly, casting vague thoughts into sequential ideas that are now forming on my lips. "So now *we* have an advantage. They'll be slow going back, keeping an eye on the forest for hostile movement. They don't know how many there are of us. They'll think we've legged it for home. *They will not be expecting us.*"

CHAPTER 34

... There is a proper season for attacks by fire and special days of a rising wind to start a conflagration.

Sun Tzü, *The Art of War*, 512 BC

We ran in single file on the deer trail alongside the river, stopping every now and then to listen. Giselle was winded, she hadn't heaved sacks of grain, ridden galloping horses or stacked hay. She filled her days in office pursuits. She lagged as we ran, breathing hard. When I stopped to listen, she'd not caught up to me when I jogged on again.

Although my arms were pumped with blood and stiff from the paddling, my legs were strong. Giselle was still a long way back down the trail when I heard her trip and fall. That's when I first heard the muted buzz of their outboard. Where the hell was she? Now I was on my own. No Guy, no Giselle, no firepower. Well, except for my trusty *Sako*. What a fuckin' disaster. Their craft was already coming around the headland before I was ready for it. Before I'd reached an overlook of the beach. Without a sound, I crouched to sit with my back against a stout Douglas fir. Placing my elbows on my knees I aligned the rifle on the water, just short of where I expected them to land. Waiting for my breathing and heartrate to settle into a more ordered rhythm.

I heard her then, the heavy rasp of her breathing came up the trail, while their craft was gaining, though far out on the water. They only had to look this way to spot her. They only had to hear her breathing over the sound of their motor.

Giselle froze when I flashed the palm of my hand and she saw me. I pointed to a low ridge of broken granite, which went to within twenty metres of the water's edge. At the last moment, too late, I realised they would reach the beach before Giselle could find cover.

That's when they cut the motor. That's what saved us.

Maybe they were nervous about where we were. Maybe they saw the beach and decided to come in quietly. Their boat drifted in, as did Giselle, worming her way forward on her belly. She found a place, lying prone behind the rocks, close enough for her shotgun — too close.

"*Wait,*" I whispered softly, "until I get Raoul."

I didn't know if she heard me, but we were going to be where we were least expected. The cammo and mozzie goop had worn off with the sweat from the run, so now sand flies and mosquitoes swarmed over me — sucking blood. Cussing under my breath, I resisted swotting them.

Their craft drifted by and turned under the blade of the man in the stern, now it's coming into the beach. I started breathing in short cycles, hyperventilating so I'd have an easy hold, lowering my heart rate for the shot. I could see the outline of Raoul's predatory figure in the prow. The others are in the dinghy, guns at the ready.

I waited until Raoul reached with his foot to the sand. Stopping my breath, aligning the i of the foresight on his chest and keeping the trigger moving. My Dad ground that sear to a light, rollover pull. Holding sights on target, waiting for the shot to break, my foresight is right on Raoul's heart.

BLAM. Giselle fires. The load takes a guy next to Raoul, square a midriff. That dangerous manhunter I'd missed with the arrow.

The boat's over, and I've missed the shot — Goddamn.

Raoul's down. Raoul's in the river! Giselle reloads with a loud CLACK-CLACK.A man leans forward over the keel and brings his rifle up, straight at Giselle! I keep the trigger going, squeezing off the shot with the foresight dead on his chest. The man slumps forward without a cry. I rack the bolt to load another high-powered round. What the hell am I doing?

The wounded man is standing in the water holding his belly — screaming. He's gut shot but not yet out of it.

BLAM. Giselle hits him with another wad of birdshot and it slams him into the river. CLACK, CLACK as she pumps that damn shotgun.

BLAM. Now she hits my guy, already slumped on the keel, with another load. The whole craft tips over flinging him in the river. Christ!

"The hell you do that for?" I shouted at her.

"That *bastard* raped me."

Damn, there's men down who could shoot back at any time. Although I understood her, I didn't like the way she's doing it, she is way out of control. She is going to get us both killed — I can feel it. Still no trace of Raoul. The water lies dark, no wind to stir its surface. Two bodies floating in slow circles in the grip of an eddy.

Are those bubbles right where Raoul's gone under? Something underwater: I fire at the spot. There's nothing but an eerie high-pitched ricochet off the water.

"Missed," I said to her. "Don't move, I think he's swum in behind that boulder."

What a fucking disaster. We still had Raoul to contend with.

Switching the *Sako* to my left hand I draw the pistol. I need the firepower. I can't stay here, Raoul knows where we are. Move damnit. I didn't like it, I didn't like it at all. What the hell happened to our ambush?

"Cover me," I said to Giselle in what I thought was a whisper.

Truth is I didn't trust myself to be accurate with the handgun, so I flicked the catch to auto, with my thumb, then moved forward. I signalled Giselle to stay put. Not daring to take my eyes off the massive boulder in front of me, I reached the beach and their wrecked boat. Saw what was left of two men, floating, bleeding out their life into the river. In that glance I rationalised what I saw, justified it, then denying responsibility — let it go.

In a few steps I reach the boulder's overhang, now I'm desperate with anticipation. A vibration registers in the air above me, almost imperceptible, something dangerous, not a sound precisely, more like a scent. I don't know what it is. That unknown something lodges in my mind. It's something that triggers fear. It causes me to look up.

The barrel of a rifle emerges as I watch. I step back, see Raoul's face and in the same instant I brought up the Glock and fire on full auto *Ripriprip*.

The pistol recoils and Raoul slumps forward over the boulder. A smear of blood runs down the granite face. His rifle falls and spears into the sand, barrel first and stays there.

Dropping my rifle I feed a fresh magazine into the Glock. *Always reload when you have the chance*, Guy had said to us when we practised in the woods.

Giselle stands up grim faced, picking her way among the rocks, holding the shotgun in both hands. She is looking down at the broken ground, taking care placing her feet. I stoop to collect the ejected shells when I feel in the air that same fear — *again*.

Hairs on my neck feel like prickles. I look up to see Giselle extending her gun, pointing.

"Duncan, he's gone. Raoul's gone!"

I whirl to where Raoul's body has lain only moments before. Staring at that bare rock before my mind catches its meaning. His rifle barrel-first in the sand and a clot of blood on the rock are the only indications he's been there.

Stepping in under the overhang I feel cold. There is nothing but the sound of my breathing. A knot of fear freezes me to the spot. A paralysing fear like that seizing the Swedish kid with the bear. I have to unlock that fear before I can take another step. Raoul is dangerous, as dangerous as a wounded bear. Where the hell is he?

Forcing the move I creep towards the water's edge, along the curve of granite. Blood stains the water as the bodies rotate in the eddy. With a death grip on the Glock I steady myself with one hand on the rock — absolutely still.

Something strikes the boulder above my head with a blast, then a whine of ricochet. Raoul leaps from the river, blood running down his face, water streaming. He swings a pistol at my face and I see his knuckle whiten as he pulls the trigger.

BLAM. A blast rips the water behind him. It's followed by a resounding CLICK. That confuses me until I realise Giselle has turned, then passed her target and misses by the time she fires.

Raoul had come up empty. That was the *click*. Now he works the slide and charges as I grip the Glock hard with both hands. When I find the trigger he is so close the water splashes me and the muzzle of his pistol is level with my face. My Glock goes off on full automatic, like a machine gun. This time I hold it low, to counter the recoil. Shots lift the gun from his groin to his chest while I fight to hold it. *Rippp*... the seventeen shot magazine runs dry in a heartbeat.

Raoul flounders as the first rounds take him, slam him over. He lies bloody in the river while I stand over him trembling from shock, the sound of gunfire still ringing in my ears.

Looking down at him, I realise that I'd crossed that fragile boundary to the other side. The dark side. I'd done something I'll never be free of. I've done something abominable.

Staring at his ruined body, I tried to put it together in my head: The first shot on the boulder must have clipped his skull and slammed him unconscious. The rest of the string had gone high with the recoil. He'd come to, then realising he'd lost his rifle, slid silently back down the boulder. Being the warrior he was, he'd drawn his pistol and slipped under water to attack from where he was least expected.

It must have been refraction that saved me. The bending of light at the boundary where water meets the air. So when he'd fired from under water, the shot had gone high. Although a gun will go off, the mechanics of the reload mechanism change in water. The slide must have jammed *after* that first shot.

Wading to him I pried the gun from his lifeless fingers. A Colt 45, standard US-Army issue. I racked the slide and saw the water had turned the gun oil and powder residue to mud, this gunk must have prevented the next round chambering.

Damn I was lucky. Lucky that Raoul hadn't cleaned the weapon after shooting ravens at yesterday's kill. I threw his gun far out in the water, took the photo of him from my shirt and tore it into tiny pieces, then cast them on the river.

Raoul lay broken and bloodied as if he'd been attacked by a bear, violated from his crotch to his crown with a brutal array of wounds. I thought of Guy. I thought of Simmone. I turned and caught Giselle as she reached me on the run. Tried to hold her, but she stepped past into the water surging in the current to Raoul. Swung her gun up.

BLAM. She emptied her last cartridge in his face.

Giselle reached her hand into Raoul's bloodied wounds and turned towards me. Her eyes locked on mine. She drew her hand across her brow leaving a smear of blood. She was *blooding*. A hunter's ritual, reserved for your first kill.

Her shot was still ringing in my ears.

"...the hell was that about?"

"I hated him. Wiped the bastard off this earth."

She was out of it, face muddied and twisted with hate, her eyes wide and angry, her whole body shaking with a demented agitation.

"Well, you've done that alright," I said. "Let's find Guy."

We found Guy in the bush face down. We could see where the rounds passed through and through. Saw the shocking exit wounds on his back, blackened and torn. A trail of ants had reached them. I put my hand on his cold arm and rolled him over. Ants formed a moving black trail through his hair, across his eyeball to the obscene trauma of gunshots in his chest.

A crow high in the trees above us called to its mate, a *Cre-craw-crawww,* the call receding at the end in its foul and feathered throat — a primal warning in defence of its prey. Giselle, looked at the moving column of ants, then up at the black row of raptors in the trees.

"We'll bury him."

I murmured assent, already knowing that it wasn't smart. When the bodies are found, and they would be, they'll know someone else was here. They will know that whoever did this survived. Still it seemed the least we could do. We dug a shallow grave in the soil with a trenching tool of the campers, and rolled him in, stomping on the *TagHeuer* to force it below ground. Bears, ants and crows would still get him, but we'd be gone. We were the ones needing ritual. I covered him with dirt and some good-sized rocks in an effort to keep the critters out. Giselle fought back tears and murmured a prayer. I just felt angry.

"Goddamn you Guy. Why were you always the fuckin' hero?" Giselle looked at me startled when I said it. I felt relieved that it was him and not me that lay there. Guilt too, that with a friend lying still, I felt relief. Relief that I was still alive.

I should have saved him; I didn't say that bit because I knew how irrational that was. Death is not a simple thing. I flung my head back and into that vast stillness of the forested wilderness let out a scream that shocked us both.

When I held my hand out to Giselle she came and took it.

We walked back hand in hand.

We collected spent shells and walked back the way we'd come. Back to Guy's canoe, back to civilisation. We'd had divine retribution, an eye for an eye. Guy had paid the price.

When we got back to our spot on the riverbank we retrieved our packs, resurrected the canoe and washed our camouflaged faces. I ditched the brass in the river as we paddled back upstream, against the current, toward the floatplane.

As we entered the lake a ghost of noise arose behind us. I turned to see a line of boiling water advancing upriver. A squall approaching. Torrential rain enveloped us with a fierce wind, it gave the water an angst we could feel through the thin skin of the canoe. As we moved along the shoreline, through pouring rain, we could see the yellow plane bobbing at anchor. A rich man's toy in the wilderness. There were no signs of life.

On landing we hauled the canoe up near the Blazer. And since we were soaked by the rain, we changed into the clean clothes we'd left in the truck. I pulled the covering net and branches off and we racked the canoe on top. Then I popped the hood and sprayed the electrics with WD-40. Finally I poured a litre of methanol into the fuel tank: stuff I'd brought with me to resolve any water condensation of the night air in the fuel.

We'd be fucked out here if it wouldn't start. With all those bodies now lying out in the bush. I held my breath as I turned the ignition; the Blazer coughed to life on the second try. We tooled out along the track. The way we'd come before, from Gladys Lake through marsh lands to the gravel road.

Giselle broke into the food hamper on the back seat. She was shivering and not just from the cold. She stayed in that uncomfortable condition as she made me a delicious sandwich — real food, well okay, peanut butter and jelly on stale home-baked bread. A can of Molson's went with it, it was real food to me.

"Rain should wash away any prints we left," I said.

Giselle broke the shotgun down in the car. She was also able to remove the bolt, though not the barrel of my rifle. I stopped the Blazer for a moment, smeared the licence tags with mud, it didn't look out of place, the truck was filthy. I dismantled the Glock, detaching the magazine, pulling the slide off against the spring and unstrapping the holster. By clamping my rifle in the tailgate I unscrewed the barrel from the wood, using a pipe wrench I had in the toolbox, which I'd brought for precisely that purpose.

Heading south on Route 37 we made side trips to a myriad lakes, wiping then hurling our gear into the water one piece at a time. Nothing of the guns, no ammunition, cammo gear or even cleaning rags remained in the truck by the time we were even close to hitting the first town. We stopped at Terrace for fuel, paid cash and said nothing. Then headed south-east again on sixteen.

We went through Jasper, not Banff, bypassing that town right on the speed limit. I didn't contact Simmone. I knew her surprise would be all the more convincing to the police if she didn't know what happened.

We pulled into Calgary, shopping for tires at the busiest place I could find, Canadian Tire on Third Street. We had four summer tires fitted, a new fan belt, points and plugs. Again I paid cash. We took the truck through a car wash that made it look presentable and Giselle vacuumed the inside. I didn't want to draw attention with a mud splattered vehicle as we drove back across the Trans-Canada.

We tried again to phone Gail, but got hubby instead.

"Can I speak to Jenny?" I said.

"Haven't seen them today," he said, "they must have gone shopping. Sunday over here you know."

Nothing to be done. Nothing, that is, but worry. We put our dirty clothes into the laundromat and ate at the Unicorn Pub while we waited. I had thinly cut roast beef with five-grain bread and salad, then some marvellous percolated coffee. I had some more coffee while Giselle rented a room. Once ensconced in the sparkling cleanliness of the room we showered, shaved and shampooed in a long warm spasm of relief.

We were ready for the run home.

That night we camped in the truck near Regina and slept the sleep of exhaustion. We built a fire, for we'd have to get rid of Guy's canoe. We knew it was an act of sacrilege to do it, but do it we must. We stood as if in mourning when we broke the canoe and fed it to the flames piece by piece. The bursting column of sparks were like fireworks. At the end we tossed our woodsmen's boots in the fire as well. I made sure they burned completely by adding fuel to them from the truck. We headed east once more, driving through the night, taking turns at the wheel — putting the Stikine behind us, putting everything behind us. We were going home.

Giselle was sullen, lost in her reflection of what might have been. We discussed events *ad nauseaum*: what was, what is, what might have been. *Who* was to blame? How could we have done things differently? Why had *I* gotten us into this mess? By now of course, it was entirely my fault.

"Guy was killed because he was brave and impulsive," I said. "He died for being macho at precisely the wrong moment."

"He saved my life," she said, staring ahead through the windshield.

"Took a hell of a risk, is what he did. You could have been killed. We nearly *all* were."

"I wasn't though," Giselle said, "that makes all the difference. He had the balls to save me, he had faith in himself. He took the chance and pulled it off. While *you* ... you did nothing."

"Guy had balls, I'll give him that. But damnit, he kept rolling the dice, he couldn't help himself — sooner or later he was bound to lose."

In my mind this was not the incident we were discussing, but instead the recurring picture of Giselle blasting Raoul with the shotgun. The way she'd dipped her fingers in Raoul's blood and wiped it across her face. It shocked me then; it shocked me now. I'm sure it shocked her too. She sat upright in her seat, tense, staring at the next bend of the endless forest rushing toward us.

"Did you love him, Giselle?"

"Of course I loved him, didn't you?"

"I wasn't *in* love with him — there's a difference."

Giselle was silent for a long time, so long I thought she wasn't going to answer.

The Chevy kept a thundering pace with my steady pressure on the accelerator.

"*I loved him*. And loved you, too. Loved you both. We didn't *do* anything. Love is as far as it went."

"Can you do that Giselle, love *both* of us?"

"No use talking about it now."

"No damnit there isn't. So what's going to happen now — to us?"

"We'll take up where we left off," she said.

Now as I drove my mind wandered, I flashed on her standing over Raoul after blasting her last load his face. The way she blooded herself afterwards with his blood on her brow. She had wanted Raoul's death, had sought it, and when it happened, she enjoyed it. Did I know her? Did I ever know her?

"I don't see how things can ever be the same," I said.

"No, not exactly the same. We can but try."

"Okay," I said, tired of the emotional effort — feeling infinitely wearied.

Giselle looked across at me. Her face reflecting a surreal glow of the dashboard with dials and gauges patterned on her skin.

It was then I realised, like suddenly seeing something take shape in a fog, that we could never go back to where we were before. Memories are such a pale imitation of the real thing: blurred greyscale photographs of reality. Just like you can't remember sex with the same emotional jolt you had in consummating the act originally. Sure you can remember the details of how it was, details of place, how it felt in that last climatic thrust. You can remember who was doing what to whom. You can think of it, but that real heart-stopping thump of reality, the emotion blasting through you is lost. The truth is gone forever. You can only know what happened and that time has passed.

There *is* no going back.

Neither of us could face sleep, afraid of reliving the whole damned thing in our dreams. We shared the driving, changing every few hours, peed beside the road, ate trail mix, drank pop and drove around the clock. At Sudbury I phoned Kirsten, told her we'd be back the next day. I made sure from now on that I put our fuel and food on my credit card. I stuffed the receipts in the glove box with the others from the trip we made up Highway 400 when outward bound. All the way we travelled home I fretted for Jenny, I fretted for *Intrepid Red,* and I fretted for our little band of brood mares.

We drove up tenth-line to the farm just on dusk. The mist was building as it does in spring, firs and maples around the house by now looked like a scene from a Gothic movie. We pulled into the driveway, sat in the truck and looked at each other in silence, when I killed the motor.

"How do you feel?" Giselle asked.

I said nothing for a moment, thinking about it, feeling unbelievably tired.

"*Haunted* just about describes it," I said. "How about you?"

"I feel like we got even."

"We lost Guy in the process."

"Yes, we did."

Kirsten walked out of the mist like an apparition and came up to speak to us, still sitting in the truck.

"Hi," I said. "Anything we need to know?"

"*Red* had a foal – a beauty. Oh, yes and there is one odd thing. A guy came to see you. Must have been just a couple of days after you left. I told him you'd gone up to Algonquin."

"Good, thanks. Who was he?"

"He mumbled something I didn't catch."

"What did he look like?" I asked, tired and kind of annoyed at the same time.

"Hmmm. Older guy, grumpy with jowls, like one of those old actors, you know the one with the boat. What was it? Ah, the *African Queen*."

"Humphrey Bogart?"

"Yeah, that's him. He sure gave me the creeps."

It made no sense. I didn't know anyone like that.

I checked on *Red* and her new foal, a filly, then slept till noon. I phoned Jennifer to reassure ourselves she was in good hands. They must be out, the phone rang and rang in the void, it wasn't answered. I wondered if she was all right. I had this anxious feeling that they might have got to her. I shrugged the feeling off and resolved to call next day.

With the new dawn came another round of recriminations, as we went about preparing for the morrow. We spoke unsayable things, things now finally said, and we could not take them back.

Giselle left for work when I started for the barn. Dawn had broken, the sky now flecked with a brooding grey. A poem of Nikki Giovanni's flicked through my head as I walked down the aisle with their feed. With no one around to hear, I spoke the words softly, like an incantation — casting a spell. A spell of love and yearning.

> ... love those with whom you sleep, share the happiness
> of those you call friends, engage those among you who are
> visionary and remove from your life those who offer you
> depression, despair and disrespect.[1]

Giselle was now offering me depression, despair and yes, in matters sexual — her disrespect. The truth is that our life was not the same, was never the same, after that. Unspoken thoughts lay between us distorting our very words. Knowing what we knew changed everything. It changed the way we were.

Giselle went ballistic at every imagined slight, her anger became a mean and bitter thing. She was now a stranger, a dangerous outsider, about whom I knew too much. From a painful distance I admired her independence — she didn't need me. I realised now that knowing her would always be at a distance. I wanted warmth and intimacy, she offered chill. I didn't know if I could handle that.

The police called the following evening. We were half expecting them, hoping they wouldn't come nonetheless. Jenny wasn't yet home. I still hadn't been able to reach her on the phone. I was snapping at Giselle, snarling at the horses. I was worried for Jenny's sake. Giselle and I had by now struck an uneasy truce.

When the knock came, I opened the door to detective Greiner, who introduced me to his new sidekick — Hackman. I looked over their shoulders to the RCMP car sprouting a forest of aerials.

"Come in," Giselle offered.

She smiled and pulled some of our camping gear off the couch, so they could sit. She offered them coffee and fetched it, while I sat uneasy at the table. They remained standing and looked around, took in the room.

"Been away?" said Greiner.

"We've been on holiday at Algonquin,"

"Ah," he said, "where did you stay up there?"

"Nowhere special; we camped around the lakes — fishing."

"So, your good friend Paigé, did he go with you?"

"Well no, we went on a second honeymoon. Why do you ask?"

And now I'm thinking, where the hell did that come from?

"You don't know where he is then."

"No," Giselle and I answered in unison.

The police looked at each other, and there was silence for a few seconds until Hackman nodded.

"He's been found dead."

"The hell you say." I couldn't stop myself. "How did that happen?"

They glanced at Giselle who had a knuckle to her mouth in shock and was making a sort of strangled noise. As if the reality of his death had only now arrived.

"Multiple gunshot wounds."

"Who did it?"

He didn't answer right away but asked instead.

"You have a gun?"

"No," I said, looking straight back at him, "Absolutely not."

I saw a glance from Giselle in my peripheral vision, neither of us acknowledged it.

"Paigé was shot out west in British Columbia. Thing is, there's five bodies at a campsite, it's a massacre. Anyway, it's now the Mounties case — it's out of my hands."

"What happened?" I said, "Who were they?"

"A Frenchman, Raoul Kelemann and his pals. Know him?"

Greiner looked straight at me. I made my face still.

"No," I said, "I don't."

"A pilot was left with the plane. He took to the air when they failed to return, spotted the bodies and radioed RCMP."

Hackman was agitated, he stood up and spoke for the first time: "Mind if we look in your car."

"Sure," I said.

Hackman moved to go, but Greiner wasn't finished.

"Paigé was shot with a nine-millimetre parabellum."

"A what?"

“Military ammo for light machine guns like the Uzi.”

“So?” I said, not able to think of anything else.

“Think of it, no guns found there were nine-mill. They did find a couple of ejected nine-mill cases though.”

Fighting to keep from looking at Giselle, I sensed the bastard was setting a trap, and the trap was for me.

“Fingerprints?” I asked as casually as I could, although I knew we had handled them with gloves.

Greiner ignored my query and added: “He was shot by the one who got away.”

“Really,” I said. “We'll need to take care of Guy's arrangements.” I said to change the subject. “There's his ex-wife Alison in Toronto and also a son I haven't met somewhere.”

“Yes, we've already seen Alison. Guy Paigé's body is still with the coroner in BC. We have a pendant from Paigé's pocket. His ex-wife said it's not hers. Do you recognise it?”

He dug around in his shirt pocket, then opened his hand to show us Giselle's turquoise pendant.

“No,” we said in unison again and Giselle shook her head.

When they finished our interview I walked out with them while they took a look at the truck. They checked the tires twice, kicking the one's on front, looked inside the cabin front and back, then they found the fuel and burger receipts in the glove box.

“Mind if we keep 'em?” Greiner said.

He dropped them in a zip lock bag. It wasn't really a question.

“Sure fine,” I said, feeling a lot less cocky than I sounded.

“Mind if we take along your boots too?”

It was then I realised he must *not* have had enough evidence for a search warrant. Hackman walked back and retrieved the boots at the back door and while he did so, Greiner leaned in close.

“Paigé was a friend of yours, a good friend — now he's dead, murdered way out west. You're into something here that smells to me like deep shit.”

This time he was right. I said nothing as they slammed the doors of their car and gunned it into a three-point turn, roaring down the driveway in second- then third- gear. I stood in the dark looking after their taillights. I had learned something.

They had no warrant,
they had no prints,
there were no witnesses.

CHAPTER 35

You cannot lead an army on the march unless you know the country and are familiar with its mountains and forests...

Sun Tzü, *The Art of War*, 512 BC

Alone at the farm I couldn't raise Jennifer on Gail's phone. Where the hell was she? The question was in my mind when the phone rang. I spoke to Gail and she told me Jenny had gone shopping.

"Damnit Gail. I told you not to leave her on her own."

"She *is* with friends. For Chrissake Duncan, what's gotten into you?"

I hung up, overwhelmed with worry. *Was she all right?* The call had only made me more anxious. I thought of Simmone. Then called McGowan, got only the duty officer instead.

McGowan phoned back when I least expected it, on the Friday when I was in the thick of the chores. He was his familiar cryptic self.

"Toronto, Sunday. Can we meet?"

"Sure, I'll drive down."

"Not the city. Somewhere nice, away from crowds."

The *nice* reminded me of the Millcroft at Alton in the Caledon Hills, one of my favourite places. I arranged to meet him on the hill behind the inn. The view at dusk can be spectacular.

Later I dropped the Blazer in the Millcroft lot and cut across the backfield where an incandescent balloon was being readied for filling. Several teenagers scurried in uniforms that made them look like sailors. They had spread out the canopy on the ground and were busy securing it to the basket standing by. The open mouth of the balloon was held above the heater in a wire frame, where the master blaster was tending it. A knot of guests in their Sunday best had assembled to watch.

It was a picture from the past, a past of a more innocent Victorian hue. The furnace was lit with a whoosh that startled me. Within minutes the balloon lifted shimmering above the grass, a sailor on each anchor holding it hard to the earth.

I moved on climbing the trail through the spruce woods, looking back from time to time to see the balloon expand, until it seemed as large as the inn itself. When I made it to the top the scenery was magnificent: farms, woods and lakes spread out before me across the valley.

There was no one waiting in the clearing. Then a movement, a flicker in the gloom. I spied Mungo leaning against a sapling birch, watching me. He was waiting to see that I was alone. He offered a hip flask when I reached him. How like McGowan to take this with him, to think a flask of gin was something he couldn't do without.

"Where is Simmone?" I asked.

"Someplace where she thinks that she is safe."

"Where pray tell, *is* she safe?"

"In this life Duncan, security is an illusion: no one is safe."

McGowan was being his usual enigmatic pain in the ass.

"Goddamnit. You won't tell me what she's doing, where she is, or even if she's safe. What the hell do you expect of me?"

"Thought you realised, old son. I want to know what happened."

"About what?"

"Don't be tiresome. I want to know what happened to Raoul."

"Fuck you."

"No, Duncan. This is how it works: I tell you something, you reciprocate with something in exchange. Tit for tat. I can offer this much for starters: Simmone is usefully employed."

"Employed, by who — you?"

"She is, if you like, somewhat the little drummer girl."

That stopped me, then I placed the reference to Le Carré's novel.

"She's hooked into your Afghan ops?"

"You need to give me something in return, old boy."

"About Raoul?"

"Yes."

"He's dead."

"I know that. I want to know the details: who and how?"

He could be wearing a wire and I didn't want to admit to anything that he could hold against me. That's when I realised that I was only going to find out about her if I traded information with him. I'd have to be careful about what I said. "Guy got him."

McGowan was silent. I didn't fill the space for him. He took his coat off and hung it on a branch, unbuttoned his shirt and removed it to show there was no wire. He turned all the way around without his shirt so I could see the truth of it. "That's not the way we put it together," he said.

"Yeah, but that's the way it was."

"We have your friend killed *before* Raoul."

McGowan replaced his shirt.

"*We*? Who is *we* exactly?"

"I want to know about the other man?"

"What other man?"

"The other man that was with you — who else?"

"To hell with that. Where is she?"

"Now is the time to give him up."

"There was no other man."

McGowan looked at me. I barely managed to meet his stare. He was angry. Despite suppressing it, anger had seeped into the hard edge of his voice. An anger belying his benign appearance, and I could see that underneath a thin veneer of civility, he was a dangerous man.

The whole idea of meeting me out here alone in the woods was now worrying. If you meet in a public place you're guarding against violence from the person you're meeting. When you meet like this on a hiking trail, with no one around, it's a perfect place for them to do you violence.

Had he planned to kill me? If I didn't tell him my accomplice, he would be reluctant to do so with that loose end dangling. Mungo took a step towards me and stopped. Perhaps he remembered that I too had been dangerous.

"Then there is nothing more to discuss."

His attention flicked to the balloon as it cleared the trees and startled us with an eerie whoosh of the dragon's furnace. We could see the faces of passengers in the wicker gondola, waving as they passed over us; two men and three women, one of them auburn haired. I saw in them a constellation of my realm. It gave an existential feel to the moment.

"I need your help in protecting my daughter ..." I said.

McGowan's attention returned to me with a gimlet stare.

"We've cut you loose. You're on your own."

"Damnit Mungo. Now I realise that I always was."

He straightened as if I'd struck him, as if I'd sullied the pristine view he had of himself as a man of principle. Belatedly I felt sorry for him and couldn't bear to see him go. Couldn't bear to cut the link.

"Can I see Simmone?"

"No. Not now — not ever. She has another life."

"Another *man* too, I'll bet. A fucking bandit — an Afghani if I'm not mistaken. That's how you're running her isn't it?"

"She's a *Borderliner* for Chrissake, what did you expect?"

"A what? *A Borderliner*? What the fuck's that ...?"

"Chaotic, sexually needy, angry, manipulative. Does that ring a bell? You must have known that she was *mad*."

"Well, I ..." then a thought hit. "You already *knew* about her, knew what she was like."

Mungo stared silently skyward at the balloon.

"Jesus, you knew all along. You manipulated me right into it. Right from the start. Right from the cop that was different. *You* wanted me to kill Raoul!"

"*Neutralise* is our word Duncan. Civilised people don't *kill*."

"No, they get others to do it for them."

"You know the drill," Mungo said.

At this point McGowan turned on his heel old soldier that he was, and with one deft look at the incandescent smudge in the sky, started hiking down the trail. I knew too many people like him. People who never reciprocate — not really, not from the heart. Those who won't negotiate, not in good faith anyway, people who have to get the best of everyone.

Even when he was out of sight, I stayed in the clearing with that anxious panicky feeling you sometimes get when you realise that you are truly alone. Where was Jenny? Right now I needed to know if she, too, was safe.

Anyway I stuck to the drill, as he put it, gave him a good five minutes, allowing him to slip away unseen on his own. I watched the balloon until it dipped out of sight, way beyond the trees on the ridge. Feeling the chill of a special vigilance, I threaded my way down through the trees along the edge of the track, a few metres deep inside the treeline, keeping out of sight. I stayed away from the light, stopping every now and then to listen, while heading in a circuitous route for my truck in the parking lot at the Millcroft Inn.

Being in London is like being at the centre of the universe, at least that's what Harry felt. He sat at a restaurant in Soho reading the *Times*. From time to time he'd glance at a table along the far wall. A table where Jennifer was dining with her friend Malcolm and his parents, the youngsters giggling over something on the table, a parcel they'd unwrapped. The father sat a touch formally, ex-army, aloft in his pin stripe suit. The wife, a trifle over weight, was explaining whatever it was the kids were unwrapping.

Harry didn't like it. He'd had to wait to get her away from her parents, now he had this lot. The holiday was perfect. Except he didn't like operating in a foreign country. He liked London right enough. He just didn't know how everything worked over here; he had no connections. Too much uncertainty for his taste. Harry liked structure. He liked a tried and tested routine. He liked to know what was going on. He liked to know details. That need, along with an ingrained patience, made him good in his profession. It also made him slow for he took his own sweet time when he tracked people down. He'd hang back and see where things lay before he acted.

Harry didn't like having to track a ditzy girl like this. Having to take her down. This was no runaway. This girl had family — a family he'd have to contend with. This was seriously messy. After he had picked up the girl's trail, after he had the details of her itinerary, he'd found her parents gone. He'd lost McKinley in Algonquin, right after he'd clocked him in Sudbury. He'd been to every damned motel and campsite within a hundred miles of Algonquin. He was almost sure they'd never been there. Sure enough for him to leave what was now a cold trail, and go after the girl. The girl for him was like pure gold.

He watched the family in his peripheral vision as he flicked through *The Times* to world news. Then an item caught his eye:

Four men shot dead in Canadian Rockies

> A French national Raoul Kelemann and three others were found murdered...

The headline screamed. Well, not *screamed* exactly, this was after all the *Times*. More like discreetly embedded, halfway down the page. Harry devoured the story and cursed aloud, then cursed again under his breath. A couple at the next table eyed him with reproof. He looked back at them and glared. They hurried back to their eating.

With Raoul dead, the deal was off. He wasn't going to get any more out of Raoul — nobody was. He didn't give a damn about the girl. He'd pocketed fifteen large already, and may as well go home. Perhaps he'd stay here until the end of the week. Have a holiday, be a tourist, take on London, have a few tarts before he went home, before he took on another job. Take some care of himself. The thought pleased him.

He smiled to himself as he reached for the menu.

Giselle left the same night the police came to the house. She'd dashed out in the revving Golf and stayed with a work friend down in Mississauga. She wouldn't tell me where. When she phoned I arranged to meet her in the Bookshop Café. A place she knew was a favourite of mine.

She was there when I arrived, seated at a table, drinking wine. She didn't sip it any more. Now she drank in deep drafts. A half-full bottle of Californian red on the table. No Perrier in sight. The pendant I'd given her, was of course, missing.

I kissed her lightly on the cheek and caught a whiff of booze as she turned her head away. When I sat down, rather than looking at me, she looked instead at the empty chair, where Guy had sat last time we'd met.

"I did not want to come here," she said.

"Then why agree to it?" I said.

"I need to know what happened."

"You know what happened. You were there."

"Did you kill him?"

I looked around to see if anyone could hear us.

"You know the answer to that. Goddamnit, you were there."

"Did you shoot Guy?"

"Don't be a fool, they set us up with that remark. He was killed with rifle fire, not with my pistol. I didn't shoot Guy. Why would you think that? *Raoul* killed him. Greiner lied, he wants us at each other's throat."

"I cannot be sure what the truth is any more."

"Think about it. The sounds you heard when he died. Remember the shots?"

"No, I was running scared. There were a lot of shots."

"There you go."

"More shots, lots more: there was an automatic."

"Look, in the heat of the moment I realised how pathetic a bolt action was in the dark, so I emptied the Glock at them on full automatic."

She looked at me doubtfully with her head on one side, "I don't know …"

She turned towards the door as if she we searching for Guy. I followed her gaze —there was no one there. She turned back and fixed me with a glare, a look so cold, so hate filled it stopped me.

In that moment, I flashed on that image I have of us deep in the forest, when she drew a bloodied hand across her face.

"Are you coming back with me?" I asked.

"No."

"No. You mean not *now*?"

"I mean *not ever*."

"I'm sorry," I said, and felt myself nearing the abyss — grieving her loss, then in that instant I let her go. Letting her go felt like that old song: a total eclipse of the heart.

"I want you to sell the farm," she said. "I want you to settle right now in cash." It was then I stood up — furious. "You will hear from my lawyer," she added.

"No, Giselle, that's not where we're going. Not now, not ever. *I AM NOT LEAVING AND WE'RE NOT SELLING.*"

Perhaps my voice rose a decibel or two from the startled looks of the diners. I leaned close to soften it.

"No lawyers, not with what we know. You'll speak to no one and deal with me direct."

She got up too with that and left in silence, her lips squeezed into a thin red line. I watched her walk away — in a suit that showed every bodacious ripple.

At home I felt as if I'd been run over. A mix of longing, anger and abandonment, yes and relief too in a wicked blend of angst. As I shook out the straw in the new stallion's stall a decrepit pickup coughed up the driveway. Ahanu Pasquale sauntered over and leant his forearms over the top of the stable door looking in at me. His face handsome and impassively Indian.

"Jenny back yet?"

"Haven't been able to reach her."

"Ah," was all he said.

"Could use a hand here though — till the snow flies."

"Sure," he said and reached for the fork. It was the very first time I'd seen him smile.

Cirrus clouds scudded across the sky when I headed back to the house. By the time I made it in the door I was being hit by wind-driven sleet, a painful reminder of winter. In Canada the weather changes awfully fast.

Inside I retrieved fresh coffee from the freezer. My favourite, an Arabica from the highlands of Kenya. I ground the beans and boiled fresh water from the cold tap. When it boiled I left it for a moment to cool, so as not to scorch the grounds. I stared out the window at the horses grazing in the home field. *Intrepid Red* was leading them to a better spot for grazing, down by the road. Her foal trotted behind as if attached by an invisible rubber band.

Having an affinity with horses; I have come to love their way of being. Living in the present, not a care for the past — none for the future. Horses have a primitive faith: a faith in the moment, no baggage, nothing to interfere with their well-honed instinct — a firm belief in their place. A faith in the core of their being.

How many times had someone recommended that to me? People telling me to have faith. Now at last I understood. They meant a faith in God, of course. I saw it instead as a trusting faith in the universe — a faith in its vast reaches. Not a religious ideological faith: no, an essential deep abiding faith in ourselves. A faith in who we are. A spiritual faith we must all have if we are to survive.

When we lose faith in ourselves, we are lost, for then there is nowhere left to go. This is what some men have known for aeons. Giselle and I had held our faith against the fiercest resistance, held to a confident faith in our own abilities. We had survived the worst, then at the end lost faith in each other.

Now I saw that we had learned to look inside ourselves — to dig deep. To find within us what was needed. We had been bold and allowed those elusive and mysterious forces of the universe to come to our aid. Giselle was lost to me, but I longed for my daughter to be by my side. Longed to know that she was safe.

I poured tepid water onto the fresh grounds, an addict reaching for my next hit. The aroma of rich coffee infused me with promise. I searched the fridge again for the delicate flavour of *Buche D'Alfinois*, a soft delicate cheese I'd bought in France.

There was none to be had. Giselle had taken even that. I managed a slice of stale bread and sawed off a week-old hunk of cheddar. I ate slow and sipped my brew, the chewy taste of cheese and coffee mingled with the dough. It was then I realised my migraines had ceased. I'd had no more since we'd left the Rockies.

The phone rang. When I picked up, a burr of long distance static came down the line, across those transatlantic miles.

"Hi Dad. You know Mum called me about your ... huh, break up."

"I'm sorry Jen. Sorry it's come to this. Sorry we couldn't hold it together for you, for us all. I feel now like ... well, feel like... that I have failed you."

"Oh Dad. Don't get maudlin, I just called to see... to see if you're alright. Are you all right?"

Before responding I paused for a moment, sifting my thoughts to see them truly. Was I all right? There was silence on the line as I turned it over in my mind. Leaning against the wall, I ran my right hand idly down that supporting arm. Felt the thick, corded muscles shift and contract. I felt strength in that arm.

"Yes," I said, in macho mode again, "I'm fine. And so is *Red* and her foal. She's had a good strong little fellow. So you'll stay with me then?"

"That's cool," she said, "I want to stay at the farm, with you and the horses. It's good to hear *Red* has a nice colt. Love ya."

"Love you too, my daughter."

"Good-bye," we said together and hung up.

Loss changed to a rush of parental feeling. All was well in this new alignment. At last I felt a sense of freedom, as if a hard decision had been taken from me and yet had still turned out well.

I strapped on my riding chaps and breathed the familiar leather smell. I was looking forward to riding Murray's new horse. I was excited by *Kikkuli's* impending arrival on the morrow. At that moment the radio kicked in with Kris Kristofferson singing *Me and Bobby McGee*. Deep inside my head, something vibrated in the same frequency as that guitar, as if he'd plucked a cord inside my soul. I cranked up the volume and sang along ...

Notes

1 Nikki Giovanni, *Racism 101*, 1994. Reproduced here with the author's kind permission.